The Way We TOUCH

USA TODAY BESTSELLING AUTHOR

TIA LOUISE

This book is a work of fiction. Names, characters, places, and incidents are products of the author's imagination or are used fictitiously. Any resemblance to actual events or locales or persons, living or dead, is entirely coincidental.

The Way We Touch
Copyright © TLM Productions LLC, 2024
Printed in the United States of America.

Illustration by Laura Moore, @LCM_designss
Design by Wildheart Graphics

All rights reserved. No part of this publication can be reproduced, stored in a retrieval system, or transmitted in any form or by any means—electronic, photocopying, mechanical, or otherwise—without prior permission of the publisher and author.

Playlist

"Galileo"—Indigo Girls

"Bones"—The Killers

"Hot Stuff"—Donna Summer

"Queen of My Double Wide Trailer"—Sammy Kershaw

"The Bluest Eyes in Texas"—Restless Heart

"Give It Away"—Red Hot Chili Peppers

"Need You Tonight"—INXS

"Spin You Around"—Morgan Wallen

"Man on the Moon"—Zella Day

"Jackson"—Johnny Cash, June Carter Cash

"Redneck Girl"—The Bellamy Brothers

"Disco Inferno"—The Trammps

"Sleigh Ride"—The Brian Settler Orchestra

"Waltz of the Flowers"—Tchaikovsky

"Least Complicated"—Indigo Girls

Listen on Spotify Here:

If you think your dream is lost, you're still here, and you
have so much to give. Fill the world with your unique
brand of spice—Logan and I are cheering for you!

"Tell me, what is it you plan to do with your one wild
and precious life…"—Mary Oliver

Chapter 1

Logan

"SO YOU WANT TO FUCK ANOTHER MAN." I lift the tumbler of whiskey, jaw tight, despite the casual smile on my lips.

"Of course, that's the first place you'd go." The cool blonde sitting across from me crosses her mile-long legs, leaning them to the side beneath the table like a giraffe.

I admit, they were the first things I noticed about her. I'm a legs guy.

"Must you always be so cocky?" she continues. "Maybe if you acted like you cared once in a while, I wouldn't have to expand our repertoire."

"I prefer only one dick at the party."

"That dick being you?" She tilts her head to the side.

"Always." Stated with my usual bravado, my calculated cool.

A light laugh slips from her glossy-red lips, but it's insincere.

Natalia van Norse is a six-foot, size zero supermodel with fake tits. Later, I learned she's also an author and a Midtown influencer, which pretty much makes her a U.S. influencer.

Tonight she's wearing a black dress covered in star-shaped sequins to match the décor of the restaurant, and her platinum hair is swept into an elegant twist off her neck complete with tiny gold stars scattered across the crown.

She's picture-perfect, ready to document the grand opening of Galileo's, the hottest new restaurant on West 53rd Street, which I was invited to attend. I'm invited to attend pretty much every opening, charity gala, red carpet affair.

I'd tossed the invitation aside, but she insisted we make an appearance.

The menu sounded like a prank, and I wasn't in the mood for camera flashes blinding me all the way inside as soon as our car pulled up at the door. But I acquiesced, and here we are.

The host whisked us away to a private alcove off the main dining room, and now we're nestled at a gilded table where midnight-blue velvet curtains separate us from the other, less-sought-after guests.

"You're so provincial, Logan, I swear, it's hard to believe you've lived in New York for eight years."

"I didn't know not wanting to share my bed was considered provincial."

I almost said my *girlfriend,* but that term hasn't felt right in a long time.

"And what about what I want?"

I roll a star-topped toothpick between my fingers thinking about the first time I saw this woman. I was out with Garrett Bradford, offensive lineman and my best friend, on our last free night before the start of the regular season.

I approached her purely out of ego. With her height and style and reputation, I decided she was the type of woman "Lightning" Logan Murphy should have on his arm.

Logan Murphy, star wide receiver for the New Jersey Pirates, most completed passes in last year's season, and on track to win the very first MVP trophy ever awarded to a wide receiver in history—if the sports commentators are to be believed.

Our relationship was rocky from the start.

She was promoting her book of essays, and I liked to read. However, when I discovered her book was actually a collection of essays about how the modeling industry only cared about her body, I made the mistake of questioning the premise.

Isn't being a model and complaining people only care about your looks the same as me being a football star and complaining people only care about my athleticism?

Sure, I graduated with honors from the University of Texas at Austin with a degree in communications, motivated by the fact that my father owns all the sports radio stations on the AM dial from El Paso to Jefferson City, but nobody gives a shit about any of that when the ball is second and goal in the fourth quarter with ten seconds left in the game.

I'm simply a player who'd better catch that fucking pigskin and get it across the line.

Then online sports betting exploded, and I was dehumanized even more.

The last time a dickhead cursed me out in the comments section, threatening my life because I fucked up a measly twenty-dollar parlay by simply doing my job, i.e., *winning*, I turned over all my social media accounts to a handler.

I'm not complaining. Much. We signed up for this life. It is what it is.

Natalia only glared at me, called me an un-evolved caveman, and we've been on the slow train to *done* ever since.

Not that I have time for a private life during the regular season anyway.

Studying the menu, I'm even less enthused about being here. Tang? Freeze-dried beef *au jus*… "It's a quirky concept, but space food?"

"My hook will be, 'It's out of this world.'" Natasha waves down our designated waiter. He's dressed in a white uniform like he's part of NASA, and he hurries over as if his life depends on keeping us happy. "I'll have another stardust martini, and may I see the kids' menu?"

"Of course." He nods, hastening away, and our eyes meet.

"I thought you promised to eat more."

"I'm not eating this." She flicks the menu with her fingernail. "I hope the children's menu will have a cheesy pasta or some version of pizza."

I hold up my hands. "It's a smart idea."

Natasha isn't dumb. She only acts that way on social media.

The man returns with a small card, placing it on the bone china plate in front of her, and she lifts it, curling her nose as she reads. "Freeze-dried carrots, potatoes, and beef cubes—just add broth. Is it supposed to be a game?"

"That does it." I take the napkin out of my lap and put it on my plate. "I'm out of here."

"Logan! We can't leave. I promised to take pictures of all the dishes and post them on my accounts."

I hesitate in my chair, irritated by this entire night—by my entire state of affairs. Maybe I'm having a quarter-life crisis, but I keep asking myself why am I still with this woman? What am I thinking I'll get? A do-over?

Reaching across the table, I place my hand on hers. Her brow furrows, and she seems confused by my sudden display of tenderness.

I'm not confused. I feel nothing, and it's the moment of clarity I needed.

I make a decision. "What do you want, Natalia?"

"Sorry?" She shakes her head, and I return to her earlier question.

"Tell me about the new dick you want to bring into our bedroom."

"Oh," Her blue eyes light, and she wiggles in her chair as if she's been planning this for a while. "Aristotle Drakos."

"Wait…" I glance to the side. "I know that name."

"You met him with Brittany on his super yacht in March, remember?"

Perhaps I am provincial, because I need to clarify. "Brittany, as in your best friend?"

"Of course! I mean, if I were to have a best friend."

"I thought she was dating that guy."

Air puffs through her lips, and she takes a long sip of her martini. "They have an open relationship. Everyone's doing it now, very *en vogue*."

I trace my finger along the base of my tumbler and consider Galileo. "Call him."

"What?"

"Give him a call. Tell him to join us."

"Okay…" The side of her lips curl into a smile, and her thumbs fly across her phone screen.

Exhaling slowly, I glance at the galaxies painted on the ceiling overhead. Galileo was an astronomer. He looked into the night sky and proved the universe does not revolve around us.

We are not the center of the universe…

They threw him in prison for it.

I think about how weary I am of the nonstop appearances, the social climbers, and the fakery. Eight years ago, my dream came true. I was a first-round draft pick, which meant I was a big fucking deal. It meant my father was wrong, and I wasn't throwing my life away on a barbaric sport.

Two weeks ago, Natalia left for a modeling gig in Europe, and I realized how much I liked *not* having her in my space. I'd already decided to end things tonight, then she suggested a threesome.

"He's on his way." She lowers her phone, stretching like a cat waking from a long afternoon nap. "You're going to like Aristotle. He's very confident in a way that immediately sets you at ease."

"It sounds like you two have a history."

Her shoulder rises, and when our eyes meet, I realize she's

fucked him already. I also realize she's on some sort of amphet-amine. And I realize I don't give a shit.

She flicks her wrist. "He mentioned something about your father being a billionaire, and how he *must* meet you. *Must* was his word."

My brow lowers. "What does he want?"

She shrugs, shaking her head with a laugh. "I'm sure it's some sort of partnership or business proposal. Everyone knows you're considering retirement, and he's wanting to get more into media."

Pulling my chin back, I study her face. I'm not sure what to make of her sometimes. "I've told you I'm not interested in working for my dad. Did you lead him to believe I was?"

"No! I don't know. He'll discuss it with you."

I motion to our waiter, and he hurries over again. "Yes, sir?"

"We have another guest joining us. Let me know when he arrives."

"Of course." He nods. "I'll alert the host."

"And put this all on my bill."

He nods before scurrying away, and Natalia leans forward, wrinkling her perfectly-crafted nose. "You surprise me, Logan. I thought you'd require a little more convincing."

"How long until he gets here?"

She glances at her phone. "Any minute, I'm sure."

On cue, a familiar man with dark hair and olive skin wear-ing a bespoke suit strides confidently across the dining room in our direction. Our waiter shows him the way, and as he gets closer, the way his eyes roam my date confirms my suspicions.

Anger heats my throat, but it's not jealous rage. He can fucking have Natalia, but he disrespected me by sleeping with her while we were a couple.

"Mr. Lightning. Your reputation precedes you."

Standing, I catch his hand in a shake, gripping it hard and pulling him closer so he can feel my strength. He's a few inches shorter than I am, and his eyes widen with surprise.

"You crossed a line." My voice is low and level. "Good thing for you, I'm finished here. You can have her, but I know."

He exhales a laugh, holding up both hands. "My apologies. I was given wrong information about your relationship."

"Yes, you were." I pass him roughly, headed for the door.

A swirl of air around me, and Natalia rushes up to my side. "Where are you going?"

"Away." I do my best to keep my voice low, trying not to be overheard, but the entire room is craning their necks to look at us. "Have a nice life, Natalia."

"But what about our arrangement?" She looks around at our growing audience.

"We never had an arrangement, and your new dick is waiting for you."

The noise of cameras clicks all around us, and I have to get out of this spotlight.

The host meets me, and I follow him to the door, hurrying out to a waiting black Escalade. As soon as I'm inside, my phone is in my hand, and my thumbs fly over the screen.

> Where are you? I'm hungry and I want to drink.

> Garrett: Lightning! Get your ass to Blondie's and get some wings. We've got a pool game going.

Garrett and I have been tight since he transferred to the team two years ago. He's a giant of a man, six-foot-four and two hundred and sixty pounds of pure strength, and he's the one person I can be completely myself around.

His family owns a pool bar and restaurant in his coastal hometown in Alabama, and that small-town, southern background is probably why we bonded right away.

He's also the best offensive lineman on the team. Without Garrett, I wouldn't be as close to the MVP trophy as I am.

Stop hustling the college kids.

Garrett: Don't blow my cover, narc.

Exhaling a chuckle, I wrap it up with

On my way.

I tell the driver where to go, thinking how only Garrett could make me laugh after this evening.

It only took a few weeks of therapy to trace it all back to my dad, Kellan Murphy, billionaire CEO of MurKo Communications.

I don't come from a family of jocks, but I knew the first time I caught a football, the first time I led a team to victory, this was the life for me.

I'd found a group of guys who cared about me, who noticed when I wasn't okay and checked up on me. I had a real family.

My mother died before I was old enough to remember her, so growing up, it was just me and Kellan—and a string of house-keepers to cover the basics, a driver to take me to school until I was old enough to drive myself.

The only time I spent with my dad was at the formal dinners we shared every night in his sterile mansion in north Houston sitting at opposite ends of a long, polished oak table.

I would push the medium-rare steak around my plate wishing I could escape, and he'd try to think of questions to ask me.

How was your day?

Fine.

Did anything interesting happen?

No.

Silence.

Eventually, he'd give up, take his scotch, and leave, and I'd dash from the table, running down to the park where guys were always playing football. They didn't care who I was or how much money I had. It was all about the game.

I'd strip off my jacket and get in the middle, calling plays and throwing passes. I wanted to be a quarterback, but when Kellan got involved, he changed my direction.

When I first told my dad I wanted to play football professionally, he'd frowned like I told him I wanted to be a professional wrestler.

Then I started making headlines when I was in college, and he started doing the math. He realized he could use my football career to benefit his broadcasting business—provided I continued to be the best.

That's when his tune changed, and the pressure began. He said I should be a wide receiver because I almost never missed a catch and I was fast. If I could run, I scored.

No wide receiver has ever won the MVP, the Most Valuable Player award, in the league, and he said I could be the first.

Don't mistake that for him being supportive and encouraging. He was simply stating his wishes before he disappeared into his ivory tower again. I was still young and naive enough to think he cared. He had a point, and maybe it meant he would take an interest in me.

So I changed directions and became a wide receiver, not considering outside of the quarterback, the wide receivers take the most hits.

Garrett has taken a lot of hits to keep me safe on the field, and I've managed to avoid serious injury and run the ball all the way to the top of the game.

The black SUV stops at the Upper West Side bar, and I thank the guy before hopping out. Outside of openings and other big events, I'm mostly left alone by the media—unless I'm dating someone interesting, like a fashion-model, author-influencer.

The bar is packed with a different game on every television, from baseball to soccer. It's a sausage party with gym bros shoulder to shoulder holding bottles of beer and talking about the upcoming season.

Garrett is impossible to miss in the back corner holding a pool cue. He spots me when I walk in and motions for me to join them. I stop off and order a whiskey neat at the bar and a classic Angus burger before heading to where he's clearing the table.

He makes a big show of not taking the guy's money before slapping my back and walking with me to a standing table in the middle of the loud space.

"LL!" He clinks the neck of his beer against my glass. "You look like you just got an extra week of vacation. What happened?"

"I ended it with Natalia." Now that I say it out loud, I actually do feel lighter.

"Thank fuck," he shouts. "Of all the boney-assed bitches you've dated, she was the worst. Always posting shit on her damn phone and always criticizing everything you did."

A petite waitress with red hair and curves hustles up with my burger and fries. She's working hard, focused, and she looks good—or maybe she's just bringing me food, and I'm starving.

"Yeah, I'm done with supermodels."

"Don't get it twisted. Some of those gals are a lot of fun. But not that one." He grabs a handful of my fries while I take a big bite of burger. "If she made one more crack about you being a country mouse, I swear to the almighty football gods… She's from freakin Hoboken!"

I laugh around my bite. Garrett is so damn loud, and I love it. I don't even want to know how he knows where Natalia is from and I don't.

I exhale a groan as savory meat and cheese fill my mouth. "We started at that Galileo restaurant tonight."

"What did you think?"

"I can't tell if it's a prank or what. You're supposed to pour hot water over everything to rehydrate it before eating."

His brows tighten. "So it's like DIY?"

Shaking my head, I take another bite. "Hell, I don't know. I didn't stick around to find out."

My burger is gone in five bites, and he waves for another beer. "What now?"

Good question. Now that I have food in me, I can think, and I don't like my prospects.

We've got a month before training camp begins, the last thing I want is to hang around the city alone. It's as unappealing as going to Houston to work with my dad, as he keeps asking.

"Know anybody with a timeshare on the moon?"

Garrett grips my shoulder. "Come home to Newhope with me." My hand is already up, and I'm ready to argue when he cuts me off. "My parents' old house is huge, and it's right on the bay. There's plenty of room, and it'll be perfect for clearing your head."

"Last thing your family needs is another football player taking up all the space and eating all the food." I know what we're like.

"Dude, it's my brother Zane and my little sister Dylan, and she loves when we're home." He waves to the waitress, and she walks over.

"Another round?" She blinks up at him, and I'm pretty sure she's flirting.

"Just the check, Wendy." Of course he knows her name. "Logan Lightning, meet Wendy the waitress. She's a single mom, working to put herself through nursing school, and she will not make you wait for more beer."

"Nice to meet you." My voice is quieter. "Good luck with… everything."

She shakes her red head. "Don't tell my life story."

"It's a good story! You should be proud."

Garrett is a giant, cocky, friendly bear with curly brown hair and a thick beard. He's casual in a T-shirt and jeans, and his dimpled grin and merry blue eyes put everyone at ease.

By contrast, I'm lean muscle, dressed in a suit jacket with my dark hair styled and a light scruff on my cheeks. I study the world with my brow lowered, and there's not many people I trust. Life has taught me to maintain a buffer.

All that to say, we're pretty much night and day.

"Grab what you need and be at my place in an hour. I want to be on the road by ten." He's not giving me time to come up with an excuse, and I don't really want to.

Escaping to a small town on the coast sounds pretty good right now.

"You know my dad has a private jet service. We don't have to drive."

"Nah, I gotta have my truck."

Garrett and his truck. "I don't know anyone who drives a pickup in the city."

"They should. Most useful vehicle on the road."

"Well, if it isn't Low-gas Murphy." The annoying voice comes from behind me, and I turn to see Ricky Berke, wide receiver for the Challengers swaggering to where we're standing.

"Bro, that is the stupidest dunk. It's not even close to his nickname." Garrett leans on an elbow and still towers over Ricky.

My nemesis is undeterred. "I noticed you weren't at the White Party this year, Murph. Losing your cool, old man?"

In the race for MVP, it's down to me and this guy, three years in and completely full of himself. Just like I was, I guess, only I'd like to think I wasn't a total asshole.

"Actually, I was in Houston with my dad for the Fourth." And it was hot as the face of the sun and humid as a fucking rainforest.

"I heard you weren't invited." Ricky lifts his chin. "No surprise. Mr. Rubin only invites the best to his parties. Not sad ole has-beens like you."

"Whatever helps you sleep at night, Dick."

I don't bother defending myself. My father and I have been on the guest list for that annual summer party in the Hamptons since before I was in high school.

"I'm surprised you made the cut this year, *Dicky*," Garrett steps up beside me, crossing his arms. "I heard *Mike* likes ass-kissing copycats even less."

Ricky and I are the same height and build, but he has bright red hair, brown eyes, and pale skin covered in freckles. I'm a little faster than he is, and my secret weapon is Garrett covering my ass and helping me make the plays that keep the commentators talking.

"Like you know anything, Grizz." He looks past Garrett. "Where's Natalia?"

This guy is always swimming in my wake.

"I left her at Galileo's. She might still be there if you're interested."

"I heard she spent last month on a yacht in the Mediterranean with some Greek mogul." Ricky smirks. "And now ESPN has you trailing me in the MVP race. It really is a drag getting old."

"It's better than the alternative." I slap his shoulder, not interested in engaging any further.

"And by *alternative* he means *you*." Garrett points at him, a laugh in his voice, and he's vibrating, hoping Ricky is dumb enough to take a swing at one of us.

He's always up for a good bar brawl—because he always wins.

I put my hand on my friend's shoulder. "Meet at your place at ten, right?" Turning to Ricky, I tip my head. "Natalia's all yours."

I don't bother adding *if it's not too late*, since she does have Aristotle on standby. Hell, he's probably fine. She's looking for a second dick anyway, and this guy is made to order.

Garrett can't let it go that easy. The little waitress walks up, and he wraps an arm across her back

"Wendy, I'm sorry we have to leave you with this guy. He's a real piece of work, and a bad tipper." He grips Ricky's shoulder. "Try to resist the urge to spit in his drink."

"Hey!" Ricky's brown eyes widen in horror, but Wendy only laughs, waving him away.

"He's full of shit. Just look at that grin." She points up at my friend.

Garrett puts a hand over his chest like he's shot through the heart, but it's all an act.

I slip an extra twenty under our check just in case Wendy actually does get stiffed on her tips tonight. Then I drag him out of the bar ready to pack and see what the place he's always raving about looks like up close and personal.

An hour later, I'm in the plush leather front seat of his maxed-out, gunmetal F-150 racing south on Interstate 95 with the radio quietly playing country music.

We're facing a day-long drive, and I'm booking a room for us to crash in North Carolina. It's the first time I've made a road trip like this since I moved to the city, if ever.

"I saw you slip Wendy that extra tip." He glances at me, returning his eyes to the road.

I stretch in my chair, doing my best to get comfortable. We're going to be here a while. "You made me worry about her."

That makes him chuckle. "You're a good man, LL. I knew it the day I met you, even if you do approach the world with your guard up."

"Likewise."

"This is just what you need." Garrett glances at the lights of New York City in the rearview mirror. "Newhope will clear your head, get you back to square one, the basics."

"Does the chamber of commerce have you on the payroll?" I tease because I love.

Garrett is the poster boy for his hometown. It's all he talks about, but the truth is, at this point, I'm up for anything to kick me out of this funk.

I think about what he's told me in the few times we've spent together, shooting the shit. He lost his mom young, like I did. He's one of four brothers—all football stars—and a little sister.

Although besides Garrett, only his brother Hendrix is still in the game.

I don't know Hendrix well, but we've met. He plays for a team in Los Angeles, and he's a bit of a rockstar tight end.

His second oldest brother Zane was a career kicker forced to retire last year after getting nailed pretty bad during a fake field goal. It was a dramatic injury, his foot dangling at the end of his leg like a freak show while he roared in pain.

It's the kind of injury you like to pretend could never happen when you're headed onto the field each week, and they played it on reruns every five minutes. Fuck, I still get chills remembering it.

"Jack said he'll be picking his fall lineup while we're in town." Garrett's large hand is propped on the top of his steering wheel, and he has a toothpick in the corner of his mouth. "I told him we could help him out, maybe give the boys a pep talk."

His oldest brother is a retired star quarterback from Texas. I remember watching Jack Bradford on the field and wondering how anyone with that much talent could ever retire. He did, though, at the top of his game. A legend.

Now he coaches high school ball. Friday night lights.

"Sure. Whatever he needs." I glance out the dark window wondering what my nineteen-year-old self would think of meeting Jack Bradford in the flesh.

Then I travel back a bit more, wondering what I would say to my fifteen-year-old self today. What would he even be able to hear? Certainly not that life at the top isn't as great as it looks from the bottom. Or that no matter where you go, there you are.

Hell, maybe I'm just depressed. I haven't slept with a woman in a long time, and the last time I did, it was with someone who was more interested in her social media following. I'm not being a hater. There was a time it was all I cared about, too.

"Dylan said Zane is laying low, but he's healing fine." My friend's jaw tightens, and he shakes his head. "It's going to be the first time I'll have seen him since that accident, and it was a fucking nightmare."

"Tell me about it." My lips tighten, and my stomach cramps.

It's a big switch to go from the nonstop schedule of a big game every week, seven months out of the year, traveling all over the country, being a celebrity to a certain segment of the population, to nothing.

Full stop.

From the roar of a stadium, to dead silence. Forgotten.

I've heard guys talk about the shock of retirement, and I'm not going to lie, I'm not looking forward to it. Even if I have been floating the possibility of this being my last year. It all depends on that trophy, even if that trophy means more to my dad than it does to me.

"That just leaves Dylan, but she'll be working at the restaurant most days." Nodding, I picture a kid living on the coast in south Alabama.

My mind travels a thousand miles down the dark road ahead of us, far from the lights of Manhattan. I think about the life I left behind when I graduated from UT.

Taking out my phone, I pull up my contacts and select my father's name. In the glow of the dashboard light, I text him what I've been thinking for weeks.

I'm not going back there.

Chapter 2

Dylan

"**G**IRL, YOU'D BETTER WASH YOUR HANDS WITH MAYONNAISE." My lifelong bestie Craig stands at my shoulder, watching as I carefully grate a small amount of ghost pepper into a glass bowl. "Olive oil. Lard."

"I have coconut oil." My voice is quiet, focused. "I only need a little bit for the recipe."

"Don't touch your eyes or your nose or your... you know." He tips his chin in the direction of my crotch, then takes a step back, holding a damp washcloth at the level of his eyes. "Or me."

I lean forward with a silent laugh before raising my gloved hands like a monster. "Craaaaig..." I make crazy eyes. "I'm going to keeel you..."

He hops back, letting out a squeal, and I snort. Then I almost drop the dangerous fruit, which makes *me* squeal.

"Stop distracting me! This is delicate work."

"I had nothing to do with whatever that was." He flicks his wrist, rounding the bar. "Threatening my life with a pepper."

Craig and I have been thick as thieves since his family moved from Mobile to the house across the street when we were kids. We bonded instantly, playing Barbie vs Bratz together every day after school. I had a Nutcracker Barbie, while he preferred the feisty Yasmin. She reminded him of a drag queen, and he's always been ready to play dress up.

My aunt Thelma, who took over long-distance parenting from Birmingham after my mom died, said Bratz dolls were "inappropriate"—whatever that means—and she would send me a new American Girl doll every year for my birthday.

It was the only time Barbie and Yasmin joined forces to take down the giant with the weird eyes. Then they'd go on "safari" together, which meant we'd take them into the backyard, and then they'd return to changing outfits and ignoring Ken.

"That pepper's going to get you in trouble." Craig tucks his nose and mouth behind his shoulder as he finishes wiping down the counter.

We're prepping for the lunch crowd at Cooters & Shooters, my family's bayside bar and restaurant. Our dad named it, and our mom got the biggest kick out of it.

I was too little to understand why my brothers all stared wide-eyed at him. It took Garrett asking why the restaurant was named after a girl's coochie for my dad to explain the original definition of the word.

A *cooter* is a large, aquatic turtle. Dad said you had your river cooter, your Florida red-bellied cooter, the northern red-bellied cooter... Our mom only laughed harder the more he listed, and the logo and interior design were set.

The restaurant is basically just a big, open dining room with strategically placed booths separating the tables from the bar area, complete with turtles in terrariums and driftwood lining the walls.

The pool tables are on the side porch with a screen door separating them from the rest of the place, and massive ceiling fans run down the center, turning their large blades lazily, keeping the humid air moving with or without the bay breeze.

By day, it's casual family dining, complete with a fenced-in, beachside play area for the kids. Parents can relax, finish their food or conversations or drinks with their children safely playing as they watch.

It was my mom's idea when she and Dad opened the place. She said she was never able to eat out after giving birth to four rowdy boys and a girl who didn't know she wasn't as big as they were.

It's true. All four of my brothers are six-foot-plus and two hundred pounds or more, while I clock in at five-foot-four. Back then, my metabolism was so high, I was as skinny as Craig still is, but these days I've got more curves.

A cool, gulf breeze wafts through the open-air restaurant, and a nostalgic smile lifts my cheeks remembering those days when we were all here together.

By night, things get a little rowdier. The bar crowd picks up, and the jukebox gets louder. It's still perfectly fine for families, but most parents with kids clear out by seven. Probably because they want the kids to sleep, and with all the nightly shenanigans, I imagine they get pretty keyed up.

I know my brother Jack's daughter does when she stays with Aunt Deedee—especially on a "Dare" night. The Dare nights have taken on a life of their own.

I got interested in hot peppers a few years back after watching a cooking show about them. I was fascinated by the heat scale, by where the spice is located in the fruit, by how long it lingers and where it appears on the tongue...

Then I was talked-slash-begged into chaperoning a four-day cruise with the high school seniors going from New Orleans to Cozumel, and while we were in Mexico, we visited a farm and learned even more about the different varieties as well as their health benefits and uses throughout history.

We got home, and I tested my first "Dylan's Dare Dish" for

the evening crowd. I made five gallons of spicy-pepper refried beans made with habaneros, which I used in a seven-layer dip. We sold out in an hour, and now I can't go a week without a new Dare.

There's always some lunatic begging me to up the ante, so I try to find a different hot pepper for each challenge. This week: ghost peppers.

"The recipe calls for an eighth teaspoon, and then it's back in the freezer with this guy." I finish grating and carry it to the utility sink where a tub of virgin coconut oil waits.

"Put a warning label on the bag."

"I will." I rub the coconut oil under my fingernails and on my hands and wrists. "Did you know ghost peppers kill the bacteria that causes stomach ulcers, and can even improve your heart health?"

"I know two people died doing the one-chip challenge."

"That was a Carolina Reaper, and two people died drinking caffeinated lemonade at Panera Bread."

"Your point?"

"The wait staff always tells them which pepper is in the dish and how hot it is." I wipe the oil away with a towel before washing my hands with soap and water. "Nobody's going to die. We're expanding folks's horizons."

"You're playing with fire, and I mean that in the most literal sense of the word." Craig points as he grabs the tray of refilled salt and pepper shakers.

"Hey, love birds!" Allie Sinclair, my head waitress and newest bestie grabs her apron off the hook by the door. "You're not quarreling are you?"

Allie is a cute girl about the same height as me with sparkling blue eyes. Her dark hair is shoulder-length, and her olive skin is tanned from the summer sun.

She moved here from New Orleans with her son Austin two years ago to be the new librarian at our old high school—or the new media specialist, as some people call her.

Newhope is so small, it didn't take long for me to hear she was having trouble making ends meet on a school librarian's salary, so I stopped by the office and mentioned how I sure could use some extra help at the restaurant. The rest is history.

It's her second summer working with us here, and she's the best waitress we have. She paid her way through college working in restaurants in the French Quarter, so she's prepared for pretty much anything.

I always hate it when the summer ends, and she has to leave us.

"Of course not." Craig breezes past her. "I never quarrel with my Clara."

He's referring to our days dancing *The Nutcracker* together.

Craig was also my ballet partner at the dance academy growing up, and every Christmas we were Clara and the Nutcracker Prince, except one year when the ballerina who was supposed to do the Arabian coffee dance got sick. We had to fill in at the last minute, and I loved it. Mostly because I adored that midriff costume.

"You two were so beautiful." Allie sighs, grabbing the tray of refilled ketchup bottles. "I could watch those old videos all day on repeat. Did Mrs. Laverne talk to you about teaching ballet at the high school next year?"

My stomach twists, and I carry the glass bowl of ghost-pepper shreds to the stove. "Yeah, she said something about it."

"And?" Allie's eyebrows rise expectantly.

"I haven't given her an answer." I swallow the lump in my throat, plastering the fake smile I use whenever anyone asks me about ballet. "It's been a long time since I danced."

"I'm sure it'll all come rushing back." Craig is one of the few people who knows how much I lost when my ankle broke that summer and my dreams of becoming the next Gelsey Kirkland broke with it.

"Like my period did that time I tried to dance without underwear?" Humor is my shield against the past.

His smile vanishes. "We swore *never* to speak of that again."

"What!" Allie yells from across the large, open dining area. "What the hell are you talking about?"

I press my lips together, fighting a laugh. "Time plus horror equals humor, right?"

"No." His response is flat.

"You know how *un*-cool it is to tease a story like that and then not tell me what happened?" Allie's black flip-flops smack against the distressed heart pine as she walks back to us.

She places the empty tray on the counter, her blue eyes narrowed. Her short ponytail bounces happily when she moves, and she's dressed in a light blue T-shirt with our logo on the front—three turtles on a log with crossed pool cues.

"Freshman year, *Nutcracker* rehearsals," I start. "We'd been reading about how the dancers in New York don't wear underwear beneath their tights when they dance, and we were all about emulating the American Ballet Company back then."

"Okaaay…" Allie's brow furrows as I continue.

"I cannot believe you're telling this." Craig walks to the PA system in the corner behind the bar.

"Of course, the first time I tried it, in the middle of a shoulder-sit…" I don't finish the sentence, and she hesitates.

Then her whole face flashes with horror. "Nooo… Not that."

"That."

"On his shoulder?" she whispers, glancing empathetically at Craig.

"You. Swore." He is not amused, but I confess, it was so long ago, I really can laugh about it now.

Allie pulls her lips in and bites them, dropping her chin to hide her face. "It's so awful."

She can barely get the words out without breaking as she follows me into the kitchen to the big stove. I take the lid off a pot of fresh salsa and carefully add half the minced ghost pepper.

I also toss in some grated onions and cilantro and give it a stir before covering it again.

"See all the knowledge you have?" She's doing her best to put an optimistic twist on the most embarrassing moment of my entire dance career. "Those teenage girls would be lucky to have you as a teacher. You could save them from… *That.*"

Our eyes meet as we return to the dining room, and we snort through our grimaces.

"You are both dead to me," Craig snips as he passes us. "Dead."

"You have to do it, Dylan," Allie begs. "We'll get to see each other every day all year!"

"I don't know." Heaviness still lingers in my chest. "I'd have to work it around my schedule here."

"Craig can keep things going during the day. This place practically runs itself."

"Do girls even care about ballet anymore?"

"Yes! And I'm sure I could get Austin and his friends to take your class if you need them. I'll say they get to lift pretty girls, and I won't mention the possibility of Aunt Flo making an appearance."

"I thought he was going out for the football team this year." Austin will be a freshman in the fall. "I'm not sure he'll have time to take a dance class."

"He might." She shrugs. "Your brother Jack is pretty… something."

A hint of a grin plays around her lips, and she sucks so bad at hiding her massive crush on my "hot" oldest brother. Too bad since his divorce, he only seems to care about that high school team and his little girl.

It's crazy how life just keeps on going no matter what it throws at you.

"I'll think about it some more."

She does a little squeal, and I smile. "Oh! Did I mention Garrett's bringing a friend home with him?"

"You did not!" Craig is suddenly back in the conversation. "Who is he? Or better yet, what position does he play?"

"He's a receiver. Logan Murphy? I think he's a big deal, but aren't they all now?" All of my brothers became stars in their own right, following in our father's footsteps.

"Lightning Murphy?" Allie yells from the opposite end of the dining room, where she's unlocking the screened-in back porch where the pool tables are located. "He is fire! I saw him on the Deux Moi Instagram with some six-foot-tall stick insect."

"I don't even know what that means," I chuckle, returning to the kitchen.

The wooden door slams behind her, and Craig has his phone out in a flash pulling up the app. Taking the pot from the stove to the large, silver worktable in the center of the room, I ladle stewed salsa into an industrial-sized blender to puree.

"Oh, come to Papa!" Craig fans his face like he'll faint. "He's a wide receiver. Just the kind I like. Look at him run."

My head dips with a laugh. "I hate to burst your bubble, but I think he's straight. Garrett said something about him coming off a breakup."

"Is that so?" He cocks his head. "Maybe he needs to get over her by getting under you. Clear some of the cobwebs off that coochie."

"No." I do not laugh.

"I know, I know, no football players." He returns to the phone. "Speaking of breakups, Davis came by the bar last night looking for you. He said you're going to have to talk to him one of these days."

"Just how drunk was he?" I puff air through my mouth, sending my hair off my cheeks. "There's nothing to say. I caught him porking Stephanie in the bushes behind Parky's."

"So many jokes just waiting to be made…"

"I haven't been able to eat grilled oysters since." I hit the button on the blender, giving it a few pulses before dumping the salsa in a larger bowl and returning to the pot.

"Honestly, I'm more mad about losing the oysters than that cheating piece of shit."

"We should beat up his Lexus with his golf clubs like that guy's wife did." Craig pulls the sleeve of his white tee higher, showing off his skinny bicep. "I've been working out."

"That *guy* was Tiger Woods, and I don't care enough to destroy his car." I shake my head, hitting the blender again, giving it a few pulses. "I stayed in that relationship way past the expiration date."

"If you ask me, it expired before you took him off the shelf."

The Dare dish is ready, and I put all the bowls in the refrigerator. We carry the small, plastic serving bowls and large bags of tortilla chips out to the bar, and when I bend down to stash them, I feel the roll around my waist.

I'm not embarrassed by my body at all, but it's a lot different than it used to be.

"I can't teach dance." It's a low musing, a nonstop continuation of the arguments swirling in my mind since Mrs. Laverne made her offer. "I look nothing like a ballerina anymore."

Craig frowns, and I gesture to my soft body, looking over my shoulder at my round booty filling my denim cutoffs.

Then I pull at my T-shirt stretched across my chest. "Ballerinas don't have boobs."

"Girl, stop." He holds up a hand. "That ass is fine, and as for up top… I can't imagine any straight boy complaining about your juicy double."

"You'd never get me on your shoulder these days."

"Just give me time, Pepper Spice. I told you I'm working out."

My eyes land on the clock, and I jump. "Shit! I've got to get back to the house and make up the guest room before the guys get here."

"Pool area's all set." Allie returns to the room with a pencil behind her ear and a pad in her apron pocket. "Tell me about the Dare dish."

"Ghost pepper salsa served with tortilla chips and a big scoop of sour cream." I count off on my fingers.

"And the warning?"

"A ghost pepper is a hundred times hotter than a jalapeño. It's one million on the Scoville scale, so proceed with caution. Expert-level tasters only." Allie's eyes widen, and she nods as I continue. "If they're in distress, don't give them water or beer. Dairy neutralizes capsaicin oil, which is why we have the sour cream."

"Got it." She does a sharp nod. "And if they're lactose intolerant?"

"Tomato juice."

"Orange juice also works." Craig hits the button and "Hot Stuff" by Donna Summer blasts through the dining hall. "Our intro music is ready to go!"

At some point, he started the tradition of introducing my Dare dishes with a pepper- or spicy-themed song. Then members of the wait staff decided to hop onto the bar and dance *Coyote-Ugly* style.

Like I said, the evening crowd gets a little rowdy.

"Aw, I wanted to do 'Give it Away' by the Red Hot Chili Peppers!" Allie whines while shaking her hips to the old disco tune.

"I have to buy assless chaps for that one." Craig says it like it's just a given.

"No assless chaps." I point at him. "We still have kids in the restaurant at night."

"Then at *least* I have to have a pair of glittery horns and gold lipstick."

"I got you, baby." Allie wraps her arm around his shoulders, laughing as they continue dancing.

We're getting closer to eleven, which is opening time. Not many people show up this early, but we have to be ready if they do.

"What are you going to do with that?" Craig points to the glass bowl holding leftover ghost-pepper shreds.

I dig behind the bar and take out a jar of local honey, setting it beside the open bag of tortilla chips.

"I saw a recipe for spicy honey and goat cheese toasts." I inhale with a little shiver. "Doesn't that sound amazing?"

"That might be too fancy for the ole Coot-Shoot." He switches off Donna and puts on quiet yacht rock for the daytime crowd.

"I'll eat it," Allie cries. "Goat cheese is the bomb!"

"Do people still say *the bomb?*"

"This person does!" Allie continues, rolling silverware in napkins and singing along to Toto on the PA system.

I'm about to go when a low voice echoes through the dining room.

"Dylan?" It's my biggest brother Garrett. "Where you at, girl? What's for breakfast? I'm so hungry I could eat a horse."

My chest squeezes at the sound of his happy, boisterous request. Every time he or Hendrix come home, I'm struck by how badly I miss them.

"Garrett!" I squeal, breaking into a run. "You're home!"

My arms are around his neck, and I dance around to jump onto his massive back. Wrapping my legs around his waist, I hang on like I could possibly hug him tighter.

"Get off me, banshee!" He laughs that deep laugh of his.

Lowering my legs, I hop around in front again to give him a proper hug. Garrett is massive, and he gives the best hugs, lifting me off my feet.

"I've missed you, Sis." He puts me down again. "You've got a little meat on your bones. Not so breakable these days."

"I've stopped playing football with ogres." I push his shoulder, and he doesn't even move.

"You look good."

In that moment, a tall figure steps up beside him, and I hiccup a breath.

"Holy shit…" The words slip from my mouth on an involuntary whisper.

Logan Murphy should come with a warning. The picture Craig showed me on Instagram didn't do him justice at all. He's as hot as a Carolina Reaper on black asphalt in the middle of July.

He's a few inches shorter than Garrett with softly messy dark hair and smoldering blue eyes. His jaw is impossibly square and dusted with a five o'clock shadow, and his biceps stretch the sleeves of his light blazer.

Don't even get me started on how the black tee underneath stretches across his chest. His waist is narrow like a runner's, and I can just picture his muscled ass with the way his thighs stretch those dark jeans.

Full lips part in a smile over straight white teeth, and a blush burns from my neck all the way to the top of my ears when I realize I've been staring at him way too long—with my mouth open, no less.

"Sorry…" I shake my head, sticking out my hand. "I'm Dylan. You must be Logan?"

Garrett doesn't even notice my reaction to his drop-dead gorgeous friend. "Craig! How's it hanging, man?" They shake and Garrett pulls him into a crushing hug. "Got anything to eat? We've been driving since 3 o'clock this morning."

"It's nice to meet you, Dylan." Logan's voice is low and smooth like that jar of honey, and he has a freaking dimple in his cheek. *A freaking dimple.* "Garrett talks about you all the time."

"He does?" I sound completely star-struck. "Can I get you something? Coffee, tea…"

Me…

"Coffee would be great."

I scurry into the kitchen to get myself together, reminding myself I don't date football players, while I also grab coffee and soft drinks, leaving them out front talking to Allie and Craig.

"Dylan, is there food at the house?" Garrett calls when I return with two coffees.

"There's food right here." I put the mugs down. "Let me grab the sugar and cream, and I'll whip up something."

I'm on my way back to the kitchen when I hear the sound of plastic rattling on the bar. "What's this? Salsa?"

I turn around just in time to see him pass a chip to Logan, and the two of them scoop into the bowl of grated ghost pepper.

Throwing up my hands, I scream *No!* Craig is close enough to slap the chip out of Garrett's hand, but it's too late for Logan. It's in his mouth, and just as fast, his eyes bug out.

He clutches his throat, dropping to one knee, and all hell breaks loose.

Chapter 3

Logan

I'M DYING.

Volcanic magma coats my tongue and throat. Tears flood my eyes, spilling onto my cheeks, and snot runs uncontrollably from my nose. Chaos is all around me, and I fall from my knees to my ass.

I try to speak, to beg for mercy, but my voice has been burned off. My entire body is burning, and I'm pretty sure these are my final moments on the planet.

From a far-off distance, I hear a woman crying. Garrett's big hand clasps my shoulder, pressing my back against the bar as the skinny guy holds a plastic glass of milk to my mouth.

"Drink," Garrett orders, but I can't.

My lips are gone, melted away by the fire of a thousand suns.

"Drink the milk, Logan!" He grasps my jaw, pulling it down and pouring the cool liquid into my mouth so fast it floods over, running down my chin and onto my shirt.

The burn eases slightly, and at the hint of relief, I grip the glass with both hands, desperately chugging the milk like my life depends on it.

I think it might.

"What have I done?" Dylan is on her knees beside me clasping a washcloth in her hands.

Someone returns with another full glass of milk, and I grab it, control slowly seeping back as the fire recedes.

"Try holding it in your mouth and swishing." Garrett's voice is worried as he studies me.

I blink my eyes, trying to regain focus as the pain slowly, slowly dissipates from my mouth and throat, but it isn't gone. Not by a long shot.

"Better?" he asks.

"My stomach…" I put a hand on my wet shirt.

The burning pain is slowly moving lower, into my abdomen.

"I'm so sorry, Logan." Dylan holds out the cloth. "Craig told me not to leave those pepper shreds out like that. I never dreamed you would try to eat them."

Her brow crinkles, and I look down at myself. I'm a fucking mess. I take the cloth, wiping the wetness off my cheeks and my upper lip. My nose is still running, and my overpriced T-shirt and linen blazer are ruined.

"Shew, crisis averted just in time to open the doors." The other woman, Allie, returns to the kitchen with the skinny guy, Craig, right behind her.

"I'll see if we have any ice cream." Garrett follows them, leaving me sitting like a wounded soldier on the battlefield.

"Can I help you up?" Dylan puts her hand on my shoulder, and I look down at myself.

How's that for putting things into perspective? Big bad Logan Murphy, *Lightning* Murphy, brought to his knees by a pint-sized woman and a tiny pinch of pepper.

If I weren't in so much pain, I'd laugh at my dumb ass Instead, I lift my hand, rubbing my palm over my brow. Even with the stop-off in Greensboro, I'm exhausted from the twenty-hour drive, and now I feel like I've fought a war.

"Are you okay?" Her eyes are warm caramel, and she blinks those damp, full lashes at me.

She's acting like she thought I might die, too. I nod, pushing slowly off the floor as she holds my arm.

"I guess I owe you one." My voice is weak, but I'm trying to break the tension.

"Atta boy. Walk it off." Garrett hands me a paper cup of vanilla ice cream as I stagger to a chair. "Bro, you scared the shit out of me. I didn't know what was happening."

"What *did* happen?" My lower stomach burns in a weird way, like I literally swallowed a burning coal, and it's making its way through me.

I'm pretty confident it's going to burn my ass off later.

"Congratulations, you just won the one-chip challenge." Craig extends his hand to shake mine. "We shall call you Fire Eater."

Garrett laughs, slapping him on the back. "Good one, Cray cray."

Yes. These people are crazy, but to be honest, I think I like it. Not the part where they try to kill me. The part where the tension is broken, and I don't have to figure out who I am here. It's pretty hard to be a hotshot football star with snot on my upper lip and milk all over my clothes.

"You ate shredded ghost pepper." Dylan returns. "I'm so sorry."

I look down, taking her in properly. It's what I was trying to do when I nearly died.

I thought Garrett's kid sister would be just that, a kid. Not a feisty pinup with long, dark hair, sparkling amber eyes, full tits, and an ass just begging for me to squeeze it. The last thing I remember, she was looking at me like she was stripping me naked. Her plump lips parted, and my stomach tightened as all sorts of unholy thoughts flooded my mind.

Nothing like a ghost pepper to torch those fantasies.

Okay, the fantasies are still there, but it's almost worse. My best friend has a fine-assed little sister, and I'm only here for a month. Raise a glass to what will never be. *Damn.*

"Aunt Deedee!" A little-girl voice rings through the empty dining area, and a streak of brown curls flies past, jumping onto Dylan's back.

I guess tackle-hugs are to be expected in a football family.

"Hey, baby!" Dylan laughs, swinging the little girl around to her waist. "Are you here with your dad?"

"Jack?" Garrett turns, a huge smile splitting his lips.

"Gary." A tall guy pulls him into a hug. "It's been too long."

They slap each other's backs then turn to face me. "Meet my buddy Logan Murphy. Logan, this is my big brother Jack."

"Jack." I clear my throat, feeling true embarrassment for the first time in years.

I grew up watching this guy dominate the field while playing for Texas. I even copied a lot of his plays when I thought I'd be a quarterback.

Now he's standing in front of me in the flesh, smiling, fine lines creasing the corners of his blue eyes, and I'm a freshly extinguished mess.

"Logan, good to meet you." He holds out a hand, giving mine a firm shake. "I've watched you play. You're a helluva receiver, and fast… Damn, that catch in the third quarter against Oregon…"

Shyness is not in my wheelhouse, but Jack Bradford saying these words to me is kind of blowing my mind.

"I couldn't have done it without your brother," I deflect, but it's true.

The ball was right on the tips of my fingers, but that cornerback was right on my heels, until The Grizzly took him down.

"You boys gonna come out and help me field a team?"

"Wouldn't miss it." Garrett reaches for the little girl riding his sister's hip. "Like I wouldn't miss seeing this peanut."

"Uncle Grizzly!" she yells, climbing onto his back.

"Who told you it was okay for you to get big?" he teasingly fusses. "I told you to stop growing when I'm out of town."

The little girl frowns. "It just happens! I don't do anything."

"It just happens?" he mimics her, jogging around the room while she squeals, her brown ringlets bouncing. "I'm going to come back and find you a grown-up girl."

"Can I still ride piggyback?" Her tone is worried.

Jack turns to his sister while the two of them make the rounds. "Sure you don't mind watching her today? I know it's last-minute."

"Of course, not. She's a good helper."

He looks over at his brother. "Kimmie Joy!" The little girl's head pops up, and he points to her. "You mind Aunt Dylan, and don't talk back."

"She never talks back." Dylan walks over to take Kimmie from her uncle.

"Cooters & Shooters' famous three-egg Mediterranean omelet with fresh spinach, Roma tomatoes, feta cheese, and a side of buttery toast." Allie sets two plates on the table where I'm standing, and Garrett immediately takes a seat.

The savory scent makes my stomach growl loudly. "Damn," I mutter under my breath.

Garrett is three bites in when he sits back and hollers, "Allie Sinclair, you are the queen of my double-wide trailer!"

She sasses right back. "You know I wouldn't live in a trailer, Garrett Bradford."

"If you change your mind, the offer stands." He returns to his breakfast, and I'm right behind him.

"You're just hungry." Allie laughs, and I catch her gaze drift shyly to Jack. "Need some breakfast, Coach?"

"Ah, thanks Allie. I've got to take Zane to physical therapy in Mobile." He doesn't even notice her doe-eyes blinking up at him. "I'll be back around three."

"Wake me up if I'm still asleep" Garrett says through a mouth full of toast.

Craig rolls the mop bucket out to clean up the milk mess while I pull out a chair.

Taking the fork and knife from the napkin roll, I exhale a laugh. "I can't get over the name of this place."

"How so?" He doesn't even look up.

I glance at him the sideways. "*Cooters?*"

"Are you insulting Snappy, Happy, and Earl?" He nods at the sign with three turtles on a log in front of crossed pool cues.

"Nobody calls turtles *cooters* anymore."

"What do they call them?" He gives me a haughty look.

"Turtles." I shake a little salt and pepper over the bright yellow eggs. "This smells delicious."

But I hesitate before taking a bite. The little girl stands right at my side watching me.

I glance at her. "Want some?"

She shakes her head no. "Why are you acting like you're scared of those eggs?"

"Kimmie J, let the men eat." Allie taps her little shoulder, but she's still watching me curiously.

Garrett pokes her side, and she squeals, slapping at his hand. "He ate one of Aunt Dylan's peppers."

That makes her eyes widen. "Did you cry?"

"Just about." I take a bite of my omelet, thankful it's not the least bit spicy.

"He didn't just cry," Garrett laughs. "His whole face exploded."

Kimmie puts her small hand on my arm. "I bit a pepper once, and I cried."

"Then you got ice cream." Dylan walks over, taking her hand.

"Sounds like Aunt Deedee needs to stop leaving hot peppers lying around." Garrett cuts his eyes at his sister.

"*Or* people need to stop walking up and eating things

without asking what they are." She squats in front of her niece, right beside me so if I glance to the left, I can see her soft cleavage stretching that white, V-neck tee.

I keep my eyes on my plate, which I'm quickly devouring. This is the best damn omelette I've had in a long time.

"Want to help me make up the bedrooms for the men?" she asks Kimmie.

"We can help you with that." Garrett is on his feet, carrying his clean plate to the kitchen.

"Well, shii—oot." I quickly clean up my language. "You finished fast."

"I'm tired, bro." He returns to his sister. "Walk over when you're done."

I look at my nearly finished plate, and exhaustion rolls over me. My near-death experience wiped me out, too, it seems.

"I'll come with you." Standing, I carry my plate to the kitchen, grabbing the last piece of toast before following them out the door.

When we got here, we left the truck parked in front of a large white house with a wrap-around porch and a yard full of blooming Crepe Myrtle trees. All our bags are still in the bed, so we stop and grab them while the girls head inside.

"My room's upstairs. The guest room is on the first floor behind the kitchen." He's talking as we walk up the steps to the front door.

Palmettos and camellia bushes mix around the edge of the porch, and a swing on the corner sways in the light breeze. Overhead, the ceiling is painted pale blue, and the scent of sweet olive and salt water hangs in the heavy air.

It's all so familiar, warm, and welcoming.

Garrett holds the screen door, and I follow him into the house. Dark, polished-wood floors line the downstairs. To the left is an open living room with French doors and lace curtains. Plush couches are arranged in front of a large flatscreen television, and a piano is in the corner.

He grips my shoulder, giving it a shake. "I'll wake you in time for dinner."

With that, he heads up the stairs, and I follow the sound of voices coming from the end of the hall in front of me. I pass the kitchen on my left. It's large and surprisingly modern with a brick oven, custom cabinets, a farm sink, and a heavy-duty gas range with a hammered-copper hood.

Looks like somebody could prepare a feast in here and probably has on several occasions.

"I got it!" The little girl's voice echoes from the other side of the door in front of me.

Peeking my head around it, I see her helping Dylan spread fresh sheets over a queen-sized bed. Dylan does most of the work, but to her credit, Kimmie Joy tries.

She puts a large pillow under her small chin, struggling to stuff it into a pillow case.

"Let me help you with that." I put my suitcase on the floor and walk over to take the pillow from her. "This thing is as big as you are."

"You can put your clothes in the dresser here, and I'm pretty sure there are extra hangers in the closet." Dylan shakes a quilt, quickly covering the bed.

I open the closet in the corner and pull the string for the light.

"Shit!" I yell, jumping back from dozens of glassy eyes staring straight at me.

Dolls in different outfits with real hair and freaky eyes stand on all the shelves, like some kind of *Child's Play* army waiting for activation.

"Sorry…" I lower my elbow, glancing down at Kimmie. "I wasn't expecting that."

"It's okay." A small hand clutches mine. "My daddy knows bad words, too."

"Kimmie!" Dylan scolds, quickly swiping the dolls off the shelves and under her arm. "Did you do this?"

"They had to go in the closet, Aunt Deedee!" The little girl lifts her hands to me, and I instinctively pick her up. "They're always watching me."

She tucks her face into my neck, and my chest tightens unexpectedly. I haven't been around little kids much, and to have her turning to me for support this way makes me want to step up for her.

Dylan puts her hand on her niece's back. "Come here." Kimmie slides from me to her aunt. "Sorry about that, Logan."

"Hey, no apologies necessary. I get it."

Kimmie starts to squirm, and Dylan puts her on her feet. The little girl takes off running down the hall, and Dylan carries the dolls to the door.

"Do you collect those or something?" I'm really hoping she says no.

"No, I was always more into ballerina Barbie, but my aunt would send me one of these every Christmas" She holds up a blonde one. "Kit Kittridge is an American hero."

"I'll take your word for it."

"You're saying she's not?" A tease is in her tone.

"I'm saying I'll sleep better knowing *M3gan* isn't in the closet waiting to murder me in my sleep."

"She's supposed to be wholesome."

"Not with those eyes."

Dylan bites her lip, fighting a grin. "If you need anything, just let me know."

"Right now all I need is sleep, but thanks. I will."

"Sorry again about the whole… ghost-pepper thing earlier." Her cheeks flush a pretty shade of pink, and she's really something standing in the doorway in her cutoffs with the soft light from the windows shining in her hair.

"I'll be sure to ask before I eat anything."

"You were only following my brother's lead." Her chin lifts, and she smiles up at me, hesitating.

"What?"

"You're not what I expected, Logan Murphy."

"What were you expecting, Dylan Bradford?" I grin, taking a step closer.

"I don't know." She shrugs. "Most of the big-time jocks I've met wouldn't be so understanding about eating a ghost pepper… And I'm not sure they'd comfort a five-year-old who's scared of American Girl dolls."

"I don't like those dolls either."

A smile curls her full lips. "You're nice."

"I'm glad somebody thinks so."

"Garrett thinks so, or he wouldn't have brought you here. And Kimmie Joy thinks so, or she wouldn't have let you hold her."

"She's a cute kid."

"She's a good judge of character."

I reach up, hooking my fingers on the top of the door, not really wanting to say goodbye. Her eyes flicker to my biceps, and she blinks down at the doll in her hands. I'm standing here in my jeans and a short-sleeved tee still damp from the milk intended to put out the fire. Only a different fire is smoldering, and I don't think milk's going to extinguish it.

Her cheeks are that pretty shade of pink again, and I'm starting to like what it could mean.

Lowering my arms, I cross them over my chest, leaning against the door jamb. "What will you do today?"

"Manage the restaurant." She holds up one of the dolls. "After I find a place to put these."

"Got any critters you need to scare away?"

She ducks with a silent laugh. "That's not a bad idea, actually. I might."

"Aunt Dee*deeeeee!*" The little girl yells from the front of the house. "Uncle Craig said stop flirting with Mr. Logan and come back to the restaurant!"

Dylan's eyes widen. "I am not… That man is so spoiled. I can't be gone for five minutes before he starts acting up."

"It's okay." I grin, taking a step back. "I don't mind a pretty girl flirting with me."

At that her face turns as red as one of her hot peppers, and she spins on her heel, leaving me at the door. It makes me laugh, and I call a goodbye after her.

"Have a good rest, Logan." She calls over her shoulder, and I watch her round ass sway in those cutoffs as she goes.

Yeah, this is going to be an interesting trip.

Chapter 4

Dylan

"PUT MORE FRIES ON THE PLATES." I stop SALINA DUCK on her way out, heaping French fries around the burgers on her tray.

"I just grab 'em the way they're served!" She shakes her brown ponytail before heading into the packed dining area.

I step into the kitchen, going to where Thomas is working at the grill, flipping fresh burgers while he monitors the frier.

"Why are you skimping on the fries, Thomas? Are we running out?"

"Nope." His full lips tighten with a frown as he shakes his head, flipping a line of Angus beef burgers on the grill. "Craig said we're cutting back on the fries for heart health."

His tone is disapproving, and my head snaps to Craig, who's standing at the refrigerator drinking Red Bull.

"What?" He glances from me to our cook.

"You told Thomas to put less fries on the plates?"

"I read an article about saturated fats and how bad they

are for us. I think it's our responsibility to look out for the customers."

"We're not skimping on the fries. Anybody in the restaurant business will tell you, 'Don't mess with what works.'" I glance at the clock, and it's after seven. "You'll put us out of business."

"Nobody's going to stop coming to the Coot-n-Shoot," he argues, and Thomas makes a noise like *I don't know…*

"Back to normal rations, Thomas." The old man nods in agreement, and I reach into the refrigerator, taking out a giant silver bowl of salsa. "Time for the Dare Dish of the Week!"

Salina returns with her empty tray. "Buddy Outlaw said it's about time you stopped skimping on the fries." She cuts her eyes at Craig. "He asked if you're trying to put him on a diet or something."

Craig puts a hand on his chest. "Who told him it was me?"

"I'm not losing tip money over your harebrained schemes."

"It's all fixed. Now let's do this." We head out to the bar where I placed the small plastic baskets earlier. "Fill these with the tortilla chips, and I'll scoop the salsa. Hit the red light, Allie."

"It's time!" Allie does a happy jump, running to cue the lights and music.

The first strains of "Hot Stuff" beat through the bar, and people start to clap and yell. The side door leading out to the pool tables opens, and the players step through the doorway to watch as Allie, Salina, Craig and a few of the other waitresses hop onto the bar to shake their hips to the old Donna Summer disco hit.

Craig gets the biggest cheers when he pulls on a shoulder-length, blond wig with flowing curls. He also pulls the bottom of his T-shirt up and loops it through the neck, turning it into a crop top. Then he starts to move like Mick Jagger.

Two old ladies run up and tuck dollar bills into the waistband of his jeans.

I shake my head, standing in front of the giant bowl of salsa and holding a ladle. We have an empty pickle jar for people to drop tips for the weekly dare dishes. Some put in a dollar, but some put as much as twenty.

My ex Davis always said it was an ignorant way to run a business, but we've always covered the cost of the weekly, off-menu items. Sometimes we even clear a small profit.

"What do we have tonight?" Buddy Outlaw walks up, dropping a tenner in the jar.

Buddy's the assistant coach with Jack at the high school.

"Hey, Bud!" I ladle the special salsa over his chips. "Ghost pepper salsa with onions, cilantro, and fresh lime." I turn the vat of sour cream. "Add a heaping helping of sour cream to cool your tongue."

"That's more like it." He cuts his eyes at Craig, who's joining me as the song ends. "None of this cutting corners."

Craig holds up both hands. "I don't know what you're talking about, Buddy Outlaw. We're all about customer service here at the Coot-n-Shoot."

I continue ladling and passing out the baskets of chips and salsa to the line of eager guests.

Allie is on the mic reciting the warning about the heat level of ghost peppers and what to do if anyone has too much. I look up to see a man standing at the back of the room scowling, and my stomach drops. He's in a pink Vineyard Vines golf shirt and khakis with a dark green visor on his head. As always, his arms are crossed.

"Take over," I say to Craig, who looks up and lets out a little groan.

"I told you he was coming back."

"I'll take care of him." Slipping off my gloves, I walk down the length of the dining hall to where my ex stands waiting.

"Shew, Dylan!" one of our regulars calls to me as I pass. "Hot stuff is right!"

"The sour cream will put out the burn, but if it's not enough, one of the waiters can bring you some ice cream. We have little cups in the freezer. Don't use beer!"

The man laughs, waving at me, and I stop when I'm standing in front of Davis. "Table for one?"

"Don't patronize me, Dylan. You know why I'm here." His entitled voice is like a hand rubbing a cat's fur the wrong way.

"Actually, I don't, unless it's to have dinner."

"I see you're still doing this sideshow."

"Customers love the weekly Dare dish."

"I guess they do. You're practically giving away free food. Who does that?"

"It's not free food, and it's not even something everyone will like." Tilting my head to the side, I give him a saccharine smile. "Would you like a bowl of ghost pepper salsa?"

If only he'd say yes, I'd put the rest of the shavings into his serving myself. I can shred more to infuse the honey tomorrow.

"No, thank you." He steps to the side, putting his hand on the screen door leading out to the children's play area. "Can we talk outside?"

"There's really nothing to say."

"Please." It's more an order than a request, and as much as I want to fight with him, I decide I'll get this over with and follow him out to the empty playground.

Anyone can see us if they're interested, but most people are too busy watching the girls dancing or they're lining up to try the weekly special.

The door closes, and he walks slowly to where the water laps at the little beach. I stop at the jungle gym, studying him in the glow of the restaurant.

Davis Kent is from an old-money family across the bay, and he went to the most expensive private schools. Even though it's less than twenty miles away, it's nothing like the small-town community we have here.

I met him the summer after I graduated from college when I worked at the golf club attached to the fancy resort hotel south of town.

He was the golf pro, and one day it was my job to run the

beer cart around the course. I'd drive around, stopping to let the golfers purchase drinks or snacks. He caught my eye because he's tall, fair, and handsome, with a lean physique and polished manners.

I liked that he was refined and smart. I liked that he wasn't in danger of getting a concussion whenever he played in a tournament. I liked that I never had to worry about him dying a slow, painful death, slowly losing his mind because of all the concussions he'd suffered for his sport.

I didn't realize I had to worry about him cheating on me.

"What's it going to take Dylan?" He turns to face me, putting both hands on his waist. "What do you want? Diamonds? A Birkin bag?"

My brow furrows, and I realize how little we have in common. "Are you trying to buy my forgiveness after I caught you sticking your dick in Stephanie Wilcox?"

"It meant nothing to me." He walks back to where I'm standing and my muscles tense the closer he gets.

"It meant something to me."

"What? What did it mean? That I was bored? That you'd been out of town or on your period, and we hadn't had sex in a week?"

"So any time you go more than five days without getting laid, I have to worry you're going to cheat on me?"

"That's not the point. The point is, it's not about us. I was blowing off steam."

My eyes squeeze shut, and I exhale slowly, centering myself so I'll stay calm and not kick him in the nuts. Because the truth is, I really don't care anymore.

Opening my eyes, I'm pleased with how level my voice is. "It was always about us, Davis. It was about us every time you'd scowl when I played with my brothers or when I ran an errand in my bare feet or when I rode my bike to meet you for dinner."

"Because running around barefoot is dangerous, and I can pick you up for dinner. There's no reason for you to ride a bike.

It's ridiculous, as is this entire dispute." His voice actually rises. "Whenever my father took a gentleman's intermission, my mother would buy a designer gown, and that would be the end of it."

"I'm not your mother, and I have to get back to work."

"I'm not finished talking to you." He grips my upper arm painfully as his voice grows louder.

I jerk it away, and now I'm pissed. "Don't touch me again. I'm not interested in an intermission. I'm not interested in the full show. It's over, and you can stop coming here to talk about it. Nothing is going to change. We're through."

The muscle in his jaw moves, and he takes a step closer. Anger radiates off him, and for the first time in his presence, a sliver of fear pierces my chest.

I swallow, straightening my spine, not wanting him to think I'm afraid. I can't imagine he'd be stupid enough to do something with Jack and Garrett around. Even injured, Zane would kick his ass if he dared to hurt me.

"You're going to regret this, Dylan Bradford." His chest heaves, and a fleck of spittle hits my cheek.

I wipe it away forcefully. "No, I'm not."

"You're going to call begging for me one of these days, and I'm going to laugh in your face."

"Don't hold your breath waiting." Turning, I walk back to the restaurant.

"This is your last chance," he shouts after me.

I hold a thumbs-up over my head as I pull open the screen door and go inside.

Craig reads my expression, and he hands the ladle over to Allie before coming to where I'm doing my best to shake off the unpleasantness of that encounter. I don't want to admit to being scared, but it was intense.

"Just shows I was right," I say to myself. "Asshole."

"Are you okay?" Craig puts a hand on my shoulder, then quickly pulls it back. "What the fuck?"

He hooks a finger in my elbow, studying the red mark on my upper arm. I look down, and my eyebrows rise.

"Did he do that?" Rage is in my friend's eyes, but I quickly tamp it down.

"It's nothing. He tried to make me stay and talk to him, but I jerked my arm away. It must've been a little too forceful."

"I'm going to show him a little too forceful. Where did he go?"

"Stop." I squeeze his arm now. "If you get the guys all riled up, it'll be a big scene, and I don't want that. I just want him to go away."

Craig's eyes narrow, and he flinches, weighing my words. "He should never put a hand on you."

"I agree, and if he ever does it again, I will help you kick his ass." I loop my arm through my friend's. "I don't think he'll be back. I made it crystal clear we're over. He just doesn't like being told no."

"He'd better not run into me in a dark alley."

I exhale a relieved chuckle, leading us further into the restaurant. Davis did scare me a little, but if any of them ever find out he did, I can't imagine what might happen. I really don't want my brothers going to jail for murder.

"What's the reaction to this week's dare?" I look around the room at the salsa bowls.

Some are empty. Some are full, while others are somewhere in the middle. Everyone's back to talking and having a good time.

"All good. Oliver Duck wants to know when you're going to give him a real challenge."

"That kid." I shake my head. Salina's little brother is always complaining the specials aren't hot enough. "I'm going to find a Carolina Reaper recipe just for him."

"You should've given him the shreds Logan ate." Craig helps me collect the empty bowls and the gallon of sour cream, carrying them back to the kitchen. "Speaking of hot, where is that fine piece of man meat?"

"Did you just say *man meat*?" I cry, leaning over the sink as I rinse the large bowl and transfer it to the dishwasher.

I might laugh a little too hard, releasing the nerves from my encounter with Davis. Craig puts the sour cream in the refrigerator and grabs two beers.

"Here. You earned it."

I take the Corona out of his hand and take a long sip. "Logan and Garrett were still sleeping when I left. I should head back and take them some dinner."

"Got you covered, Boss." Thomas winks, handing me a box. "Two burgers, medium rare with our special sauce and extra fries."

"They are going to love you. Garrett might walk over here and give you a hug."

"Oh, no!" Thomas throws up his hands, laughing. "If I see him coming, I'm gonna run."

Craig slides a hand across my upper back. "I'll close tonight. Take care of your brothers."

Leaning to the side, I give him a hug. He knows me so well. He knows how much I miss Garrett when he's in New York, but most of all, he knows I need a minute after that interaction with Davis.

Chapter 5

Logan

THE SOUND OF VOICES ROUSES ME FROM A DREAMLESS SLEEP, AND for a second, I blink in the darkness trying to figure out where I am.

"You didn't bring me any salsa? After all we went through?" Garrett's voice pulls a smile across my face, and I sit up, tossing the blanket aside.

Glancing at the clock, it's almost nine. "Shit," I swear under my breath. I hope I'll be able to sleep tonight.

Stopping in the small bathroom, I splash some water on my face and run my hands through my hair. Not too bad.

I pull a clean T-shirt over my head and step into a pair of sweatpants from the top of my suitcase before opening the door and going into the kitchen.

"It's aliiive!" Garrett cries, holding up both hands like I'm Frankenstein's monster or something.

"Shut up." I shake my head, laughing. The scent of

something delicious hits my nose, and my hand instinctively covers my stomach. "Dang, what's that smell?"

"Thomas, our cook at the restaurant, made hamburgers for you two." Dylan walks around the bar, looking even better than she did earlier today.

Her dark hair is loose now, and it hangs long down her back. She's done something to her eyes, because they seem to glow even more, and her lips are a glossy pink. The scent of coconut drifts around her, reminding me of a sunny day at the beach, and for a second, I forget how hungry I am.

"Here, let me put it on a plate for you." Turning, she walks away, into the kitchen, and my eyes land right on her fine ass.

She changed out of the cutoffs, but the denim skirt she's wearing is equally short, showing off her shapely legs. They're toned and smooth, and she moves with controlled grace like a dancer.

"You all right?" Garret's tone has an edge, and I snap the fuck out of it.

"Yeah." I rub my hand over my eyes then stretch both arms to the sides like I'm still waking up. "I guess it's too late for coffee."

"Only if you actually want to sleep tonight." My oversized friend laughs. "Have a Guinness. It's like coffee."

"Right." I nod, taking the can of beer from him.

"How's that?" Dylan sets a thick hamburger and a pile of fries on the bar in front of me and one in front of her brother.

Garrett scoops up his. "You tell Thomas I'm coming for him."

"I did." She laughs, pouring herself a beer.

He groans, loudly. "So good. Just like I remember."

"We wouldn't dare touch that recipe."

"See what you think." He sits back on the barstool, pointing at my plate.

I take a big bite, nodding at the perfectly charred beef laced with a tangy, zesty flavor that makes me want more. "Damn good."

"Thomas has a secret ingredient he won't tell anyone." Garrett finishes his last bite. "I think it's plain ole black pepper."

"Nah, that's too simple." Dylan shakes her head, taking another sip of dark beer. "It has to be some kind of Worcestershire blend."

"Whatever it is, it's delicious." I stuff a few fries into my mouth. "I'm pretty sure this is the best burger I've had in a long time."

"Try ever." Garrett stands, slapping my shoulder. "And after all you went through, my sister here didn't even bring us any of that ghost pepper salsa."

My chin jerks, and I give him a look like he's crazy. "I'll pass, thanks."

"Are you telling me you don't like hot stuff, Murphy?" Garrett grabs another beer. "And you're from Texas?"

"Really?" Dylan's eyes light. "What part? I've only been to Dallas, but I'd like to get out to San Antonio eventually. Get some authentic Chile Pequin."

"I have no idea what that is."

"You don't know peppers?" Dylan leans on her forearms, watching me. "How is that possible?"

"My dad wasn't into Tex-Mex." I think of dinners served on fine china with cloth napkins and silver utensils at a long, formal table. "He was more they Wagyu beef and lobster type."

"Fancy!"

"Something like that." The old bitterness attempts a return, but Dylan curtails it.

"Well, that's a damn shame." Her tone is sassy, and her cute nose wrinkles with a smile. "What about your mom?"

"Not sure." I take a sip of Guinness. "She died before I knew her."

"Oh, I'm so sorry." She touches my forearm briefly. "We lost our mom when I was thirteen. Cancer."

"Yeah." I nod, wishing I didn't keep bringing down the conversation. "Garrett told me."

It was another of the things that bonded us right away—small hometowns, lost moms, and him laying out any football player who got in my way.

"Zane, hey, bro!" Garrett hops around to the long hall leading to the front door. "Where you been?"

I look up to see a tall guy with dark hair standing just inside the front door like he's trying to avoid being seen. He's about my height but slim in that way former athletes get after they stop training hard.

"Garrett." His voice is low and final, and he goes to the stairs.

Garrett, of course, isn't taking any of that. He hustles down the hall, pulling his brother into a hug. "I've been waiting for you. You weren't with Jack when he picked up Kimmie."

"I had some errands to run." Zane slaps his back before taking a halting step away.

He looks up to where Dylan and I stand watching in the kitchen, and his eyes are a striking shade of blue, clear like water. Still, they're haunted, and even though he turns away quickly, the pain is evident.

"Are you hungry?" Dylan calls to him, and her voice is softer than it's been all day, laced with something like caution.

I wonder if that's why he seems to want to escape. I don't know how I'd feel if my career was cut short the way his was, my entire world turned upside down in the blink of an eye. I sure as fuck wouldn't want everyone treating me like glass.

"I got something earlier. I'm just heading up." He grips the bannister, but Dylan goes to where her two brothers are standing.

"How'd it go today?" she asks.

"Fine." Again, he says the word like it's the end of the conversation.

"Did they say how much longer you need the crutches?"

He's not on crutches, but I notice a pair propped in the corner. Zane's square jaw moves as the muscle flexes, and I imagine Dylan is the only person who can get away with pressing him like this.

I turn and go back to the bar, feeling like I'm intruding in a situation where I don't belong.

"They said I can stop now." His response is low.

"That's good! We put Logan in the guest room, but if climbing stairs is too much—"

My ears perk up, and I return to the hall. "I can stay upstairs. It's not a problem. I haven't even unpacked yet."

"I'm good." Zane nods at me. "You must be Logan? Welcome."

I nod in return. "Thanks. Big fan. I watched all your games…"

My voice fades out, and I feel like an asshole. I'm sure the last thing he wants to be reminded of is the game.

"Thanks." Is all he says, and he grips the railing, using it to help him climb the stairs. "Have a good night."

Garrett returns slowly in my direction, his eyes on the floor, but Dylan stands at the foot of the stairs, her lips tight as she watches her brother go. Eventually her chin lowers, and her eyes meet mine as she walks to the kitchen.

"How's he really doing?" Garrett's voice is quiet when she enters the room.

"I don't know. Jack takes him to PT, and he's got pain meds. He's supposed to be talking to a therapist, but he stopped going after two weeks. Said reliving it over and over wasn't helping him any."

Garrett glances at me. "I'm going to head up, bring him a beer. Sometimes people will talk more at night when it's quiet."

I nod, understanding completely "What time do we need to be ready in the morning?"

"You know the drill. Summer camp starts early." He smiles

like the thought of picking a high school team takes all the pain away.

"Bang on the door, and I'll be ready."

He grabs a beer and leaves us. I turn around to see Dylan collecting his plate and pint glass off the counter. Worry lines her face, and as much as I can't imagine losing everything in an instant, I also can't imagine being one of the people trying to support him.

"I can help with that." I hustle around to where she's standing, and she smiles in a way that doesn't quite meet her eyes.

Carrying my stuff as well, I try to break the tension. "I'll probably be awake all night. My days and nights are all mixed up."

"I can't believe Garrett talked you into making that drive."

"And my dad has a jet service."

"He does?" She switches on the water, taking the plates from my hands. "How does that work?"

"It's like a timeshare. You put in a request, and they find you a plane with a pilot. Saves having to own a jet."

"That's really smart." She hands me a clean dish, and I dry it with the towel.

"That's my dad."

"Are you two close?"

"No." I exhale a bitter laugh, taking another plate from her hands. "He's sort of an asshole. Or maybe he just never wanted kids. I like to think I was my mom's idea, then when she died, he didn't know what to do with me."

"I'm sorry." She hands me another dish, giving me a worried glance.

"Don't be. I survived my childhood, and now I guess he finds me interesting."

"Because you play?"

"Yeah, and he's betting once I retire, I'll bring all my fans to his channels."

"Is he in entertainment?" She turns off the water as I dry the last dish.

"He owns MurKo Communications. It's a big sports radio network."

"Ah." Her chin lifts. "You'll be a commentator, then."

"Not if I can help it." I put the last dish on the stack beside me on the counter.

"That's funny." She picks up the stack of dishes and carries them across the small space. "Most guys I know would love to talk about sports all the time as their job."

"Sure, I'd like that part. I just don't want to work for my dad, and I don't want to move back to Houston."

Reaching overhead, she opens the cabinet door, but I step up quickly, taking the plates from her hands and putting them on the shelf where they belong. My chest brushes against her side, and she steps away with a light laugh.

"Such a gentleman. Thank you."

"You're welcome." I grin down at her, and I notice a light bruise on her upper arm. "What happened here?"

"Oh…" She quickly covers it with her hand almost like she's embarrassed. "It's nothing. I… uh, caught it on a door knob in the restaurant. Moving too fast."

I nod, wondering why it feels like she's not telling me the truth. Then I dismiss the thought. Why would she lie about it?

Still, her mood shifts, and she reminds me a little of her brother Zane—suddenly wanting to escape.

"Well…" She claps her hands together, taking a step towards the hallway.

"What happened to your dad?" I don't move, hoping by giving her space, she'll decide to stay a little longer.

I'd like her to stay a little longer. I like talking to her. I like watching the way the light plays off her soft hair, the way her full lips move when she speaks. I like the light in her almond eyes that are sexy and sweet at the same time.

I want to change our memories from me falling out on

the floor or being afraid of dolls to something a little more…
interesting.

"Well," She exhales heavily. "The doctors said it was a stroke, but he'd been having memory problems, irritability, headaches…"

My stomach pits. I know those symptoms well—we all do, and it's scary as fuck. "CTE?"

Chronic Traumatic Encephalopathy, or the football disease. A brain condition thought to be linked to repeated blows to the head.

"Nobody wanted to call it that, because then we'd have a case." An edge is in her tone, and I get it. Families suffer as much as we do when it comes to injuries.

"It's a tough sport. We know a lot more now than we did back then."

"Yet they all continue to play." She nods, then she seems to shake it away, looking up at me brightly. "It's why I only date golfers."

"What?" The word jumps from my mouth, a cross between a laugh and a protest and a few ticks louder than our conversation.

Her pretty eyes widen, and a small dimple appears at the side of her mouth as she fights a smile. "Do you have a problem with that, Mr. Murphy?"

You bet your ass I have a problem with it, but I'm not about to say it out loud.

"Not at all, Miss Bradford. Date who you want. I just can't imagine somebody like you settling down with a golfer."

"What's wrong with golf? It's a sport that requires skill and patience, and it involves zero physical contact." She counts on her fingers. "I don't know a single golfer who's sustained a concussion playing the sport."

"If you call that a sport," I quip.

"How many golfers are at risk of getting CTE?"

Holding up my hands, I straighten. "You got me. I'm just

saying, from what I've observed, you're not shy about physical contact."

And it's sexy as fuck.

"I'm not getting hit in the head, and I'm not watching them get hit in the head either."

My brow furrows. "You don't watch the games?"

She shakes her head no. "It's too hard after what happened to our dad and knowing the risks. I wish they'd all retire, but you can't tell my brothers what to do."

I'm not sure how I feel about this new information. No, I do know how I feel about it. I don't like it one bit.

Gentling my tone, I take a step closer. "Life is uncontrollable, Dylan. I could walk out the door tomorrow and get hit by a car."

"Don't say that," she whispers, lifting her hands as if she'll say a prayer to ward it away.

"My point is, you've got to do what you love, and we love the game."

"Trust me. I know."

"You can't control who you love or what happens. Saying you only date golfers is silly."

"Maybe, but if I don't date football players, I'm not at risk of falling in love with one."

Our eyes meet, and the air grows quiet and still. My stomach tightens, and somehow I've gotten close enough to touch her again. She's standing in front of me in that short skirt and tight shirt, and her soft breasts rise quickly with her breath.

It's been a while since I've been around a woman so open and vibrant and full of life. Someone who likes to play and dance and experiment with hot peppers.

A woman who has no business settling down with a man who plays golf.

Fuck that.

My hands are at my sides, and I tighten them into fists,

exhaling a breath and taking a step back. What's crazy is me talking to her this way, thinking about her this way.

As previously noted, Dylan is my best friend's little sister. She's completely off-limits, and even if she weren't, she lives here in this tiny coastal community, and I'm headed back to the East Coast in a few weeks.

One month, and I'll be a thousand miles away.

Clearing my throat, I fix my eyes on the floor and not on her sexy little body or her pretty eyes or her long hair I want to thread around my fingers.

"I'd better try and get some sleep if I'm going to help your brother tomorrow." My hand instinctively goes to my stomach like it does when I'm hungry.

"You'd better." She nods, slipping off her shoes at the door and walking to the hall. "If there's anything you need in the night, just make yourself at home and get it."

Her toenails are painted red, and fuck if my mind doesn't fill with images of what I might need in the night. What I want to get. Her soft curves pressing against my hard angles, her silky hair falling around us in a curtain as our bodies move together.

"Thanks, I'm good."

That's a fucking lie. I'm very, very bad, but at least I know what's right.

I'm here for a break and to get my head on straight, not to create more problems than I already have—or give my giant of a best friend a reason to kick my ass.

Chapter 6

Dylan

I AM NOT OBSESSED WITH LOGAN MURPHY. HE'S A FOOTBALL PLAYER.

Not to mention, I almost killed him with a ghost pepper the first time we ever met.

Yet all night, I tossed and turned, thinking of his strong hand gripping the front of his shirt, fingers digging into his stomach as if to keep them from digging into me.

I failed at blocking out the heat in his dark blue eyes as he towered over me, telling me I couldn't control who I fell for and I was crazy to think I could.

He didn't need to tell me. My hormones were screaming it in my ears.

He's not like the other jocks who hang around my brothers. He's smart and thoughtful. He notices when I need help and gives it to me.

To be honest, he got me when he picked up Kimmie Joy without hesitation. When his large hand rubbed her small back as she buried her face in his neck.

My niece has never taken to a stranger that way, and I can only guess she did it because they're both hot pepper survivors.

Riding my bike to Jack's house this morning, I glance out over the bay as the sun slowly rises in the east. A group of pelicans glide in a *V* formation over the water, and a hazy mist in the distance is colored pink and yellow and bright blue.

No one was up when I left the house, and I almost tapped on Logan's door to be sure he was awake. I don't know if he was able to sleep last night, or if he was even affected by what happened between us in the kitchen.

Maybe this is all in my head, and I'm imagining this intense pull between us. It's possible he's simply being friendly, offering advice, joking around like anyone might do. Perhaps I was with Davis so long, I lost sight of what it's like to be around someone not trying to control me or press me into some mold that doesn't fit.

It doesn't matter. He might be the hottest guy I've ever seen in my entire life, and he might be thoughtful and kind and great with kids and notices when I need help with the dishes. He's Garrett's best friend, and on top of all of that, he's a football player.

I don't date football players.

"Hey, good morning." My brother holds the screen door open as I park my bike by the porch. "There's coffee in the kitchen. Kimmie's still asleep, so you'll have the place to yourself a little while longer."

"You ready for today?" I trot up the steps to where my oldest brother waits.

"Ready as I ever am." He gives me a brief hug before heading out to his old red truck.

I know he has a love-hate relationship with this time of year. As much as he enjoys coaching and fielding the strongest possible team, he secretly hates having to tell boys they're not starting material or worse. They didn't make the cut.

I know that's why he's glad Garrett is here. If anyone can give bad news in a way that will leave you smiling, it's Garrett.

Jack is so much like our dad with floppy brown hair that hangs over his eyes. He's tall and lean like the former quarterback he is, and he's every bit the natural-born star our father was. Dad was a legend, and Jack followed right in his footsteps.

It's a thought that tightens my stomach when I think about how our dad died. Jack was only twenty. He'd just graduated early from State, and he was the first-round draft pick for the Texas Mustangs.

He stood in front of that casket, we all stood there, knowing our lives would never be the same. Then he straightened and told us all what we were going to do. He went on to Texas, playing five years before retiring at the top of his game.

Zane was old enough to keep an eye on us when Jack went away. He went to college across the bay while the rest of us got four years older. It was the time required for me to mature into taking care of myself, and when Garrett graduated, he was able to leave for college in Tuscaloosa.

Hendrix went to USC and never came back. He loves sunny California and living like a rockstar. He's only a year older than me—Irish twins is what they called us—but we couldn't be more different. I've grown to love the quiet, small-town life here with my friends and family.

Losing our parents was the hardest thing we'd ever gone through. To me, it was second only to the loss of my dancing dreams, and it bonded us in a way nothing ever could. We held onto each other and didn't get into trouble. We looked out for each other, and I always knew I had four guys protecting me no matter what.

It helped we lived in a small community that rallied around us as well. Ten years later, I can see how lucky we were to be in Newhope.

On this rare cool morning in July, looking out over the bay, I can still hear my mamma singing "The Bluest Eyes in Texas."

We didn't know when she passed our father would follow right behind her. I only knew when you see someone you love in so much pain, all you want is for that pain to end. Even if it means having to say goodbye.

Sitting in a swing on the screened-in back porch at my brother's house facing the water, I think about how everyone in town was ready to lift us up and bring us casseroles.

That's one thing you learn early living on the Gulf Coast with hurricanes blowing in every other year and folks needing help and getting older and trees falling and whatnot. Not the casseroles part, the taking care of each other part. We always come together in times of need.

Just like Kimmie Joy, who became like my own daughter after her mother took off one fall night without a word. Jack found her living in Oklahoma, shacked up with some old boy and singing in night clubs on the weekends.

He didn't care about any of that. He only wanted her signature on the papers that said they were divorced and giving up any claim she had on their sassy little girl. Now she prances around here just like I did, thinking it's her job to keep all the big people in line.

"Good morning, Sunshine," I tease as she walks out onto the back porch, rubbing her eyes and frowning before climbing into my lap.

Her curly head is on my shoulder, and I swing us gently, sliding my hand up and down her back. She's never been much of a morning person, but I like waking up slowly, too.

She'll be marching around here soon enough.

The cool of the morning evaporates with the rising sun, and when she starts getting sweaty, she slides off my lap.

"Are you going to make pancakes for breakfast?" She takes my hand so I'll get off the swing and get cooking. "Austin always makes pancakes on Friday. He says it's T-G-I-F."

Allie's son has been babysitting Jack's daughter the last two summers since his mom started working with me at the restaurant. In the past, Kimmie stayed with me during the summers, but I think my oldest brother saw the same way I did their little family could use the money.

Now with Austin going out for the team, I'm back to babysitting, which I don't mind at all. In fact, I've missed her funny little ways.

"You're coming with me to the restaurant. I'll make cheesy scrambled eggs or if Uncle Craig is there, you might be able to convince him to make you pancakes. If you ask nicely."

She nods slowly. "I know how to ask nicely. Daddy taught me."

"That's good." I pat her bottom. "Run get dressed so we can get going."

We're pedaling up to Cooters & Shooters a few minutes later with her behind me on my bike in a detachable plastic seat and a bike helmet on her head.

Allie's already in the kitchen, drinking coffee and chewing her nail when we enter. I go straight to the coffee pot as my niece runs all around looking for Craig.

"You okay?" I pour myself a cup of coffee. "Need one of these?"

"If I drink any more coffee I'll get the shakes." She goes to the dishwasher and starts unloading utensils.

I dump half and half in my coffee and grab a stack of napkins, frowning as I watch her. "Are you worried about Austin?"

"It's his first time trying out, and he's been practicing so hard. Every afternoon, he throws that football through the tire. He jogs all the way to the bay and back. He watches all the old games, studying the way Jack played."

"He wants to be a quarterback?" I grab a fork and a knife and roll them in a napkin.

Kimmie returns. "He's not here."

"Sit tight, and I'll scramble some eggs for you."

Allie takes over rolling up the utensils while I take a carton of eggs and a container of shredded cheese out of the refrigerator.

"He doesn't just want to be a quarterback, he wants to be a Jack Bradford quarterback."

"And he's never played before?"

"His elementary school had flag football." She grabs a napkin and rolls up another set of utensils. "He played that."

She's moving so fast, we'll have enough utensils rolled up through Sunday. I crack two eggs into the warm pan and sprinkle cheese over them, waiting for them to bubble. Kimmie joins me, taking a piece of bread and putting it in the toaster like I've taught her.

"Flag football is actually much safer for younger players." I don't like to keep harping on the same old string, but if I had sons, it would be hard for me to let them play tackle football with their brains still developing.

"I don't know where this sudden interest in the game is coming from. Do you think it's because of his dad?"

Allie hasn't told me much about her ex, other than he was into drugs and now he's in the state penitentiary. He was a dealer, but from what she hasn't told me—what I've only gathered by observing her cautious behavior—he was also abusive.

Their divorce was finalized before she ever came here, but she said he threatened to find her when he got out. The good news is his chances of getting out are slim to none, according to my friend.

A big part of her motive for moving to Newhope was to start over where his threats and bad reputation weren't hanging over their heads.

"I've never known a guy who didn't want to play football." *Other than Davis*, I think, and I see how that worked out for me. "Jack does have that father vibe on lock, though. He slid right into the job when our dad died without missing a beat."

She chews her lip, rolling the last set of silverware. "What's going to happen if he doesn't make the team?"

"Hey." I put my hand on her arm. "The good news is my brother rarely cuts any of the boys who try out. He always finds a place for them, even if it's only third string."

"Austin will be devastated if he's third string."

"If he's been working as hard as you say, Jack will see it." I glance up at the clock, thinking about what's been on my mind since last night.

I'd love to see Logan in action, and Allie will feel better if she can get a peek at how her son is doing.

"It looks like you've got us more than ready for the lunch crowd."

"I couldn't stay at the house alone, so I came up here after Austin left this morning."

"What if we took a little break and rode out to the high school to check on them? We could bring the coaches coffee or something. Or just blame Kimmie Joy." I slide the cheesy scrambled eggs into a small paper to-go box, quickly buttering her toast.

"What did I do?" Kimmie frowns up at me, and I forget she's not three years old anymore.

"You want to see what your ole buddy Austin is doing, don't you?" I muss her curly hair.

"He's just running up and down the football field like they all do." She wiggles her body side to side as she nibbles her toast.

"Let's pretend you want to see what he's doing. Or your daddy."

"Daddy's just blowing the whistle and yelling at them to go long or follow the method or keep your eyes on the ball!"

The way she says it is so much like my brother, I can't help a laugh. "Then just eat your eggs, and don't blow our cover."

Her button nose wrinkles, and I haul her onto my hip, my heart beating faster at the prospect of seeing Logan again.

"Good catch, Jordy!" Garrett slaps the scrawny kid on the back. "You'll make first string in a few years for sure with that hustle."

"Thanks, Mr. G!" The boy beams, and it's official. My brother can break bad news to anybody and leave them smiling. It's all in the delivery.

Standing at the fence, I watch the boys running up and down the field. Logan is beside Jack on the sidelines. They both have their arms crossed, brows lowered watching. Garrett is out there with Jack's assistant coach Buddy Outlaw, laughing and pointing, calling plays, and throwing the ball.

Buddy works the defensive line, and he has Garrett showing the bigger boys how to guard the runners or block the passes.

"It's a lot of boys." Allie's voice is worried, and I spot Austin on the line, waiting to run at the snap.

"It looks like they've got him as a running back. I can't tell if that's wide receiver or tight end." I sip my coffee, and Kimmie wiggles to get off my hip.

"That's more than I know," Allie quips.

"Don't go on the field." I call after my niece as she skips away from us.

"I know." She shakes her head like *duh* then she takes off running in the direction of Jack and Logan. "Daddy! Daddy! We brought you coffee!"

My teeth clench, and I'm afraid he's going to fuss at me. His arms uncross, and she's on his hip in a sweep, his eyes never leaving the team. He says something to Logan, who nods and jogs onto the field while my brother walks in our direction.

"Everything okay?" Jack frowns, and I know he's confused about why we're here.

I know as well as anyone this is an intense week for him, and he doesn't appreciate distractions.

"I wasn't sure if you got any breakfast before you left this morning." I hold out one of the breakfast burritos we grabbed along with the coffees when we went through the drive-through.

"I don't really have time to eat right now, Dylan."

"How's your first day?" Widening my eyes, I tilt my head to the side in the direction of Allie, doing my best to play it off like I'm cracking my neck.

He puts his daughter on her feet, pressing his lips together. I know he doesn't like talking about his process, especially not with parents, but they're a special case.

"We've got some good talent on the field this year." He nods, glancing out to where Logan is talking to the running backs. "A lot of potential on the offensive line."

Relief breaks across Allie's face, and her eyes glow as she watches my brother. She so obviously adores him.

"We shouldn't be bothering you." She touches my arm. "Come on, Dylan, let's get back to the restaurant."

"We can stay a few minutes longer," I argue. "Let's watch them get off a few plays."

"It's okay," he says. "You can stay."

Allie chews her bottom lip, and Jack walks to the side, giving his whistle a brief tweet. Garrett claps, and he says something to the bigger boys, who line up in front. The boys are split with half playing offense and half playing defense, and the way they practice is how they'll play on the field during games.

It's all second nature to me after years of hanging out with my dad and my brothers, listening to them talk. I might not watch them every week, but I know how it goes.

A taller boy I recognize as Harry Wilcox, cousin to Stephanie, stands in the middle calling the play.

"I'm pretty sure Harry's a junior this year," I tell Allie. "Jack will probably make him QB-1."

Her brow furrows, and I explain. "First-string quarterback."

"Right, I knew that." She nods quickly. "That makes sense if he's a junior. Austin is only a freshman."

"If he makes the team as a freshman, that's a really good

sign. Jack doesn't just put guys on the team he doesn't believe should be there."

Her eyes are wide, and she nods. I'm not sure I made her feel better.

My eyes go to Logan. He's on the other side of the field watching them, studying how they respond, their decision-making skills under pressure. How instinctive they are or aren't.

Today, he's in jeans and a white tee, and his muscular arms are crossed. His square jaw is tight, and he has that same air of concentrated leadership as my brother. It's hot as fuck, and it makes me wonder if he was a team captain at some point in his career.

I do not think how I'd let him be captain in my bedroom.

Okay, I do, but he's a football player. I have boundaries.

The boys break and start to move, and his large hands go to his hips as his eyes scan the players. My lips part, and I wish I didn't fantasize about how they'd feel pressing against mine, against my skin…

I just have to be strong for a few more weeks, and he'll be gone, back to New York with my brother. A whisper of sadness sneaks through my chest, and I exhale a little groan, tearing my eyes away from his physique.

"He's going long!" Allie's voice tenses.

She grabs my arm, and my attention flickers back to the field, where Austin is making a break from the line.

Garrett yells to one of the bigger boys, who makes a quick pivot to block a defensive tackle headed straight for Allie's son. Harry rears back and fires off a tight spiral. Allie and I grab each other's hands, holding our breaths and gripping the other tightly as the ball shoots through the air like a bullet.

Austin reaches out. My stomach pitches, and Allie whimpers as it bounces off the tips of his fingers. It looks like it's a fumble, until at the very last second he seems to stretch an additional inch. His hand curls, and he grabs it, pulling the ball tight into his chest as he crosses the line.

"He caught it!" I scream so loud.

Allie jumps up and down beside me, coffee splashing through the top of the white lid as she cries. "He did it! He completed the pass!"

Even Kimmie Joy is jumping up and down and pumping her little fists over her head. "Austin! Austin! Austin!"

The guys gang up, slapping each other on the back. The bigger boy who blocked the tackle lifts Austin off the ground, and Garrett is right in there, giving out compliments and making constructive notes with equal measures of enthusiasm.

I'm smiling so hard my cheeks hurt, and I'm breathing like I just finished a sprint. Damn football. I wish it wasn't so destructive, because it's thrilling as hell.

Logan's eyes land on mine, and a zip of electricity shoots through my stomach. He smiles, lifting his chin before jogging across the field to where we're standing.

My breath tightens in my chest the closer he gets. I blink away from his approaching frame, and now I'm the one having trouble keeping still. I shove a lock of hair behind my ear, and I scramble, trying to think of something to say.

"Hey." He's not even winded when he reaches us. "Austin's looking good out here today, Allie. That's your son, right?"

She nods, her face glowing with pride. "He's a freshman."

"Jack told me that." He glances back at the field.

"He did?" Her voice rises, and I can tell she's pleased Coach Bradford is keeping tabs on him.

But of course, he is. My older brother might not see her obvious crush, but he knows Allie is my friend. He knows their situation, and he's empathetic.

The big heart my oldest brother hides behind his stern exterior is one of the things I love most about him.

"He's got a lot of natural talent," Logan continues. "He just needs training."

Allie is positively beaming. "He's hoping to be a quarterback one day."

"It's not out of the question." Logan straightens, and his confidence melts my insides. "I expect Jack will find a place for him."

Our eyes meet then, and my mind blanks. He's so tall and handsome, and he's being really nice to my friend… And the way he looks at me sometimes makes me forget where I am.

Snap out of it, Dylan. I've never been like this with a man before.

"I thought you didn't watch the games." He gives me a sly grin, like we're sharing a secret.

"I can make exceptions." I do my best to be coy.

"Good to know." He leans his forearms on the fence. "What's in the bag?"

I blink up at him, stretching like a flower in the sunshine. "I wasn't sure if you and Garrett had any breakfast. I left before y'all were up this morning."

"No ghost peppers, I hope."

"Not today, Fire Eater." I can't resist teasing him with Craig's nickname. "We only make the Dare dish once a week."

"That's Lightning to you, and I've learned my lesson about touching things without permission. You're dangerous." I'm pretty sure he means it as a joke, but we hesitate when our fingers brush as I hand him the bag.

Jack's whistle tweets again, breaking the spell, and Logan takes a step back, pointing at me as he breaks into a trot. "I still owe you one."

Heat flushes my cheeks, and I clear my throat so I don't giggle. I need to grab the reins, because I'm acting as obvious as a high schooler. If I'm not careful, people will start to notice.

Allie nudges me with her elbow, and when I look at her, she's giving me the side-eye.

Too late.

"I guess we can get back to the restaurant now, Miss Dangerous. I'm sure Craig will be wondering where we are."

"Let's go!" I lift my chin, doing my best to dish it right back.

"I'm glad you're feeling better. Coach Bradford seems to have that effect on you."

Her eyes widen. "I don't know what you're talking about."

She spins away, heading for the parking lot, and I huff a laugh. "I'm sure you don't."

I call to Kimmie, waving to the guys before leading her back to my friend's waiting car.

Chapter 7

Logan

WE KEEP GOING UNTIL SUNSET, WITH ONLY A SHORT BREAK FOR lunch. I'd forgotten how hot it gets in the deep south in late July, and after running up and down the field all day in the blazing sun, I'm a hot, sweaty mess.

A quick shower and wardrobe change later, and we're at Cooters & Shooters for dinner. Garrett makes a big show of hugging Thomas, lifting him off the ground while the older man protests.

"You're going to break my back!" he cries, and I shake my head, taking a long drink of beer while I scan the large dining area—just checking out the place, not looking for Dylan.

"Never!" Garrett growls.

The older man gives us platters of burgers and fries, and I think if I ask where his sister is, Garrett will be onto me. He almost busted me earlier when she and Allie stopped by for a visit.

Seeing her this morning made me so damn happy, it took a

minute to get my game face back in place, but the guys were all pretty focused on the kids who were trying out and running plays.

I learned through the day a lot of the boys came from little places all around, some from outside the county limits, to work with Jack Bradford. Some from families with hardly any money, for whom football could be their only hope of going to college, all because of Jack's reputation.

It's a reality I know well, even if I never had to confront it myself. From what I know of Garrett and his brothers, football was their ticket to security as well, although they had the advantage of a celebrity dad.

"We've got another early day tomorrow." Garrett slaps my back after we've finished eating, as we walk back to the house. "Ready to do it all over again?"

"Yeah," I laugh, looking up and wondering if Dylan will be inside.

"He's got a good group of boys this year." Garrett continues, holding the door as we jog up the back steps. "It's not always like that."

"You're pretty good at giving feedback, even when it's not so great."

"I'm just honest. Everybody appreciates a straight shooter, and I try to be fair. The truth is some of these guys just need time."

He has a point. I've seen boys come back after a summer and be a foot taller and totally filled out. What matters is the boys like him, and they respond to his instruction.

"Need anything?" He pauses in the kitchen, grabbing a bottle of water out of the refrigerator.

The house is empty, and a ribbon of disappointment slips through my chest. "I'm good."

"In that case, I'm heading up to shower. I'm beat, and I need to see what Zane's been doing all day."

I know he's worried about his brother, who disappears most days when he's not hanging out in his bedroom.

"I'm turning in, too." No reason to hang around by myself.

We say our goodnights, and I walk into the guest room. I'm restless, which is incredible after how hard we worked and how hot it was today. I wait to get undressed, thinking I could just happen to venture into the kitchen if I hear anyone rustling around in there.

Anyone like Dylan.

Next thing I know, I'm waking up fully dressed in the dark.

I sit up frowning and go to the door. The house is quiet, and I'm pretty sure I missed Dylan. Opening the door, I glance down the hall lined where dim lights illuminate the floor. I'm thirsty, so I'll grab a bottle of water before changing clothes and getting a real night's sleep.

Creeping into the quiet kitchen, I'm about to open the refrigerator when a gasp stops my heart.

"Fuck, who's there?"

"Logan?" a soft voice whispers.

My chest tightens when I see her sitting on the other side of the bar with a laptop open in front of her. Her long hair is pulled up into a ponytail on the top of her head, and her eyes are wide like I've caught her doing something embarrassing.

"Hey." I can't help a smile, and with the way she's acting, I can't help a tease either. "What are you doing? Watching porn?"

"What?" Her voice goes high, then she looks at the computer and exhales a laugh. "Oh—no. I was…" She clears her throat, closing the computer. "Just watching some old videos."

I don't want to invade her privacy, but I am glad to see her. "We missed you at the restaurant tonight."

"I was helping Jack with Kimmie, getting her bathed and putting her to bed." She's dressed in a long-sleeved tee and shorts, and she's really pretty, nothing like the women I've been wasting time with. She's fresh-faced and so real. "What did I miss?"

"Not much, I imagine. Your buddy Craig is hilarious, and Thomas is a gem."

"Yes, he is." She nods, leaning on her arm. "He's been at the restaurant since I was a little girl. He and my dad played ball together when they were in college."

"I figured he was older than he looks."

I take a bottle of water from the refrigerator, leaning against the counter across from her.

"You looked like a natural out there today." She watches me, a light in her eyes. "The boys really respond to you and Garrett, and I know Jack appreciates the help. He acts hard as a brick wall, but he's a softie."

"I had a good time." My eyes drift to the counter as I think about working with the boys and their excitement. "It reminded me of being that age, just getting started in the game. Falling in love for the first time, how it feels like anything could happen."

"Very poetic, Mr. Murphy." She's playing with me, and my eyes return to her face.

Am I poetic? I never have been before. Yet something about this woman makes me want to say what I'm thinking rather than hide it. Is it her? Is it this place? I can't seem to curb this drive to understand, as if it's the key to what's not working for me.

"Garrett said I'd get my head straight here, and I'm starting to think he's right."

"Why was your head crooked?" Her eyes crinkle at the corners, no judgment, only curiosity.

"I don't know." I exhale a chuckle at her phrasing. "Maybe it was just burnout. I still love the game, the strategy, the teamwork. Of course, I love winning."

"Of course."

"It's all the other things around it weighing me down. The fake friends, the flashing lights, the online gamblers. God, they're the worst, but even the women…"

"Are you thinking of switching teams? Craig will be thrilled."

"What?" My eyes snap to hers, and I grin. *This girl.* "No, I just meant the women I dated. It always feels like they're using me to get to the next level, to elevate their brand or get more followers. It's all a numbers game now, and it's sucking out the joy."

"That makes sense." Her voice is quiet, a little sad, and I straighten.

"I'm sorry. You were out here peacefully watching porn, and here I am dumping all my shit on you."

"I wasn't watching porn!" Her laugh is a little louder, and her cheeks blush.

The ends of her ponytail bounce around her shoulders, and her full lips part over straight white teeth. Her feet are bare, and fuck me with those red toenails.

"Then why did you act so guilty when I caught you?"

She exhales a little *argh* noise, opening her laptop again. "I was watching my old dance videos."

"You danced?" I push off the counter, rounding the bar to where she's sitting.

"For thirteen years. Now the assistant principal at the high school wants me to teach it as a PE course, and I was just…" She bites her lip, hesitating.

"Pregaming? Watching your old moves?"

"More like trying to remember something I worked so hard to forget. It's scary."

Up to now, I've only seen her smiling and playful. We've skimmed around heavier topics, but seeing a real note of sadness in her expression, hearing her voice change, a different emotion twists in the center of my chest.

It's something I've never experienced before, and similar to how I felt when Jack's little girl buried her face in my neck, but stronger, more persistent.

I want to gather her into my arms and press my lips to her head. I want her to tell me what's making her sad, what's stealing that pretty light from her eyes. I want her to lay it on me so I can fix it, so I can tell her I'll take it away and keep her safe. *What the hell?*

Swallowing this rush of feelings, I lightly place my hand on her shoulder instead. "Why would you want to forget it?"

She wrinkles her nose as if she'll try to smile. "I guess sitting here, alone in the dark, the memories hit me harder than I expected."

"Good thing I showed up." My thumb moves back and forth across the top of her arm. "Let's see "

Her slim fingers hesitate over the touchpad, almost like she's afraid to start it. After a moment, she swipes and the dark screen blinks to life. The video is of a practice room with a couple standing in the center, perfectly positioned, chins lifted. The girl is in a pink leotard with black tights and pink pointe shoes. The guy is in navy joggers and a gray tank.

It only takes a second to recognize a much younger Dylan and Craig. She taps the play icon, and they begin to move. Dreamy piano music surrounds us, and he backs away from her holding his hand out as if drawing her to him. She backs quickly *en pointe* until they both stop at the exact same time.

Then they spring into action. He steps forward, lifting her off her feet, and her legs straighten into a perfect split. He moves her through the smoothest arc over his head, and when he lowers her, their arms extend and entwine. His fingers lift beneath her elbows, and her arms stretch into a line, one hand resting on his bicep as her leg lifts behind them.

"Holy shit." I watch them fold and unfurl, crossing the stage quickly then stopping for another lift in perfect, flowing rhythm. "This is really good. It's like you're reading each other's minds."

"Craig was an amazing partner." Her voice is quiet. "He had a playful style of dancing, but he never missed a beat. He was slim, but so strong. I knew he would never drop me, and it gave us the confidence to be daring."

"I can see his muscles." We're both almost whispering, as if we're watching something sacred, and the way he holds her, the way he gazes in her eyes, burns in my chest. "It's making me jealous."

"Of his muscles?" Her eyebrow arches, teasing.

I'm embarrassed I said that out loud. "This is really special,

I mean. I can't believe you'd stop. I know how hard it is to give up a sport you love."

"Funny you should say that. Nobody ever calls ballet a sport."

"Are you kidding? Sure, it looks delicate, but you guys are working hard. I imagine you had to practice all the time. It's a lot like what we do."

She leans back, all teasing gone. "You're an interesting man, Logan Murphy. I'm sorry I almost killed you."

"I thought you didn't."

"You're right, I take it back. You did that to yourself."

I huff a laugh. "You should come with a warning, Dylan Bradford."

"I'd say the same to you."

Her eyes meet mine, and the temperature in the room shifts. We've both tipped our cards a little, and my heart beats faster.

Watching another man holding her, touching her, even a gay man, has my inner caveman coming alive. I want to claim her like she's mine…

But she's not mine.

Shaking these thoughts away, I nod at the laptop. "So what happened? I mean, unless it's none of my business?"

I'm asking her these questions like I have a right to know her past, like I expect her to tell me. At the same time, I want to know everything about her.

"It's okay." She touches my arm, and my entire body lights. "It was special. Craig is my best friend, and he's always been there to help me get back on my feet."

"Were you hurt?"

A ghost of a smile is on her lips, and her teasing game isn't as strong now. "Yes. Once again, all thanks to football."

My brow furrows. "What does that mean?"

She closes the laptop again. "I was seventeen. It was senior year, Thanksgiving break. All the guys were home, and we thought it would be fun to play a family game in the backyard." Her eyes drift away, past the device holding her history, now quiet on the bar. "It wasn't anybody's fault... Jack threw a pass, and I ran to catch it. The ground was uneven, and the guys are naturally competitive. I stepped in a hole, and a two-hundred-pound giant came down on top of me."

"Fuck," I hiss a sharp inhale. "You broke your leg?"

"My ankle and a bone in my foot." She looks down at her foot on the chair. "It was a career-ending injury."

"Shit." I step back resting my hands on my head, and I remember what her brother said the first day we got here. "Garrett landed on you?"

"Zane, actually. He was a bit thicker when he was younger."

"He must've felt like shit." As much as I can't imagine my career ending, I can't imagine ending someone else's—especially not someone I loved, someone so talented.

She nods, looking down. "It changed my life. I haven't found anything I love as much since."

I lower my arms, stepping forward. Now I really really want to pull her to me. Instead, I touch her shoulder. "I'm sorry."

Forcing a smile, she looks up at me. "What do they say? Don't cry because it's over, smile because it happened?"

"Does that make it better?"

"No." Her gaze lowers to her lap, and I can't hold back anymore.

I reach out and take her hand, and we both look down at my fingers wrapping around her slim ones. "I don't know what to say."

"It's okay." Her thumb slides across my skin. "There were times I wished I'd never danced at all. I wish I didn't know how much I loved it, because then I wouldn't know how painful it is not to have it."

Touching her chin, I lift her face so our eyes can meet. Every breath, every heartbeat, draws us closer.

I slide my thumb down the line of her jaw. "Do you still feel that way?"

"Sometimes?" Her brows clench. "I said I'd never dance again, but when I see us, I remember how beautiful we were…" She blinks away, and I can almost see her rebuilding her walls. Her tone changes. "Which is why I'll say yes to teaching. It's what Jack does. It's what all of you do to hold onto what you love, to pass it on to the next generation."

"Maybe sharing your love can heal the loss?"

Her cheeks flush, and her tongue touches her bottom lip. I was talking about her love of dance, the way I'd been talking about my love of football… I think?

Now I'm not so sure. Is it like Garrett said—something about the night, the quiet, makes it easier to say what's on your mind.

So I say it.

"You're very beautiful, and you're very strong. I think you'll be an amazing teacher."

Our bodies are close, and this pull between us is undeniable. It's been growing since she knocked me on my ass, and now with her sitting on this barstool, her face right at my shoulder, I feel like I can't resist.

I'm a man of action. I'm used to taking what I want when I want it. Leaning closer, my lips are heavy. I could dip my chin and capture her mouth with mine, but I'd never force her.

She places her palm flat against my stomach, and my muscles tense. Have I ever responded to a woman this way? Have I ever craved someone this much? It's a low fire simmering in my veins, fueled by the most primitive of urges.

It's so elemental, it makes me ask questions I've never considered before. Was this meant to happen? Is it why I came here?

A door opens upstairs, and the spell breaks. Someone shuffles across the hall overhead, and another door closes. As if waking from a dream, she pulls her hand back abruptly, gathering her laptop to her chest.

"You'd better get some rest." She slides off the stool not meeting my eyes. "You've got another long day tomorrow."

In her bare feet, her head only reaches the center of my

chest. I picture myself sweeping her into my arms as her legs wrap around my waist so gracefully.

My hand is on her upper arm. My intention is for it to be friendly, reassuring, but her skin flushes, and she trembles. Her response is like a drug, and I'm already addicted.

She lifts her chin, and her dark lashes flutter before her eyes meet mine. With a groan, I withdraw my hand.

"You'd better go to bed before I do something I can't take back."

"Would you want to take it back?"

"No." I step away. "Goodnight, Dylan. Thank you for sharing that with me."

"Goodnight." Her voice is quiet.

She steps into the dark hall, but hesitates, looking over her shoulder at me once more before disappearing into the darkness.

Chapter 8

Dylan

I ALMOST KISSED HIM.

I wanted to kiss him.

All night, I tossed and turned in my bed wondering if I made a mistake not going for it. What would he have done? *Something he wouldn't want to take back…*

A shiver moves through my shoulders, and it definitely was not a mistake to leave. To run is more like it.

I can't kiss Logan Murphy.

I can't kiss him because he's a football player, and even if that excuse is getting pretty weak in the heat of our growing attraction, he's only here for a little while. Then he's gone. I don't want that kind of pain.

But every time I look at him, my muscles flash with adrenaline. My head gets light, and I'm hot around my ears. The intensity of his presence consumes me. He's sexy and kind, and when he touches me… *Lightning.*

I definitely can *not* kiss Logan Murphy. I might never recover.

When I got home last night after taking care of my precious niece and making sure my older brother had dinner and was hydrated after a long day in the blistering sun, I'd planned to have the kitchen to myself.

I'd prepared to watch those old videos of me dancing at the height of my skill, my dreams of being the next Gelsey Kirkland oozing from every pore, permeating every step and facial expression. I was so damn earnest. I was going to open that old wound, have a good sob, maybe eat some ice cream, face those old demons then email Mrs. Laverne to say I'd take the job at the high school.

Then he emerged from the darkness like a fairytale prince on a mission to carry me out of that dark place and heal my broken heart. *You're very beautiful. You're very strong…*

Outside of my big brothers, I've never known a professional player who wasn't just that—a professional player. They're really into the game and the football-star swagger, the celebrity, and showing off their status as superjocks, and aren't I so impressed?

Logan isn't like that.

He's easy to talk to, easy to tease, and surprisingly deep.

I've turned over what he told me about longing for something true all day. I've thought about him on the field with my brother, working with the boys, and encouraging them. I've thought about him talking about falling in love.

I've thought about his warm hand holding mine, his touch on my cheek while his heated gaze burned my skin as it moved from my cheeks, to my lips, to my breasts. He was electricity and warmth pulsing in my veins. He's strong and skilled and thinly veiled desire.

We got so close…

"Have you boned him yet?" Craig's voice jolts me out of my thoughts.

"Shit!"

He shakes his head, disappointed. "I can tell by that pensive look you haven't."

"I'm not going to bone my brother's best friend." I swipe my finger roughly across the face of the forgotten iPad.

"So you say." He nods, like he's waiting for me to confess what I was just thinking.

I'm not confessing anything.

It's just the two of us at the restaurant this morning, getting ready to open. Allie is at school prepping the library for the fall. She took Kimmie Joy with her, because my little niece loves books, and she's super Type A when you give her a project.

Also, even if she won't admit it, Allie is in love with my brother, so naturally she wants to love his daughter as well. I guess that's not always natural, but Allie is awesome.

I'm browsing hot pepper recipes on the Internet, searching for inspiration for next week's Dare dish… when I'm not obsessing over Logan.

"I've decided to say yes." His eyes light, and I quickly add. "To teaching ballet at the high school. If you can manage here without me during the day, that is. What do you think?"

His shoulders drop, he shakes his head. "Somehow I manage."

"It's only four days a week, a few hours in the afternoon. No Fridays."

Puckering his lips, I worry he might argue with me. Instead, he lifts my hand off the counter and holds it in both of his.

"Can you do that?" Lowering his face, he catches my eyes.

"What do you mean?" I swallow the knot in my throat, lifting my shoulder and pulling my hand out of his.

"I was there, Dylan, I remember how you cried." Reaching up, he slides a piece of hair behind my ear. "I'd only seen you cry that hard two other times."

It's true. If anyone would know how big of an ask this is for me, it would be Craig. His question is real, and I stop to really consider it. The ceiling fans turn overhead, and a lone seagull cries on the bay. I gaze out at the big, empty dining hall.

"I think I need to do it." I remember Logan's words when we talked last night. "I think teaching might help me heal."

You're very beautiful. You're very strong… Maybe I just needed to hear someone say it? The conviction in his voice as he said the words, as he looked directly in my eyes, stirred something deep in my soul.

"Those kids will be so lucky." Craig wraps his arms around me, pulling me into a hug. "You were good, Dylan. Real good. Legendary good."

My breath tightens. "I loved it so much."

"I didn't." His voice lightens. "I was just having fun."

"Liar." I pinch his waist, and he hollers, releasing me.

"You are so abusive." He returns to sorting the menus. "I'm not lying. It's why I'm still here. I loved dancing with *you*, but when it all comes down to it, this is my home. I never wanted to be a New Yorker. That was your dream, Balanchine."

"Well, I never could have gotten that close without you."

"Not true, but I'll let you think that if you want." He flicks his wrist.

"How can you possibly say it didn't matter to you? You had so much style. Have you watched those videos lately? You were amazing."

"Do you know how much money *danseurs* make?"

"Less than you make here?"

"At least I get tips here, and I wake up every day in paradise with people I've known all my life. Who wants to starve in a broom closet behind an elevator in New York?"

"That's a very specific reference."

"You know it's true, though."

My lips press into a smile, and I remember being at Jack's yesterday morning. "Don't the people make the place? You'd have been there with me."

"That would've helped, but this is where I belong. Just look out there. The ocean recharges my battery."

I gaze out the screen back door at the blue water. It's a hot, full-sun day, and I can't argue with him. Although, the blazing sun reminds me…

"Speaking of batteries, they're adding solar panels to Miss Gina's roof. I'm not sure how I feel about it. Can they do that to a historic building?"

"You are obsessed with that old lady. Why does she even need lights? She's blind."

Miss Gina Rosario lives in a massive home on the bluffs north of town overlooking the bay. It's a beautiful, historic place with brick and wrought-iron fencing, travertine tiles, and a huge mermaid fountain out front.

Her well-established yard is full of succulents, tropical plants, gardenias, and crepe myrtles with trunks as thick as my waist. I've only been inside a few times, but I remember it even has an elevator.

"Her caretakers aren't blind." My voice is wistful. "I would love to live in that old place. Have you seen her gardens?"

"She's never seen her gardens. How sad is that?"

"She can smell the flowers and the roses." I chew my lip trying to remember the last time I visited her.

Her history is as obscured as her vision. My dad said her family were some of the original town founders, who came here and tried to form a utopian society. They shared the land and everything on it, but at some point it fell apart.

Another story is that she's the descendant of old Spanish pirates who came to this area centuries ago. The story is her ancestors built that big house and buried treasure on the grounds. Even wackier is the suggestion that her father was a mafia kingpin or that she's a lost Spanish princess.

She just laughs at the stories, says her father was a kind man, and never disputes anything. I suspect she enjoys the creativity of bored, small-town imaginations.

"She's really sweet. Every time I see her, she tells me to come for a visit."

"So go visit. Take the Peanut. Old people love little kids. Maybe she'll leave you her big house."

"Don't say that. I really like Miss Gina." I watch him pulling out the silverware. "But she is always so happy to have company."

"Who rolled all of these?" He digs in the bin. "We're set for a week at least."

"Allie was nervous about Austin's first day at summer camp. All the condiment bottles are filled, the salt and pepper shakers are topped off, the toilet paper is stocked. I think she even alphabetized the spices."

"Shit, that's who did it. Thomas was pissed. The man has a system."

"My lips are sealed."

Picking up the iPad, I turn my back to the counter. "So what's going on with Closeted Clint?"

Craig stops, holding up a hand. "I told you we're not calling him that anymore."

"Has he told his family he's gay yet?"

"No, but they're very strictly religious. And his brother bullies him into silence."

"You're always criticizing my love life, yet you continue to date this guy."

"He's very… nice."

"He's got a big dick?"

He doesn't answer, and I start to laugh, holding my nose so I don't snort. "You are so ridiculous. You won't let me date anybody, but you'll stay with a guy who can't be honest about who he is because he has a big dick."

"And he knows how to use it." He circles a finger around my face. "And there's only one person I don't want you dating. A certain golfer, who if he puts his hands on you again…"

"We're not talking about that anymore." I turn, starting for the door. "Can you cover the lunch crowd? I'm going to pick up Kimmie Joy and pay a visit to Miss Gina."

"Of course." He waves me away. "Tell Allie I appreciate her

hard work, and she's very smart to get close to your mini-me. Best way to bag the dad."

"First, I think Allie really loves my niece, and two, wouldn't she be great for him? He's completely oblivious, of course."

"Your brother needs to get over the past and see what's right in front of him."

His future…

"He's so focused on those boys and that little girl, he's forgotten how to be a man."

"He hasn't forgotten." Craig slides up beside me. "And I know two people who can create happy accidents."

Puckering my lips, I nod, thinking about this idea. "Put it on our to-do list. We'll plan a meet-cute after I sort out my shit."

"We can't possibly wait that long."

Shaking my head, I flip him the bird as I slip out the door.

"Dylan! What a lovely surprise!" Miss Gina sits on a black wrought-iron bench surrounded by a fragrant gardenia bush and several tall peace lilies.

Her white hair is gathered in a bun, and she smiles, her blue eyes gazing past me towards the sky like she's seeing the angels.

I can tell Miss Gina used to be a great beauty. Even now with lines covering every part of her face, her smile has so much radiance and her features are so bright, she's timeless.

"I'm sorry it's been a minute since you invited me over. I've been pretty busy with the restaurant, then my brother Zane came home…"

"Oh yes," Her smile dims. "I heard about that, poor man. People underestimate the importance of a good kicker, and he was one of the best."

"How did you know that?" I exhale a short laugh. There's no way she could've watched his games.

"My gardener Steven likes to keep up with all the local boys. He was a big fan of your father's."

"Oh right." I nod, looking down. Everyone knew my dad.

Everyone was a fan, and after my mom died, when he started going down fast, they all surrounded us with love and food.

"Do you see something?" Kimmie Joy's little voice is curious as she climbs onto the wrought-iron bench beside Miss Gina, turning her head to follow the old woman's gaze.

"Who is this?" Delight fills Miss Gina's tone, and her wrinkled, spotty hand feels around until she finds my niece's. "Is this Kimmie Joy Bradford?"

"It is," I smile, watching them.

"That's such a beautiful name. How old are you now?"

"I'm five." Kimmie nods her head side to side. "I'm starting kindergarten with Mrs. Patience in August."

"What a perfect name for a kindergarten teacher." Miss Gina pats her back. "Patience."

"She's also very young." I lean closer to the old woman, lowering my voice. "Patience and energy."

Miss Gina's eyes close and she laughs almost like she's remembering being that age.

"Do you really have an elevator in your house?" Kimmie traces her finger over the flower pattern of Miss Gina's shawl.

"I do. Want to see it?"

My niece nods frantically, and I'm about to translate when the old lady stands. "Come with me."

She waits for my niece to take her hand, then she leads her expertly across the patio to the French doors leading to the house. I don't even ask how she does it.

"Aunt Deedee said you can't see anything." Kimmie hops along beside her. "Is it like the middle of the night all the time? I don't think I'd like that."

"It's not my first choice." Miss Gina takes her hand. "But it's not darkness. More like a white sheet blocking out everything, like someone pulled the wool over my eyes."

She chuckles like she cracked herself up. It's so unexpected, it makes me smile.

"Like if I put a blanket over my head?" Kimmie asks.

"I think so." The old lady opens the door and steps to the side for us to enter. "The downstairs was designed for entertaining. This is the formal living room, and behind it is the formal dining area. All the bedrooms are on the second floor."

Her posture is straight, and she moves with confidence, motioning with her hands as if she can see perfectly. "And here is the elevator."

She stops at the black, wrought-iron cage that has a small bench inside. "Want to ride it?"

"Yay yay yay!" Kimmie jumps up and down before running inside the ornate cage.

"Did you grow up in this house?" I watch as she directs my niece how to press the buttons.

"I lived here until I left for college at eighteen. Then my father died, and I moved back to take care of my mother when my sister left."

"I didn't know you went to college." I try to imagine her navigating a campus the way she navigates this house.

I think about all those old stories about her, and they all seem so silly now. The only mystery that stands out is this house—and what I assume is the money to go with it. Maybe her family were descended from pirates. I'm pretty sure she's not a Spanish princess, but who knows?

We stand beside the wrought-iron elevator shaft, and I watch as Kimmie rises to the second floor. "Come right back down," I call to her, and she waves at me through the grated floor.

"We never had children here—other than my sister and me, of course." Miss Gina's tone is quiet. "When I was young, I never gave it any thought. Now that I seem to be outliving everyone,

I'm beginning to understand that line about the kindness of strangers."

"From Streetcar?"

"That's the one," she chuckles.

The elevator returns to the first floor, and Kimmie hops out when it stops. "Can I do it again?"

"Let's go back outside." I reach for her hand, but she takes off running ahead of us.

As we return to the patio, I think about her words. "Are you okay, Miss G? Do you need help with anything?"

"Well…" Her voice quavers. "My nurse is retiring. Steven is in his mid-seventies, and last week he said he'll have to retire soon as well. I don't know who I'll get to help me with the roses and all my million repair jobs around here."

When we walk outside, Kimmie has her face in a large rose bush. "They smell like roses!" She cries excitedly.

"That's good!" The old lady laughs. "Sometimes they don't smell like anything."

Standing beside her, I think about her predicament. "I don't know any nurses, but my brother Zane was always pretty handy. If you'd like, I could ask him if he'd be interested in helping you. He needs something to do."

Reaching out again, she grasps my hand tightly in hers. "What a wonderful offer! I'm sorry if I sounded a bit maudlin just now. I was worried, but I trust your recommendation. Tell your brother, I'll gladly pay him for his time."

"If he can't, I'll ask around for you. We'll find someone, don't worry."

"You are such a dear." She holds my hand to her chest. "Don't worry about the nurse. I have a new girl coming to live with me this fall."

"You do?" My chin pulls in. "Who is it?"

"She's a friend of my niece's from Birmingham. She finished her degree in physical therapy, and she's always wanted to live near the ocean."

"Well, she'll be in the right place for that. I can't wait to meet her."

"I think she's about your age." Her eyebrows rise, and she nods. "Maybe you can be friends. And knowing someone is lined up to replace Steven is such a relief. I have such a good feeling, like something wonderful is going to happen."

"You sound like a mystic."

She tilts her head to the side mischievously. "They say the blind have special gifts."

"Is that true?"

Her face scrunches, and she leans closer. "No." Then she chuckles, "but you live to be my age, and you start to notice patterns. Just wait and see."

Chapter 9

Logan

"YOU'RE WHERE?" MY FATHER'S VOICE IS STERN ON THE LINE, LACED with impatience.

"Newhope. It's a small town on the coast in Alabama."

"What the hell are you doing there? You were supposed to come back this summer and work with me at the office."

Groaning internally, I can't think of anything worse than spending the last of my summer in hot as Hades Houston or being stuck in that high rise in a suit with him every day of the week.

"I never said I'd do that." My tone is flat.

"You're acting like a college student. How is the staff supposed to get to know you if you're gallivanting all over the Gulf Coast with your friends?"

"I'm not gallivanting." I do my best to keep the snap out of my tone. "I'm visiting Garrett's family. His brother is Jack Bradford."

I almost hear the record scratch as his tone changes. "Jack Bradford the quarterback?"

Silence fills the line, and I know he's impressed. I spent every fall into winter watching the games with him, watching him covet Jack's celebrity.

"He's head coach at the high school here. We're helping him field a team."

"See if you can talk him into doing an interview. A lot of people were disappointed when he retired the way he did. He had at least five more good years in him. It took the Mustangs a while to recover from that loss."

The Mustangs did just fine, as I recall. My mind drifts to Dylan.

I thought about her all last night as I lay awake in my bed. Now I'm thinking of her fears for her brothers and the risks of being a professional quarterback.

"Pretty sure he had his reasons."

"I'm not interested in your theories. Listeners want to hear it from the horse's mouth. Maybe he can hop on a zoom with Mario. See what he says."

My brow lowers. "You know I graduated with honors in communications from UT, right?"

"You're saying *you* want to interview him?" The scoff in his tone bristles my skin. "Let's leave that to the professional talent. Your place is in the boardroom with me."

The last place I'd ever want to be.

My jaw tightens, and I gaze at the bay from the back porch of Garrett's brother's house. They're inside sharing a beer, breaking down the game, discussing the team, but I stepped out when my dad's name appeared on the face of my phone.

We spent another long day today at camp, but I feel energized. Jack had Garrett and me talk to the young players, and I was impressed by their mature, thoughtful questions.

They wanted to know if we still thought a college degree

was as important as going straight to the draft once they had a name.

The answer from me was an obvious yes, get your degree. Garrett's answer was a little more nuanced. I didn't know he'd struggled with dyslexia, and his grades in school were bad. That got several of the guys' attention.

His point was, if you're not a strong student, but you're a big strong athlete like he is, perhaps it's better to make the most of your good years and bank as much money as you can before retirement.

"It's your year," my dad continues, drawing me back into the conversation. "You're going to win that trophy, and then you can retire and take over for me."

"Or maybe I'll keep playing." The words are out before I can stop them.

I usually keep my thoughts to myself. I've been around this rodeo long enough to know where it leads if I don't.

"What's that supposed to mean?"

Here we go.

"It means I've still got a few good years left in me, and I'm not ready to trade it all in for a suit and tie in a sterile office all day." *With you.*

He exhales heavily. "You said when you started this barbaric endeavor it would only be for five years. Now you're up to eight. Win the damn trophy and walk away while you still can."

"I'll think about it."

"Every time you go onto that field, there's a chance something could go wrong. You saw what happened to Jack's brother, the kicker."

Zane. I think about the broody fellow who lurks around the house and keeps mostly to himself or his room. I think about Dylan. Again.

Beautiful Dylan who gave me a peek behind her dark curtain last night. Funny how we only think about ourselves when it comes to career-ending injuries. Ballet is a beautiful sport, and she was amazing.

She is amazing.

Her full lips and soft skin haunted me as I tried, and failed, to sleep. Every time I closed my eyes, I saw her pretty amber ones burning with passion, laced with sadness. I should've kissed her.

"Did you hear me?"

"Sorry, what?"

Another impatient noise. "Let me know when you're back in New York. I'll see about making the trip there and we can talk business."

"Yeah, I'll do that."

We disconnect, and I lean against the post on Jack's porch. It's hot as fuck, but at least there's a breeze. It's always moving, keeping the stagnation at bay and carrying the scent of possibility.

"Are you going to give it a try?" Garrett sits across the table from me, and it's the night of Dylan's Dare dish.

"Aunt Deedee said Oliver Duck is going to pee his pants tonight!" Kimmie Joy jumps to her feet on the bench beside her uncle, climbing onto his back as he explodes with a laugh.

"Dylan said that?" Garrett squints over his shoulder at his niece.

The little girl's lips press together. "I wasn't supposed to repeat it. Aunt Dylan said, 'Kimmie Joy! Don't you dare repeat that!'"

She does a pretty good imitation of Dylan's voice in her little-girl scold, and her uncle lets out another big laugh. Then he points at me.

"You'd better sit this one out, Buttercup. Don't want to melt your face off again."

"Don't call me Buttercup," I clap back. "Speaking of, what's Dylan's middle name?"

"Why?" Garrett frowns.

"Kimmie keeps calling her *Deedee,* and I was wondering…"

"Lynn."

"So the extra *D* is for *Danger?*"

"Dylan Danger?" Garrett laughs more. "I love it."

"Danger Dylan!" Kimmie shouts, hopping off her uncle and taking off in the direction of the kitchen.

I imagine she's going to tell Dylan what I said, and I watch where she goes, hoping to catch a glimpse of her aunt. I'm starting to feel like *Deedee* might be avoiding me after our late-night near-kiss. She's gone every morning before we get up.

I know she's helping Jack with his daughter during camp, but I haven't even seen her in the evenings.

Garrett gave me her number a few days ago—so I could text her to get him some Icy Hot from the store. I've thought about using it again to apologize. The only problem is, I don't want to apologize. I'm only sorry for *not* kissing her.

Kimmie disappears around a corner, and my eyes go to the bar, where Craig is popping the tops off of longneck beers as fast as he can. It's a busy night, and everyone seems to be humming with excitement over the new dish.

I'm about to say fuck it and just ask Garrett if he knows where his sister is when rainbow disco lights flash above the bar, and Craig pulls out a mic I didn't know existed.

"Are you readyyy to get heated?" he announces in a Michael-Buffer, pro-wrestling style.

Whistles rip across the room, and some people shout. The door to the patio where the pool tables are located opens, and patrons stream into the diner as a line of waitresses in cutoffs and tank tops carry out large bowls of what looks like mac & cheese with an orangey crust.

"I love that guy." Garrett laughs as Allie takes over on the mic.

"Tonight's dish is experts-only, folks. Dylan brought the heat with a special Carolina Reaper mac & cheese!" A low roar ripples through the crowd. "In case you missed it, the Reaper is listed in the Guinness Book of World Records as the hottest pepper in the world. But if you still want more, *Oliver Duck*, she made this special sauce of pure Reaper to shake on top."

Everybody laughs as Kimmie takes the bottle from Allie and marches with it to a table in the middle of the room where a teenage boy sits with his arms crossed and an obstinate expression on his face.

"We've mixed it with heavy whipping cream and cheese, but that doesn't kill the burn," she continues. "As always we have ice cream cups and tomato juice. Don't use water or beer to put out the flames. Let's do this!"

My chest tightens as Dylan emerges from the kitchen, and I feel like a kid seeing his favorite toy on Christmas morning. My jaw clenches, and I'm on my feet. Then the music changes to The Red Hot Chili Peppers' classic "Give it Away."

"Aw, shit," Garrett growls from behind me, getting out of his seat. "Let's do this!"

I think he's going to get us a bowl of the fiery dish, which the waitresses are scooping as fast as they can into plastic cups, while wearing plastic gloves.

What I don't expect is half of them to drop the utensils, remove the gloves, and climb onto the bar led by Craig now wearing a blond wig, horns, and metallic lipstick.

They're all dancing to the music like some kind of sexy *Coyote Ugly* dance line, and I shout with a laugh when Garrett stomps out of the kitchen in his own platinum-blond wig. He hops onto the bar behind Craig and starts grinding along with them.

I make my way closer to the commotion, unable to hide my laughter. "What the hell?"

Garrett makes a motion like he's slapping an invisible ass in front of him, and waitresses grind on each of his sides.

The entire restaurant is dancing, with some brave souls eating the mac & cheese dish and immediately yelling and shaking their heads. A few of the men run to the side bar where two teenagers are frantically passing out birthday-party-sized cups of vanilla ice cream.

I watch as a guy rips the lid off and holds it directly onto his tongue.

Dylan is bobbing side to side with Kimmie on her hip, her eyes glowing with laughter, and I'm drawn to her like steel to a magnet. Our eyes meet, and I forget about the bodies writhing around me. All I want is her.

She's the flower, and I'm the bee.

It takes a minute to navigate the impromptu dance floor, but finally I reach her. We're both smiling and breathing fast, and Kimmie wiggles to get onto the bar with her uncle.

Dylan turns to deposit the child on the counter, and Garrett sweeps her up at once. When she turns back, I reach up to slide a lock of wavy dark hair behind her ear. "Dance with me?"

Her cheeks warm attractively, and damn, I want to lean down and kiss her. Instead, I wrap my arms around her, pulling her soft body close to mine.

She clutches the top of my shoulder, and I have to lean down to spread my hand over her lower back. My other hand clasps hers, and I spin her around, making her laugh.

I wish I was skilled enough to lift her off her feet like Craig did in those old videos, but I'm not. Still, I'm content to hold her this way, her face glowing and my heart expanding in my chest.

It could be fucking Mardi Gras going on around us. All I know is we're in the middle of the inferno, and I want to do nothing more than melt with her.

"Danger Dylan?" she shouts up to me, arching an eyebrow.

"Isn't that why Kimmie calls you Deedee?" My hand tightens on her waist, and I love pressing her body against mine.

"No!" Her hand tightens on my shoulder. "I'm not sure why she started calling me that."

"That's why."

"That's not why!" A push from behind moves us closer to the bar.

It's impossible to dance the way I want in this ruckus, but I've still got her. Her back is to the bar, and I'm leaning down. My nose traces against her hair, and she smells like lavender and vanilla. She feels like heaven.

"Are you hungry?"

Jesus. She has no idea.

Pressing my lips together, I don't say what I'm thinking, even if it would go nicely with the chaos all around us. *Give it away…* Now. To me.

"I had some of the non-deadly mac and cheese."

She shakes her head. "I wasn't trying to kill you."

"How much longer do you have to stay here?"

I want to take her home and find out where she's been, what she's been doing, how she's been thinking and feeling. I want to see if she'll let me kiss her this time.

"I could probably take off in an hour."

A large hand grips the top of my shoulder, and I look up to see Garrett rotating his hips in time with the final beats of the song. "Get up here and dance, LL!"

I jump. Hell, I'd pretty much forgotten he was in the room. Good thing he doesn't seem to be paying attention to us.

I hold up a hand and yell back, "Not me."

"Dylan," he warns, "don't make me come down there and get you."

"You know I don't do all that." The song ends, and a new one starts.

This time it's INXS's "I Need You Tonight," and Cooters & Shooters is in full-on dance mode. I look around and everyone's rotating their hips and singing along with the song.

Garrett bends down and lifts his sister onto the bar in one fluid motion. She lets out a little yelp, but now she's standing above me, her muscular legs on full display, her ass barely covered in denim cutoffs, and her long hair swinging down her back.

"Dance!" Garrett orders, and she shrugs.

Then she lifts her arms over her head and starts to rotate her hips in a way that short-circuits my brain.

In her ballet videos, she was a girl—delicate, thin, and dainty as a Christmas snowflake. Now she's all woman and pure sex.

She bends her knees and does a little hip thrust, and my dick springs to life in my jeans. Her tanned legs dip and flex, and her plump ass bounces in those shorts.

My lips are parted, and I'm surprised my tongue doesn't roll out like one of those cartoons. My mind floods with images of all the dirty things we could do together. *I need you tonight…*

Everyone on the bar dances in time, including the two men in wigs, but she's the only thing I see.

She turns around, her hips still moving to the beat, and when she turns back, her eyes are closed. Her chin lifts, and she raises her arms, rolling with the music and twisting her narrow waist. Her full tits bounce in time to the music, and that does it.

The last of my resistance goes up in flames.

"I'm sorry if I got a little dark on you last time we were together." Dylan's voice is soft, and we're back at the house. She's sitting across the bar from me in the kitchen, a pint of Guinness in her hand, and everyone's gone to bed.

She's amazing, and I've been on edge since her sexy dance on the bar. Holding her in my arms and swaying to the music was great, but she took it to the next level with her *Coyote Ugly* moves.

"I've never talked to anyone about what happened that day," she continues, seeming oblivious to her effect on me. "Except, Craig, of course."

"Your brothers never checked on you or asked how you were feeling?" I'm leaning on the cool granite across from her.

I want to extend my hand, slide my fingers up and down the soft skin of her forearm, wrap them around her wrist, and pull her to me.

"I think they felt guilty, Zane in particular, and maybe he thought it would make me feel worse if we talked about it."

I consider her brother Zane, and his response to therapy. "Still, they should've asked if you were okay."

"I can put on a pretty good show of taking things in stride." Her voice isn't as fragile tonight, and I'm glad. "I'm pretty good at pretending everything's fine when inside I'm falling apart. I guess we all are."

"It can be a relief to focus on what you're good at, on the things you can control, instead of what you can't."

Her head tilts to the side. "You sound like you have experience with it. What fell apart on you?"

Exhaling, I take a chance, extending my hand across the bar in her direction. Her brothers are all in bed or at their own homes. It's just the two of us, sharing like we always do after dark.

Now I'm reaching out for more, but she hesitates. I don't move, giving her the chance to consider, to say yes or no, as every muscle in my body tenses.

Her amber eyes are on my hand, and her tongue touches her bottom lip. I know her fears, but I'm so far past wondering if this might be a mistake. She danced across that bar and stole my heart tonight, and I don't care about the consequences.

I know she doesn't date football players, and I know I'm asking her to bend her rules. At the same time, we've shared so much. It's a risk, but something tells me this risk is worth taking.

This connection we share is different. It's real. Things can change. We can change them together.

Seconds tick past. I'm on the razor's edge of letting her go, chalking it up to what might have been, to nothing ventured, when she moves.

The air in my lungs stills as she slowly leans forward in her seat. She puts her elbows on the bar and lowers her pint glass.

Then, with her eyes fixed on my hand, she moves hers over it. My heart beats faster, and it requires all my control to take it easy. I turn my palm so hers slides against it, and I do my best to act casual, not like something monumental just happened.

What did she ask me? My experience with life falling apart.

"I would see my friends with their dads throwing the ball, laughing, going to movies. One friend's dad took us to see the Spider-Man movie, and he was as into it as we were. Then I got home that night, and my house was empty."

Her slim brows furrow, her hand still wrapped in mine. "How old were you?"

"Twelve."

"I'm so sorry, Logan. Didn't you have anybody?" Her thumb moves lightly from the knuckle of my forefinger to my thumb, and I try to remember.

Have I ever had anyone until this moment?

"Yeah, ahh… I had a really nice housekeeper named Anita. She would bring me leftover cookies after her kids had birthday parties. I think she felt sorry for me."

My gaze moves from our hands to her eyes, and she's so sad.

"Shit," I laugh. "And you thought you were dark. This is ridiculous. I want to kick my own ass right now."

"Stop it. You're not ridiculous. I hate that for you."

Releasing her hand, I circle the bar so I can stand in front of her, between her legs. She's still sitting in that chair, and her head is at my chest. I want to lift her onto the counter so our faces will be level. I want to lift her arms around my neck and kiss her like I've been dreaming of doing every damn night since I got here.

"Football became my family, and I became a dick." Leaning down, I trace my nose along the side of her hair, inhaling her delicious scent.

Her breath quickens, and her hand is on my stomach again, half-heartedly holding me back. "Why do you do that?"

"To protect myself. I locked up my feelings, and I dated models or socialites who wouldn't ask too much of me or get too close. If they did, I'd shut it down and move on. I wasn't letting anyone hurt me again."

I grew up to be exactly what my father taught me to be, cold and distant. Pursuing cold and distant relationships that wouldn't challenge me.

I blamed the women for using me, for not caring enough, for only wanting to build their brand or steal a pinch of my stardom for themselves. The truth is, it was me. I chose them precisely because they wouldn't ask for anything I didn't want to give, and with each passing year, I turned into him more and more, growing more and more miserable as the years rolled by…

Until Garrett brought me here, to this place. To her.

"You have a pretty clear picture of yourself."

"I didn't until now." Another hit of lavender. "Until you knocked me on my ass and burned all that shit out of me."

"Stop it," she laughs, pushing me gently. "I didn't!"

"Garrett said seeing a real family would get my head straight, and he was right. I'm seeing a lot of things I didn't know I wanted. Things I didn't even know I was missing."

"Logan," she whispers, and the pressure of her hand against my stomach increases, as if she'll make me stop.

Fuck, I don't want to stop. "I really want to kiss you right now."

Her chin lifts, and our eyes meet. The pull between us is so strong, I swear it sparks. My entire body sparks. It's a heat unlike anything I've felt—right up there with that ghost pepper I accidentally ate.

Her pink tongue touches her bottom lip, and my dick is fully hard in my jeans. "Is something stopping you?"

"Other than you?" I lean closer, tracing my lips lightly across her temple.

She shivers, and the fist in my chest tightens. I am hesitating because of her, and it's not just her hand on my stomach.

Dylan is everything I want, from her sassy little attitude to her sexy little body. I love her humor and her caring, the way she takes care of her brothers and her niece and Craig and that restaurant. Even her obsession with those fucking killer peppers fascinates me.

I want to protect her from anything that might hurt her, and it fucking terrifies me. If I keep going down this road, I can only see two outcomes—I'll come back with something real and lasting, or I'll come back with permanent scars, more painful than the ones I already have.

"And if I wasn't stopping you?" Her voice is sultry.

Our eyes meet, and I level with her. "I've never felt like this before, Dylan, and I'll never forgive myself if I let you down."

"How would you do that?"

I put my hand over hers on my stomach. "I've never had a good role model. I never saw how a good man is supposed to act, and you deserve the best kind of man."

Her hand twitches as if she'll pull it away. "So you're not a good man?"

Memories of cold dinners filter through my mind, sitting on opposite ends of that long, polished table, longing for a relationship I'd never have.

"I want to be." Lifting my chin, I look out the window at the night sky. "How much of a foregone conclusion is it that I'll end up being exactly like my father?"

Her fingertips lightly touch my neck, and I look down at her pretty face. Understanding breaks in her eyes, and her smile is everything I want.

"I think you know who you'll be." Her tone is gentle. "Some things are either inside you or they're not, like the love your mother gave you, even if you don't remember it. I've seen you on the field with the boys, and you're good with them. I've seen you with my niece, and you're so sweet to her. It says a lot about a man when children and young people know they're safe."

Safe.

"There's nothing safe in the way I feel about you." The low growl in my voice flushes her pretty cheeks, and I lean closer. "The things I want to do to you scare me, but I swear to you right now, I'll never let anyone hurt you. Not even me."

Her hand rises to my cheek, and she places her thumb on my bottom lip. Her lips part, and she blinks slowly. "If you don't kiss me now, I might hurt you."

A hungry laugh lingers on my breath as I close the space between us, covering her mouth with mine.

She whimpers softly, and I lift her out of that chair, moving her ass to the counter. I'm between her legs, and I wrap one arm around her narrow waist. The other I use to cradle her head.

My fingers slide into the side of her hair, and my thumb is on her chin. Pulling it down, I open her mouth so I can taste her. Our tongues curl together, and a little explosion goes off in my brain.

She's rich chocolate and spicy pepper. She's lavender and vanilla and the ocean and the sky. She's every beautiful thing I've ever wanted in my life.

Her legs wrap around my waist, and my cock is a steel rod against her core. My hand moves from her waist to her ass, and I cup it, squeezing and moving her against me. I want her to feel my desire. I want it to set her on fire the way she's burning inside of me. I want to make her come.

"Logan," she gasps, lifting her chin as my mouth slides down her neck.

I pull her skin with my teeth, and she whimpers. Her nipples are stiff little points in her shirt, and I slide my palm over one, circling my thumb over it through the thin fabric of her T-shirt. Her body jumps, and her legs tighten on my waist.

"Oh," she gasps, and her mouth is on mine again.

Her hand is behind my neck, and she's kissing me now. Her

fingers thread in my hair, and she pulls. It sends a rush of sensation prickling through my arms. I can't need her more than this without acting on it.

My chest rises and falls rapidly, and I manage to stop myself from consuming her right here on the bar in this kitchen.

"I want you so much, Dylan. I want to fuck you all night and have you begging for more. I want to take you through that door and pull you onto my lap. I want to watch your breasts bounce as you ride me, then I want to lift and devour them. I want to squeeze your ass and taste your pussy until you scream my name."

Her eyes are dark, and she's breathing fast. Her full lips are parted and swollen, and it's almost more than I can take. It's physically painful when her hand moves to my chest and she shakes her head.

"We can't do this here." She slides off the bar, not meeting my eyes. "Not yet. We're tired, and we need to rest. We can talk more tomorrow. Goodnight, Logan."

She leaves me standing in the kitchen, practically running to the stairs. I'm breathing like the wind has been knocked out of me, like I'm standing with every nerve ending in my body activated.

I do the only thing I can. Turning on my heel, I go straight to my bedroom, pushing the door closed as I strip out of my clothes and go to the shower. I flick the water on hot, grab the conditioner and put some on my hard. Then I grip my cock.

Chapter 10

Dylan

MY BODY IS ON FIRE. MY NIPPLES COULD CUT GLASS, AND MY INSIDES are slick as butter.

Pushing through my bedroom door, I lean my forehead against the wood doing my best to catch my breath. I was so close to fucking him right there in the kitchen. What's gotten into me? Anyone could have walked into the room and caught us.

But this heat, this lust, this burning need…

Rubbing my thighs together, I unbutton my cut offs and shove my hand inside my underwear, between my legs.

It doesn't take much to get me there. My fingers are slick with my arousal, and I rub up and down, around and around. I can still feel his soft lips pulling mine. I can still hear his voice low and groaning in my ear. *The things I would do to you scare me…*

"Oh, fuck," I gasp as the orgasm tightens in my pelvis.

I want him to do those things. A thrill zips through my core at the thought, and I want his beard scuffing my skin again. I want his ragged voice speaking dirty words to me… *I want to squeeze your ass and taste your pussy until you're screaming my name.*

He lifted me onto the bar in a sweep, and it was all over. I was lost to him. I was lost to his large hands kneading my breasts, his thumb sliding back and forth over the stiff peaks of my nipples.

My eyes squeeze shut, and a low whimper rips from my throat. I grasp a hand over my mouth to muffle my moans as my knees tremble and bend, my pussy flutters, and I wonder why the hell I ran from him. Who cares if they catch us? Who cares if it's impulsive and too soon?

Sliding down the door to my knees, I'm breathing fast, coming down from that rocket high fueled by fantasies of Logan. I'm clenching and pulsing with fading orgasm, and I know why I ran from him, *dammit.*

He's hot as fuck, and I'm so far past caring he's football player. But he lives in New York. He's leaving to go back to his life in two weeks. What am I, a masochist? Am I really considering doing this?

Reaching out, I hold the wall to help myself stand. My legs come together, and I feel it at once like a lit match touching my clit. The burn is unmistakable.

"Shit!" I shriek, dashing across the hall to the bathroom.

The clock is ticking as I fling open the cabinet doors, digging past the tampon boxes and extra bars of soap and shampoo and toilet paper.

Nothing.

"No no no no…" I jump to my feet, not even caring that my cutoffs are on the floor in my bedroom, and I'm only wearing a thong.

My pussy is burning, and I fly down the stairs at top speed. Dropping to my knees, I rip open the cabinets under the kitchen sink. I shove the dish soap aside and the Cascade bin and the Lysol spray and the garbage bags.

The fire is burning hotter, and I'm almost crying. I've got to find the extra tub of coconut oil.

I spin around the room trying to think. There's only one last place to check. I don't have time to worry about the consequences. Running into the guest room, I bang on the bathroom door and push through it at the first sound of his voice.

I barely notice him standing with a towel around his waist, water running down the lines of his muscles in rivulets. His face is stunned to see me in only a cropped tee and black thong.

"I'm sorry!" I fall to my knees, flinging open the doors of the cabinet beneath the sink. "Oh my God! Oh, thank God!"

I rip open the coconut oil and jam my fingers inside before quickly falling back on my ass and shoving them between my legs, rubbing them all over my blazing clitoris.

Leaning my back against the wall, my knees are bent. My eyes are closed, and I'm breathing fast as I grab more, rubbing it all over my burning pussy until the fire slowly begins to dissipate.

The pain starts to subside, and my hand drops to the floor beside me. My breasts rise and fall rapidly, nipples still erect, and I look up to see Logan standing over me, eyes bugged, lips parted. He might be drooling.

"Fuck me," he murmurs. "What was that?"

Then it hits me what I did—what he watched me do.

For all he knew, I ran in here and masturbated on the floor at his feet. I was in a panic, but all he saw was me with my legs spread wide, rubbing oil on my pussy like a sex-crazed nympho.

Now I'm on fire with embarrassment. Jerking my knees to my chest, I wrap my arms around them and bury my head against my forearms.

"I'm sorry!" I wail. "I had no choice—I was desperate!"

"Don't ever apologize for doing that… Shit." I can't look at him, but I can hear his confusion. "It was the hottest fucking thing I've ever seen."

I exhale a groan, trying to imagine what was going through his mind. "I can never see you again as long as I live."

"Damn straight you're going to see me again. You are literally the sexiest woman I've ever known. First that dance, and then…"

"It was the Carolina Reaper. Some of the oil must've gotten under my fingernails or I didn't wash long enough. It got there… in my coochie."

He huffs a laugh, kneeling beside me. Large hands gently grip my arms, and he pulls them away from my face. I try to turn away, but he won't let me. His finger hooks under my chin, and he forces me to meet his amused eyes.

"Are you saying you were touching yourself?" My lips tighten, and I hesitate, which only makes him more smug. "Did this have anything to do with me?"

My knees straighten, and I stand quickly, wanting to run away. But he holds me. "Let me go, Logan."

"I will, but answer my question first. Did you get Carolina Reaper on your pussy because of our kiss?"

He's kneeling on the bathroom floor, and I'm standing in front of him in the tiniest scrap of underwear, throbbing with post-orgasmic, post-hot pepper-panic adrenaline.

Looking up at me, he slides a large hand up the back of my bare thigh. "Answer me, Dylan. Were you fucking your hand and thinking of me?"

"Are you trying to embarrass me?"

"I would never embarrass you. I want to be sure you're okay." His palms are flat against the back of my thighs, and he's looking up at me. "Are you?"

"I think so…"

"Want me to double-check?"

My lips part, and I look down into his lusty gaze. I'm pretty sure I know what he means, but still, I ask, "How would you do that?"

His left hand slides higher up the back of my thigh, and I gasp softly. My heartbeat is in my core as his fingertips trace the curve of my bare ass. He dips the index finger of his right hand in the tub and lifts a dab of coconut oil to the front of my thong.

"Is this okay?"

Oh, god… My back is to the wall and I only hesitate a moment before nodding. "Yes…"

His eyes darken, and he slides my thong to the side before placing his finger over my swollen clit. My body jerks to life, and a little cry escapes my throat as he starts to stroke me up and down, around and around.

I rock higher onto my toes with every touch. My mouth opens, and I exhale a soft moan. He meets it with a growl, and a fresh orgasm tingles in my thighs, snaking higher with every circle.

"Better?" His voice is rough, and I respond with a moan. "I should clean this off you so it doesn't stain your clothes."

"Okay," I gasp.

"Will you let me use my tongue?"

Shit shit shit… My stomach trembles, and I want it so much. I'm gasping, and this is my last chance. If I say yes, everything will change between us. But I'll be damned if I'm going to say no.

"Yes."

Large hands grip my ass, and he pulls me forward as he covers my pussy with his mouth. My fingers dive into his hair, and I wail, arching my back as his tongue slides up and down, licking my clit and sliding all over my pussy.

My knees are liquid, and I groan out a *Fuck* as my hips rock in time with his movements, as the orgasm twists and builds tighter in my lower belly. I'm grinding against his mouth, pulling his hair, and riding his face as primal need takes over.

He's eating me like a coconut cream pie with a dash of spice, and I'm whimpering and moaning like a cat. His thumb dips into my dripping core, curling and sliding in and out, and I cry out his name as I clench around it.

I'm fucking his face. I'm fucking his finger. I'm frantic and wild, moving all over him as the pleasure blazes through my bloodstream, until it's too much to contain.

The orgasm rips through me like a current. It blanks my mind and shakes my legs. Shudders ripple through my belly, and he groans against my center as I ride it out, jerking against his mouth.

His thumb continues plunging in and out, working me, and he doesn't stop until I'm too sensitive to go on. My legs are weak, and he eases me down to his lap.

Resting my cheek against his firm chest, my breathing gradually returns to normal. Strong arms encircle me, and he gently smooths my hair away from my cheeks. I feel his lips softly tracing the line of my hair. He's holding me, soothing me as I slowly drift down to this planet.

Blinking a few times, I realize he's still only in a towel, and his cock is a lead pipe beneath me.

Lifting my chin, I meet his lusty eyes, and the palpable desire in them tingles my stomach. He's sweet and loving, and dirty as fuck. His full lips are shiny from the coconut oil and my come, and I reach up to slide my thumb over them, wiping it away.

"You're a mess," I whisper, straddling his waist with my knees.

"I think it's fair to say we're both a mess."

My hard nipples press through thin cotton against his bare chest. He grips my ass in both hands, and I thread my fingers in his hair again, pulling gently.

"Is it okay if I kiss you?" I tease.

He reaches up and grabs the back of my neck, closing the space between us. Our kisses are frantic and raw. Our lips part, and our tongues collide and slide, curling together as we consume each other.

He's delicious, soft coconut and hard muscle. His cock taunts me against the back of my thighs, and I reach down, to stroke it. He's thick and long. My fingers don't meet around him, but I smooth them up and down. I slide my palm over the tip and a deep groan vibrates in his chest.

Large hands move from my ass beneath my T-shirt, and he lifts my heavy breasts, holding them to his mouth so he can suck and rake his teeth over my tight nipples. My core clenches, and I need more.

We're past the point of no return, and I want him inside me. I want that fat cock stretching and massaging me.

Kissing my lips across his cheek, I speak in his ear. "Do you have a condom?"

"Yes." His lips are on my jaw, sliding down the column of my neck.

Cupping his face, I lean back to meet his gaze. His dark hair is a sexy mess from my fingers, and his lips shine from the oil and my kisses. We're vibrating and ready, but my brain sends up one last warning flare, one last chance to retreat.

As if he can read my mind, he moves his hands to my arms. "What's the matter?"

"I need you to be straight with me." I tremble asking this question, but I have to know. "Is this just a game, a summer fling to you? Or is it something else?"

"It's not a fling, and it's definitely not a game." His brow tenses. "It feels… real. I've fantasized about being with you since the day I got here, since the moment you looked at me like you'd never seen a man before."

Heat flashes in my cheeks, and I fail to hide my grin. "I'd never seen a man like you before."

"But that was all lust," he continues. "Now that I know you, I don't want to be something you regret. You made a few things very clear to me from the start, and I don't want to let you down."

My stomach drops. "How would you let me down?"

"I can't lie to you, Dylan." His tone is serious, and I feel sick. "I'm not a golfer. I don't even know the game."

"What?" I squeal, and he breaks into a laugh.

"I'm only a football player. I know it's not what you want. Maybe I can take lessons…"

"Logan Murphy!" Diving forward, I wrap my arms around his neck, pressing my lips to his again.

I feel his smile as our mouths open and our tongues slide together. Is it possible this feels so good? Is it possible he's stealing my heart right now?

"Get those panties off and get in my bed," he growls. "It's taking every bit of strength not to take you right here on this floor. You're even more beautiful and sexy and responsive than I imagined, and my dick is so fucking hard right now."

"Dylan?" Garrett's deep voice at the bedroom door sends us both scrambling.

"Holy shit!" I'm off Logan's lap so fast, I should be called lightning.

"Dylan, are you in here? I thought I heard screaming."

Logan's on his feet as well, wrapping the towel around my waist and cinching it. "Get out there."

I'm shoved through the bathroom door, which he closes behind me, just in time to greet my oversized brother as he sticks his head into Logan's bedroom. Thankfully, only the bedside lamp is on behind me, or I'm sure he'd see the scuff marks from Logan's beard on my cheeks and neck.

"Hey, girl, what are you doing in here?" His voice is a stage-whisper, and he's in a large white tee and maroon boxer briefs. "I thought I heard yelling and cabinet doors slamming."

"Yeah," I force a laugh, scrubbing my fingers over my forehead and wishing my heart rate would return to normal. "Somehow I got Carolina Reaper in my… nose."

No way in hell I'm saying I got it on my pussy. I'd never hear the end of it.

He exhales a blast of air through his lips, shaking his head. "Oh, shit! Are you okay?"

"I am now, but I almost lost it trying to find the coconut oil. There wasn't any in our bathroom upstairs or in the kitchen—"

"Yeah, Craig took that tub we keep in the kitchen last week, and I carried the one from the upstairs bathroom down here." He presses his lips together, not even questioning my presence in his best friend's bedroom in only a towel and a T-shirt.

Everyone in my family knows the pain of capsaicin oil.

The door opens behind me, and I feel the heat of Logan's body enter the room as distinctly as if he'd touched me. "Hey, man, your little sister was in here in a panic."

"I can believe it! I've gotten that shit on my junk before, and I thought I was going to have to go to the hospital."

"Apparently I had the coconut oil in my bathroom."

"I searched the whole house." I wave my hands, like it's so bananas.

"Well, I'm glad everything's okay." Garrett stands at the door, waiting for me to return upstairs.

We all stand around for a solid two seconds before I huff a laugh and turn to give Logan a little wave. "Thanks again," I say, not daring to meet his eyes for fear I'll lose it.

"It was my pleasure." The hint of a grin in his voice makes me spin away before I blush.

Even in a white undershirt and black boxers, he's the hottest fucking thing—he might be even hotter. I can only assume he had those clothes with him in the bathroom.

"You didn't do shit." Garrett's loud voice contains a laugh, and he has no idea what Logan did and how good it felt.

Still, he's waiting for me at the door like a great big cock blocker. I guess he is a blocker on the field.

"Okay, then," I say one more time, stepping into the hall and walking to the stairs like a child who's been told they have to wait until Christmas morning to play with the gifts they've already found.

Garrett follows me, and when I get to the bottom of the stairs, I look over his shoulder to where Logan stands in the doorway watching me. I'm pretty sure he's thinking the same thing I am. *Dammit.*

"Night, sis." My brother squeezes the top of my arm as I go into the upstairs bathroom.

Flicking on the light, I see my scuffed cheeks in the mirror. I gasp when I see the red marks on my neck, thankful the dim light in the hall apparently hid them from Garrett's sleepy eyes.

My pussy clenches again remembering how they got there, and where else Logan's beard marked me. Looking down, there's no mistaking the pink marks on my inner thighs.

I remember his strong hands gripping my ass as I rode his face. I remember his strong arms wrapped around my waist as he kissed me on his lap. I remember my fingers wrapped around his cock, sliding up and down as he groaned in my ear.

If my brother hadn't walked in when he did, we'd be fucking right now. I'd be boning my brother's best friend like I told Craig I wouldn't.

Yet, here I am.

"What am I doing?" I laugh, rolling my eyes.

It's too late for that question, and I know it. I've drunk from the well, and there's no going back. The cap is off the bottle. The milk is spilled, and I intend to ride this wave to the end.

Grabbing a washcloth, I quickly step into the shower to wash the arousal, the orgasm, the makeup, and the rest of the day off my skin.

Chapter 11

Logan

GARRETT STOOD THERE LIKE SOME GIANT PRISON GUARD LEADING her away, and it was all I could do not to reach for her. I listened as they went upstairs and the doors closed. I heard the sound of the shower running.

Now I'm in my bed, thumbs flying.

> I used to tell your bro he was the best blocker on Earth. He has no idea.

Gray dots float, and I wait impatiently for her reply.

Dylan: I'm pretty sure my heart stopped.

> Coconut will forever remind me of you coming on my tongue.

Dylan: Coconut oil is very good for you, and it's organic virgin oil.

> My memories are not virginal.

I use a devil emoji, to which she sends a sweaty red face.

> Dylan: I want to sneak down again, but I can't think of a good excuse... More pepper?

> I could come to you. I'm pretty heated...

> Dylan: No!

She includes a laughing emoji.

> Dylan: We're too loud when we're together.

Fuck me. I slide my hand over my hardening cock before replying.

> We could still finish together if you want.

> Dylan: What do you mean?

Tapping the screen, it switches to FaceTime, and she answers before the first ring. Her face is freshly washed, and her hair falls around her cheeks in large waves. She's fucking gorgeous.

"Hey, beautiful. Show me your tits."

Her chin dips, and she covers her laugh with her hand. How is it possible that everything she does is so adorable?

"I think we'll be even louder this way," she whispers, hopping off her bed and going to her door.

"I've never seen your bedroom. Show me."

Her lips twist, and she holds the phone over her head, turning it so I can see the pretty white and navy room. "Here it is! My bedroom."

A queen-sized bed with white bedding is in the corner, and a desk is across from it. Beside the desk, a tall, narrow bookshelf is filled with books and more books stacked on top of each other.

"You need a bigger bookcase."

"I know." She walks over to the narrow piece of furniture and lifts a book with a muscular man on the cover.

"What's that you're reading?"

"Just some spicy romance. This one's about a man who pushes away everyone who loves him because his father was abusive."

"Sounds vaguely familiar."

"Then he meets a feisty redhead with a killer bod, and he can't keep his hands off her."

This time I slide my hand inside my boxer briefs to stroke my erection. "He's a man after my own heart."

Her bottom lip goes between her teeth, and she walks to her bed. "Are you saying you want to put your hands on me?"

It's a shy request, and it activates the beast. "Damn straight. I want you to touch yourself the way I want to, and I want you to keep that phone where I can see you come."

Her eyes flare, and her smile turns naughty. "Okay."

I watch as she climbs into the bed. She falls back onto her pillow, and her dark hair spreads around her shoulders.

Then she smiles, blinking up at me. "Now what?"

"Pull up your shirt and tuck it tightly under your arms so I can see your breasts."

She does what I say, and her pretty, rosebud areoles are visible. Her arms clench at her sides, and they squeeze together in a way that makes precome slide from my dick. I mix it with the coconut oil at my side for lube.

"That's right, damn. You're making me so hard right now."

"Show me," she whispers.

Lifting the phone, I move it down so she can see me sliding my hand up and down my cock, circling the tip. She whimpers, and my eyes squeeze with a groan.

"I love to hear you moan." Her confidence is growing. "Tell me how you'd touch me if you were here."

"I'd start with those pretty tits. I'd pull them into my mouth and suck them hard. Then I'd tease your nipples with my teeth before sliding my tongue all over them and doing it all again."

"Oh…" she exhales, tracing her fingers over her breasts and tweaking the tips until they harden.

My dick jumps, and another surge of precome appears. "You're a fucking pinup, Dylan. I'll never get the sight of you on my bathroom floor rubbing your pussy with your back arched and your breasts bouncing out of my mind. It was the hottest thing I've ever seen. "

"I was putting out the fire."

"You were lighting another one. Do it for me now."

She sucks her bottom lip into her mouth, and I watch as her body starts to move. The phone moves away from her face, and she lets me see her hand in her undies, her fingers circling fast over her clit.

My fist picks up speed, and I groan watching her massage herself. Soft whimpers fill the air around me. Her hand moves faster, and her hips rock in time. Breathy moans fall from her lips, and I wish I was in the room to see all of her.

"Tell me what you're thinking about." It's a rough order.

"Your tongue," she gasps. "It's so warm and demanding. I love the way it slides over my clit again and again, not stopping." She exhales another moan as her hand continues. "I love how hungry you are."

"Fuck…" I'm straining as my own orgasm radiates tighter in my thighs, snaking through my pelvis. "That's right, baby, I'll eat your pussy until you scream."

"Your cock is so big… I want to feel it stretching me. I want to feel it all the way inside me, hard and wild."

"I'll bend you over and fuck you til your legs shake."

"Oh… oh, I'm coming. Make me scream, Logan!"

"I'll make you forget your name." My hips rise off the bed

as I picture her soft body riding mine, her hair falling all around us, my cock driving deep, stretching her clenching core.

I can't forget the way her pussy sucked my thumb when I was eating her out in my bathroom.

"I'm coming…" She drops the phone, but I watch her silhouette.

I watch her back arch and her breasts rise. I watch her stomach tremble as she moans louder. Then her legs start to shake, and it sends me flying. My dick pulses and warm liquid spills onto my belly, again and again.

I'm moaning, and my eyes close as the sensation blinds me. I stroke faster until the pulses of pleasure turn painful, and I have to stop. Then my hand drops to the side, and I'm breathing hard, coming back from another plane.

On my phone I see her hand moving slower, circling gentler, until at last she cups her fingers over her core. She rolls to her side, and her cheeks are flushed. Her pretty eyes meet mine, blinking slowly, and she smiles.

"I've never done that before." Her voice is slightly hoarse. "Did you finish?"

"You kidding? I couldn't watch that show and not finish."

"Can I see?"

Another little surge spills onto my skin at her request, and I move the phone so she can see the come on my lower belly. On the screen, her eyes flare, and she pulls her lip into her mouth.

It's the second sexiest thing she's ever done.

"I wish I was there with you," she says.

"Me too."

"What do we do now?"

I grab tissues to clean up myself. "Are you always working at the restaurant? I'd like to take you on a real date if you have a night off."

"I could take off Monday. It's always a slow night in the summer."

"Put me on your calendar. I'll meet you downstairs at seven."

Her nose wrinkles, she rests her cheek on her hand. "What will we tell the guys?"

After everything that's happened between us, I want to say I don't give a damn, but I know that's not true. She cares about her brothers as much as I do.

"I'll talk to Garrett. It'll be okay."

"Will it?"

"Either it will or he'll kick my ass. I'm going to see you again, regardless. I'm not letting your brothers keep us apart."

Her expression relaxes into a contented smile, and my stomach tightens with warmth. "I really wish I could hold you right now."

"I do too. I like the way you hold me." She reaches behind her and pulls a large pink body pillow between her legs and up to her cheek. "In the meantime, I'll pretend this is you."

"Damn, lucky pillow. It's right where I want to be."

A happy laugh floats in the air around me, and she blinks her eyes away. "Good night, Logan."

"Goodnight, Danger." That gets me another little laugh. "Dream of me."

"I will."

I'm pretty sure every day of camp is hotter than the day before. We've chosen the first and second string for the varsity and even picked the guys who'll be on the junior varsity team.

Garrett was the friendly bear, letting the guys who didn't make the cut know what they needed to work on to make the team next year, and as far as I could tell, none of them walked away devastated.

Sure, they were disappointed, but he gave them so many

helpful tips and so much encouragement, I imagine they'll all be back next year. Unless they pick up another sport.

"That Sonny Langston needs to be on the track team." Garrett chuckles taking a sip of beer. "He's a great runner, but he can't throw for shit."

We're back at Jack's place doing post-mortem. His brother walks out onto the back porch, Corona in hand, and leans against the railing. "What do you think about that Austin Sinclair kid for QB-2?"

Garrett's eyebrows rise, and he puckers his lips. "Allie's son? He's a natural talent."

"He makes good, snap decisions, and the other guys seem to like him," I add, remembering my days as a quarterback in high school. "He's not nervous or indecisive."

"He's got the makings of a star." Jack nods, taking a long sip.

"Hell, you ought to know!" Garrett laughs.

"We'll train him." Jack nods. "I think he's mature enough to handle it."

"Allie's going to cry." Garrett leans back, and his older brother's jaw flexes.

It's the first hint we've gotten that he's not as oblivious to Allie's feelings for him as he lets on. "In that case, I'll let you break the news."

"Don't tell me Coach Jack is afraid of a few tears." Garrett's voice turns teasing. "Afraid she might put her arms around your neck and try to kiss you?"

I rub my hand over my mouth to hide my laugh.

His brother exhales a growl as he goes through the screen door into the house, leaving us alone on the back porch.

"Why don't you go home. It's late." He calls to us. "Quit drinking all my beer."

Garrett laughs louder, tilting his head back before standing. I grin watching them, wondering what it would've been like to have siblings. Wondering how I'd feel if Dylan were my little sister, and someone like me came calling.

If he knew what I wanted to do to her—what we've already done—he'd probably want to kick my ass. But I know how I feel about that beautiful woman, and there's nothing I won't do to make her happy and make her mine.

"Come on." He grips my shoulder, and I follow him down the back steps to the path leading along the bay.

We're close enough to walk to his family's home, and I figure now is as good a time as any to rip off the Band-Aid. We stroll past a group of kids playing frisbee in a small, grassy park, and we pause a moment to watch them.

"You seemed distracted today," Garrett says as we start walking again. "Preseason's about to start. Thinking about next year?"

"Some." I have been thinking about next year, but not for the reasons he assumes.

"Ricky's got it in for you, but I've got a good feeling about it. We're going to get you that MVP trophy." He grins, shaking my shoulder, and I nod. "What? Has your dad been busting your balls again?"

"No more than usual." I clear my throat as we take a few more steps.

I'd planned out a few different ways to bring up the subject, but none of them feel particularly subtle.

So I just go for it. "Dylan's really nice. I've been talking to her, and I really like her."

"Yeah, she's a great kid. She's an even better cook. I've been encouraging her to go to culinary school, but she's so stubborn."

"You have?" I feel a little miffed this is the first I'm hearing about it, but I don't let it distract me. "I was just wondering why she's not dating anybody."

"Oh, she was. Some dickhead golfer who cheated on her. That asshole better not show his face around here while we're in town."

I second that emotion. Why didn't I know about this either? He'd better not have made her cry. The thought of Dylan crying has my temperature rising. My fists clench, and I'm ready to find that fucker and kick his ass.

"I didn't know."

"Yeah, Davis Kent. Doesn't he just sound like a douche?" Garrett shakes his head. "She needs a man who'll treat her like a queen."

"I think so, too." We take a few steps, and my throat is dry. "Speaking of, I was thinking about asking her out, maybe taking her somewhere nice for dinner."

"Really?" He squints at me. "That's really thoughtful of you, LL. Need a recommendation? Want me to go with you?"

"Ah, no." I exhale a laugh. "I wanted to go alone, because I want to spend time with her. I like her."

"Everybody likes Dylan." His brow furrows, and this dumb oaf still doesn't get what I'm saying. "She's a great girl."

"I think so, too, and I want to spend more time with her. On a more serious basis."

He takes a few more steps as the words sink in, then he stops. A frown tightens his forehead, and my muscles tense.

I do some quick, mental math on his size versus my size, and yep, Garrett could seriously beat me to a pulp if that's the direction he decides to take it.

Flexing my hands, I brace for the worst.

"You want to date my sister?"

"Is that okay?"

Shaking his head, he starts to walk, this time he's moving faster. "I don't know. You're kind of a player, Logan, and Dylan's not like the girls you normally date. I'd hate to have to kick your ass, because I consider you a really good friend, a best friend."

"I feel the same. It's why I'm talking to you." I swallow the desert in my throat. "I have no intention of playing with Dylan. She's real and sweet and beautiful. She's kind, and she makes me want to be a better man."

"You're damn straight you'll be a better man. You'll be the best man."

"That's what I said."

We walk a few paces in silence. "My little sister is special. She's the kind of woman you marry."

I think about her sweet face and satisfaction unfurls in my chest. "I know."

Damn. She really is.

"What are you going to do when we have to go back to New York?"

And the dread rushes in. "We haven't really gotten that far. This is all pretty new."

"Well, you'd better get there. We're only here a few more weeks."

Fuck. "I know."

"Are you going to try and do some sort of long-distance thing?"

"Maybe? If she's up for that." I rub my hand over the back of my neck. "I'd like to try."

"Can you do that?" He glares at me, and I cut my eyes up at him.

"Yes." I'm dead serious.

He is, too. "If you tell her you will, you won't *try*. You *will*."

"You think I'd be talking to you this way if I wasn't serious? You, of all people?"

He's satisfied with that answer, and we're approaching the restaurant. "How did this happen?"

"Have you seen your sister? She's amazing." He doesn't answer, and I look out at the bay. "You told me if I came here, I'd find what I was looking for."

"So you're blaming me for this?" His voice rises.

"Maybe I am. You're my best friend, and she's your sister. It makes sense I'd like her better than I like you. She's a lot prettier than you are."

"Let's get one thing straight now." He stops walking again, and I turn to face him. "As far as all that goes, you're waiting until marriage to touch her. No, I take it back. You are never sleeping with my sister. Even if you wind up having kids, they're getting dropped off by a stork. I'm not thinking of you with Dylan."

"I mean, I'm going to touch her—"

"Ah-ah!" He points a thick digit at my nose. "I don't want to hear about it. You read me?"

I hold up both hands and laugh. "Loud and clear."

We're at Cooters & Shooters, and I see her inside laughing and talking to Craig. My whole body lights up, and I want to go to her. I want to pull her into my arms and kiss her. I think about what Garrett said about kids, and my chest tightens. What would she say if I told her about it? That's nuts, and way too fucking soon to even think about.

I'm not thinking about it now…

"Just remember, always keep in mind every second of every day…" Garrett's voice is a low warning. "If you hurt her, if you make my little sister cry, I'll beat your ass so bad—"

"I'll gladly take it if I ever make her cry."

"So long as we're on the same page." He glances at the restaurant. "Let's get cleaned up. I'm kind of looking forward to you being on your best behavior."

"I'm always on my best behavior compared to you."

"Sounds like some bullshit to me."

A smile curls my lips, and I let him take off a few steps ahead of me while I linger behind, watching her inside the restaurant waving her hands and shaking her head so her pretty dark hair swishes down her back.

Calm is something I haven't felt in a long time, if ever. But standing here, gazing at my future, I'm just as calm as a perfect day on the water. Not a cloud in sight.

Chapter 12

Dylan

MY BROTHER ZANE IS TALL WITH DARK HAIR LIKE MINE AND STUNNING blue eyes. He's naturally muscular, and he has our dad's square chin and our mom's wide, perfect smile with a deep dimple right in his cheek.

It's a smile I haven't seen since he came home six months ago.

Zane is five years older than me, but way back when I was three and he was eight, he was the only one of my brothers who'd sit and read to me.

He wasn't as rowdy as Hendrix or a brute like Garrett, who was already huge at six and throwing me over his shoulder, running around like I was a football. He didn't have Jack's raw talent, but he loved the game.

Being a former team captain, our dad was constantly watching and working with his boys. Zane was a good teammate, but he didn't want to be the star. He liked to do his own thing and be left alone, which is why Dad steered him to kicking.

Dad would say the kicker is one of the most important

members of the team. An entire game could turn on a single field goal or an extra point. Zane was consistent and accurate, he could get good height and rotation on the ball, and it gave him space.

He went in the first round of the draft, and by the time he made it to Baltimore, he was one of the highest paid kickers in the league.

Then the accident happened, and his entire life turned on a single fake field goal. Now he's always alone.

"Zane?" I tap on his door, waiting in the quiet hall in the middle of the day.

A rustling noise from inside precedes the door opening a crack. "Dylan, what's up?" His voice is low and scratchy, like he was asleep.

"Come down to the restaurant. I made more pulled pork than we can sell tonight. It's your favorite." I smile, doing my best to pry him out of this cave.

"Thanks, sis." He straightens as if he'll close the door again. "I'm not really hungry."

"Wait!" My hand shoots out, and I stop the wooden barrier. "Just come down and sit with me. I miss talking to you."

He inhales slowly, releasing the door and stepping away. I push it open, stepping inside his neat bedroom. A box in the corner holds several discarded trophies, and the walls are bare.

A large bookcase is mostly empty, and I walk over to see it holds fabric-covered hardback classics. Pulling one down, I read the spine, *A Separate Peace.*

"Are you reading this?"

"No." He walks over and sits in a chair beside the polished-oak desk. "I'm pretty sure that was Dad's."

It makes me sad, because I know how much he loved to read, but I'm not going there. "I'm going to steal this bookcase. Mine's overflowing."

"Go for it." He waves a hand.

His beard is thicker than Logan's, but still trimmed and

tight. The thin T-shirt he wears lets me know his muscles are still toned, and a sleeve of tattoos covers his right arm. His eyes are tired and lately they've been so distant.

"Remember when we were little kids, and you'd read to me?" I smile, tilting my head to the side. "What was that book you always read?"

"*Everybody Poops.* Mom said it would help you relax and go potty."

"She told you that?"

"Yep." He exhales, stretching in his seat. "I was the only one who'd sit still long enough for her to talk to. Until you got bigger."

"I miss talking to you." I walk over to put my hand on his shoulder. "We all miss you down at the restaurant. Craig asks about you all the time."

His smile is more of a wince. "I don't like how people look at me when I'm there, and if one more person speaks to me in that voice…"

"What voice?" I lean down, imitating the high-pitched, sing-song sympathy tone. "The one where I'm soooo worried about you?"

"Stop." He flinches away from me.

"Does your footie-woot hurt weel weel bad?"

"I'm going to start flipping tables."

"Don't do that." I drop the baby voice. "The Coot & Shoot has gotten rowdy enough after dark. I'm starting to rethink the whole concept of my Dare dish. Last time it broke out into a full-on, dirty-dancing party, and we still had little kids there."

"It's your thing. Customers love it."

"Only a small group of customers love it. Most of them can't even eat it. We throw away more than we give out." Exhaling a sigh, I walk to the door. "I'm starting to think maybe Davis is right, and it's a dumb idea, both from a business and an accounting perspective."

"Davis Kent is a jackass."

"And the *Coyote Ugly* routine is probably a health code violation.

If anybody complains, we could get fined or whatever they do with those."

"Nobody's going to complain about pretty girls grinding on a bar."

"I don't know. Some people get real mean when they're titillated."

That manages to draw a ghost of a smile from him. "They can eat somewhere else."

Bobbing my head side to side, I'm not giving up on him so fast. "We could probably tone it down some. It would be nice to have a calming presence, though."

"You mean a distraction?"

"You're not that distracting."

"Everyone in the world saw my injury. It's all they see when they look at me."

"I think you're being a little dramatic. Not everybody in the world watches football, you know." He cuts me a look. "Just around here, and you need to get out of this house."

"I do get out of this house." He presses on his knees, rising slowly. "I go for drives…"

"After dark, which is weird and stalkery. People are going to think you're a serial killer."

"I'm not a serial killer."

"Good, because Miss Gina has a job for you. Steven is retiring, and she needs someone to help with her garden and minor repairs. I told her you were available."

"Dylan," he groans.

"Well, you are, and she's blind so no pitiful looks. It's the perfect thing. She's the sweetest little old lady, and she needs help with that big ole house."

"I can't be running up and down all those stairs. Aren't they marble?"

"Good news: She has an elevator."

Quiet falls around us, and he leans on the doorknob, which

I guess means it's time for me to go. His chin lifts, and he seems to acknowledge defeat.

"Fine, I'll swing by and talk to her."

"You've already got the job. She even said she'll pay you."

"How much?" His brow furrows, and I shrug.

"I didn't ask her. That's your business."

"Oh, now it's my business." A low chuckle gives me the smallest bit of relief.

He's not a total lost cause, and I have faith in Miss Gina. Reaching out, I slide my hand over his wrist, giving him a squeeze.

"Thank you, Zane."

I start for the door when he stops me. "I'm sorry I hurt you, Dee. It always weighed on me... I guess karma took care of that."

Sadness twists in my chest, and I look up to meet the ghosts in his eyes directly. "I have never once held what happened against you. It was just one of those things—a freak accident."

He nods, turning away. "How did you get over it?"

It's a quiet question, and it breaks my heart. I don't like to think of him up here struggling alone. Craig would never leave me alone that way, and I'm not leaving my brother either.

Exhaling a laugh, I do my best to stay upbeat. "Who says I did?"

Before I leave, I pause, looking around the small but clean space. "Are you sure you don't need to move downstairs? We could put Logan up here—"

"Across the hall from you?" His voice rises, and he becomes a touch more animated. "Sounds like a good way to burn the house down."

My eyes widen. "What do you mean?"

"I'm not blind." His eyebrow arches. "Or deaf, Miss Phone Sex."

Heat races up my neck behind my ears, and I hustle through the door. "Good, because Miss Gina needs somebody who can hear."

His deep laugh follows me down the stairs, and I wince. I

might be embarrassed as hell, but it's not too much to drown out my relief. I think that might have been a little breakthrough.

Maybe that old blind lady is right. Maybe something good is coming.

"Your brother didn't kick my ass." Logan's forearm is braced on the door frame above my head, and my back is against the door.

After stealing little touches and thrilling looks all night, we've managed to sneak out to the empty playground behind the restaurant. The moon is almost full, and a breeze lifts my hair around my shoulders.

"I'm glad to see it." He's so tall, I have to tilt my head to look up at him, and I can't keep a silly grin off my face. "What did he say?"

He reaches up to slide his thumb lightly from my chin down my jaw. "A lot of things I didn't know."

The warmth in his eyes makes my stomach squeeze. It makes me cross my arms over my waist.

"Like what?" I'm a little breathless.

"He said you should go to culinary school."

"Oh," I shake my head, rolling my eyes. "I don't have to go to culinary school to learn new recipes. That's why God made YouTube."

A low laugh rumbles in his chest, and it's a vibration straight to my core. "Maybe you can teach me some new reci-pes. Something other than ghost peppers."

"I can do that." I give him a little wink. "I'll take it easy on you."

"Not too easy." He leans closer. "I like my girl to have an edge."

"Your girl?"

"That's what I said." He's so close, his fresh, citrusy scent surrounds me.

My lips are heavy, and I reach up to tug the front of his shirt, bringing him closer. "Do you mean me?"

"You know I do."

Rising onto my tiptoes, I seal my lips to his. His hand goes around my waist, and he pulls me flush against his hard body. His mouth opens mine, and when our tongues slide together, I exhale an aching whimper.

He groans in response, and heat saturates my core. I rise higher, pressing my body closer as I thread my fingers in his soft hair. I wrap my arms around his neck, and for a moment, it's as if we're melting together. It's only us and the touch of skin against skin, the warmth of our lips pulling each other's.

His hand finds the bare skin at my waist, and I arch my back. I want him to move that hand under my shirt, lift my bra and play with my breasts, but a loud laugh from inside the restaurant cuts through the haze.

"Fuck," he groans, moving his lips to my eyebrow. He kisses my forehead and the top of my head before wrapping me in a hug. "I can't get enough of you."

My cheek is buried against his chest, and my eyes close as I hold him, inhaling his body all around me. I know the feeling, but I also know I've got two brothers inside and a restaurant full of people.

"I'd better get back in there." I lift on my tiptoes once more to kiss his lips. "I'm looking forward to our date."

"Wear a dress."

The naughty grin on his lips is another flash of heat to my slippery core, and I drop my chin with a laugh. "I will."

Hurrying through the dining hall, I give the place a quick sweep before heading into the kitchen where Thomas is at the stove. Craig is at the sink rinsing a large pot with the hand sprayer.

He's dancing and singing along to an old Indigo Girls song, and when he sees me, he lets out a loud, "She boned him!"

"Craig!" I yelp, going straight to him, lifting my hand like I'll grab his mouth.

He turns fast, holding the nozzle at me like a gun. "Don't make me spray you."

"Stop saying that—Kimmie will hear!"

"She doesn't know what it means." He finishes up with the pot.

"No, but she'll repeat it, and her uncles know what it means."

That makes him snort. "Logan is a brave man… but you're worth the beat-down they'll give him."

"Nobody's beating anybody. We're going on a real date, and we have not had intercourse."

"Don't play games with me, Danger-girl." His eyes narrow. "You've had something. You're glowing."

Pressing my hands to my cheeks, I look in the mirror over the sink. I can't see a difference, but I do feel happy, and I don't know how I'm going to make it to Monday.

Craig's face appears over my shoulder, and his teasing expression is gone. He's studying me with all seriousness. It's a look I haven't seen since my injury.

"You really are glowing. That asshole better watch his back."

"That's a switch." I frown at him, crossing my arms and turning to face him. "I thought he was hot as a ghost pepper, and he was supposed to get the cobwebs off my coochie."

"That was before. Now you have a look like…"

My chest tightens so fast, I hiccup a breath. "Like?"

"Like that boy'd better be serious. I know at least five men who will hand him his ass if he plays more than football."

"At least five?"

"I don't know how invested Thomas is." He says it loud enough so our old chef can hear him.

Thomas's reply comes calm and easy. "I'll bring a shovel."

Chapter 13

Logan

STANDING IN THE FOYER AT THE BOTTOM OF THE STAIRS WAITING, I haven't felt this way since I was in high school waiting on my prom date. My palms are sweaty, my collar is too tight, and I keep expecting Allie or Zane to step out with a camera.

Okay, not Zane. All of Dylan's brothers have given me a version of the "hurt her and die" speech. I expected it from them. I did not expect it from Craig, who I think might be the most dangerous one of all.

I can actually imagine Craig sneaking up on me in a dark alley with a knife. He'd shank me and wouldn't even look back, and old Thomas said something about bringing a shovel. I think they're in cahoots.

"Hey, sorry I took a little longer than I expected." Her voice is soft, and as she skips down the stairs, I have to reach out to hold the rail for support.

She's so fucking gorgeous. Her long hair flows in smooth

waves down her back and over her shoulders. Her lips are glossy pink, and her full lashes are lowered over her eyes.

She's wearing a dress as requested, but it's not just any dress. It's red with a zipper that runs all the way up the front, filling my head with images of unzipping her, and she's pulled a light denim jacket over it.

Her shapely legs end in high-heeled, strappy black sandals with laces wrapped around her ankles, and those red toenails again…

"Damn, girl. You really are dangerous."

She stops on the bottom step, putting her face almost level with mine. Her nose wrinkles with her smile, and she shakes her head. "I'm not so dangerous."

Her hand is on my shoulder, and I put both my hands on her waist, unsure what to make of these feelings she stirs in my chest.

"Yeah, you're dangerous." Leaning closer, I slide my nose along the side of her hair, speaking low in her ear. "To my mouth and my heart."

She shivers, and a shuffle on the landing above draws our attention. "Drive safe, kids. Don't stay out too late, and don't get into trouble."

We move apart, and her expression brightens at the sight of Zane leaning heavily on the railing at the top of the stairs.

Lifting her chin, she teases, "Don't worry, *Dad*."

He's coming out a bit more, which I know is a relief to all his siblings. He was even at the restaurant last night for a little while, until more people started approaching his table wishing him well, and he said goodnight. I've learned he doesn't like to be fussed over.

I don't blame him.

"Thanks for loaning me your Jeep," I call up to him. "Sure you don't need it?"

"Nah, I've got an early day tomorrow, heading over to Miss Gina's. I know it's more fun to drive than Garrett's big rig."

"You're going to Miss Gina's tomorrow?" Dylan's voice rises excitedly.

"Yeah, so don't bring it back empty."

"I won't." I give him a wave before catching his sister's hand and leading her out the door. I'm ready to get her fed and get her alone.

Garrett recommended a restaurant on the bay south of town. The drive down the old highway takes us through the sweeping live oak trees and blooming crepe myrtles. The top is on the Jeep, but the doors aren't. I drive slower, so the wind doesn't beat us up too much.

"It's so different here from Texas."

"How so?" She glances up at me, and I hesitate a moment, watching the wind lift a curl around her cheeks.

Then I shake it away. "It's greener, closer together."

"Texas is pretty huge."

It's a nice night, not as hot as it has been, and I pull into the gravel parking lot. Hustling around, I help her out of the vehicle, holding her arm as we walk on the rocks so she doesn't turn an ankle.

"Not the best footwear for gravel." She clutches me, and we take it slow.

"I like those shoes. They're nice."

They're practically invisible with the thin straps over her red toes, and I consider sweeping her off her feet and carrying her inside. But I don't.

The small restaurant is in a renovated old house with a weathered wood exterior and deer antlers for door handles. Inside, the place is all exposed wood, from the floor to the walls. The wide-plank ceiling is adorned with twinkle lights wrapped around long branches of driftwood, and a brick fireplace is in the center.

It feels like an old hunting lodge, and it smells like expensive food.

We take a seat at a square table covered in a white tablecloth.

The waiter takes our drink order. Dylan orders a smoked Old Fashioned, and I have a plain ole scotch.

The dining room is very small and dimly lit with jarred candles on the tables and shaded lamps mixed with the twinkle lights overhead. It's cozy and romantic, and only a handful of other diners are present.

She leans forward, eyes sparkling in the light. "We're not in Cooters & Shooters anymore, Toto. This is fancy!"

I exhale a laugh. "Let me order for us. Garrett gave me the inside scoop."

"He would know." She lets me take her menu. "He was sweet to cover for me tonight. I told him it wasn't necessary, but he likes to hang out with Craig and Thomas. They'll turn the whole night into a party."

"He has a tendency to do that everywhere." I think about his dance moves on the field after we score a touchdown.

The waiter returns with our drinks, and I order marinated crab claws and halibut for her, the five-ounce filet for me, and two glasses of their best pinot noir with our entrees.

Before he goes, he takes out a small blowtorch and lights the top of Dylan's old-fashioned. I guess that's the "smoked" part.

Her eyebrows rise, and she cups one hand beside her mouth. "Now that's dangerous." She points at the flaming tumbler.

"Not as dangerous as you."

Lifting it, she holds it out for a toast before bringing it closer and blowing on it. "How do I drink this?"

"Here." I lift a metal lid off the table and slide it over the top of her glass until it extinguishes the flame.

"I didn't see that." She lifts it again and takes a sip. "Mmm… it's warm and spicy."

"Just like you like it." My hand slides across the table, and this time she doesn't hesitate.

She puts her hand in mine, and it feels so natural, so good.

"Tell me about your parents. I know your dad was a big football star, but what about your mom?"

Dylan's head tilts to the side. "She was the head cheerleader in high school. They were the total stereotype, and when they graduated, he was prom king and she was his queen."

"They were the same age?"

She nods. "They went to the same college. Dad played ball, and she got a business degree."

"Smart."

"They got married right after graduation, and he went pro while she stayed home having babies."

"Was that okay with her?" My brow furrows.

I've heard too many stories about women sacrificing their careers for their husbands, and I agree it's unfair. I wouldn't ask Dylan to do it.

If I were asking Dylan to do anything… *What the hell?*

"Yeah." She looks up at me with a smile. "Mom loved babies. She wanted a big family, and she really, really wanted a little girl. I was her last chance. If I'd been a boy… Well… She probably would've tried one more time."

She starts to laugh, and I smile, squeezing her hand. "I'm glad she got you." She blinks down, shyly, and I thread our fingers. "How did the restaurant happen?"

"Mm…" she nods, sipping her drink. "After Dad retired, he didn't know what to do with himself. They were going to open it with some friends, but the friends fell through. Mom said they could do it themselves, so they took a leap of faith and put us all to work, Thomas too."

"Ready-made crew?"

"Yeah." Her eyes drift over my shoulder. "I think that place was as much for her as it was for him. Mom put her business degree to work, and it really took off—helped, of course, by Dad's celebrity status."

"Of course."

The waiter returns at that moment with our entreés, which he places in front of us. Cracked pepper for Dylan, none for me. I slice a piece of perfectly cooked steak, and it melts in my mouth. Dylan picks up a crab claw in her fingers and expertly slides the meat off with her teeth.

"This is really good." Her eyes widen, and she turns the plate. "We should have crab claws at our place. They're not hard to make."

"Garrett does want you to go to cooking school, after all."

She shakes her head. "Garrett." Then she tilts her head to the side. "What about you? What did your mom do?"

"She was a beauty queen. Miss Texas."

"Wow." Her eyes widen. "That's impressive. Texas is a big state."

"Then she went into broadcasting. She was the six o'clock news anchor. It's how she met my dad." Lifting my glass, I study the light red wine. "From what I've heard, he really loved her. Maybe that's why he acted the way he did."

I'm starting to feel like I could understand not getting over someone, how their loss could cast a long shadow over everything good in your life.

Only, if I still had a piece of her, a child we shared, I can't understand not loving that piece as much as the whole.

"I think that's what happened to our dad, too." Her brow furrows, and she studies her wine glass as well. "He went downhill really fast after Mom died... Or maybe it was already happening, and we were too young to know? Now that I'm older and I'm at the restaurant all the time, I realize she covered for him a lot. He wasn't there nearly as much as she was."

Setting my glass down, I reach out and take her hand again. "I'm sorry for what happened to him. From what I've read and seen, your dad sounded like a great guy, and now that I know you, I'm sure your mom was amazing as well."

"They were." Her voice is soft as if remembering.

A moment passes, she sips her wine then presses her lips into a smile, looking up at me. "And you're up for the MVP award this year. That's exciting."

"I've never been this close, and I owe a lot of it to your

brother. If that giant weren't on the field blocking for me, I wouldn't be able to make half those plays."

"I don't know. He says you're the fastest receiver he's ever seen, *Lightning*." She gives me a wink. "How fast are you?"

Grinning, I take another bite of steak. I'm usually pretty cocky when it comes to my career and the game and my stats, but Dylan comes from football royalty. She's surrounded by star players—whom she doesn't even watch play.

"I'm pretty fast for a tall guy."

"You're being humble." Her eyes narrow. "I've never known a league player who didn't brag about his abilities."

"Yeah, but you're from a family of great athletes. I know it doesn't impress you. But if I could play golf…"

"Not that again!" She covers her face, but her eyes glow.

She's so pretty. I think about what it would've been like to have her cheering for me in high school. I think about her in a cheerleader uniform, and damn, that's a new fantasy.

Then I think about her in my box watching me play, maybe even wearing my jersey. I wonder how it would feel to look up to see her there. It's something I've never had or even really thought about, but I like it.

I like it a lot.

It's only a few miles down a narrow, two-lane road until you reach the end of land and the start of the ocean.

I pull the Jeep into a public parking lot near an abandoned beach bar one of the hurricanes ruined. It was never rebuilt, and now it stands as a monument to the past.

Taking her hand, we walk down the sand to where the water rolls gently onto the shore. It's a constant, soothing rush, like the ticking of a clock or the swinging of a pendulum.

The wind is stronger here, right on the front lines of the

Gulf, and when we reach the end of the dry sand, I drop to my knees, pulling her down to my lap. She sits in front of me, her legs wrapped over mine, bare feet in the sand. We left our shoes and her denim jacket in the Jeep, and I'm thinking about that zipper on her dress.

She's so beautiful with the briny air turning her hair to waves. She's so sweet and funny and unexpected and fucking sexy. I can't deny it any more. Dylan Bradford is in my blood. She's in my veins, and all I want to do is make her happy.

Tonight is the start of something—or I really want it to be. Yet, a growing frustration churns in my chest when I think about what she's told me and how she feels.

My feelings for her have grown so fast and so strong, but I can't ignore the truth. We have a problem, and no matter how I turn it over in my mind, I can't find the solution.

We laugh and joke about it, but I see the sincerity in her eyes when she talks about her father. She doesn't want to be with a football player, but I can't give it up.

Not that she's asked me to give it up. She doesn't ask anything from me, and that almost makes it worse. I want to give her everything. I want to make her as happy as I am when I imagine us together.

At the same time, I can't just turn off what's driving me, my unfinished business.

Reaching up, I thread my fingers in her hair, but when our eyes meet, her brow furrows. She can see it in my gaze. I'm as turbulent inside as the waves being tossed about by the wind and gravity and the pull of the moon.

"What's wrong?" she asks over the sound of the surf.

"I told you before I don't want to hurt you."

"How would you do that?"

"I'm not ready to quit, Dylan." I cup her face in my hands. "It's still inside me. I still want to play."

Her lips part, but I don't give her a chance to speak as I continue. "I have to prove to him that I'm better than what he thinks. That I'm the best, and he missed out on not wanting to spend time with me." I look up at the black-velvet sky full of stars. "Inside I'm still that dumb kid wanting him to love me."

The waves crash, and I exhale heavily. These are words I've never said out loud to anyone other than my therapist. To be honest, I can't believe it still matters so much to me, but it does. To this day.

Soft hands cup my neck. Slim fingers thread in the back of my hair. I swallow the thickness in my throat and meet her pretty eyes. They're full of acceptance and warmth.

Her lips press together, and she smiles. "Okay."

I blink several times before repeating it back to her. "Okay?"

"I understand."

"You do?"

"You're not a dumb kid, Logan. You're so much more than that." Her fingers tighten on the back of my neck, and she scoots a little closer. "I want to say forget about your father, but I also understand needing to prove yourself—if only for yourself. We're a lot alike in that way."

She blinks a few times, and I reach up to touch her chin. The moon is full tonight, and I see the sparkle on her lashes. It's like a punch in the chest.

"Are you crying?"

Her eyes roll, and she tries to look away. "No?"

"You are." I cup her face in my hands, sliding my thumbs over the tops of her cheeks. "I'm sorry. I didn't mean to make you cry."

"It's not that. I want you to be honest with me about who you are. Honesty doesn't hurt me." She looks at the sky, doing her best to quell the tears.

"What is it, then?" I feel like an asshole.

How could I be so forceful with her on our first date, when we're just getting close? Now I really want to kick my ass.

"I'm crying because you're leaving. There's no point to this. I knew it from the start, but I did it anyway."

Energy rises in my chest at her words. *She did it anyway?* "What did you do?" Her head is turned, so I gently catch her chin, guiding her gaze to mine. "Tell me."

She blinks up at me, and I'm on edge, needing to hear her say it. "These past few days have been a dream, but I told myself not to get attached. When it's over, you'll go back to New York and forget all about me."

I almost laugh. "Forget? Do you honestly think I could forget you? You're the first woman who's ever made me struggle with who I am and what I want to do with my life."

It's too soon to tell her she's the first woman who's made me think about things like having a wife and kids. She's the first woman who's made me feel like I deserve those things or that I might even be capable of having them and not fuck it all up like my dad did.

I think with Dylan by my side, I'd be able to do anything, and even more, I'd want to do everything.

"When I close my eyes, I see your face. No matter where I am, something reminds me of you." My hands are on her shoulders. "Don't you see?"

Her pretty lips pout, and a fresh stream of tears lines her cheeks. "What are you saying to me?"

"I want you to be my girl, Dylan. I want you on the sidelines cheering for me. I want you at home watching me when you can't be at the games. I know I'm asking for something you said you'd never to do, and it kills me that you'll say—"

"Okay!" She cuts me off, and for a moment, I can't speak.

We're sitting in the sand holding each other with the noise of the surf crashing before us, and my chest breaks open.

"You will?"

She nods slowly, her eyes never leaving mine, as if she's making a promise. I know this girl will keep it, too, because this girl is not like anyone I've ever known.

So I make my own solemn promise. "I'm going to win that

trophy, and I'm going to retire. Then I'm coming back here for you."

A smile lifts her cheeks, and her eyes are glassy. "I've never had a long-distance relationship before."

"Me neither, but I want it with you. So that's what we're doing."

Her chin drops, and she exhales a laugh. "Oh, we are?"

"Yes, now kiss me."

Reaching for her, I slide my hands under her soft ass and pull her closer. Her hands move between us, and she grasps the zipper at the hem of her dress, sliding it higher, until I see she's not wearing underwear. Desire surges straight to my dick.

"Dylan," I groan, and my hand tightens on her ass, lifting her even closer.

She's off the sand, sitting on the tops of my thighs, and she takes my hand, moving it between her legs to her bare pussy. "I've been thinking about you touching me here all night."

Fuck me, this girl.

"You're so wet." I slide my fingers up and down, and her eyes close as she moans.

I quickly strip off the linen blazer I'm wearing and place it on the sand before rolling her onto her back. She's so beautiful. Her knees are bent, and she's looking up at me as I loosen my belt and jeans, easing the pressure on my straining cock.

She grasps the top of the second zipper and slowly lowers it to allow her bare breasts to spill out, and with a groan, I drop to my forearms, dragging my face over her beautiful body.

I cup her breasts in my hands and lift them, holding them together as I pull a nipple between my teeth gently. She squirms and moans, and I can't resist.

"Your body is so beautiful." I kiss across her breasts and repeat the ravaging on the other side. "I think I'm more a fan of *Coyote Ugly* Dylan than *Nutcracker* Dylan."

"*Nutcracker* Dylan didn't have her boobs yet," she laughs, threading her fingers in my hair.

"Don't get me wrong, you were always beautiful."

She hums softly. "I know what you like."

"I know what you like."

I talked her through coming in her bed, and I'm going to give her the fantasy. My mouth moves down the center of her chest to her soft stomach, and her sighs melt into moans.

I pull her skin between my teeth, giving her a little nip as I make my way lower. She gasps my name, and I lean forward, wrapping my arms around her thighs and lifting her to my mouth. Then I slide my tongue up the center of her pussy, tracing slow circles over her clit.

"Logan!" Her fingers stab into my hair, and her back arches as she moans loudly.

Her words in her bedroom echo in my ears, and I slide my tongue hungrily over her clit as she moans my name. It's the best sound, and my cock is so hard.

Everything is different now. Now is the start of something new. It's the start of something I've never had yet always tried to find.

I built a family with my teammates, but that was different. I had no idea how good it could be to have it with a beautiful girl whose eyes are warm whiskey and whose body is sweet honey.

Sliding my palm over her stomach, her muscles quiver beneath my touch, and soft whimpers rise to louder moans. I slide my mouth higher, dragging my beard across her sensitive skin as I kiss my way up her stomach.

Her knees jump and sexy noises fall from her lips. When I reach her face again, I look down at her, wrapping my arms under her shoulders and pulling her tight against my chest. "I'm going to kiss you gently, then I'm going to fuck you hard."

Her chin lifts and she cups my face in her hands. "You can kiss me hard, too."

I start to laugh, but she rises off the ground to meet my mouth. Our lips seal together, and we fall back, sliding our tongues along each other's. It's the hottest, most amazing feeling. Her hand is on my bare stomach, and she moves it lower, rubbing my cock through my boxer briefs.

"It's so big." Her voice is husky, and her eyes are blazing. "I want to see it."

I rise onto my knees, looking down at her sexy body on my jacket in the sand. Sitting on my heels, I shove my underwear down my hips, and my cock breaks free, hard and heavy.

Her eyes are on me in a way that has precome slipping from my tip, and I slide my hand over my erection, giving it a slow tug.

Her eyes widen. Her bottom lip goes between her teeth, and her knees rub together as she watches me.

"Do you have any idea how sexy you are?" I groan.

"As sexy as you?" A naughty grin is on her lips, and I quickly take the wallet out of my pants to grab a Magnum, rolling it on fast.

Gripping her thighs, I spread her out before me. "Touch yourself."

Her eyes are on mine as she does what I say, and I hold my cock in my hand, guiding it to her slippery core. She's circling her clit, and when I insert the tip, her lips part. She exhales a deep sigh, and her fingers move faster.

"It's so big," she gasps, and a pulse moves through my cock.

I slide deeper, watching her body stretch to take me. Feeling her quivering as her orgasm rises.

"Fuck, Dylan," I groan softly. "You take me so good."

When at last, I'm fully seated, I hold, allowing her to get used to my size. Leaning forward, I kiss the base of her neck, that little space between her collar bones, and her legs start to shake.

Lifting my head, I meet her eyes, and she moves beneath me. "Fuck me, Logan," she whispers. "I'm about to come."

At that, my control slips. My hips move, and I thrust easy, steadily, until she's ready. Soft whimpers slip through her lips, and she's so warm and soft and wet and perfect. I kiss her lips before moving my cheek to hers.

Her knees rise, and she bucks against me, meeting my thrusts.

Her whimpers turn to low moans, and her body clenches and tightens around my cock. My eyes squeeze shut, and the pleasure radiating through my pelvis is undeniable. I can't hold back anymore.

Three more thrusts, and I hold, gripping her body as a violent orgasm rips through me. I pulse, filling the condom, and she moans, shuddering beneath me. My arms are around her body, and she's flush against me. We're soaring to the highest altitudes together, wrapped in each other's arms. It's incredible.

I hold through the final pulses, through her soft whimpers, and as we drift down together, I lift my chin to claim her lips again. Her tongue curls with mine, and it's so good. It's everything.

Sliding her hair away from her face with my fingers, I kiss her lips, her cheeks, her damp eyes. "Yep," I whisper. "This is what we're doing."

"It's going to be hard to be apart." A wistful note is in her tone.

After that orgasm, I know it's true, and I'm doing the math on how to get around it.

Chapter 14

Dylan

"H E'S NUMBER 12." I LEAN OVER THE iPAD LOOKING AT THE ONLINE store for a jersey with Logan's number on it. "Look, it even has his name!"

"I can't believe you're just discovering this." Craig frowns standing beside me. "They're all over the stadiums during the games. You really never watch any of them?"

Pain twists in my stomach, and I shake my head. "I still wouldn't watch them, but it means a lot to him."

"You don't like long distance. You don't like watching football…" He's counting on his fingers.

"Correction, I'm *afraid* to watch the men I love play football." I rub my palms up and down my arms. "I don't want to see them hurt. And long distance just sucks any way you cut it. But a lot of people do it. What if he was in the military?"

"I suppose." My friend exhales heavily. "He'd be in scarier situations, and you wouldn't have the option of visiting him or seeing him on TV."

"You're right. That would be worse." I play with a thread on my sweater.

My bestie straightens, reaching for my hand. "The time will pass so fast. You'll be teaching and running the restaurant, and he'll be playing every week and practicing. Hell, you'll blink, and it will be February."

"I hope so."

I've never been in this situation, where the thrill of new love twists painfully with the aching dread of separation.

Last night, I slept in his bed, not that we did much sleeping. After our declarations on the beach, he told me how all of my brothers and Craig and Thomas had pretty much threatened his life if he hurt me. It was sweet, and it made me laugh.

It also made me realize I'm a grown woman, and I can sleep with whomever I want in my own house. When I opened my eyes this morning, two strong arms were wrapped tightly around my waist. My head was tucked beneath his chin, and I'd never felt so cherished.

When I had to get up to get ready for work, he playfully wouldn't let me go. He kissed the top of my shoulder, and it was a shock of joy all the way to my stomach.

I thought about how rigid I used to be. I thought if I made the rule never to date a football player, I'd never be in danger of falling in love with one.

It's too soon to talk about love. We're only dating, but it's there, just waiting to consume me. I can't. We need to take it slow. We need to get to know each other better, despite all the promises. I will be smart.

"I've never even googled him." I laugh, taking out my phone. "I don't even follow him on social media!"

"Don't." Craig is at my side, eyes wide.

I frown up at him. "Why not? It's fun."

Opening my Instagram app, I tap in Logan's name and navigate over to his profile. I hit the Follow button as soon as I'm there, then I begin to scroll. Image after image of him and different women. One is a statuesque blonde in a shimmering dress. In fact, almost all of them are tall blondes. They're all so thin, they could be dancers. I spot one brunette like a fly in the buttermilk. She's wearing a chambray shirt tied at her waist and pantyhose for pants. An inch of light is between her thighs.

"So many models…" I try to laugh, but even I can hear it's forced. "Oh, he dated Natalia van Norse, the influencer. All the way up to… now."

"He's been here a month, so it couldn't be now."

My neck is hot, and I wish I had never started down this silly path. "You're right! It's really none of my business."

I put my phone facedown on the metal work table, and I feel Craig's eyes on me. I also hear a shrill, small voice echoing through the dining hall.

"Aunt Deedee!" Kimmie yells. "Where are you? *Aunt Deedaaay!*"

I try to forget what I've just seen, but it's too late.

Looking up, I see Logan walking through the kitchen door with my niece riding on his back. His dark hair is messy, and his straight white smile seems to glow. He's in faded jeans and a gray T-shirt that stretches attractively across his muscular chest, and his muscles flex as he holds Kimmie behind his back. *Dammit*, he's so hot, and I'm sure my poker face is not working for me.

"Lightning McQueen got me ice cream, then he said we had to come see you before you get too busy." She tilts her little head to the side, speaking right in his face. "Are you going to marry my Aunt Deedee, Mr. Lightning?"

Logan's eyes are on me, and his brow quirks at my expression. "I'm not sure she'll have me." He sits Kimmie on the counter and walks to where I'm standing trying to get myself together. "What's that face about?"

"She looked at your Instagram," Craig answers before I can play it off or even say a word.

I cut my eyes at him, but Logan only laughs. "Oh, man. What have they posted now? I had to pass that account to a handler. The online gamblers were pissing me off—"

"Models." Craig continues. "Lots and lots of models. Sooo many models…"

"Will you stop?" I widen my eyes at him.

"No." He shakes his head. "Honesty is imperative in relationships, especially long-distance ones, and if I'm going to root for you two, I'm going to sing like a stool pigeon."

"Do stool pigeons sing?" I snip at him. "I thought they just blabbed their big mouths."

"What's a stool pigeon?" Kimmie's little nose wrinkles, and Craig grabs her by the waist.

"It's a bird. Now come with me, big ears. We're going to the playground."

"My ears aren't big!" She shouts as he picks her up. "Your ears are big!"

"Not as big as your mouth." He tickles her waist, and she squeals louder.

"Aunt Deedee said *you* have a big mouth," she argues.

I wince, looking up at Logan, who is studying my expression. His lips tighten, and he closes the space between us, standing directly in front of me and caging me in with both hands on the metal counter. "What's going on in that pretty head?"

"Nothing!" My voice is too high, and my stomach is churning.

"Somehow I'm not convinced." He dips his chin to find my eyes.

I turn to the side, but there's no escaping his strong arms. "It just… it looks like you have a type is all." *And I'm not it*, I don't say out loud.

"I haven't looked at that account in a year, but I get invited to a lot of events that require a date. I don't remember half of who I take to them."

"Natalia van Norse is in a lot of the photos all the way up to now." I hate that I sound like a jealous girlfriend. Waving my hand, I duck under his arm and walk around so the counter is between us. "You know what? This is silly. It's not like we didn't both have lives before you came here."

"It's true. I still haven't met that golfer."

"Hopefully, you never will."

He walks around the counter to where I stand. "Look at me, Dylan. I don't give a shit about Natalia van Norse. She was in Europe all summer, and the last night we had dinner, she proposed a threesome with the guy she'd been cheating on me with." He slides a finger under my chin, lifting my eyes to his. "There is nothing there."

I blink a few times, trying to be strong and not get lost in his blue gaze. "I'm sorry that happened to you."

"I'm not." His hand moves to my waist, and he pulls me against his chest, lowering his face to my ear. "You were my type from the moment I saw you… fucking me with those pretty amber eyes, dancing around here in those hot little cutoffs, teasing me with that ass."

"Stop." I laugh, feeling my ears heat. "I was not."

"You were. Then you melted my face off. I should sue for sexual harassment."

"You don't work for me."

"Wouldn't that be interesting." He winks, reaching down to lift my hand. "I got you something." He takes a delicate, woven-leather bracelet from his pocket and slides it on my wrist. It has dark-blue glass beads threaded in the strands, which he pulls to tighten it. "Kimmie and I were walking along the bay, and a girl was selling them."

I turn my hand side to side. "I love it!"

"I'll get you something nicer, but I couldn't resist. Look." He turns my hand so I can read the word *Mine* stamped on the side.

My nose wrinkles, and I slide my finger over it. I love it so much, it might as well be made of twenty-four-karat gold. Reaching forward, I slide my arms around his waist, pulling us together.

"Logan," I sigh heavily. "I'm afraid we're moving too fast."

His hands are on my back, one at my waist and the other sliding higher until his fingers thread in the back of my hair.

He presses a kiss against the top of my head, and my eyes close as he takes a long inhale. "We might be, but I've never felt more sure of anything in my life. Besides football."

Leaning back, I look up at him. "Maybe we should just keep in touch and not call it dating. That way nobody gets hurt."

A half smile lifts the side of his mouth. "Is that possible for you? I'd be pretty pissed if some golfer came along and stole you away from me while I was gone."

Exhaling a frustrated growl, I press my head against his chest. "Nobody's going to steal me away from you."

"We'll just call it dating then. To keep things straight."

My eyes close, and my head is still against his chest. "I'm afraid. What if you get hurt?"

His large hand slides over the back of my neck again, and he kisses my head once more. "Your brother would never let that happen."

Miss Gina sits on the black, wrought-iron bench in the middle of her sweet olive bushes. She's in a straw hat, and she has a pink shawl around her narrow shoulders. Kimmie runs back and forth behind her, trying to catch an orange kitten, who's hiding under the outdoor patio.

"Come on, kitty-kitty, I have a treat!" My niece rubs her little fingers together as if she has something in them. She doesn't.

"I've found that if I sit very still, eventually, she'll come out and attack my shawl. Try that." Miss Gina calls to her before turning to me. "Your brother has done so much around here since he started, I'm almost glad Steven retired. I'm not sure he was doing anything!"

Her blind eyes narrow with her laugh, and she stands slowly, reaching for me. I take her hand, leading her to where Logan stands beside Zane, holding the side of a pergola while my brother finishes attaching the roof.

Climbing down slowly, he slaps Logan's back. "Thanks for stopping by to help me with this. It's really more of a two-person job."

"No problem." Logan takes the hammer while Zane packs up the rest of the tools.

The wooden structure stands at the back corner of the patio over a slightly raised platform, and Miss Gina slides her hand up the smooth wooden posts. "Rachel is going to love this. She can set up her massage table here and take clients. Wouldn't a flowering vine be nice wrapping around these columns, Zane? What do you think? Maybe a Bougainvillea or a Sweet Pea?"

"Sure." My brother nods, squinting up at her. "Whatever you want."

"Is that the friend of your niece?" I'm so excited. "When do you expect her?"

"Not until the fall, but she's going to love all the new additions." The old lady's eyebrow arches, and I glance over to see my brother's back is turned.

He motions to Logan, who helps him carry the tools to the small shed behind the house.

"I'm really glad it's working out. Zane had me worried."

The old woman nods, pressing her lips together. "He's still carrying some baggage, but he's a hard worker. Like you!"

"Help me, Lightning McQueen!" Kimmie yells from where she's on her hands and knees at the side of the patio. "The kitty is right there!"

"He's lovely." Miss Gina slips her hand into the crook of my arm. "He sounds very handsome."

"I don't know how someone can *sound* handsome." I tease her. "Are you saying he's not?"

"No, he's really hot." I duck my head, and we both laugh.

"A football player." Her brow arches. "I remember when you said you'd never date one of those."

"I was always so worried after we lost our dad, and after all he went through and suffered. The guys are all I have left."

"I know." Her voice is quiet, and she pulls my hand into her arm as we walk back to the bench. "But loss can happen anywhere at any time. You have to face your fears to learn they can't defeat you. You've survived all the pain life has thrown at you, and here you are, finding new happiness."

Chewing my lip, I watch as he pulls the small, orange feline from under the patio for a cheering Kimmie. The tiny cat's claws are visibly digging into his hand, but he doesn't even flinch as my niece pets its little head, cooing at it and showering it with unwanted affection.

He looks up, and when our eyes meet, it's an electric charge through my entire body.

"I'm not sure I'd survive if something happened to him." My voice is quiet.

"You would." The old woman pats my hand. "But you can't live thinking that way. You have to know that you would, then let it go and enjoy the time you have together. That's what makes life worth living."

He finally releases the small cat, and it dashes under the patio again with my niece right behind it. Standing, he walks over to us, gorgeous in those faded jeans and a maroon tee.

His dark hair is brushed away from his face, and his possessive smile sends heat rising in my body. "What are you ladies talking about?"

He wraps a muscled arm around my waist, and I tilt my head against his shoulder, inhaling his clean scent of citrus and sandalwood.

"I heard Dylan took the job at the high school." Miss Gina lifts her chin in our direction. "I'm sure the students are so excited. You were such a beautiful dancer."

"Now you're just being nice." I laugh, nudging her side. "You never saw me dance."

"But I was in the audience. I heard the music and the gasps of the people around me. They were amazed."

"It was all Craig."

"Don't believe her." Logan leans down, taking a deep breath at the top of my head and sending chills skating down my arms. "Craig was good, but Dylan was breathtaking."

The old lady's eyes shine with delight, and she presses her lips into a satisfied smile. "Yes, you are quite lovely. It's all going to work out."

Logan gives me a confused smile, but I shake my head. There she goes again.

Chapter 15

Logan

Tʜᴇ ʀᴇsᴛᴀᴜʀᴀɴᴛ ɪs ᴘᴀᴄᴋᴇᴅ, ᴀɴᴅ ɪᴛ's ᴏᴜʀ ʟᴀsᴛ ɴɪɢʜᴛ ɪɴ ᴛᴏᴡɴ. I'ᴠᴇ spent every night with Dylan since our date, and as much of every day as possible with her running the restaurant.

I help out where I can—where it doesn't require knowledge or experience. Thomas showed me how to hold a knife properly so I could help him slice carrots, onions, and celery, which he calls the *mirepoix*.

At night, we walk down to the bay holding hands. She tells me her plans for the school year, and her worries about never having taught before and whether the kids will respect her or listen to her.

I do my best to reassure her. She was an incredible dancer, and those kids want to know what she knows, they want to be there. It's an elective class as well, so I doubt they'll be disrespectful.

She listens to me with so much sincerity, I feel proud I can reassure her. From what I saw in those videos, she was so fucking good. If any of those kids have done their homework, they'll be in awe of her.

Then we'd end up sitting, fingers intertwined, her dark head on my shoulder. The small breakers created a soft hush on the sand, and I'd lean closer, nuzzling my face behind her neck, memorizing her fresh, slightly herbal scent as I kissed her warm skin.

She started wearing skirts all the time, and when she'd straddle my lap, I'd trace my fingers under them, squeezing her soft ass before shimmying out of my jeans and sinking deep into her hot, sexy body.

I love her sleeping in my bed with me. We don't sleep much, to be honest. Having her so close in the night inevitably leads to more, but it isn't only sex. Holding her, talking to her is our ritual.

I don't know how I'll go a single night without her in my arms now, tracing her finger along the line of my hair, looking up at me like I'm a fucking hero.

Glancing at the closet, I remember a time she was telling me I could probably handle a Serrano pepper. Then she started teasing it with her tongue, saying how it wasn't even that hot, and I had to back her into the supply closet and take her right there against the wall, *hard*.

Fuck, that was hot.

And I've got to shut down those memories before I pop a boner right here in the middle of Cooters & Shooters.

Tonight, I'm hanging back as Dylan skips around the kitchen, taking large platters of pizza out of the ovens.

"Is this Dare dish too lame?" She frowns up at me.

"It smells delicious." I grab the pizza wheel to help her cut the large pies into small, servable squares.

"No need for gloves with this one, but I double-washed my hands just in case." She gives me a wink. "Chocolate habaneros are one step down from the ghost pepper."

"I'll take a pass."

"Are you saying you'll never be a guest on *Hot Ones*?"

"Is that the show where they interview celebrities while making them eat hot sauce?"

"That's the one!"

"No, ma'am."

She breaks into a laugh, but Kimmie pouts as she rests her little chin on the tops of her fingers watching us. "I thought there was going to be chocolate."

"They're called chocolate habaneros because they're brown." Dylan leans down to kiss the top of her head. "They're hotter than jalapeños, which means they're too hot for you."

The little girl makes a sad noise, and Craig walks over to place a chocolate kiss on the counter in front of her. "Don't tell your dad."

Her eyes light, and she scoops up the silver-wrapped candy. "Thanks, Uncle Craig!"

"Good girl," he teases. "Are we ready? I've picked out a special song for tonight."

"Something less stimulating than last week, I hope." Dylan looks up at him. "Things got a little out of control."

In the very best way, I want to add, but I don't.

"That was your fault pulling out the Carolina Reaper." Craig bumps her with his hip. "You're going to like this one. It's special. Come on, KJ, let's do this."

He grabs the little girl's hand, and Allie breezes in as the two of them head out.

"Sorry I'm late!" She grabs an apron and drops it over her head. Her eyes are shining, and her smile is so big. "You're not going to believe what Garrett just told me!"

I know what he told her.

"What?" Dylan straightens, brow furrowed.

"Austin is QB-2!" Her voice goes so high, I'm surprised glasses don't break.

"QB-2!" Dylan meets her pitch, tossing her pizza wheel aside and running to her friend. The two of them jump up and down before falling into a hug and swaying side to side. "I'm so happy for you! My big brothers are the best."

"Logan is, too!" Allie grabs my arm, pulling me into their hug. "Austin said it was so cool having two real live Pirates at camp this year."

"He's a talented kid." I straighten, patting her arm. "I expect to see him go far."

"Thank you, Logan." Warmth is in her eyes as she picks up the platter Dylan has just filled with small pizza squares.

She practically skips out to the dining hall, and Dylan finishes stacking the rest on the second platter.

She straightens, but before she can scoop them up, I scoop her up. Pulling her into my arms, I lean down to steal a kiss. She exhales a little noise as I part her lips, and when I slide my tongue against hers, her muscles relax. She wraps her arms around my neck, and for a moment, we're lost in bliss.

Then I pull her lips with mine a few quick times before lifting my face and smiling down at her.

She blinks a little breathless, and her smile is the best thing. "What was that for?"

"Just wanted to do it while I still can."

Her smile melts into a little pout, but her eyes are still shining. "I can live with that." Rising onto her toes, she kisses me once more before pressing her hands against my arms. "I've got to get out there."

Craig's voice is already on the mic, and I hear the whistles cutting through the room.

"I'll help you carry this." I pick up the heavy platter of pepper-pizza, and she turns, leading me into the big, open space filled with smiling faces.

"The chocolate habanero is about five hundred thousand on the Scoville scale," Allie explains on the mic. "It's one step down from the ghost pepper, so proceed with caution. And as always, no water or beer! We have ice cream, milk, and tomato juice up here."

Craig hits the switch. Orange, yellow, and red lights flash around the room as a fast guitar starts thumping, and Johnny Cash and June Carter Cash launch into the country classic "Jackson."

A few whoops echo, and people bounce up to the servers for a slice. Craig and the girls on the bar are wearing cowboy hats and boots, and while the dancing isn't as wild this week, people are clapping in time, and the atmosphere is still pretty joyous.

Dylan steps back, and I put my hands on her waist, holding her back to my chest. She's smiling, watching the scene, and I get why Garrett wants her to go to cooking school. It's clear how much she loves making these dishes and watching the response from the crowd.

"You didn't start without me?" Garrett strides in from the kitchen, and he hops up on the end of the bar, dancing with one of the female servers.

He's not wearing a cowboy hat, but no one cares. Dylan shakes her head, and when her gaze returns to the pizza line, I feel her body stiffen suddenly, almost like she's been shocked.

I'm instantly on alert, looking around for what could've upset her. Leaning down, I'm about to ask, when a tallish guy with medium blond hair walks up to where we're standing.

His hands are on his hips, and he's wearing a pink golf shirt and khaki pants. A visor is on his head and a pair of sunglasses sit on the band. His entitled sneer reminds me of my father's asshole friends who think the world belongs to them simply because they have a lot of money.

"What's this all about?" He jerks his chin at me, and I'm ready to punch him in the face. "You're dating a football player now, and you expect me to believe he had nothing to do with your decision to end it?"

Dylan steps out of my arms as if she'll confront him. "You mean my decision not to date a cheater who acts like he's too good for me all the time?"

The guy sniffs at her, sticking a hand at me. "Davis Kent. I take it you're Logan Murphy?"

I don't shake his hand. "You must be the golfer. I was wondering when you'd show up here."

"I'm going to give you a little advice, friend." He leans in as if he's sharing a secret. "She's really pretty, and you probably think all this pepper crap is quirky. Let me tell you, it gets old fast."

"Tell you what," I smile, straightening to my full height, which is about three inches taller than him. "I'm not your friend, and if I wanted your advice, I'd ask for it."

He holds up both hands, leaning away. "Just a tip from a guy who's been there."

Dylan's eyes are throwing fire, but I'm not letting this douche think he's got something on her.

"I don't like you, Kent, and I don't take tips from a guy who doesn't know a good thing when he has it." I reach out and grip his shoulder hard enough for him to feel my strength. "That's from a guy who isn't going anywhere. Now have some pizza or get the fuck out of here."

His eyes narrow, and he glances at Dylan. I take a step between them, blocking his view. "The pizza is this way. Or I can show you to the door."

"I know where the door is." He turns and stalks out of the restaurant.

Watching him walk away, I'm still a little amped, and I'm not sure that asshole has gotten the message. Dylan grabs my arm, pulling me around to face her.

"That was really great." She's smiling, and she hops onto her toes to throw her arms around my neck. "Kiss me, big guy."

"That's Lightning to you." I lean down to wrap my arms around her, lifting her off her feet.

Her legs go around my waist, and when we kiss, cat-calls and whistles break out across the room. It breaks our kiss when we both smile, and she leans her face against mine before hopping out of my arms and onto the bar.

I stand back and watch, and tonight, her eyes are on me as she dances to "Hot Stuff" by Donna Summer. It's the same song that played the first time I was here, but tonight everything is different. Tonight, she's mine.

I watch her shake that ass, looking over her shoulder at me, and damn, I realize I've found something I like better than football.

She's in my arms when Garrett knocks on the door before dawn, letting me know it's time for us to hit the road. He wants to be through Huntsville by lunchtime. It's a six-hour drive, but it's only the start of our trek with a grueling preseason waiting on the other end.

And no Dylan.

Her cheek is against my chest, and I lift my hand to slide a lock of soft hair off her cheek. Her eyes are closed, but her full lips press into a pout. We've only just fallen asleep after losing ourselves in each other's arms more than once.

"No," she whispers. "It's too soon."

My chest squeezes, and I lift her gently, rolling her onto her back and moving my body over hers. My hands are on her shoulders, and I hold her like she's something precious I've only just discovered, like lost treasure or a rare pearl from the sea.

She puts her hands on my shoulders, frowning as she blinks her eyes open. "I don't want you to go."

Her words send an ache through my stomach, and I lower my face to kiss her. Our lips slide together, and I move mine to her cheek.

"I'm going to be pretty slammed for the next two weeks,

then the season will start. If you want to come see me, I'll schedule the plane."

She threads her fingers in the side of my hair. "I have to run
the restaurant, and school's starting."

Nodding, I look down at her small body in my arms. Dipping
my head, I kiss her neck, the hollow at the center of her throat.

She sighs, "But I'll do my best to find a weekend soon."

Another tap on the door twists the ache in my chest, and
I don't want to let her go. Leaning down, I kiss her again, this
time slower, doing my best to memorize every sensation, every
scent. Lavender and vanilla, warmth and sweetness, whiskey
eyes and honey kisses.

I had no idea when I got into that truck with Garrett in New
York all those weeks ago, my life would change. Now I'm headed
back, and I'm trying to remember why. Outside the game and
the team, everything I want is right here.

"Go back to sleep. I'll call you from the road."

She told her brother goodbye last night when we loaded up
the truck. We knew it was going to be like this, but it doesn't
make it easier.

I step out of the bed, grabbing my jeans and pulling them
over my hips. It's followed by my shirt, and I lean down for one
more kiss before I go. She sits up, and the blankets fall to her
waist, giving me one last look at her beautiful body.

Wrapping her in my arms, I kiss her shoulder, sliding my
hands along the soft skin of her back. "Don't melt anything
while I'm gone."

"I only do that for you." Her face is against my shoulder,
and her voice is pouty.

It makes me chuckle. "Yeah, you do."

I hug her one more time, holding her a little longer. The
words are right on the tip of my tongue, but it's too soon to say
them. I'll hold that thought in my heart a little longer.

One more kiss, and it's time to get the show on the road.
Garrett and I have a mission, and the MVP is in our sights.

Chapter 16

Dylan

"**S**TAND IN FIRST POSITION, AND WE'LL START WITH A GENTLE WARM-up." Classical piano music comes from the record player, and I'm standing in front of the class in a black leotard and pale pink tights with a ballet skirt, leading them through the movements. *First position, plié, toes out, slide…*

My class of high school dancers is bigger than I expected, twelve girls and Austin and Josh from the football team. Jack said he would give them extra credit for "helping me out."

The girls are at all skill levels, which I'm used to from my days at the dance academy. Their PE uniforms are pink leotards, pink tights, and basic, pink ballet shoes.

The boys are in black nylon joggers and black undershirts, and they have no idea what they're doing. Still, they're interested, and I can work with that.

Their main job is to hold the girls steady, and if they're fast learners and strong enough, we might attempt a few lifts.

Craig has been texting me nonstop since I got here.

Craig: Let me know if you need me to be there.

I need you to be at the restaurant making sure everything runs smoothly.

Craig: This place could run itself during the day. Can Allie walk over?

She has to run the library. I'm fine. Stop worrying, Mother Hen.

Craig: It's a media center, and that's Uncle Hen to you. I know this is a big step.

I love you, and I've got this.

The truth is, I've been taking a lot of big steps in the past few weeks.

I dug my ballet skills out of the locked chest I put them in years ago, and I have a date with the gang to watch Monday Night Football tonight at the restaurant.

I'm not going to lie, my heart beats frantically at the thought, but I promised Logan I'd be watching, wearing my Number 12 jersey with his name on the back.

As soon as it arrived in the mail, I called to give him the fashion show. It's navy and red and enormous, and the shine in his eyes when I spun around in my room for him to see unleashed a kaleidoscope of butterflies in my stomach.

Naturally, it was the only thing I was wearing.

"That looks really damn good, Dylan." He laughed, low and naughty as he wiped the sweat off his brow. "Too bad I'm at practice or I'd let you model taking it off for me."

I replied with a sassy, "Call me when you're done."

And that's just what he did.

My ears are hot as I guide my students through the basic barre warmup. "First position and demi plié, straight. Demi, straight. Now grande plié, straight, bend forward, all the way up." I lean down and touch my toes, then I arch back before moving to second position. "Let me see you do it."

I leave the bar and count as I walk through the line of barres arranged in the center of the small studio. Watching the young dancers concentrate and move shifts something in my heart.

The days when I was in their place, a student, are over, and now I'm on the other side, a teacher, sharing a gift with them I hope will bring them the joy it used to bring me. It's an unexpected, but welcome response to my first day back at the barre.

"That's very good, Mia." I stop beside a slim young woman with excellent form. "Remember to keep your chin parallel to the floor."

Her cheeks lift with a smile, and she holds her head straighter. Returning to the front of the room, I look down the lines of straight posture, pointed toes, curved arms. I see so much beauty and so much potential here.

The music continues, and I go to where the boys are doing their best. Neither of them has a very good turnout, but Josh is able to get some real height in his sautés. Austin's posture is good, and his arms are strong from football training, which is a promising sign for lifts.

We have a way to go, but I expect they'll be able to perform some basic *Nutcracker* choreography by Christmas. Anticipation of the show, something I haven't done in so long, forms a lump in my throat—of happiness. I'm so surprised, my eyes tingle.

"Very good, Class." Real joy is in my voice as they finish their combinations. "Please move the barres to the side, and line up in the corner of the room."

I lead them through a very simple walking routine with a grand jeté jump at the end. I'm able to do the small move, and when I finish, their eyes are all round.

"It's just a basic move." I exhale a laugh. "You'll get it."

Mia is the best going through the line, and I give them all lots of encouragement before moving through another simple move, the *pas des chat*, or *step of the cat*.

The ninety-minute class passes so fast, and by the time I dismiss them to change into their school clothes, I'm lighter than I've been in years. They're hard workers, and they're very invested in learning.

Picking up my phone, I tap out a quick text to Craig.

I actually really loved being back in the studio. It was so… good.

The word doesn't convey how I'm feeling, but it's the best I have at the moment. I'm still trying to get over how healing it was to be here sharing what I know, not allowing all those years to be lost.

Craig: I should've been there.

I needed to do this on my own, and I wonder why I didn't do it sooner.

Craig: You know why, but I'm glad you feel this way.

I'm too old to be Gelsey Kirkland anymore.

Craig: It's true, and you're much better fed now.

My nose wrinkles, and I lean forward with a laugh.

Are you calling me fat?

Craig: Never! I'm saying Logan can take over lifting you. Now get back here so I can see your face.

He wants to verify I'm not crying, more like it. I only shake my head.

I'll be there soon.

My next text is to Logan, even though I know he won't see it right away, especially on game day. It's basically the same thing with a little extra thanks for encouraging me.

I did it, and you were right. It was so good to be back in the studio. Thank you.

Smiling, I try to think of what it would've been like if we'd been in high school together. I would've had the biggest crush on him, but I'm not sure he'd have noticed me. I was not a cheerleader, and I pretty much avoided the entire football scene. It was too fresh after losing our dad.

My brothers, by contrast, were completely enmeshed.

"How did it go?" Allie meets me at the door to the media center on my way out. "Was Austin a complete disaster?"

I'm still in my ballet uniform, but I've swapped out my ballet shoes for flip-flops. I'll bike back to the house and change before heading to the restaurant for the dinner shift and game viewing.

"He did his very best. I could tell he was concentrating on the steps. They both were."

"How are you feeling about tonight?" Worry is in her eyes, and my chest squeezes.

"At least I'll have all of you with me."

"That's not really an answer."

Inhaling slowly, I think about losing our dad, the day I swore off football forever, even though it was practically inescapable in my life. "I guess we'll see. I hope it will be like returning to the studio—worse in my mind than in reality."

She reaches out and catches my hand. "We'll all be there with you."

I force a smile. "I know."

"Mrs. Patience has a baby boy named Jack, just like my daddy!" Kimmie has been talking nonstop since her first day of kindergarten, and it's clear she's very impressed by her teacher.

"She said his name is really John, but they call him Jack." Her little brow furrows. "Why don't they just call him John?"

She's sitting on a stool at the large silver work table. A small bowl of shredded cheese is beside her, and she's putting it between two bite-sized flour tortillas.

"I'll be honest, Peanut, I have never understood the whole Jack-John situation."

"Is Daddy's real name John, too?"

"Nope." I point to her little plate. "All done?"

She nods, and I carry it over to Thomas to give a quick grill. Stopping at the fridge, I take out a ramekin of mild salsa made with no peppers and carry it to her.

"Take this out to the table, and I'll bring your quesadillas when they're ready."

It's a regular Monday night at Cooters & Shooters, which means it's pretty slow. All the young and single football watchers are at the sports bar in town, and now that school is back in session, our family customers are home for the start of the week.

Only a few older people and a couple of tourists are dotted around the large dining room, and Salina runs around taking care of them.

Craig is off work after covering the day shift, but he's here along with Jack, Zane, Allie, and Austin for the big night. My first viewing of Logan.

Thomas hands me a platter with four hamburgers and Kimmie's dinner. I decided to wait until after the game to eat. My stomach is in knots.

Logan: About to head out on the field. Glad your first day went well. Wish I'd been there.

I reread Logan's text several times, and every time I do, my heart does a little skippy beat.

I wish you were here too, but for different reasons.

He replies with a devil emoji, and I exhale a laugh. Then he sends me one last message.

Logan: If they show me on the field, this means I'm thinking of you.

He sends a hand emoji with the thumb and index finger crossed. I'm not sure what this means, but I send back a selfie of me in his jersey doing a thumbs up.

Have a great game!

Logan: Man, I wish you were here.

His reply sends heat through my stomach, and I shove the phone in my pocket before heading out with everyone's dinner.

All four flatscreen televisions over the bar are tuned to the game, and the aggressive music makes my heart beat faster. The announcers are all animated, talking to each other about the stats of the major players. As they go through each one, a large photograph of the player being discussed appears on the screen.

"Uncle Gary!" Kimmie yells when they show Garrett's face along with his height, weight, experience, and age.

The team of brother-sportscasters talks about what makes a good offensive lineman and how hard it is to quantify. They're going on about my brother's ability to open a path when the screen changes, and Logan's image appears. My heart jumps to my throat.

"Lightning McQueen!" Kimmie yells, holding up both of her hands.

He's not smiling, and he's incredibly hot in his shoulder pads and jersey. On a line under the screen they list yards, touchdowns, and first downs in addition to height, weight, and the rest.

"Look at those numbers." Zane's voice is low as he pours ketchup on his fries. "No receiver's that fast. When the ball is coming, he's there, and Garrett's going to clear a path every time."

A warm sense of pride moves from my stomach up to my neck, and I'm standing behind my brother's chair gazing at the screen.

"We'll get a feel for what they can do tonight." Jack leans back, crossing his arms like a coach evaluating the situation. "The Allstars are a tough team, and I'm sure they've done their homework."

Austin sits behind them, quietly watching, until Kimmie hops down and climbs into his lap. "Will you be on TV, too?"

Allie's son pats her back. "Maybe," is his quiet reply.

His eyes never leave the screen, and I know that look. He already sees himself there, which means it's only a matter of time. Logan said he's going to go far.

The cameras cut to the sidelines, where the guys stand around, helmets in hand, waiting to take the field. My hands are clasped, and I watch as Garrett goofs off, getting in a fellow lineman's face, smiling broadly.

They do a little friendly rough-housing, revving each other up, and beside him, Logan stands calmly watching the field. His fingers are hooked in the neck of his shoulder pads, and he's so focused.

"How are you doing?" Craig is at my side with two beers.

He hands one to me, and I take a sip before answering quietly, "This is worse than ballet."

The Allstars have the ball first, so I take the opportunity to check on Salina and make sure Thomas has everything he needs. Salina reports the three tables are almost done, while Thomas sits alone on a stool in the back of the kitchen. He's watching the game on a small, black-and-white television with an antenna.

"I don't think we'll have any more orders tonight if you want to watch with us on the big screens." I call to him.

He only waves me away. "I always watch in here on this TV. It's good luck."

I hold up both hands. "Okay!"

I know not to mess with sports superstitions.

Clapping and cheering echoes in the dining room as I return to where everyone's watching. "That was quick," Zane laughs.

It's time for our guys to hit the field, and a knot is in my throat. My stomach is queasy, and I thread my fingers, putting both hands on top of my head. *Why did I say I would do this?*

They all line up, and the music is driving my heartbeat faster. I'm having trouble breathing, then the snap happens. They all break into play, and as the cameras zoom out, my eyes stay on Garrett and Logan.

I can't inhale deeply as my massive brother drives forward like a bull, meeting an equally huge guy head-on. A soft *Oh!* jumps through my lips, and I step behind one of the posts in the center of the dining room to peek out at the screens, as if I'm watching a horror film.

All eyes are on the quarterback, and the minute the ball leaves his hand, cameras flash to Logan, Number 12, at the ten-yard line. Sure enough, he's wide open, but a big guy is barreling down the field right at him.

"Oh, shit! Oh, shit!" I clasp my fist, holding it over my nose to partially block my view.

Logan slows down to make the catch. The defensive lineman

is looking at the ball, but it's clear he's making a drive for Logan. Every muscle in my body braces for the hit.

"He's going to take the penalty." Zane's voice is tense.

My throat knots, and my hands flatten on my forehead above my eyes. Right when it looks like the guy will grab him, Garrett's there to take him out.

The room erupts into shouts as the pass is complete and Logan easily runs it in for the score. A red banner flashes across the bottom of the screen with the word *Touchdown* in all caps. The stadium is going crazy, and I'm trying to catch my breath. My hands are shaking, and my muscles are weak from the rush of adrenaline.

Allie runs to where I'm leaning my forehead against my hiding-post. "You okay? That play was amazing."

"That's how they make history." Jack and Zane are on their feet, and while my oldest brother is pacing, Zane only takes a beat before returning to his chair.

The rest of the game is pretty much the same. I nearly have a panic attack every time Logan is approached by a defensive lineman. I have to look away every time Garrett slams into another player as big as he is.

A few times, I have to go into the kitchen and watch with Thomas. His little television is much less "in your face," and I wonder if that's why he prefers it. He's known us all our lives, and maybe he doesn't like to see my big brother getting beat up either.

The Pirates win easily in the second half, and navy and red confetti rains down on the players. People flood onto the field, and we watch as the reporters mix with the players to get sound bites.

The guys are all in front of the camera. Garrett lifts their quarterback off his feet, and when the camera pans to Logan, he grins, holding up one hand with his index finger and thumb crossed just like the emoji he sent me.

My heart jumps to my throat, and a breath hiccups in my

lungs. Nobody knows it's for me, but my ears are hot anyway. Automatically, I twist my fingers at my side, even though he can't see me.

They talk to the coach and the quarterback before sticking a mic in Logan's face and asking if he's going to make history this season.

"That's the plan." He grins, and his voice squeezes my stomach.

His eyes glitter, and he's so sexy. I can tell he's riding the high of their win, and I think for the first time, it would be so good to be there with him.

"Everybody get together for a photo!" Craig calls, and we bunch up with the screen behind us as he takes a selfie. "I'll send it to the group chat."

"We've got to get home. School tomorrow." Allie gives me a hug. "See you there."

"Thank goodness for afternoon classes." I'm only half-joking.

The way my heart beats out of my chest, I don't know how long it'll be before I'm calm enough to sleep, and I have a phone date with Logan.

"One down, sixteen to go." Craig wraps an arm around my shoulders. "And that's not counting the playoffs or the big game."

"Sixteen…" My chin drops, and he rolls me into his chest. I can't help it. I start to laugh. "I'm going to need medication."

"You okay?" Jack's deep voice is optimistic, and he puts a hand on my shoulder.

"Why do I feel like I just played football for four hours?" I laugh, and he grins, giving me a squeeze.

Kimmie is asleep on her daddy's shoulder. "Danielle was always on edge during the games."

"That's because everyone hated her," Craig quips, and I elbow him in the side.

My brother is unfazed. "Try not to let it get to you. We live for these games. It's a high you don't find anywhere else."

"You did it right, though." I put my hand over his.

I don't elaborate how my brother retired before any serious injuries out of consideration for Zane. He's not quite "in the light" yet, although working for Miss Gina seems to have improved his spirits. He still disappears at times.

"I had more important things to consider." Jack puts a large hand on his daughter's back, and I know what he means.

My oldest brother has always prioritized taking care of his family.

"You're a good daddy." I grin, giving him a hug and rubbing my niece's little back.

"Glad you finally came around and joined us." Zane limps up to where we're standing, a welcome grin on his handsome face. "We'll get you through the season, don't worry."

"You'd better." I tease, sliding my hand in the crook of his arm. "I'll see you back at the house."

They all head out, and I fall back to close up the restaurant. Then I have a FaceTime date with my man.

Chapter 17

Logan

ENERGY SURGES THROUGH MY LUNGS, AND I'M SURROUNDED BY MY brothers on the field. We're hot and sweaty and fired up and starting off strong. I caught ten passes for two touchdowns, but only 190 yards. It's not the best, but it's pretty damn good.

A few of their linemen tried to play dirty, but Garrett was right with me the whole time blocking them.

Craig made a group chat and sent a photo of all the gang watching at Cooters & Shooters. Dylan was right in the middle wearing a huge smile and my Number 12, and pride surged in my chest. Damn, she looks good in my jersey.

I'm fast on the field, but I'm even faster getting cleaned up and changed and in the black SUV taking me to my place. The guys are all going out tonight to celebrate our win, but I'm headed to my apartment for a date with my girl.

I grab my iPad Pro and quickly pull up her number. When her bright smile appears on the screen, my entire body relaxes. She's sitting in her bed still in my jersey with her hair down and her legs crossed. Her pretty eyes shine, and when she smiles, she steals my breath a little.

"You were amazing out there tonight!" Her excitement tightens my stomach, and I'd give a million dollars to have her in my arms right now. "Garrett was right. Lightning."

That makes me chuckle. "Did you watch the whole thing?"

"Yes, from a safe place behind a post in the dining room."

I laugh more at that. "What were you doing behind a post?"

"Hiding from you getting tackled."

"They only got me a few times. Garrett had my back."

"I didn't like seeing Garrett getting tackled either."

"From what I understand, he did most of the tackling."

"How are you feeling?" Her voice is quiet, and she lies on her side, resting her head on her hand.

"Pretty good. I need to get my numbers higher, but it's only the first game of the season." My fingers ache to touch her. "I don't want to talk shop. Tell me about your day. How'd it go?"

She exhales a little groan. "It was fine—so much better than I imagined. I really built it up in my head."

But I push back. "Don't do that. Your injury was a big loss for you. It changed everything."

"I was just a kid, though. I had my whole life ahead of me." Her voice gets quiet. "I faced much bigger losses."

Damn, this distance. "If I were there, I'd have you in my arms right now."

Her lips press together, and she blinks up at me. "I'd like that a lot. I saw your signal on camera."

"Yeah?" I grin. "What did you think of that?"

"It was kind of perfect." Her chin dips, and she almost seems embarrassed. "In the middle of everything happening around you, you thought of me."

I want to say I'm always thinking about her, but that feels like a lot. "Johnson's wife is organizing a charity gala next month. Think you can get your fine ass up here and go with me?"

"I can try." Her eyes brighten. "Text me the date. I don't

have class on Fridays, and I'm sure Craig and Allie will cover for me at the restaurant."

"You forget, Allie's doing the Friday night lights now."

"Oh, shit!" She slaps her hand against her forehead adorably. "I keep forgetting Austin's in high school. He was really great in class today. They all were. As I was watching them, it was just like you said, my love for the dance seemed to heal the pain in my heart."

She's so thoughtful and pretty. "You're going to be the best teacher for them."

"Do you remember that old saying, 'Those who can't, teach'?" I nod and she continues. "I'm pretty sure it was supposed to be an insult, like you weren't good enough to do the thing, so you had to teach it?"

"You're right." My jaw tightens, and I'm not sure where this is going.

"I have a whole different perspective on it now." Her brow furrows, and I can see she's struggling with her emotions. "As much as I want to, I can't dance the way I did before I was injured. It's not because I'm older and out of shape. I literally can't go up on pointe… But I can teach."

Her chin quivers, and I'm on my feet. "Hold that thought. If I can get a plane, I'll be there in five hours—"

"Wait!" Her voice is high, and she taps her fingertips under her eyes. "You don't understand. It's like I've reclaimed that dig. I can't dance, but teaching dance is such a gift to me now. I understand why Jack coaches. The students are so precious, and they want to learn from someone who knows how hard they're working and understands their dreams."

My shoulders are still tense, but I exhale slowly. "Are you sure you're okay?"

"I am." Her eyes are still misty, but her smile is genuine. "I'm really happy."

Sitting heavily on the foot of the bed, I lean my forearms on my knees. "You're a really great girl, you know that?"

I can't get over her strength. I mean, I was pretty sure it was in her the night we talked about it, after she told me her story. Here she is proving me right.

"I'll tell you what else." She lifts a finger to her mouth, sliding it over her bottom lip. "It made me wonder what it would've been like if you'd been in my ballet class in high school."

"I'm kind of tall for a ballerina."

"Male dancers are called *danseurs*."

"I'm still kinda tall."

That makes her laugh, and it's the best sound. It relaxes the fist in my chest at seeing her almost cry. Shit, that was rough.

"I would've been so into you in high school." She leans on her side in the pillows, a naughty smile curling her lips. "I imagine your big hands lifting me in only a leotard and tights. Maybe you'd be shirtless, and I'd slide down your chest. Mmm…"

Her eyes close, and she does a little shiver.

"Now we're getting somewhere." My voice is low and growly. "If I'd had my hands on you in high school, they'd have kicked me out of the class."

"Why?"

My eyebrow arches. "You know why."

"Show me." Her voice is sultry, and my dick stirs in my pants.

I walk over to place my iPad on its stand, then I step back and start to unbutton my shirt. She jumps up, flipping onto her stomach with her chin resting in her hands and her eyes wide.

"Take it off!" She yells, and I start to laugh.

Reaching behind my head, I pull my shirt off in a sweep. She puts her fingers in her mouth and does a perfect taxi whistle, which causes me to stop mid-strip.

"I didn't know you could do that."

"Stop stalling and show me that dick!" Her carnival-barker voice is fucking hilarious.

"You're going to wake Zane." How did I become the old

school marm in this situation? *Redirect.* "Shut your yap, Danger, and show me that pussy."

Her eyes flare, and she scoots to the end of her bed, placing her laptop on the desk across from her. I watch as she stands and lifts my jersey, revealing white lace panties that rise over her hips.

"That's more like it." My cock is at full attention now. "Have I mentioned how good you look in my jersey?"

She turns and wiggles her soft booty wrapped in white lace before threading her fingers in the sides and slowly lowering them down her hips.

Looking over her shoulder, she blinks her eyes. "What do you want me to do, Lightning?"

I've never thought my nickname was sexy until I hear it dripping off her lips. "I want to watch you touch yourself while I come."

She walks forward, climbing on all fours onto the bed, and I lube up before wrapping my fist around my erection.

Leaning her back against the pillows, she lifts the jersey over her bare tits and spreads her legs so I can see her touching herself.

"Damn," I groan, moving my hand up and down my cock.

Orgasm builds in my pelvis, tightening my ass as I watch her bite her lip and moan. Her lids flutter, but her eyes are fixed on my hand.

"That's so hot," she moans. "I want to hear you come."

My breath grows heavier the faster I pump, and I brace the desk, exhaling a groan. She moans in response, rubbing her knees together as her fingers circle her clit.

It's a surge straight to my cock. "I'm close," I groan and now my eyes are fixed on her bare pussy.

She slips two fingers inside and moans. "You're so big. I wish I could put you in my mouth and suck…"

"Fuck," I groan, reaching for the box of tissues on the counter as I continue jacking off for her.

Her eyes narrow, and her back arches. "I'd slide my tongue

all over your tip, then I'd pull you all the way to the back of my throat."

It's another surge of pleasure. "I'd bend you over the bed and fuck you so hard."

"Yes," she moans. "I'd twerk my ass up and down your cock…"

"You take me so good. I'm so hard."

"Oh!" Her legs jump, and I watch her orgasm. Her mouth opens, and her stomach shudders. "Logan…" she cries, and I groan deeply.

I start to jerk, and I grab a tissue to cover the tip.

"Let me see it…" She gasps, and I move to the side allowing come to spill over my fingers. "Oh my god."

I exhale another groan as my hand slows, and her thighs tremble. My arm bends, and I give my cock a final tug before stopping with a hiss. "Too sensitive."

She rolls to the side, cupping her pussy with her fingers. We're both breathing fast, and she hums, a smile curling her lips.

"You are five million on the Scoville scale," she teases.

I take a step back, sitting on the edge of the bed with a heavy exhale. "Which pepper is that?"

"It doesn't exist." She lifts up onto her elbows, resting her chin on her hand. "It's the Logan Murphy pepper."

That makes me laugh weakly. I'm sitting on the foot of my bed buck naked. My dick is still pulsating on my leg from that orgasm. "Damn, I wish you were here. Hearing you say my name while you come in nothing but my jersey is a real-life wet dream."

"Is it?" Her eyes are wide and excited.

"Yeah, but it's not the same. I want to touch your body."

"Text me the date of the gala. I'll be there."

The thought tightens my chest, and I think about her here, in my place, making love all night. "I might lock you up and never let you leave."

"Hmm… I might let you."

Chapter 18

Dylan

"WE WERE SO EXCITED WHEN WE HEARD YOU'D BE TEACHING THIS year." Mia's mom twists her paper schedule in her hands as if she's meeting a celebrity. "She watches your videos on the YouTube all the time. It's her dream to go to college for dance, but we can't afford extra lessons."

I was so nervous getting ready for tonight. I don't have a teaching certificate. I'm only here because the PTA is paying my salary, and I worried parents might question my ability.

Instead, everyone has been so kind, and grateful parents like Mia's mom make me feel so protective of them and my little class.

"I don't mind working with her after school if she wants. I know the dance academy is expensive, but she has a lot of natural talent."

I can't help thinking about Austin and Allie and their situation. His only hope for college is a scholarship or borrowing money and hope he makes it to the pros so he can pay it back.

"You would?" Her mom's eyes widen, and her hand flies to her mouth. "She has my permission!"

I exhale a laugh. "I'll talk to her about it next class. She just needs to polish a few things and learn a few more advanced steps. Things I won't teach in the regular class."

There's no way those beginners could learn to pirouette or fouetté, but Mia will need to know them if she wants to be considered for a college or a company.

"I'll help her with an audition video, too." I do my best to recall everything she'll need to apply. "I can teach her a short scene from *The Nutcracker* or *Swan Lake* to perform."

It was all the things I was in the process of doing when my dance career fell apart.

"Oh, thank you," her mother whispers, and I look up to see her eyes are filled with tears. "Having you here is such a blessing to us."

Her words put a lump in my throat. They reinforce my reclamation of the "those who can't, teach" insult.

Stepping forward, I give the woman a brief hug. "It's my job. I'm here to help my students learn and grow."

When I get home, I have my phone out to FaceTime with Logan while I make myself dinner.

"And when her mom started to cry, I almost cried with her." I'm grating cheese onto a bowl of black bean and corn *Maque choux* Thomas sent home for me.

"You've got to stop with the crying while we're apart." He's rubbing a towel over the side of his wet hair. "I don't like it."

He's in a white tee and sweats, and he's holding the phone as he walks to his refrigerator to take out a plastic cup containing a dark green liquid. I'm pretty sure it's Garrett's "signature" protein shake that he endorses for sports radio.

"They're happy tears." I take my dinner out of the microwave and a Guinness out of the refrigerator. "Are you drinking Garrett's special formula?"

He nods, taking a long sip. "The man is a beast. He nearly killed me at leg day today."

"I can't tell." I take a sip of my own beverage. "You're looking like a snack tonight."

That makes him laugh, and my stomach squeezes at the sound. "You're looking like a teacher I'd like to…"

"Hey, Logan." The loud voice from behind me almost makes me toss my phone across the room.

"Zane!" I fuss. "You scared the shit out of me."

"I do still live here." He takes my beer off the counter before continuing down the hall. "Night, you two. Try and keep the noise down."

Shaking my head, I go to the refrigerator and pull out another beer. "Craig said he's got me covered the weekend of the gala. I can leave Thursday after class and stay all the way til Monday morning!"

"I'll arrange a jet to pick you up." He takes out his iPad and starts tapping.

My nose wrinkles. "I'll have to fly all by myself?"

"You'll be amazed how fast you get used to it." He has that snobby tone he gets sometimes, more and more now that he's back in New York.

It reminds me that he's always had all the money in the world, unlike my redneck family. Davis always curled his nose when I'd show up in bare feet or talk too loudly, but so far, Logan doesn't seem to mind. He's a little obsessed with my red toenails, and he's best friends with Garrett, after all.

"What's that face about?" He's also the most observant boyfriend I've ever had.

"Nothing." I force a laugh. "I was just feeling nervous or something."

"Don't be nervous. I'll send you everything you need to do and the flight attendants will take good care of you. I'll make sure of it."

I grab the bottle of Louisiana Hot Sauce and shake a few

drops into my bowl. "What about your friends at the party?" My voice is quiet. "What if they don't like me?"

He pauses a moment, and I appreciate him not dismissing my question as childish or silly. "I know my friends pretty well." He walks over and sits in the chair. "The guys will love you, and Johnson's wife Maddy is from a little town in Georgia. She's dying to meet you, and Garrett will be there. I'll be there."

The fear in my chest relaxes a little. "That sounds good."

"I'm not going to lie, I don't intend to stay very long at that gala. I've got other plans for your visit."

His gaze darkens, and my stomach flips. "Okay."

"Be sure to pack that jersey."

"It'll be the first thing I put in my suitcase."

The last thing I put in my suitcase is my pack of birth control pills.

I made an appointment with my gynecologist when he left and got a blood test and a prescription. It's been three weeks—three agonizing nights watching football games, three wonderful hours after school working with Mia on her advanced ballet steps. She's a fast learner, and she hangs on my every word as if I'm a ballet oracle.

I've talked Austin into staying after a few times to work with us on lifts. He's also a fast learner, and his hands are strong. He's used to making sudden turns from football, and I'm already planning how I can modify the dance of the Snow Queen and her Cavalier in the Nutcracker for them to perform.

Three weeks, and I'm finally walking into the small Callahan terminal an hour east of our home.

"Miss Bradford?" A woman in a pale gray uniform greets me as I walk through the glass doors. As I expected, I'm the only person here besides the crew.

"This is for you." She hands me a small, robin's-egg blue bag.

"Thank you." My voice is quiet as I roll my suitcase.

"I'll give your suitcase to the porter, and you can come right this way."

I nod, following her out another door to a small jet with a short ladder in front of it.

Once I'm onboard, she puts a flute of champagne on an oval table in front of me. "I'll be right up here if you need anything."

"Thank you." I take out my phone and send a text to Logan.

> I feel like a princess.

Logan: Did you get your gift?

> I haven't opened it yet.

Logan: I'll wait.

My lips press into a grin, and I remove the white tissue paper. A smaller, light blue box with a big, white-satin ribbon is inside. I slide the ribbon off, and the word *Tiffany & Co.* is stamped in black on the blue lid. My fingers tremble as I remove the lid. I might be from a small town, but I know what Tiffany means.

Inside is a beautiful pearl bracelet and matching earrings. My heart jumps, and I whisper, "Logan…" even though he can't hear me.

Picking up my phone, I quickly tap the button to call him, and when his handsome face appears on the screen, my chest squeezes.

"They're so beautiful."

Although, not as beautiful as the smile he gives me. "I told you I'd buy you something better."

Looking down at the leather bracelet on my wrist, I shake my head. "I told you, I don't need anything better."

"I'm thinking those pearls, my jersey, nothing else."

The low growl in his tone clenches my core. "Sounds good to me, and I can't wait for you to see my dress."

"I can't wait to see you."

Anticipation hums in my veins the entire five-hour flight. I do my best to watch the in-flight movie, but I'm not really interested in the familiar rom-com. I finish my glass of champagne, but I decline another. I try to read a spicy romance on my Kindle, but it only makes me want to see Logan more.

It's dark when we finally begin our descent into the Teterboro Airport. I can see the Manhattan skyline, and a wave of nerves steals my breath. We touch down, and I shoot Craig a quick text.

Why am I so nervous to go back to NYC?

He replies so fast, I wonder if he was holding his phone.

Craig: Because I'm not with you.

It would help. Why didn't I bring you again?

Craig: Somebody has to serve the Fire Eaters, and your rich boyfriend wants you all to himself.

My stomach tightens, and I chew my lip.

I have stage fright.

Craig: It's going to be the best reunion.

Maybe he's forgotten what a hot mess I am.

Craig: Slip him a pepper. He'll remember.

That makes me snort a laugh.

Love you, Bish.

Craig: Love you, Deedee.

The plane stops, and the flight attendant opens the door. My nerves have twisted a knot in my throat, and my fingers tremble as I collect my things. I'm just walking down the short staircase when I look up and see a tall, handsome man in jeans and a blazer waiting on the tarmac.

His hands are in his pockets, and his dark hair moves in the breeze. He's watching me with that straight white grin, and the desire in his blue eyes turns the nerves in my stomach into frantic butterflies.

I run straight into his arms, and he lifts me off my feet. Our mouths seal, lips part, tongues slide together, and the longing in my chest almost makes me cry.

I swallow back my emotions, but my voice still cracks. "I've missed you."

So much… I don't say it out loud, but I'm pretty sure he knows.

"I hired the fastest SUV to get us back to my place." His voice is low, and he lowers me to my feet. "I'm not sure I can wait that long."

His arm is around me as we walk to the vehicle, and he holds me securely to his side. On the drive to his apartment, he holds my hand, occasionally lifting it to kiss the back of my fingers. It's a rush of warmth in my veins every single time.

"What's the Dare dish tonight?" His eyes trace my hair, and I want to get out of my seat and straddle his lap.

"Shrimp-stuffed jalapeños."

His dark brow quirks. "That seems tame for a Dare dish."

"Craig's calling it his Disney Dare." That makes Logan chuckle, and I explain. "He doesn't like to handle the really dangerous peppers."

"That's only for my girl."

His girl. It's another fizzy rush of warmth in my veins.

Finally, we're at his building, and the moment the Tahoe stops, he's out of his seatbelt, helping me out of mine. Large hands span my waist, and his eagerness makes me laugh. It has my insides hot and slippery.

"What about my things?" My hands are on his shoulders as he helps me out.

"I've already paid Fred to get them to the doorman. He'll have them delivered to my suite." He practically carries me across the sidewalk.

"Welcome home, Mr. Logan." A man in an embellished coat and hat holds the door as we hurry through it.

"Thanks, Klaus." He barely gets the words out before we're at the elevator.

He presses the button repeatedly, and I can't stop laughing. "Are you going to throw me over your shoulder?"

"I might." He turns to look at me and the need in his eyes echoes mine, pulsing in my veins.

Seeing it reflected back at me is the most uniquely satisfying emotion I've ever experienced. He's missed me as terribly as I've missed him, and as soon as the elevator door opens…

And we wait for an elderly lady to collect her little dog and pick up her umbrella and pick up her bag and double-check she didn't leave anything behind and slowly exit the small compartment…

"It's like she didn't know she was getting off," he mutters impatiently, and I have to hold my nose to keep from exploding with a laugh.

I can't seem to stop the excitement bubbling higher in my chest. At last, we're alone in the elevator, and he exhales a growl as he presses my back to the wall, covering my mouth with his and lifting me off my feet.

My fingers are in his hair, and our mouths consume as we shoot higher to his penthouse suite. We're sloppy in our haste, licking and pulling each others' lips. Nipping and breathing faster.

I barely hear the ding. I'm still wrapped around him, my mouth on his neck, as he crosses the short foyer and unlocks his door.

The door slams, as he carries me straight to his bedroom. With feverish haste, he rips off his blazer followed quickly by his black tee. A satisfied hum slips from my lips at the sight of his lined torso.

I've shoved off my leggings and my hoodie, and I'm ripping off my undershirt when large hands cover my hips.

"Oh," I gasp as his lips touch my stomach.

"Give me this." He rips my panties down, and his face is buried in my crotch as I drop my shirt to the floor.

"Logan!" I cry at the first pass of his tongue over my clit.

All the weeks we've been apart, the hours on the plane, the minutes driving here, getting up to this room, it's burning anticipation, and it has me on the edge so fast. My lips part, and my legs are shaking. He doesn't stop.

Large hands cup my ass, and he slips two fingers into my drenched core, forcing a deep moan from my chest.

"You're so wet for me." His mouth moves to the crease of my leg, and the scuff of his beard across my sensitive skin makes me gasp.

"I need you inside me." I slide my hands over his shoulders. "It's been too long."

I need to feel his hard body pressed against mine, his hard cock inside me moving fast, feverish. He passes his tongue over my clit once more, and my thighs jump.

Standing, he catches me around the waist, pulling me tight against his body as we move higher onto the bed. My legs part, and he pauses, looking into my eyes. We discussed birth control, getting tested, and we shared our results.

"No more condoms?"

I cup his face in my hands, lifting my lips to his. "No more."

With a groan, he captures my mouth, and our kiss is ravenous. We're starving for each other. I lift my knees, and he reaches between us, lining up the tip. With a low groan, he presses into me slowly, stretching me wide, arching my back as he fills me.

"Oh, god," I gasp as my pussy starts to spasm. "Logan…"

I've never been this way, responding to every breath, every touch, the smallest whisper. His mouth covers mine again as he starts to thrust. The way he fills me makes me cry out. My arms are around his neck, and I'm right on the edge.

"I'm going to come." He groans. "You feel too good."

His hips pick up speed, jerky and desperate. I'm right there with him, gasping and lifting my hips to meet every thrust. Muscled arms are around my waist, and he rolls me to be on top of him.

I reach forward to grab the headboard, and my hips glide up and down, taking him from root to tip. His hands grip my ass, squeezing and spreading me, grinding my body against his, but I'm lost in my own sensations, chasing the orgasm swirling and tightening in my lower belly.

His deep moans, his hands gripping my ass and moving me faster, drive me higher. I jerk on the headboard as I keep pace, sweat trickling down my neck, slipping between my breasts. I'm right there, balancing on the edge of the cliff when his tongue slides up my ribs to my nipple.

He teases it with his tongue and teeth, and I break with a deep, shuddering cry, almost feral. My body jerks then bows forward. My thighs tighten at his waist, and I grasp his shoulders.

He continues to move me up and down his cock, and I feel him pulsing as he groans, his voice breaking as he comes. Leaning forward on his chest, I hold him through the shudders, through the trembling bliss of orgasm. We're together, finishing in each other's arms.

He holds me so tightly, and I listen to his heart pounding as fast as mine. We're panting as we start to come down. My hands are on his chest, and my eyes close. Strong arms hold me, and I nuzzle in the cocoon of his embrace.

Soft lips press against my head, my neck, and my shoulder. He rolls us to the side, and we both seem to be fumbling with the intensity of what just happened. All those nights of looking through screens, needing to touch each other, longing to feel each other's bodies have brought us to this place. It's like a dream come true.

Lifting his hand, he traces my hair off my cheek with his finger. "I can hold you now."

"Every minute."

Scooting forward in the bed, I press my face against his warm skin. I inhale his scent of citrus and sandalwood and soap and sweat. Salt is on my tongue from kissing and biting and licking his body. Strong hands hold me like he'll never let me go, and he gently strokes my hair.

I could fall asleep this way, and I almost do when I feel him stirring. He stands, scooping me into his arms and carrying me to the bathroom.

Chapter 19

WARM WATER RAINS OVER US, AND DYLAN'S HANDS PRESS AGAINST the stone wall of my shower She's gasping my name, moaning loudly, and my eyes roll shut as I grip her hips, driving my cock deep into her drenched pussy.

Her ass twerks against my pelvis, and I reach around to circle my fingers over her clit. It isn't long before her knees buckle, and I catch her around the waist. She feels so good taking me. She's tight and hot and wet, and when she breaks into orgasm, my mind alters.

My teeth are against the skin of her shoulder, and she trembles in my arms. I'm holding her up and finishing, three more solid thrusts, before the orgasm shocks me rigid, causing me to still as the pulsing fills her, until it's spilling down our legs.

Her head falls back against my collarbone, and I kiss her neck, pulling the skin between my teeth. She tilts her face, and I capture her mouth again, licking my tongue against hers.

She's my drug, and I can't get enough. Hell, I wouldn't be surprised if we stay in this apartment for the next four days doing nothing but fucking.

Turning in my arms, her soft breasts press against my chest, and I wrap my arms over hers, looking down into her pretty amber eyes.

"You okay?" My voice is so warm with affection. *Have I ever spoken to a woman this way?*

"I'm better than okay." She grins, and that dimple is at the corner of her mouth. "I'm in heaven."

"Let me clean you up." I reach for the loofah and put my shower gel on it.

It's masculine and woodsy, but I like her smelling like me, *like mine.*

I slide the sponge over her shoulders, but I use my fingers to clean between her legs. Her cheek is against my shoulder while I work, and that lazy smile curls her lips.

"Are you trying to make me come again?"

"I plan to make you come all night, but first, let's get clean."

Reaching for the shampoo, I gently rub it into her hair, working up a lather. Then I hold her head as we step under the shower spray to rinse. Her chin lifts, and I cover her mouth with mine, fresh water mixing with our kisses.

When we're done, I shut off the faucet and wrap us both in oversized towels. Dylan takes a smaller one and wraps it around her head like a turban.

"I ordered food." I lead us from the bedroom to the small foyer area where we left her suitcase. "It's probably sitting outside the door."

"I'll get changed." She smiles, catching my arm and rising onto her tiptoes for another kiss.

I lean down and hold her lips with mine for the space of two heartbeats. It's such a relief to be able to touch her. I'm realizing how much I've wanted to do it since we said goodbye what feels like a million years ago.

Two medium-rare steaks with asparagus and a light lemon sauce are plated and reheated. I've changed into gray sweatpants and a white T-shirt, and she walks into the kitchen in her feet bare wearing nothing but my navy and red jersey.

I have to stop and admire her. A giant red 12 is on her chest, and her damp hair is over her shoulder. Her lips are swollen from my kisses, and possession burns in my chest.

"Damn, Dylan." My hand covers the ache in my stomach. "I just want to fuck you again."

She leans forward with a giggle and skips over to me. Rising onto her toes, she wraps her arms around my neck. I lift her onto the bar so I can kiss her properly, sliding my tongue with hers and slipping my hands under her top to feel her warm skin, her soft breasts.

Her lips break away, and she gives me two quick kisses. "You have to feed me first, because I haven't eaten since lunch."

I grin at her sassy tone, kissing her once more slowly before releasing her.

"Is that what you're wearing to the gala?" I walk over to uncork a bottle of red wine.

"Of course!" She holds out her arms, looking down at the shirt. "And those beautiful pearls you gave me."

I'm pretty sure I'll be smiling all weekend. Everything she says, every sound she makes is the sweetest music to my ears.

"Here." I hand her a glass of wine. "To staying in bed all weekend."

"Mmm…" She clinks her glass to mine. "That sounds like a dream."

I wish it were possible. The reality is, I have practice tomorrow and a light workout Saturday morning, but having her here, waiting for me when I get home, is the best reward.

"I can't believe I haven't seen my brother yet," she calls from behind the closed door.

We spent our first night wrapped in each other's arms. Friday morning we shared coffee and a light breakfast before I left for practice.

When I got home, she met me at the door in my jersey, so of course, I carried her inside and bent her over the couch. Again, I ordered dinner in, because we couldn't seem to stop touching each other... or maybe that was just me touching her.

She'd spent the day running around Midtown then stopping by the American Ballet Company offices to see about getting an audition invitation for Mia.

"It's the only way to get in," she'd told me as I held her in my arms last night.

"All you have to do is ask for one?" I confess, I know nothing about ballet.

"Anyone can ask, but Constance Westwood carries a lot of weight in the community." My brow furrows, and she explains. "She was my teacher when I was at the dance academy in Mobile. She's an alum, and I hope saying she taught me, and Mia is one of my students, will get her toe in the door."

"Wow." My eyebrows rise. "I get why Mia's mom was crying now."

Her lips pressed into a smile, and her cute ears turned red. Naturally, I had to roll her onto her back and make sweet love to my beautiful, generous girl.

My girl. I'm not sure when I started calling her that, when the words first appeared in my mind, but they're so right.

I can't stop touching and tasting her. When we sit, I pull her into my side, inhaling her silky hair, and when we sleep, she's wrapped in my arms. We're like two stars pulled together by inescapable gravity.

Now she has me outside the bedroom door waiting while she puts on her dress for the gala. She went out this morning when I was at training to have her hair and makeup done—not that she needs any of that. Dylan is so naturally beautiful.

"You'll see Garrett tonight. He had a pretty hard practice yesterday."

"He texted me asking if we were ever leaving this apartment."

"I hope you told him no."

A soft laugh drifts from her to me, making me smile. "We'll have to have brunch or lunch with him tomorrow."

Her voice approaches the door, and I straighten, ready to see her again. I'm like a little kid unhappy when even a thin plank of wood keeps me from the object of my affection.

It took me a whole five minutes to pull on my basic black tuxedo pants, tie, and jacket, and when she opens the door, my breath disappears.

"Fuck…" The word slips from my lips on a whisper. "We're not going anywhere with you looking like that."

Her dress is floor-length and flowy, made of a nude, seemingly transparent fabric that's covered in glittering sparkles. It has spaghetti straps, and the front is a V-neck wrap. It's low cut to allow the swell of her breasts to taunt me. Hell, the whole damn dress taunts me.

Her cheeks flush pink, and she looks down, lifting the sides of her skirt in her fingers. "It's like I'm wrapped in starlight."

"You look amazing." I walk to where she's standing, lifting her hand in mine. "I'm going to have to beat up every guy who looks at you."

"You are not." She laughs, placing her palms flat against the lapels of my jacket.

The pearl bracelet I gave her is delicate on her wrist, and the diamond-tipped pearl earrings warm her cheeks. Leaning down, I kiss her glossy pink lips. Her dark hair is pulled up on the sides, but it hangs in flowing mahogany ripples down her shoulders and back.

I trace my thumb lightly across the top of her cheek. "I'm really glad you came this weekend."

She leans her cheek against my hand, blinking thick lashes up at me. "In case you haven't noticed, I'm having a wonderful time."

"I guess we have to make an appearance at this party, but don't expect to stay too long."

Her nose wrinkles, and she leans closer to kiss me softly. "You're the boss."

"I like the sound of that." My voice is a low growl. "Maybe a little too much."

She steps away, holding my hand. "We'd better go or we never will."

The Gala for a Cure is packed with celebrities and influencers. The entire football team is here, since it's our quarterback's designated charity.

Photographers wait for us to step out of the SUV, and I wish I could protect Dylan from this part of my job. The gossip sites and the entertainment reporters are always in our business, and their opinions and comments can be really shitty at times.

I don't want Dylan to lose her privacy, and I fear as soon as they see this beautiful mystery woman on my arm, a feeding frenzy will erupt.

Flashing lights blind us as we step out, and photographers shout my name. I lift the side of my jacket, doing my best to hustle us up the red-carpeted stairs and into the venue as quickly as possible. Dylan holds my arm and the side of her dress, as she tries to keep up with me in her heels.

"Where's the fire?" She laughs, pushing her hair back when we stop inside the foyer of the ballroom.

"I hate those guys." I straighten my coat, and she reaches up to fix my collar.

"My brothers hated them too." Her voice is calm, matter-of-fact "Well, all except Hendrix. I think he really enjoys being the center of attention. He likes to say it's because I came along and stole the spotlight when we were babies."

"When I was his age, first starting out, I thought it was cool. Like I was a rockstar. Now I've learned you never know what they're going to say about you, and you can never get them to take it back."

"I'm not worried about Internet gossip."

"Finally, there you are!" Garrett's booming voice greets us as we enter the ballroom.

Dylan's eyes light, and she lifts the side of her dress again before skipping over to hug her brother. "I can't jump on your back in this thing," she laughs, hugging him.

"Good thing." He lifts her off the ground in a bear hug. "You're getting chonky."

"I am not!" She slaps his back, and I chuckle at the two of them.

A tall, size zero brunette reaches for his arm, and my brows rise when I recognize Lainey Smith at his side. Lainey is one of Natalia's model friends, and I'm surprised to see her here with the Grizz. At least she isn't constantly taking pictures and posting on her socials.

"Hi, Lainey." I reach out to shake her hand.

"Logan." Her slim brow arches, and she inspects Dylan. "Who's your lovely date?"

"Ah, Lainey Smith, meet my little sister Dylan." Garrett puts his hand on Lainey's upper back. "She flew in from Alabama so this guy could attend."

"Yes, she did." My voice is warm as I look down at my girl.

"Sounds serious." Lainey's gaze goes from Dylan to me. "How did you meet from so far away?"

"Brought him home this summer to meet the fam," Garrett quips. "And Dylan nailed him with a ghost pepper!"

"Garrett!" Dylan punches him in the upper arm then shakes her hand. "Ow!"

"It's a slab of granite." He flexes his bicep, grinning.

"You okay?" I take Dylan's hand in mine and gently massage it.

"Yes." She shakes her head. "It's really nice to meet you, Lainey. I don't know what you're doing with my two-headed brother."

"She's only met the one head so far." Garrett is on a roll.

"Garrett." This time Dylan only pushes his arm. He doesn't move. "What would Mamma say?"

"She tried." He laughs, elbowing my chest.

Lainey rolls her eyes at him then blinks to me. "What's this about a ghost pepper?"

"It was just a silly accident." Dylan cuts in. "Are you really a model? Have you met Anna Wintour?"

"Yes and no." Lainey smiles, slipping her hand into the crook of Dylan's arm. "Let's get a drink. You seem like fun."

"Oh… ahh…" Dylan's eyes flash to me. "Is that okay?"

Hesitating, I'm not entirely comfortable with Lainey taking her away and giving her the third degree so she can report it all back to Natalia. At the same time, Dylan can handle herself, and I want everyone to know about her.

"Go ahead." I give her a wink. "I'll be right here."

She smiles, and I watch as she walks to the bar with Lainey. She's a curvy, delicious bundle of sexy spice wrapped in starlight, and I like Lainey a little better for being nice to her.

"I'll take a ghost pepper to a glacier any day," I say absently.

"Even if she melts your face off?"

"She's melted more than my face."

His brow furrows, and he momentarily drops the bravado.

"You're really serious about my little sister. What does that mean?"

I know what I want it to mean, but all I say is, "We're doing our best to take it slow."

"Doesn't look slow to me."

I can't argue in view of how we've spent the last two nights, but he doesn't want to hear about that. Instead, I follow him to the nearest open bar, and I wait as he orders a beer for him and a whiskey neat for me.

"What are you doing here with Lainey?" I take a sip of my drink. "You always said you hated skinny women."

"*Hate* is a strong word, my friend. I needed a date for tonight, and Lainey was available." He takes a drink. "She's the least annoying of Natalia's friends, but you're right. Give me a redneck girl with a nice ass, and I'll be a happy man."

Assman, I chuckle to myself. "What happened to Wendy? She seemed to fit the bill."

"Would you believe she went and got a boyfriend on me while we were down south? I swear, you can't go out of town these days."

I exhale a laugh. "At least you're not here with Natalia."

"Speak of the devil." Garrett coughs into his sleeve.

I turn just in time to see my ex walking up with Ricky (the dick) Berke.

"Hello, Logan." Her voice is cool confidence.

She steps forward to put her hand on my arm and kiss my cheek. I don't recoil, but I don't really appreciate the gesture. I don't want Dylan to think I'm still interested in her.

"Natalia." I nod curtly. "Ricky."

Garrett puts a hand on my shoulder, pointing at the two of them. "Are you two dating or is this just for the gala?"

"What do you think, Grizz?" Ricky puts his hand on Natalia's ass, and I notice her flinch.

I dated Natalia long enough to know she doesn't appreciate public displays of affection. Or pretty much any physically attentive behavior. I'm half waiting for her to bite his head off when Dylan's sweet voice joins us.

"Sorry, I didn't mean to run off on you the minute we got here."

My shoulders relax, and I slide her silky hair off her shoulder before putting my arm around her. "No apology necessary. I want you to have a good time and meet people."

"And who might this be?" Natalia studies us. "Not Garrett's little sister I've heard so much about?"

"You've heard about me?" Dylan's eyes blink wider, and she steps forward with her hand extended. "Natalia van Norse, I'm so pleased to meet you."

To her credit, Natalia is caught off guard. "The pleasure is all mine, I'm sure."

"Sorry," Dylan's chin dips. "I'm Dylan Bradford. Garrett's sister, and, ahh…"

Her eyes flicker to me, and I reach for her hand. "My girlfriend."

Natalia's eyes widen. "*Girlfriend?*"

I have no idea why she's pretending to be shocked, but I explain. "We've been seeing each other since July."

"We were at Galileo's in June."

I want to ask how it went with the Greek guy, but Dylan speaks first. "I confess, I'm a little starstruck meeting you. I always check out your Instagram for fashion ideas. I absolutely adored the dress you wore to last year's Met Gala."

Natasha's lips part, and she seems thoroughly confused. She can't possibly fathom someone as genuinely kind as Dylan.

"Thank you." Natalia clears her throat, tugging on Ricky's arm. "We're just going to get some drinks. I hope you all have a wonderful evening."

Dylan watches them go before turning to me and slipping her hands in my arms. "Everyone's so nice. I was so worried they'd treat me like a hick."

"If anyone treats you like a hick, you let me know." A low growl is in my tone, and amusement shines on her face.

"I won't, but I really like this protective side of you."

Placing my thumb on her chin, I hold her gaze. "I won't let anyone hurt you."

"Logan! I've been searching for you everywhere." I recognize Maddy Johnson's voice. "Where is my new best friend?"

Maddy is in a flowing white dress that reminds me of a toga, and she has a gold belt around her empire waist and a gold headband on her blonde head. Both hands are extended to Dylan.

"When Logan told me you were from Alabama, I squealed, didn't I, Logan?" I nod as she continues. "It's so good to have someone from home to talk to."

"I know just what you mean." Dylan pulls her into a hug. "This is an amazing event. Did you do it all yourself?"

"Lord, no!" Maddy shakes her head. "We have a team of party planners handling all this. Let's get more champagne."

She drags Dylan to the bar, and I hang back, watching her fit into my world.

"Those accents, heavens!" Natalia holds her hand beside her ear as if she's getting feedback. "I know some people find it charming, but it's like nails on a chalkboard."

My brow lowers. "Jealousy's not a good look on you."

She holds up both hands. "Easy, big guy. I was only teasing. I actually walked over to say you're different. You seem happier than you've ever been—or at least than you ever were with me."

"We had very little in common." I take another sip of whiskey.

"Is that true?" Her eyes narrow. "I'd say we have very much in common. We're both from wealthy, detached parents. We're both smarter than the professions we've chosen."

"I've never cared for stereotypes."

"Still, they have a basis in fact. Models and jocks are not typically geniuses, but you and I notice things."

"What have you noticed?" Not that I particularly care.

"You're dating this little girl from the country. I can't think of a better way to get back at your father. I'm sure he's so proud."

I study her, trying to figure out if she's joking. Anyone close to me knows I don't have that kind of relationship with my father.

"You know me so well." I can't keep the sarcasm out of my tone.

"I'm simply trying to say she's very sweet, and you seem happy. That's all."

"In that case, have a nice evening."

I want to find my girl and dance with her in that dress.

Chapter 20

Dylan

THE GALA WAS A FAIRYTALE. WE STAYED LONGER THAN I EXPECTED, spinning around the dance floor in a swirl of starlight. Logan held me in his arms like my very own handsome prince, and when we finally got home, we barely made it through the door before he had me pinned against the wall.

Our reunion has been ravenous and aggressive, and I've loved every second of it.

We had brunch with Garrett, who claimed he took Lainey home after the event. I don't know why he feels like he has to explain himself to me. He can date whomever he wants, even if he's never really been the supermodel type. I don't judge.

Strolling through Central Park, Logan and I hold hands. He buys me a bouquet of fresh-cut flowers at a little newsstand, and we stop off at Ray's for pizza before walking to his apartment, where we spend our final night in each other's arms.

Our beautiful getaway weekend comes to an end with us

standing on the tarmac at 7 a.m. in the misty rain with the chill of winter lacing the gray air.

"I hate to say goodbye." Blinking against the fog, I fight my tears.

"We're not saying goodbye, although I am starting to see the drawback of timeshare planes." He grumbles, holding me firmly in his arms at the base of the small staircase. "If it were my plane, I could fly back with you."

"You couldn't do that." I force a smile. "You have a game tonight."

Leaning down, he kisses the side of my cheek. "I really like thinking of you watching me play. I wish I could look up and see you in my box."

I don't want to tell him how difficult it would be for me. Instead, I simply say, "One of these times."

"Thanksgiving?" He slides a finger along my jaw, gazing into my eyes. "We have a game on Black Friday every year."

In the past I'd be shopping or hiding out from where Jack and Zane (and Craig and Thomas) would be glued to the screen all weekend. I'm part of the club now, knotted stomach and all, and I can't tell my gorgeous boyfriend no.

"Then I'll be here."

A different flight attendant gently clears her throat. "I'm so sorry to interrupt, but we do need to get going if we're going to stay on schedule."

He leans down to kiss me for real. Our tongues curl together, and I can't hold back a little sob. He pulls my lips before kissing a line to my cheek where a stubborn tear has fallen.

"These tears." His voice is rough, and he slides his thumb over the top of my cheek. "They hit me hard."

Reaching up, I brush a fresh one away, doing my best to smile through the ache of leaving. "Would you rather I didn't cry?"

"I'd rather you stayed." He pulls me to him again, exhaling heavily. "It's harder to let you go this time."

"I know." My voice is quiet. *I love you…* But I save those words for a better time, and instead I rise on my toes once more to kiss him. "I'll be watching you tonight."

"I'll be thinking of you."

I text Craig as soon as I'm alone on the plane.

> He introduced me as his girlfriend.

> Craig: Sounds serious.

> We're so different, but we're so good together. How did this happen?

> Craig: You're not so different. He's BFFs with Gary. I think you have more in common than you think.

> But he comes from so much wealth and privilege, and I come from… Cooters & Shooters.

I can't help adding a crying-laughing emoji. Even though I still ache to be with Logan, my tank is so full of fizzy, happy love.

> Craig: You're both driven and talented and hot.

> You think I'm hot?

> Craig: Hotter than a pepper sprout.

> I'll be home before noon. Sweet talk Thomas into making me a hamburger. I didn't get breakfast.

Craig: Thomas will happily make you a burger, no sweet-talking required.

You're both too good to me.

Leaning back in my chair, I consider how different the flight home is from the flight to New York. I'm content, calm, missing him like crazy, but utterly full—and after four nights barely sleeping, I crash the minute I put my phone down.

It's a different world standing in the kitchen at Cooters & Shooters in my cutoffs and bare feet, eating a delicious hamburger Thomas made for me.

"I have to get ready for school, but I wanted to tell you what I did."

Craig is moving around the kitchen, setting up plates for the lunch crowd. Mondays are typically slow, but we still have a decent lunch crowd. Salina swings in with a fresh order she pins to Thomas's line.

"Tell me." Craig stops and puts a hand on his hip.

I put my burger on the plate. "I went to the American Ballet Company and requested an audition for Mia." Then I grab his arm and shake it back and forth with a squeal.

"You think that will work?" He's less enthusiastic.

"I find your lack of faith disturbing. I name-dropped Ms Westwood and everything."

"Ms Westwood is dead. Anybody could walk in and say they knew her."

"Why would anybody walk in off the street and say they knew her? No one would even think of her unless they were down here with us."

"Okay, okay." He holds up his hands. "You're a genius, and Mia is lucky to have you."

"I've got to get to school." I take a last bite of hamburger. "Thank you, Thomas!"

He gives me a wave, and I skip out the back door of the kitchen, heading to the house to put on my leotard and tights.

It's so much warmer here than in New York. As soon as I got home, I dropped my suitcase in the guest room and changed out of my warm clothes. Then I ran down to the restaurant.

"Hello, Miss?"

"Oh!" I squeal, jumping to the side.

"Sorry!" A youngish guy with blond hair and brown eyes holds up his hands. "I didn't mean to scare you. I'm just visiting. That's some name."

He nods at the sign, giving me a sly smile, and my shoulders drop. He looks harmless enough, dressed in starched jeans and a long-sleeve button-up shirt. *Who starches their jeans?*

"Welcome to Newhope." I wipe my hand on the back of my denim shorts before reaching out to shake his hand. "A *cooter* is another name for a turtle. I'm Dylan Bradford."

"Callum Cross." He shakes my hand, and that stops me.

I tilt my head to the side. "Have we met? Your name is familiar to me…"

He briefly seems startled, but he covers it fast, which is weird. "I don't think so. I'm not from around here. I, ah… I heard this place has spicy food?"

"Yeah, we have a spicy special every Thursday night at seven." I do a little wave. "You could come back then or stop in now. The regular menu is pretty delicious, if a bit tamer."

He glances down, seeming embarrassed. "I heard they also do *Coyote Ugly* dancing?"

I hesitate, wondering what he's after. "Also only on Thursdays."

"Do *you* dance?"

"No, it's just something the staff started doing for fun."

"Too bad."

Is he trying to flirt with me? Sorry, Callum. I am *so* taken, it almost makes me smile.

"Well, I'm late for work. Maybe I'll see you around."

"You will."

I take off for the house. I've got less than an hour to be at school for ballet class.

The rest of my day goes like the last six weeks—teaching, working with Mia. I do not tell her about what I did in New York. I don't want her to be nervous or distracted or intimidated the way I would've been at her age.

Then after school, I ride my bike home, change into my cutoffs and flip flops again before heading to the restaurant to work. It's Monday night, which means I'll be hiding from the game in a few hours.

"Garrett said y'all had a good visit." Jack hugs me when he arrives with Kimmie Joy holding his hand.

She runs forward, wrapping her arms around my waist and hugging me like I've been gone a year. "Uncle Craig made stuffed jalapeños, and it still burned my tongue."

I squat, making a pout. "Let me see." She sticks out her little tongue, and I lean in close, pretending to examine it. "I don't see a blister. I think it's going to be okay."

"He said I must've got a seed. Then he gave me ice cream."

I hug her, kissing her soft cheek. "Uncle Craig probably thought you were a jalapeño expert since you already bit one."

"I'm not." Her eyes are huge.

Zane walks up behind Jack, and I stand to give him a hug. "Did you do okay by yourself this weekend?"

"The house was so quiet. I actually got some sleep."

He's teasing, but I pinch his side. "I moved downstairs so I wouldn't disturb you."

"We need better soundproofing on those old walls."

Craig joins us, placing a platter of beers on the table and a root beer float for Kimmie. "Who are we supposed to cheer for tonight?"

I cringe, clutching the sides of my hair. "I can't believe we have to watch all three of them play." My brother Hendrix is a tight end for the Los Angeles Tigers. "The only good part is they're all on offense, so they won't face each other."

"Where's Allie?" Craig walks over to lean on the bar beside me.

"Austin has an exam tomorrow, so she's home with him. Hey, did a little guy stop in here today?"

He shakes his head. "Why?"

"I ran into this man asking about spicy food and *Coyote Ugly* dancing."

"You're infamous." Zane taps my shoulder. "Which means *more* than famous."

"Not me." I hold up my hands. "You know I don't get on the bar."

"You got on the bar when Logan was here." Craig gives me the side-eye, and heat flushes my belly at the memory.

Yes, I did…

Jack steps up to take a beer and Kimmie's dessert drink. She'll be asleep before halftime, but we have a little palette made up for her in one of the booths. I'd hold her, but I have to take my place behind the column in the center of the dining room, a safe distance from the large screens.

The Monday Night Football music blasts through the room, and my heart jumps in my chest. Colorful lights flash on the screen, and the commentators excitedly launch into where things stand mid-way through the season.

Logan's face appears on the screen, and my chest squeezes. Then Hendrix's face is right beside him on a split screen.

They talk about their stats in excited voices and who's in the running for the Big Game, and I rest my cheek against my old friend the column.

Last week, I pulled a chair over here, and Craig brought me beer and snacks while I did my best to tune out the clashing of helmets and the loud grunts of the players. Oh, and don't forget the nonstop instant replays.

"He's such a showboat," Jack shakes his head at a clip of Hendrix dancing in the end zone after a score. "They should make him be a team captain for a year, show some responsibility."

"You can't force a square peg into a round hole," Zane replies calmly.

I think about the two of them, the oldest of our clan, and how they sit and talk like I imagine our parents might. Jack is the grumpy oldest, while Zane is more patient.

Garrett was the youngest for so long, his over-the-top personality is cemented. Then Hendrix arrived, followed eighteen months later by me.

"Dylan, I know you're cheering for Logan," Jack notes. "Zane will cheer for Garrett, and I'll root for Hendrix."

He acts grumpy, but Jack was always sweet to us younger ones. It's just like I told Allie—he's hard on the outside, but a total alpha-roll in the middle.

"Hello?" Craig pipes up. "Way to leave out Thomas and me."

"Nobody tells Thomas what to do." Zane chuckles, taking a sip of beer.

"Craig can help Zane with Garrett. He's big; he needs more support. Dylan's in love enough to cover Logan."

"Yes." Zane nods. "I can vouch for that."

"I want to cheer for Uncle Grizzly, too!" Kimmie walks up to her dad, climbing into his lap and rubbing her eyes.

"KJ, come sit with me." I hold out my hand to her. "You can help me cheer for Lightning McQueen, so he doesn't feel lonely."

She hops off Jack's lap and crawls into mine. Once she's asleep, I'll put her on her little makeshift bed. Then I can duck and squirm without disturbing her.

"Is the restaurant open?" A tenor voice draws my attention, and I sit straighter as the man from earlier walks through the door.

"Callum, Hi. I was just talking about you." I flash my eyes at Craig, who is on his feet at once.

"Hi, there. I'm Craig." My bestie holds out his hand. "I heard you were looking for some spicy food?"

"Yeah… what's going on here?" He surveys the room. "Watching the game?"

"Ah, yeah." I stand, shifting Kimmie to my hip. She lets out a little grunting noise, burying her face in my neck. "You're welcome to watch with us if you want. Both of my brothers are in this game. Craig can bring you a menu if you'd like to order some food? Or have a beer?"

He smiles, and I can't shake the feeling he's making mental notes of everything. It's peculiar, but not necessarily bad. Maybe he just wants to remember the place?

"Are those your brothers?" He nods at Jack and Zane, who are watching the opening discussion and ignoring us.

"Yeah, that's Jack and Zane Bradford."

"Jack Bradford?" Callum's eyebrows rise. "Shit… Oh, sorry."

Kimmie lets out a little-girl snore, and I exhale a laugh. "Looks like you're safe."

"Are you hungry?" I glance towards the open kitchen door. "Thomas is watching the game, but he could fry up a burger for you real quick."

"Best burger on the coast," Craig adds.

"Is Thomas related to you?" He steps over, craning his neck so he can look through the doorway.

"He might as well be," I exhale a laugh, walking over to the blankets we arranged in the booth and placing my niece on them gently. "He's been with us since we were kids."

"I see…" Again, Callum appears to be making mental notes. "Sure. I'll have a burger."

"Got it." Craig heads for the kitchen. "Anybody else need a drink or anything?"

"I'll take another beer if you're getting them," Jack calls.

Zane holds up a hand, but I shake my head. I have to work tomorrow, and I plan to be awake to talk to Logan tonight. My battery recharge is wearing down, and I've been thinking about him all day.

The game starts, and it's just like before. My brothers shout and cheer. They complain loudly when a ref gets it wrong, and they're on their feet at every close play, which is pretty much all four hours.

I hide behind the column, peeking out and hiding again any time one of my brothers or the man I love gets pummeled or nearly pummeled.

My stomach is in knots, and my feet are in my chair so I can hide my face in my hands.

Callum walks over towards the end of the game. "I can't tell if you're enjoying this or not."

My hands are over my ears, and my eyes are pressed against the top of my knees.

"Oh." I exhale a laugh, casually uncurling from my stress-clench. "It's great. They're all such talented athletes."

I'm pretty sure he's not buying it for a second. It doesn't matter, because right then Zane and Craig break into a loud cheer and start high fiving. I realize I missed something big, so I peek around the column to see the instant replay.

Garrett took out a cornerback making a beeline for Logan, and my gorgeous man jumped as gracefully as a gazelle, cupping the ball against his chest and falling into the end zone for the winning score.

The stadium is bananas. The Pirates are on a winning streak with zero losses so far in the season, and Logan has just logged the best numbers of his career.

Confetti rains down on the field. Garrett lifts Logan off his feet, running with him in his arms to the mob of players jogging to meet them. Logan's helmet is off, and his smile is so big it makes me smile.

Then right there in the middle of it all, he holds up his hand, thumb and forefinger crossed, and I huff a laugh as tears spill onto my cheeks.

Chapter 21

WE'RE WINNING EVERY GAME, AND ALL EYES ARE ON US. THERE'S talk of us winning the Big Game, and we're all buzzing with anticipation.

Ricky is chasing after me hard in the rankings, and every now and then I hear a commentator saying he's going to catch me.

He's not. Grizz and I are unstoppable.

I celebrate our wins briefly with the guys, but I have a one-track mind after every game. I want to see her smiling face, hear her enthusiasm, see her waving her hands while wearing my jersey, then see her sexy body come undone for me.

The guys who had high school girlfriends act like I'm trying to recapture something I lost in my youth, but I'll tell you. If I'd had a girl like Dylan cheering for me in high school, we'd have been just like her parents. I'd have never let her slip away.

She'd have gone with me to college, to the pros. We'd have had five children—at least. Hell, I'd probably keep her pregnant. My life would be so different.

As it is now, we're just getting a late start.

"You should've heard the guys when you made that final score. Even Craig was yelling his head off. I'm surprised we didn't wake Kimmie."

"The Peanut wasn't watching me?" Ever since she put her little hand in mine and shared her jalapeño encounter, we've been tight.

"She fell asleep." Dylan makes a disappointed face. "Kindergarten is hard work."

"That's okay. I understand." I'm feeling so good right now.

She sits on her bed in my jersey, and I'm buzzing with the win and with seeing her now and thinking about how I'll see her again in just a few more weeks.

"The sports guys say your stats are making history!"

"The sports guys?" I can't help teasing her.

She laughs. "Whoever they are!"

I don't bother filling in their names. "Yeah, they say that, but they're also talking about Ricky catching up with me."

"He won't catch you."

I love the confidence in her voice. I love knowing she's there, watching every game, supporting me.

I also don't want to spend the whole time talking about me. I want her to know I care about her career, too. "How's it going with Mia?"

"I didn't tell her about the possible audition. I mean, it might not happen, and I don't want her obsessing over it like I would've at her age."

"I think you made the right call."

"Otherwise, it was pretty much the same. Some guy showed up asking a lot of questions about the restaurant and spicy food and *Coyote Ugly*."

My brow lowers. "Was he trying to steal my girl?"

"No!" She falls back with a laugh. "Now that I think about it, he might be one of those undercover restaurant reviewers. I'll have to tell Craig if we see him again to be on our best behavior."

"Just give him one of Thomas's burgers. You'll get a Michelin star for sure."

Rolling onto her side, her whiskey eyes turn deep. "I saw your hand. In the middle of my brother hauling you all over the field, you were thinking of me."

"I'm always thinking of you, Deedee."

"I wish I could kiss you right now."

"I wish I could put my hands under that jersey."

"I wish I could get on my knees in front of you like I did at your apartment."

"Fuck, that was hotter than one of your peppers."

Our conversation takes a sexy turn, and before long, we're flushed and sweaty and sated—or as much as we can be from a thousand miles apart.

We don't say goodbye. Instead, we fall asleep with our phones on our pillows. I talk to her until I hear her breathing become slow and rhythmic, and I know she's asleep. Then I close my eyes. When I wake in the morning, my iPad is dark. I hate it, but I know what I have to do.

I have to put my head down and work, practice, play. I talk or text Dylan every chance I get, but I've set my goal for this season. I have to stay focused on accomplishing it.

My numbers are improving every week, and she's right, I'm setting records. But "the sports guys" are right, too. I've got players on my tail, and this is a competitive field with athletes out to beat me.

If this is going to be my year, I can't let up on training, so I push myself every day, not even taking our optional days off.

I'm doing this for us and our future, because I want to be with this beautiful girl, and I've got a plan.

Thanksgiving is just around the corner. I'm in the gym with a bar across my back doing squats when the door slams open, and Garrett barrels in like a raging bull.

His hazel eyes are shooting fire, and I straighten, letting the heavy bar drop to the cushioned mat with a crash.

"What the fuck, Logan?" He shoves his phone into my chest, and I take it from him.

Swiping my finger again and again, I shake my head. "What is this?"

"That's what I want to know. Did you talk to these assholes?"

I tap the top of the screen and I see it's the feed of *Too Much Information,* TMI for short, one of the most notorious gossip sites on social media, and one of the meanest.

"They've got pictures of the two of you on your balcony."

"The fuck?" I scroll quickly to the bottom of the story where they posted a grainy photo of Dylan on her knees.

I'm sitting in a chair with my head tilted back, and a blur bar is across my lap where her head is located—when she gave me the best blowjob of my life.

"What the FUCK?" My voice goes louder. "They can't print that without permission. How did they even get it?"

There's a reason I live on the top floor in one of the tallest buildings in Midtown. *Privacy.*

"I don't want to talk about *that.*" He snatches the phone back, reading the caption. "Trust-fund baller Lightning Murphy might be setting records, but it won't stop this gold digger from sucking him dry."

Heat flashes through my chest and neck followed by cold. My ears roar, and I'm moving. I'm not even thinking. My phone is out, and I tap the numbers on the screen as I push through the door.

"Where are you going?" Garrett follows behind me.

"Tell Coach I have a family emergency."

Chapter 22

Dylan

"AND PLIÉ AND THREE FOUETTÉS THEN ARABESQUE. AUSTIN, YOU'LL come in quickly for the lift, then lower, turn, and down." I move the slider on my phone to the number where we'll start the music, then I press play. "Four, three, two, one…"

Mia lifts her arms, rising en pointe and begins the scene. It's a short number from *Giselle*, and I hope they'll be ready to perform it at the Christmas pageant, a little more than a month away.

We've worked on this choreography since we started staying after, and they're really improving. Standing back, I watch as they glide across the stage. Austin lifts Mia with ease, and she comes down on her toes, doing three little hops before lifting her leg behind her.

His hand braces her thigh, and she goes up. Then she wobbles, then she turns and slides, falling down his chest.

We all let out a disappointed noise, and I tap the pause button on my phone.

"My bad!" Austin calls, holding up his hands. "I didn't have the grip like you showed me."

"It's looking good, though!" I try to keep our spirits high. "Lifts are hard, but your posture and form are great."

If they're not ready for Christmas, we can do it at the spring showcase. It will also be great for an audition video.

We rehearse until Austin has to go to football practice, and Mia needs to rest.

"After a while, it really is good to break and do something else." I give her a brief hug as Austin jogs out the door. "You've come a long way fast. I think you're going to have your pick of schools in the fall."

"Thank you, Miss Bradford." She smiles as she removes her pointe shoes. "I don't know how I'd have done this without your help."

"You're an excellent dancer." I press my lips into a smile. "It's very gratifying to help you achieve your dreams. It's a little like I'm achieving mine."

Her voice is quiet as she looks up at me. "Maybe I'm helping you, too?"

Nodding, I squeeze her arm. "I think you are."

It's Thursday, and I've got to get to the restaurant to prepare tonight's Dare dish. I've picked out a recipe that calls for Trinidad Scorpion, which is between the Carolina Reaper and the ghost pepper on the Scoville scale. It's a new one, and I'm interested to see how the regulars handle it.

When I work with Mia and Austin after school, I come back in my work clothes. Parking my bike at the house, I jog down to the large, sprawling white restaurant with the wrap-around porches my dad affectionately named after the saltwater turtles who always sit on a log down by the bay… and the pool players, *not* irresponsible drinking, he'd said.

For Thanksgiving, we've decorated the place with stalks of corn and orange and white twinkle lights. Craig made little pilgrim hats for the turtles, and Kimmie insisted on a huge, inflatable turkey for the playground. The restaurant will be closed for the holiday, and I'll be far away in New York with Logan.

The thought of another four days like our last visit has me so excited, I skip through the back door into the kitchen. I'm happy with Mia's progress, I'm happy about the crisp touch of fall in the air, I'm happy about my upcoming trip…

It all crashes down on my head when I enter the room.

Craig meets me at the door, eyes tight with worry. Allie's face is pale like she's seen a ghost, and my heart drops to my feet.

"What's wrong?" My hand is on my throat. "Is it Thomas?"

"Not me," the old man growls from where he's standing beside the stove shaking his head.

He seems disgusted, and I don't know what to make of that. It's not a game night, but that doesn't rule out my brothers. Or even…

My head gets light. "Did something happen to Logan?"

Allie rushes up to me, taking my hand. "Oh, honey. You'd better sit down."

My eyes widen, and I almost scream. "If somebody doesn't start talking—"

I might throw up. Acid is in my throat.

I'm not a paranoid person, but life hasn't exactly been kind to us, and my friends don't look at me this way ever.

"*TMI* just published a story." Craig walks over to where I'm barely holding it together, the iPad in his hand. "Written by *Callum Cross*."

My face snaps up to his. "I knew I recognized that name!"

"It's not a very nice story," Allie says quietly.

"It's a fucking smear job. It's one of the worst things I've ever read, and it's all lies and speculation and garbage. Clearly clickbait."

I reach out my hand, not caring if my fingers tremble. "Show it to me."

Craig hesitates, holding the iPad to his chest. "I'm only showing you this because you need to know."

"Does she?" Allie's voice cracks.

She looks like she might cry, and I don't wait for his response. I take the device from my friend and look down at the headline stretching over the screen in heavy block letters. *Logan Murphy's Mystery Lady Revealed, and She's After His Booty!!!*

"That's just silly. Three exclamation points?" I glance up at Craig, and his mouth is pressed into a tight line.

"He's just getting warmed up."

A dry ache is in my throat as I quickly scan the article. It spends a lot of time portraying Logan as cultured and rich, dating models and attending black-tie events, and me as a redneck gold digger only in it for his money and fame.

"*She's no barefoot contessa, but she is barefoot—all the time!*" I exhale an embarrassed laugh, the muscles between my shoulder blades tightening. "I guess they're not wrong."

"They're assholes." Craig's voice is simmering fury.

"They interviewed Natalia?" My stomach sinks as I read her words.

"*I can't imagine what they have in common,*" van Norse said. "*They're worlds apart.*"

When asked why he might choose someone so far beneath his wealth and status, van Norse speculated, "We broke up in June, and he started dating her in July. Clearly it's a rebound."

"A rebound?" I want to argue with the phone.

"*Either that or he's getting back at his father. What better way to send a 'fuck you' to the old man than to take up with the poor little sister of his redneck best friend?*"

Lainey's quote cuts the deepest. "*All I'll say is Logan Murphy has a type, and that's not it.*"

They're basically the exact words I said when I saw his Instagram feed, and I can almost hear them snickering behind my back.

"She was so friendly at the gala." Now I actually do feel

dumb—for thinking they wanted to be my friends. "Is that what they were saying about me?"

"They're a bunch of jerks." Allie's voice is louder.

"Oh, my God, he interviewed Davis?" I can't keep the horror out of my tone.

"He's the douchebag who called you a gold digger!" Allie shouts.

"With her brothers moving out and moving on, she's grabbing at any wealthy man she can find." My forehead is hot and tight. *"She holds weekly dance parties at [restaurant name redacted], complete with a near-striptease all in an effort to entice the affluent and vulnerable..."*

My upper arm tingles when I remember the way he grabbed me. "As if Davis Kent has ever been vulnerable."

"Will you let me beat up his car with his golf clubs now?" Craig is fuming.

The article is littered with candid photos, and I'm at the bottom when I reach the one that turns my blood cold. It's from my visit to New York, and it's the night we were on the balcony. My head is in Logan's lap, and it's very clear what I'm doing.

I have to stop myself from throwing Craig's phone across the room.

"Everyone's going to see that." I shudder. "The school, my brothers... People who don't know me will read those quotes and think it's the truth."

"We'll sue." Craig slaps his hand on the counter. "It's an invasion of privacy. You have rights."

"Do I?" I look up at him with round eyes. "Logan's a celebrity."

I walk over to lean my back against the kitchen wall behind the dishwasher. The strength drains from my limbs, and I slide down it until I'm sitting on the floor with my face against my knees.

My friends rush to my side.

"What are you thinking?" Allie sounds nervous.

What am I thinking? My head is spinning, and I think about everyone discussing this story and me. I think about it spreading across the Internet. I think how much it sucks to go viral.

"I think Davis is an asshole, but Natalia? Lainey? They said what they thought." I can't forget the images on his Instagram feed—model after model after model. "We are from completely different worlds, and I'm not his type."

Of course, I fell in love with him. He's handsome and rich and polished and sexy, but what am I? A redneck girl miles away with bare feet, no plans, and a weird hot pepper fetish. I'm a curiosity, not something you bring home to Papa, no matter how much you hate him.

Or maybe it's what Natalia said: you do it, *because* you hate him.

"Stop right there." Craig's voice is sharp, and he squats in front of me. "Not a single word of this story is true."

"I don't feel so good." I place my hand on his shoulder, and he helps me stand slowly. "Would you mind covering for me tonight? I have a recipe and ingredients set out, but you can do whatever you want."

"You are not believing this story, Dylan," Craig orders, following me to the back door. "I won't allow it."

"I don't want to believe it." My heart twists in my chest. "But maybe it's a warning."

"It's bullshit."

Nodding, I hold out my hand. "I just need a minute."

I feel like the wind has been kicked out of me. Or like somebody found the biggest bruise on my body and punched it as hard as they could. Using their knuckle.

Or like I broke my foot all over again, and my world is crashing down on my head once more. I dared to dream, to reach for something that seemed impossible, and Fate noticed and slapped me down again.

Craig watches me with impatience. "Dylan…"

Turning away, I head for the house like I'm walking through

a bad dream. My mouth is dry, and I don't want to talk. I don't want to think about all the people seeing that story.

The house is dark, but I don't turn on the lights. I put my phone on the kitchen counter and go to the living room. A small, portable wet bar is behind the couch. We don't use it often, so the bottles of whiskey, gin, and vodka are pretty full.

I grab an unopened bottle of tequila and carry it to the guest room where I've been sleeping. Then I shut the door, twist off the top, and collapse to the floor.

Chapter 23

Logan

MY FINGERS ACHE BY THE TIME WE APPROACH THE SMALL AIRPORT east of Newhope. I've spent the entire five-hour flight gripping the arms of my chair. The flight attendant offered me a drink to help me relax, but I just said no.

I don't want a drink. I want Dylan.

Then I want to beat the shit out of Callum Cross.

It took longer to get out of New York than I'd hoped. We weren't in the air until after seven. I tried FaceTimeing her, but it rang several times before going to voicemail.

It's Thursday, which is always a busy night. It's possible she doesn't have her phone with her. It's possible she's having fun at the restaurant, and I'll get to her before that fucking article does.

Is it possible she hasn't seen it? Then I remember how much she knew when she was with me in New York. She knew all about Natalia's book. She knew about the Met Gala…

At the same time, she didn't know about me until I walked into her restaurant. It's possible…

Staring out the window into the darkness, I can't imagine what she's thinking. Rubbing my fingers over my forehead, I add that asshole Davis Kent to my to-do list.

She knows he's an entitled asshole, but Natalia, Lainey? Tightening my fist, I worry their words hurt her.

She seemed a little starstruck by my ex, and I know she had a good time with Lainey. Hell, Lainey was Garrett's date. I exhale a growl remembering how sweet Dylan was to everyone. How beautiful she was in that glittering dress, and how they all knifed her in the back.

Again, my fingers tighten on the arms of my chair.

What's worse is knowing this is my fault. If she hadn't gone to that event with me, she wouldn't be in this situation. She'd be anonymous, a private citizen. Now, her family will see that photo of us on the balcony—so will her coworkers, her students.

Protective anger burns in my chest, and as soon as we touch down, as soon as the flight attendant lets me off, I hustle into the SUV I ordered before we left five hours ago.

Speeding through the night, I try calling her again.

Again it goes to voicemail.

When I finally arrive at the house, it's after midnight. No lights are on and the doors are locked, but Garrett told me where to find the hidden key the last time we were here.

Quietly, I unlock the back door and slip off my shoes. She told me she sleeps in the guest room now. The last time we FaceTimed after one of my games, she said she moved down here for Zane's sake.

Hesitating outside the door where I spent that entire, golden month, I tap softly. "Dylan?"

My voice feels loud in the quiet house, but no one responds.

Turning the handle, I open the door and step inside. My eyes adjust slowly, but in the dim light from the bathroom, I see her lying on the floor beside the bed. She's curled up on her side, and a bottle of tequila is beside her. It looks like a quarter of it has been drunk, and I glance around for food, limes, salt. Even a shot glass?

I don't see any of those things, and I know. She saw the article.

It hits me like a punch in the gut, and I bend down, hating that she's in pain because of me.

"Dylan?" My voice is soft, and I lift her in my arms.

Her head wobbles, and she murmurs something I don't understand.

Placing her on the bed, I dash across the hall to the kitchen to grab a bottle of water from the refrigerator. It would be great if I could get her to eat something, but I don't know if that's going to happen tonight.

When I return, she's curled into a ball again, and it hits me just as hard the second time. It's such a self-protective pose, an ache moves through my chest.

I want to be the one to keep her safe from whatever tries to hurt her. Instead, I've brought shame into her life.

Sitting on the side of the bed, I reach out to touch her cheek. "Dylan, babe? Will you drink some water?"

She doesn't move, and with a sigh, I put the bottle on the nightstand. I stand and slip off my jacket. I take off my T-shirt and jeans, stripping down to my boxer briefs.

I manage to get the blankets down on one side, then I move her over to do the same on the other side. I slide into the bed behind her, wrapping my arms around her soft body and pulling her tightly against my chest.

A fist grips my lungs as I lower my mouth to her shoulder and kiss her skin. Then I inhale the soft scent of her hair, lavender and vanilla. I kiss her behind her ear, and she stirs with a little noise.

Loosening my arms, I let her shift to face me. She blinks a few times, confused, before focusing on my face.

"Is this a dream?" Her voice is rough.

"No, honey, I'm here."

"Why?"

I swallow the knot in my throat. "Because I need you."

Her head bows, and she seems to close in on herself. "Do you?"

"Yes, Dylan. I need you in my life more than you know."

"Even if they're right?"

"How could you ever think any of those words are right?"

Her shoulder rises in a shrug. "Because it's true—you're all those things, and I'm… nothing."

Reaching up, I slide my hand over her forehead, moving her hair back and lifting her face to mine. "You are not nothing, Dylan Bradford. You're everything to me. I dream about you every night. I ache for you every day. Nothing any of those assholes say will change the truth, and the truth is, I love you. Everyone else can go to hell."

She hiccups a breath, and I'm worried she's crying again.

"What is it, beautiful?"

"You should come with a warning." Her voice is small.

"Why?"

"My heart just exploded."

The knot in my throat unfurls, and I pull her to me again. I slide my hands slowly down her petite frame, and I make a vow to fix this.

If it's the fucking last thing I do, I'm going to make this right. She's not going to be humiliated for being with me. Those assholes are never going to hurt her again. They'll be too scared to.

Garrett: Coach is blowing a fuse. I said family emergency, but what family? Your dad?

Garrett's text is on my screen when I open my eyes.

Dylan is curled into my side, and warmth spreads through my chest. My instinct is to text back *My wife.* Instead, I leave her brother on *Read* and turn back to wrap her in my arms again.

The situation isn't fixed, far from it, but I didn't lose her. She didn't tell me to go to hell or say she didn't sign up for this or say all the things she could've said. All the things she had the right to say.

She doesn't deserve to be treated this way or spoken about like that, or have pictures of our intimate times published on the fucking Internet. That's the main one that has me seeing blazing red.

I've already left a message with my lawyer, even though I know what he'll say. I'm a celebrity. I've given up my right to privacy. Embarrassment isn't the basis for a lawsuit.

Fuck it. I'm trying anyway.

"Oooooh, why did I drink all that tequila?" Dylan cringes in my arms, curling forward.

"What can I bring you? I've got water here, ibuprofen." I slowly lift us to a sitting position, taking the tablets off the nightstand.

She blinks up at me, squinting through bloodshot eyes. "How are you here? Don't you have practice?"

"Take these." I hold out the pills, waiting as she takes them then handing her the water. "Don't worry about me."

"I am worried about you." Her voice is quiet, and I recognize the low tone—it's hangover volume. "They'll fine you for missing practice, and you can't miss practice!"

"Look at me." I put my finger under her chin. "Do you remember what I told you last night?"

Her lips press together, and she nods, blinking fast. "Every word."

It's a thick whisper, and I dip down to kiss her lips. "You needed me last night. And I needed you."

She reaches out to thread her fingers in my hair. "It means a lot to me that you're here. It feels so good to be in your arms."

I hug her closer. "I should've done a better job protecting

you from them. I've asked a lot from you, and I never want you to be sorry you're my girl."

"You didn't ask for anything I didn't want to give you." Her hand moves to my cheek. "And I love being your girl."

"I can't wait to have you in my box at Thanksgiving." The thought of looking up and seeing her watching me play sends a surge of adrenaline racing through my veins. "Do you want to sleep a little longer? Are you hungry? I can bring you coffee, toast…"

She shakes her head, exhaling a laugh. "I have to get out of bed. I've got class, and you have to get back to New York."

"New York will be fine without me."

"Maybe, but you've worked too hard for TMI to knock you off track, and I've met that Ricky guy. He's gunning for you." She steps out of the bed then puts her hand on her head, sitting down again. "Damn, what was I thinking last night?"

"You were hurt." I stand in front of her. "I'm going to do what I can to get them to print a retraction or at least take down that damn photo. It's going to be hard, but I've messaged my lawyer."

"We'll just have to deal with it." She slowly rises to her feet again. "I remember when Jack went through it. He was so upset, and I didn't really understand. I understand now. It's brutal."

"Get back in bed. I'll bring you some toast. You've got time."

She's standing right in front of me, and her head only reaches the center of my chest. If anything, what happened has made me more sure than ever this is where I want to be. I want to be with this little firecracker who's stronger than she knows.

Then she reaches up to touch my face. "About what you said last night…"

"Yeah?" My brow furrows.

"I love you, too, Logan Murphy."

Her whiskey eyes hold mine, and I cup her face in my hands. I seal my mouth to hers, parting her lips, and we're lost together in our little paradise.

Chapter 24

Dylan

"It's like he got a second wind. He's playing better ball than he's played all season." My brothers sit in their usual spots in front of the big screen televisions in the restaurant, and the crowd for football night has grown.

Ever since the story was published, the community has rallied around us like they always do when a storm hits. It was almost like they saw the big city gossip sites coming after us, and they decided Logan and I needed their help.

We're a village that faces down life-threatening storms every couple of years, so dealing with a sneaky take-down artist is small potatoes. Even if I'm still embarrassed that photo of me blowing Logan is out there for everyone to see.

Unexpectedly, I've had a few of the older ladies give me knowing nods and elbows, like we all share a secret now. The worst was Salina Duck's mom telling me it's important to keep your man happy.

"I wanted to die." I grab Allie by the arm as I hide behind

my friendly column. "I was just delivering the leftover Carolina Reaper sauce I made for Oliver that night, remember that?"

It was the same night the little brat finally said I'd made the Dare dish hot enough.

Allie nods, her eyes fixed on the screens above the bar. "Oliver Duck has a crush on you. That's why he acts the way he does. He'd melt his ass off to get your attention."

"He's fifteen."

"I'm surprised he didn't take your ballet class. Probably didn't want you to see him in tights beside Austin and Josh."

"Well, anyway, I figured he was the only one who'd want that leftover sauce. Then his mom just came on out and started telling me about how when Mr. Duck was going through his midlife crises, the one way she kept him from philandering was with tantric massage."

My friend's eyes cut to mine. Mine are wide, and I press my lips together in a grimace.

"Dylan Bradford, that is a visual I did not need in my head."

"Tell me about it."

Waldorf Duck is shorter than I am, round, and always sweaty. We both shudder then start to laugh, but it's short-lived.

"Oh my god oh my god oh my god!" Allie is on her feet jumping up and down.

The guys are all standing as well, and even Austin is jumping around yelling. Logan is making a 50-yard run to the end zone.

We all scream when Garrett goes down, taken out by a defensive lineman.

"Oh, no!" I cover my face, not wanting to see my gentle giant of an older brother tackled by an even bigger giant. "Is he okay?"

"He's okay." Allie holds my forearm, rubbing my back.

"It was just a matter of time," Jack grumbles as we watch Garrett clawing the grass, doing his best to get back on his feet. "They're all studying the two of them."

It doesn't matter. The play is happening. The cornerback is

headed straight for my man, and Logan is so focused on completing the pass, I'm not sure he even knows Garrett is out.

He's off his feet, arms extended, gliding through the air. The entire room holds its breath as we wait to see if the defensive player, also reaching hard, is going to block it.

It's the final play of the game. Garrett is on his feet again, and as the ball descends, two hands reach out.

"Get it, Logan!" I scream, and in that instant, his fingers stretch.

The ball sticks like velcro, and he rips it to his chest. It's an off-center catch. One corner of the ball sticks up to his shoulder, but he's got it. He continues flying through the air until he lands on his side, just at the corner of the goal line.

"It's good!" Zane yells louder than I've heard him since he's been home.

The entire restaurant bursts into screams and cheers. People are hugging and jumping up and down. It's as wild as a Dare night. Craig laughs, running over to lift me up and spin me around.

When he puts me on my feet, he slaps both hands on the tops of my shoulders. "Did you see that?"

I'm laughing so hard, I can only nod my head. "I saw it!"

The field is in chaos with all the people running out to congratulate the players. Again, my brother has Logan off his feet in the air, but this time, he doesn't make the signal.

This time he struggles to get down, to get to the reporter on the field. When the blonde woman asks how he's feeling about the MVP award, he puts his hand on the neck of the mic, looking straight into the camera with his blue eyes so focused.

"Dylan Bradford, I love you. You are the perfect woman for me, and I want everyone in this town to know it. You're exactly my type."

Heat flashes from my head to my toes, and I cover my face with both hands as everyone in the restaurant turns to look at me. They're all smiling, pride in their eyes, and I know I don't have to prove anything in this place. We've all suffered and cried and supported each other through all of life's ups and downs.

Still, that was on national TV.

Even if he can't see or hear me, I hold up my hand, my thumb and index finger crossed, and say it loud, "I love you, Logan Murphy!"

Everyone breaks into applause, a taxi whistle cuts through the air, and the celebration continues.

"How will I celebrate Thanksgiving without you here?" Craig sits on the silver worktable in the kitchen. "You know my parents drive me crazy."

"So come with me! We haven't been to New York together since we were kids, and it's going to be all decorated for the holiday. We can run around Midtown together, catch a show, ice skate at Rockefeller Center."

"Logan would love that." He rolls his eyes.

"He wouldn't mind!"

"I am not horning in on your love nest. You two have sex all over the damn place. I've seen the photographic evidence." My eyes narrow, and he holds up both hands. "Too soon?"

"Way too soon."

"Sorry." Craig hops off the table to give me a hug. "You know I'm the biggest fan of LoDy... DeeLo? DeeLight?"

"You are not combining our names... but I like DeeLight." We both snort a laugh. "What about Closeted Clint? Why don't you do something with him for Thanksgiving?"

"I've put him on notice." Craig holds up a hand, shaking his head. "He either owns our relationship, or it's over."

My eyebrows rise. "Strong words from someone so infatuated."

"I'm not infatuated, and I deserve a man who'll fight for me, too."

"I couldn't agree more." I hug my bestie. "You're worth fighting for."

I think about how Logan is fighting for me. He forwarded to me his lawyer's reply to his lawsuit request against *TMI*. It basically said exactly what he predicted it would, but he was still angry.

Logan: It's not right these dickheads can get away with printing shit like that.

We were careless going onto the balcony.

Logan: I should've known better, but you're hard to resist.

That makes me smile.

Everyone in town has been so great. I don't know how many of them read the article, but they've all been coming to C&S for the games and supporting us.

Logan: That does it. Newhope is our new home.

I think they're doing it for my parents.

Logan: They're doing it for you, Dylan.

His words make me pause.

I don't know why it's hard for me to believe I matter that much to people. My brothers have always been the ones everyone pays attention to. They're the celebrities, not me.

Still, in the last two weeks, my greatest humiliation has turned into my greatest source of peace. Jack pulled me into a hug and told me I could talk to him any time. Zane told me Miss Gina wants me to come for a visit. I told him to tell her as soon as I get back from New York.

Climbing the steps to the small plane, I wonder if I'm growing up or if I'm simply becoming less afraid of the future. I'm not the type to sit around and consider my life choices, what I've done and what it means. I typically go with my instincts.

The one time I did lean into the direction my life was going, when I dedicated myself to ballet, I learned very quickly life does what it wants. We can work hard and make plans, but we can't control everything

At the same time, working with Mia, even being with Logan, I'm starting to feel like I *am* important, and I can make a difference. I'm letting go of the notion that I can protect myself by not wanting things so much.

It's okay to dream, to take risks, and if a door closes, look around for the unexpected door standing wide open. Most of all, I have people there to catch me if I fall. I always have.

Stepping off the plane this time, when I see him standing there just like before, waiting with his hand in his pocket and that smile on his face, something shifts. Up to now, this has felt like a beautiful dream.

Now it feels real. It feels like forever.

We're less frantic than last time, thanks to Logan's visit two weeks ago. Still, my hand never leaves his as we make the drive from the airport to his apartment building, and he holds me tight to his side as we ride the elevator to the top floor.

Stepping into his luxury apartment with its soft pine

floors, large, white sectional sofa, granite countertops, and brushed stainless appliances, I'm struck by something new.

"You put blackout shades on all the windows." I walk into the living room, sinking my bare feet into the plush, white rug.

You can take a girl out of the country, but you can't make her wear shoes. I slip off my fluffy coat, tossing it onto the chair so I'm only wearing a short, sage-green dress with thin straps and no underwear.

The heat of his body is at my back, and he places his hands on my upper arms. "No one is going to violate your privacy this time." His voice is low, determined. "I want you to feel safe here."

My heart squeezes, and I turn, reaching for his shoulders. "You're the one who's not safe, remember?" It's a sassy tease. "We established that on Day 1."

It breaks the tension like I'd hoped, and he laughs, lifting off my feet. "I'm still going to protect my dangerous girl."

"You're such a caveman." Leaning closer, I pull his ear with my teeth, humming a happy noise. "Love me like nobody's watching."

"I'm going to love you so hard everyone will know." His hands grip my thighs under the tiered skirt of my dress, and heat is in my veins. "They just won't have pictures."

Our mouths unite, and his tongue invades, possessive and hungry like always. He carries me to the sofa to sit, pulling the straps of my dress down my arms.

My breasts spill out, and he groans, lifting and squeezing them, covering my body with kisses. I wiggle out of my top, reaching for the buttons on his shirt, quickly unfastening them so I can slide my fingers over his chest.

His cock is hard in his jeans, and I rock my body over it, feeling the heat rising. His hands slide to my bare ass, and he groans a swear. Rolling me so my back is on the cushions, he lifts my knee before burying his face between my legs.

"Oh, fuck," I gasp, threading my fingers in his hair.

Fire blazes through my veins with every pass of his tongue over my clit, and it's not long before I'm soaked and aching for him. He's on his knees looking down at me, blue eyes dark with desire, and I watch as he unfastens his jeans, releasing his erection.

Pushing up onto my elbows, I wrap my fingers around his shaft, holding it to my lips and tracing my tongue around the mushroom tip. His dick jumps, and he exhales a low groan, sliding his fingers lightly along my jaw.

I take him as far as I can, bobbing my head and sliding my hand to meet it. His hips rise and he groans. His fingers curl in the side of my hair, twisting tighter, until he lifts me onto his lap.

"I need to be inside you." It's a rough, animalistic order.

My knees are beside him on the couch and my breasts flatten against his chest as I ride him. I lift onto my knees, sliding all the way to his tip, almost out, then I drop again.

His head drops back and he jerks with a loud groan. It sends a charge of orgasm racing through my core, and I do it again. Large hands grip my ass, and he starts to move me up and down.

Our movements are feverish, and I'm lost in the sensations swimming in my veins. Sweat trickles down his cheek, and I kiss it. Salt is on my tongue, and I curl it into his mouth.

He groans into my kiss, and his hips rise off the couch. The hair on his chest tickles my sensitive nipples, and my second orgasm grows tighter in my core.

"Fuck, Dylan, I'm coming." His body jerks, and he drives deeper.

It's so deep, his cock strikes a place that fires orgasm through my veins. My eyes squeeze, and my body stiffens. My back arches, I'm jumping faster on his lap, doing everything I can to get more of the sensation.

His fingers tickle my ass, and his stomach shudders. "Oh, God, Dylan."

I'm in another world, doing my best to keep going as my body gradually finishes, as the spasming of my muscles subsides.

Falling forward on his chest, my body is limp, and I start to giggle.

"What?" A grin is in his tone.

"I think I just rode the lightning."

We both start to laugh, and he wraps his strong arms around me. My face is tucked against his chest, our hearts beat in time, and I guess we're both dangerous.

"Nobody interviewed me." Maddy crosses her arms roughly. "I'd have told them what a wonderful person you are, and how you're exactly Logan's type."

"Aw, you're sweet to me."

We're both wearing our navy jerseys with big red numbers on the front. Hers is 18 for Charlie—who I don't call *Johnson*. I'm in my Number 12, and we're standing in the glassed-in box together overlooking the field.

"It's just the truth. The only reason they went after you is because you're interesting. Models are all the same. They have to have mass appeal, so they can't be too spicy."

She gives me a wink, and I smile. "Thanks, Mads. You're the best."

"Us girls have to look out for each other."

A small group of people are with us, including Charlie's parents, and we have snacks and drinks. I'm holding a beer, and I'm a little nervous not to be hiding behind my lucky pole.

But I'm determined to be strong for this game. I'm going to smile and cheer and wave and give Logan our signal.

The guys are on the sidelines, and right at that moment, he looks up at me.

I wave and cross my index finger over my thumb, holding it up and wondering if he can even see it. He grins and signals back, and I'm as happy as a kid on Christmas morning.

"Oh, y'all are so cute!" Maddy wraps her arm around my waist and gives me a side-hug. "Charlie and I should do something like that."

"You know what this means?"

"Sure! It's the Korean hand signal for *I love you.*" She shrugs. "I mean, I guess it's anybody's signal now, that's just where it started."

Clasping my hands together, I think about how long he's been doing it on camera, telling me he loved me in front of the whole world before he even said the words to me.

"Do you think Logan knows what it means?"

She slants her eyes at me. "Yes. It's a heart, see?"

She makes the signal, and I see it now. "I just thought it was fun and went with it."

"It's adorable. Just like y'all are."

Any insecurity I might have been feeling at returning to the city fades, and as the players take the field, the only nerves I have are watching the guys.

Chapter 25

Logan

THE INTENSITY OF THE GAMES GROWS FIERCER THE CLOSER WE GET to the playoffs. We haven't had a loss this season, which means we're a shoo-in for the Big Game. Still, competition is high, and it's evident the other teams are studying Garrett and me. Last week's tackle has us on alert.

Today's game is against the Challengers, Ricky's team, and he's giving me death glares from across the field. We're both putting our best running games forward, and on both sides, the defensive line is a wall.

My muscles tweak with energy, and when I look up at our box, my adrenaline spikes even higher. Dylan waves, and I can see her big smile. She holds up her hand, making our little *I love you* signal, and it's better than I thought it would be to have her here.

I confess, it makes me want to show off a little.

Yesterday, we had Thanksgiving dinner in bed. I haven't really wanted to venture out on the streets with her, not since that fucking article was printed. I don't like people saying bad things about her simply because she's with me, and that's all it is. She'd be anonymous otherwise, and I don't want her to decide being with me is too difficult.

Still, we went for a walk in Central Park with Garrett later in the day. He wanted to see his little sister, hug her, and tell her Lainey's a double-crossing jerk he couldn't believe he thought was cool.

Dylan was graceful, as always. Told him not to worry about it, said she was glad to see him, she missed him.

It was gray and breezy, and the few people who were there gave us space. In the past it was easy for me to move around the city unnoticed, but since I've been breaking and setting records, everything has changed.

It's probably why I got sloppy, and she got hurt.

It won't happen again.

Jogging onto the field, Garret bumps my shoulder pad. "Keep your head in the game."

It's a rough order, but he's right. Having Dylan here is great, but the Challengers aren't fucking around. They're thinking about the Big Game as well, and I'm sure we'll see these guys a few more times this season, vying for the championship ring.

We don't make much progress on our first possession. Johnson is sacked, and Garrett has a penalty that sends us back five yards. We leave the field looking like amateurs.

"We gotta do better than that if we're going to win." Charlie pulls us all together, and calls out a new play we've been working on this week.

He gives me the signal, and I know he's going to have his eye out for me next possession.

The only problem is I can't get open. Garrett is held back, and I'm off my feet before Charlie even has a chance to pass. He's forced to run, and we lose more yardage.

It's pretty much the same every time we get the ball. The only saving grace is our defense is holding back the Challengers just as well.

Coach hands us our asses at halftime, but it doesn't do much to improve our game. Our tight end runs the ball in for a score, and the kicker gets the extra point. We get a field goal in the third quarter, but in the final minutes, we're still 10-13, with the Challengers leading by three.

Every time I look at the box, Dylan has her hands clasped in front of her mouth, and she and Maddy are on their feet, glued side by side in the window. Seeing her there is everything. It's more than any trophy, more than all the cheers when we score. I'll win this one for her.

It's the final play of the game, and I glance up at her one more time. She holds up her fingers, and I give her a nod. We break the huddle and Garrett leans in as we hustle down to the lineup.

"They're putting a lot of pressure on me, but I've found my guy's weakness. Keep your eyes open." I nod, and we take our positions.

The guys chatter in the line, but I hear Garrett's growl above them all. "Let's do this!"

My entire body is tense, and at the snap, I keep my eyes on my friend. Garrett barrels forward with a loud yell, and sure enough, he breaks through. He takes down a guy two inches taller and at least fifty pounds heavier than he is.

As soon as I see the opening, I dig in and zip through it at top speed. I'm flying to the red zone. The field is clear ahead of me, and I turn to look back at Johnson. He's waiting, watching, and our eyes lock when he sees I'm open.

Whipping back his arm, he fires the ball to me, and I dig in harder. Intuitively, I calculate the speed of the pass and where I need to be to complete it. It's a perfect spiral, and this is it. I'm right where I need to be.

A flush of satisfaction unfurls in my chest. Not only are we going to win this game, it's going to be a career-making play for me.

This one will be on instant replay all week long, and it's going to be so sweet.

I'm at the height of my career. I've got my girl, she's here with me. I've made it to the top of the mountain. Everything I want is in my hands. The ball arcs down, flying straight to me as if guided by a string. Reaching up, it's mine.

Just as I catch it, as it lands in my fingers, I lift my eyes to see Dylan's face. Her hands are fisted, and she holds them to her cheeks as if she'll hide. It makes me smile. *No fear, baby, I'm winning this.*

My feet touch the ground. All that's left is to run it in for the score, when *BAM!*

I spin around and everything goes dark.

Voices drift through the haze. They're speaking low and urgent, and I try to understand what they're saying as I open my eyes. The white room blinds me initially. I'm in a hospital bed, and I'm surrounded by softly beeping monitors.

My first instinct is to sit up, but as soon as I try, large hands grip my shoulders, forcing me down again.

"Hold it right there, Murph," a deep male voice scolds, and I squeeze my eyes as I try to focus, to see what's happening. "Glad to see you're back with us."

I'm so weak. I try to move again, but when I look down, a flash of dread hits my stomach. My leg is wrapped around a brace, and I can't bend my knee.

"What happened?" My throat is scratchy, and now the large, dark hand holds a straw to my lips.

My nurse places his other hand on my shoulder to help me lean forward. "It was fucked-up, man. That corner is out for the season, and looks like…"

He stops abruptly, but I know what he was going to say. I know what a knee injury means.

"Looks like I am, too." An ache moves through my chest.

It's over.

His lips press into a grim line. "Let me get your people in here. They've been waiting to see you."

He goes to the door, and I lean back in the bed, driving my fingers into my hair. Sickness is in my stomach, and when I breathe, my lungs feel like they're lined with tiny shards of glass.

"Logan?" Dylan's soft voice fills the room, and I do my best to sit up again. "You're awake."

"Hey." It's a weak greeting, but seeing her eases the pain a little.

"Wait, let me help you." She takes the control from beside the bed and presses the button, raising the back to a sitting position. "Is that okay?"

"Yeah." I'm sitting up now, and I can see the swelling around my knee. "I don't remember what happened."

She slides her fingers through mine. "It was awful, a hip-drop tackle. You suffered a mild concussion, and your knee…"

Her voice fades, and my lips tighten.

I swallow the shout bubbling in my chest, clenching my teeth instead. "Hip-drops are illegal."

She nods, her eyes fixed on my hand. "Garrett got into a fight on the field. Ripped off the other guy's helmet and started punching. It was chaos."

Thinking of my oversized friend doing his best to beat up the asshole makes me feel slightly better. Until my doctor enters, with a tight expression on his face. He's an older man in traditional scrubs, and I wait as he clips X-rays to a screen.

"The good news is, you'll be off crutches in a week to ten days, but here's the problem…"

He circles my knee with his pen and goes on to describe the injury and what it needs to heal, finishing up by essentially saying if I follow his orders, I'm looking at a full recovery—but this season is done.

"You'll be able to walk and live your life normally. You just can't run fifty yards or fly through the air or zig-zag out of the way of a defensive tackle…"

"Or basically do anything related to my job." My tone is bitter.

He exhales a chuckle and stands. "Only for six to twelve weeks. The physical therapist will decide when you're ready. You're very lucky."

He leaves the room without saying the silent part out loud. It's over. My record, the trophy, everything I've worked so hard to achieve, all ended in one illegal play.

"I could kill that guy." I exhale heavily.

Dylan's fingers tighten around mine, and she nods. "I'm pretty sure that's how everyone feels right now. Even Ricky."

"Ricky?" My eyes snap to hers.

"He's out in the waiting room. He wanted to talk to you when you woke up. He's really pissed. Not as pissed as Garrett, but close."

I press my head against the bed as sickness spreads through my stomach. I don't want to see anyone. I don't want to be in this hospital room. I want to be as far away from all of this as possible, then I want to throw things and break things and roar.

Clearing my throat, my eyes are fixed on my leg. "How long do I have to stay here?"

"Just a day or two." She strokes my hand, and I watch her slim fingers sliding up and down mine.

The sound of the monitors is around us, and I can't think of a thing to say.

A light tap on the door and Ricky steps inside the room. He's in jeans and a thin, long-sleeved sweater, and he looks like he spent the night here.

"Logan…" He doesn't approach my bedside, but I can tell he's agitated. "I won't stay. I just needed to say something in person. We're all sorry about what happened. Peter is trying to say he did it for me, but that's bullshit. I'm pushing to have his contract terminated. I don't even want to be on the same team as that guy."

Peter Krall. Now I'm even more angry. That asshole's got a reputation for targeting runners. I'm not his first illegal tackle, and I hope he *is* kicked out of the league.

"Thanks, Ricky." I attempt a smile, but it's more of a grimace.

"I wanted you to know just in case you saw any lies in the gossip feeds."

I glance at my girl by my side, her fingers threaded in mine, silently holding me together. "I've seen a lot of lies on the gossip feeds."

Rubbing the back of his neck, he stands taller. "Well, I wanted to beat you fair and square. I didn't want to win the trophy this way, by forfeit."

"You haven't won anything yet." Garrett's tone is pissed as he walks through the door, coming straight to my side. "How's it going, bro? You're pretty swole up, but you'll heal. No worries. We'll get you back out there."

I expect nothing less from my best friend, but I can't tell him how I really feel. I'm not even sure yet, so I only shake my head. One thing I do know, I never expected to see my biggest rival so wound up in my defense.

Ricky exhales a noise, holding up his hands. "That's all I wanted to say. There's always next year."

The words hit me like a punch in the chest. I press my head against the stiff pillow behind me again, squeezing my eyes shut. Next year *wasn't* the plan.

"May I speak to my son, please?" The polished voice draws all our attention to where my father has replaced Ricky at my door.

He's wearing a suit, as always. One hand is in his pocket. The other is on his stomach. Dylan stands immediately, but my hand tightens around hers.

"Wait." It's a quiet order.

"Oh, yeah," Garret's voice is mildly sarcastic. "Your dad's here to see you."

I look up at my friend, and he shrugs.

"If you wouldn't mind." My father's eyes narrow. "I'd like to talk to Logan alone."

Dylan leans closer, pressing her soft lips to my brow. "It's okay. I'll be right outside."

Garrett follows her, and soon I'm in a room facing the death of my proudest season with the man who never believed in me in the first place.

Anger is hot in my blood, but I don't want to give him the satisfaction of being right. I don't want to come across as a sullen child.

"You had a good run this year." My father's eyes are on the monitor instead of me. "I've been very proud of you. I'm not sure I've ever told you that."

"You haven't."

He nods. "Well, I'm telling you now."

The words don't give me the satisfaction I once thought they would. I don't even care to acknowledge them.

"Did someone call you?"

His eyes finally meet mine, and impatience permeates his tone. "I don't have to be called to be concerned about my son."

I shift uncomfortably, wishing I wasn't trapped in this bed. "That's new."

"Dammit, Logan. I saw you lying on that field not moving, and I worried you might not get up. I wanted to be here if you needed anything."

"You could've saved yourself the trip. I don't need anything." Not from him, at least.

"I'm glad." Clearing his throat, he walks over to the rolling stand that holds my water cup. "I was thinking on the flight here, you might want to come home while you recover. You could work in the office. I'd always hoped you might take over for me one day."

He attempts a smile, but I don't know how else to make it clear I don't want that.

"Thanks, but I'll probably just stay here."

"Who'll look after you?" He glances at the door. "That little girl?"

"Her name is Dylan." I level him with a glare.

"I saw the article about her, and I can't say it portrays your relationship in a very flattering light."

"Dylan is an amazing person. She's strong, and she's very special to me. That article was a disgusting work of fiction."

He holds up both hands. "I was simply saying—"

"Look, I appreciate you coming here, but I'm not going back to Houston. Once I speak to my doctor and my coaches, I'll have a better idea of what I'll be doing, but it won't be that."

Silence fills the room. It's a heavy silence that presses on my temples, and makes me tired. I want the people I care about with me now, not this man who has only ever seen me as an asset or worse, nothing at all.

As if reading my mind, he turns his back, putting his hands on his hips. "We never had that kind of storybook, father-son relationship. I tried, but—"

"No, you didn't." The words escape on a bitter laugh, and I regret them almost at once. Even if they're true.

"It wasn't easy. You were so much like your mother as a boy, it was difficult even to look at you in those days. Now… it seems you're a lot like me."

"I'm nothing like you."

Something like regret tightens his features. "No, you're not. You're better."

I don't answer. There was a time when I would've sincerely appreciated him saying these words. As it is now, with everything coming down on me like it is, he needs to read the room.

Walking to the door, he stops before exiting. "Take care, son."

Chapter 26

Dylan

"Has he been going to therapy or something?" Garrett is at Logan's bedside, waiting to help the large male nurse get him into the wheelchair.

I stand at the door with his bag of clothes and toiletries.

"Don't know." Logan slides to the edge of the bed.

"Was he drunk?" My brother teases.

"I've never seen my father drunk." Logan looks up at the man in scrubs gripping his arm. "Is this really necessary? I can walk on the crutches just fine."

"It's the rules," the nurse says.

"They're all out there." He gives the guy a look of *please*, but nobody's getting anything past Logan's nurse.

I almost wonder if that's why he was assigned to my tall, dark, and stubborn boyfriend.

"We have security on standby if we need it." The man nods to Garrett, who steadies Logan's other side.

Logan drops into the wheelchair with a frustrated grunt,

and my brother and I follow as we slowly make our way to the elevator. Nurses and staff smile and applaud, and Logan forces a smile, nodding his thanks.

We're safe inside the hospital, but when the elevator doors open at the first floor, hoards of fans and spectators are visible through the glass doors. They've lined the streets, hoping to catch a glimpse of the injured celebrity.

He looks up at me. "You want to go on ahead?"

"Do you mind?" I reach down to hold his hand.

"It would actually make me feel better, since I'm stuck in this chair. It's going to take forever to get me out of it and into the SUV, and I'd rather not have you standing around exposed."

"Okay. I'll be waiting for you." I lean down to kiss his cheek before hustling ahead of him to the waiting vehicle.

I brace for my exit from the lobby. Logan's driver sees me and stands waiting with the door open. As soon as I emerge from the hospital, I duck my head against the throng.

Some people call my name and cheer, but others boo and yell at me. I've never had people vocally dislike me this way, and it's a shock. It hits me hard every time, twisting my stomach and making me want to hide.

I'm a nonstop topic of discussion with some people saying I'm a real person, just what he needs. Others say I'm a gold digger or at the least, a distraction. Since his injury, a new group has emerged, blaming me for what happened.

They point to the replay where he looks up at me after the catch, just before he gets hit, as proof I distracted him. Like I'd want him to be hurt that way. Like I'd want his career to be cut short.

Those shouts hurt the worst. My heart hammers in my chest as I reach for Fred's hand. He helps me into the black SUV, and as soon as I'm inside, I go to the very back doing my best not to cry.

Logan gets so angry about all of it, and he's got enough on his mind right now. He hasn't said much about how he feels, and I know from personal experience, he's still processing this injury and what it means.

When I broke my foot, it wasn't until the day I was supposed to return to ballet practice that it hit me. When I realized I wouldn't go anymore. Ever again.

Then it all came crashing down at once. It was a painful, black day, and I'm ready to hold his hand through it.

I know from watching my brother Zane, the men think they have to be strong all the time and never show their emotions, but I'm hopeful.

Logan and I started our relationship sharing our hurts and dreams and disappointments. It's how we grew close in the early days. I'll be here when he's ready to talk.

I hate that I have to go home tomorrow. I took an extra week off school to be here for him until the doctors released him, but Christmas is coming. I have the school show, Mia and Austin have been working hard, and I can't abandon them as much as I want to be here for Logan.

Cheers and clapping break out, and I know it means Garrett is bringing him out of the hospital in the wheelchair.

The look on Logan's face tells me all I need to know about how he feels about being wheeled out in front of all these on-lookers. He hates it.

"Easy…" Garrett locks the brakes as he tries to stand.

Logan's not as big as my brother, but at six-foot-two, two hundred pounds, he's not easy to manage.

I get on my knees inside the vehicle holding out my hand. "Can I help?"

"It's okay." Logan's face is red from exertion.

He's not as strong as he's used to being, and I see the anger rising in his chest. I move back to my seat to give him space.

I hear my name yelled, but I block it out. This isn't about me. It's about him and making his transition as easy as possible.

Finally, the door slams and Garrett falls hard into his seat.

"I'm going to pop one of those motherfuckers if I hear another word about Dylan."

The muscle in Logan's jaw moves, and my heart hurts. I feel like I'm causing him even more stress than he needs.

"It's okay." I lean forward in my chair. "I don't care about them."

"I do," Garrett grouses, shifting in his seat. "Assholes."

I place my hand lightly on Logan's shoulder. "The team hired a nurse to check on you. I know Garrett will be there, but if you need something, you can give her a call."

Blue eyes flash to mine, and he frowns. "Where will you be?"

"I have to get back to Newhope." I blink rapidly. "I have my classes, the restaurant…"

"Right. Of course." He looks down, and guilt floods my chest.

My cheeks grow hot, and I look at Garrett in a panic. He gives me a subtle wink and nods like it'll be okay. Only, I know what's coming for Logan, and the last thing I want is to leave him alone—even if he'll eventually recover. He's lost the best season of his career.

"Maybe you can come for Christmas? We'd love to have you."

He doesn't speak, and I swallow the knot in my throat. I'd drop everything and stay here with him if I could, but people are counting on me. I can't let Mia down.

Back at his apartment, he watches quietly as I pack my clothes into my suitcase. Outside it's gray and rainy, and I wish I could think of something encouraging to say.

"I'm sorry I asked you to come here." His voice is quiet, and my heart falls.

I do my best to keep my voice even. "You are?"

I imagine him doing what Zane did, building a wall and shutting us out. *Don't push me away, Logan…*

"I watched the replay. It was pretty bad." His tone is grave. "It was everything you told me you never wanted to see, and

I asked you to come and have a front-row seat to your worst nightmare."

Dropping the dress I'm holding, I rush over to where he's sitting. I kneel beside him, taking both of his hands in mine.

"Yes, it was horrifying to see you hurt. It was my worst fear realized, and I almost broke when you didn't get up…" My heart races in my chest, and my thoughts jam together in my mind. I take a slow breath to calm myself before continuing. "But it would've been a million times worse if I'd been at home. Here, I could hold your hand and be by your side. Being here for you is the most important thing to me."

Reaching out, he puts his hands on my shoulders, pulling me to him. I rise onto my knees to hug him, and I'm surrounded by citrus and cedar and his warm, hard body.

I tighten my arms around his neck, nestling my face against his, and with a deep exhale, his muscles relax. My heart breaks, and heat floods my eyes. For several moments, we simply hold each other. Our hearts beat in time, and I thread my fingers in his soft hair.

Turning my face, I kiss the side of his jaw, and his arms relax, allowing me to sit back on my feet. Holding his hands, I look up at him and smile.

He reaches down to trace the hair off my cheek. "I'd like to go back with you to Newhope, if that's okay?"

My heart squeezes, and I nod. "I would love that."

Chapter 27

Logan

THE RESTAURANT ISN'T NEARLY AS CROWDED AS USUAL, WHICH DYLAN explains is normal for a football night. Still, a decent-sized group is here, sitting at tables facing the large TVs over the bar.

"The crowd has actually grown since that *TMI* article. Before that it was just the guys and Allie and me and one or two other people."

She told me about that, and I really love the way this little village comes together to take care of its own.

When I enter on crutches, they all stand and clap for me, which hits me unexpectedly hard.

An older fellow gently pats my shoulder. "That was the worst thing I've seen since Zane's injury, and his wasn't intentional."

His words poke at the anger still simmering in my chest about what happened. I'll have to train my ass off once I'm back on my feet, and at my age, it's not a prospect I relish. Then, even with all the training, there's no guarantee I'll ever see the stats I was racking up this season.

"Thank you." Is the best I can manage.

I make my way to the table where Jack and Zane have a front-row seat to the enormous, center flatscreen behind the bar.

Salina moves through the room taking care of the customers, and I look for Dylan. I find her wearing my jersey, but she's sitting in a chair behind a column several feet away in the middle of the restaurant.

Allie sits beside her, but she's not hidden.

I turn and crutch over to them. "What are you two doing back here?"

Dylan hops up and carefully holds my shoulders to give me a kiss on the cheek. "You sit up there with Jack and Zane. I do better watching from back here."

My brow furrows, and I glance at Allie, who shrugs. "She does it every week."

"Every week?" My eyebrows rise.

"Sometimes she goes to the kitchen to watch with Thomas."

"Why does Thomas watch in the kitchen?" I take a step back, glancing through the open door.

Sure enough, Thomas is on a stool in front of the metal table with his arms crossed. A small, black-and-white TV with rabbit ears is in front of him.

"He's superstitious," Dylan explains. "But sometimes it's easier to watch on the small screen than up there, where it's all… in your face."

Leaning one of my crutches against the column, I hop over and grab a chair from an empty table, putting it beside my girl. "I'll sit right here with you."

Allie smiles warmly and hops up. "I'll grab us all a beer."

She disappears, and I reach over to cover Dylan's twisting fingers with my hand. The leather bracelet is on her wrist, and her eyes are in her lap.

"You did this for me every week?"

Lifting her pretty, pretty eyes to mine, she blinks a few times. "It was important to you, and I want to support you."

I can't find a way to say how much it both aches and warms me to know she was here, doing her best for me. At the same time, I file it away along with all the other things going through my mind these days as I contemplate our future.

"All this time it was horses?" A week has passed, and I'm standing on the edge of an arena connected to a large horse farm south of Newhope, watching Zane lead a gorgeous thoroughbred through its exercises. "But why keep it a secret? Jack and Dylan would be relieved to know you're doing something so… positive."

I know my beautiful girl has been worried about her broody older brother since he came home and started disappearing every day. It's part of what prompted her to suggest he help Miss Gina.

He shakes his head looking down. "To be honest, I hadn't planned to keep doing it, but after a while, I couldn't seem to let go."

I lean on my crutches behind the rail as I watch him slide his hand over the brown neck of the purebred animal. "They're beautiful."

He nods, scrubbing his fingers under the horse's mane. "They come here because they're useless once they're injured. Just like… people."

I'm not sure if he was going to say *just like us* or *just like me*. Either option is pretty dark, so I let it pass.

"What do you do?"

"Exercise them, brush and feed them. I help out when the therapy kids come here, holding them and guiding the volunteers. I was surprised by how well the kids respond to them."

"Like troubled kids?"

"A few, but more like injured and neurodivergent kids. The horses are very calm, almost like they can sense the person's needs. You might try it."

"Sounds pretty woo-woo to me," I tease, but he stiffens.

"It's not." His reply is curt. "Equine therapy is well-documented in clinical research."

Clearing my throat, I straighten on my uninjured knee. "Sorry, I didn't mean to imply it wasn't."

I'm only just getting to know Zane, and I want to continue building the bridge. He and I are in a similar boat—only my career isn't over like his.

"We'd better get going. Miss Gina has some new problem for me."

I exhale a laugh. "I think she likes having you around."

"I know she does."

He leads the tall horse back to its stall, and I start the trek to his Jeep. I do my best to keep pace with him, but it takes me longer to do just about everything with these crutches. I'm trying not to be pissed as hell about it.

It's worse knowing it was an intentional foul, but I got a slight reprieve when I found out Peter Krall was suspended from the league pending further review.

It's not complete retribution, but it's close. They said if my injury had been career-ending, it would've been worse for him.

As it is, I'm healing fast. The physical therapist said I'll be off the damn crutches in a few more days, but I still have to wear a brace—and figure out what comes next.

Zane drives us north along the scenic road, headed to the old lady's mansion on the bluffs. It's a cool day, but we have the top and doors off the vehicle. I'm not sure, but I bet it's to curtail the need for conversation.

Dylan's brother isn't much of a talker, which is fine by me.

I look through the live oak trees mixed with magnolias at the sparkling water of the bay. It's cool, and the briny scent of saltwater is in the air. A lone sailboat drifts past, and it's restorative, peaceful.

In addition to being with Dylan, being here helps to loosen the fist of anger in my chest, about a lot of things.

Traveling along the old scenic highway, I notice a small cinder-block building with a low roof and a giant satellite dish in the backyard. It's painted white, and it looks like it's been here for a century.

"What's that?" I shout over the wind, nodding at the building.

Zane glances, then leans to the center to answer. "The old AM station. Been around for years."

"Does it still broadcast?"

"Some." He shifts in his seat. "It's mostly for storm warnings, local stuff like that."

Nodding, I think about this as we continue our journey.

"Won't all the ladies be jealous?" Miss Gina's high voice wobbles with laughter. "Now I've got two handsome football stars working for me. I really must be a long-lost princess."

"Now you're just feeding the rumors," I tease, moving slowly on my crutches with her hand on my arm. "How do you know I don't have cross-eyes and a pot belly?"

I tease her every time she compliments me, because she's *blind*.

It only makes her laugh more, which to be honest, is kind of nice. Her whole face lights up when she smiles.

We pause at the French doors leading out to her patio, and I open one, doing my best to hold it for her while allowing her room to pass.

She hesitates then walks through the opening. I hop out

and close the door behind me as she waits to put her small hand on my arm again.

"You have a refined air about you, Logan Murphy. What in the world got you interested in football?"

Her question prickles my skin. "I get that question a lot."

"By someone you don't like." Her chin lifts. "A family member?"

I swear, the entire village has it all wrong. Miss Gina is a psychic. "By my father mostly."

"Ah," she nods. "Fathers and sons often have difficult relationships."

"Or none at all."

"Is he still alive?"

"Yes, ma'am." I can't keep the annoyance out of my tone, but she squeezes my arm.

"Then there's hope."

She's a kind old lady, and I don't want to argue with her, so I don't.

"At least I was able to impress him this year, even if I didn't finish the way I'd planned."

"I'm an old woman," Miss Gina nods her head slowly. "One constant I've learned is no matter what, life always changes. The best way through is to accept the fact, and move to the next great thing."

"How do I know it'll be great?"

She gives me a wink. "It always is."

We're slowly making our way to where Zane is on a ladder beside a large glass and wrought-iron structure filled with a variety of plants.

"The heating duct on my greenhouse failed." She puts a hand on her chest. "It's a good thing Rachel was using it for her hot yoga or I'd have lost all my orchids!"

"Rachel?" My brow furrows.

"My new nurse. She was supposed to be here in August, but

she had some problems getting out of Birmingham. She started a few weeks ago—Zane has met her…"

"Are you talking about me?" A young woman walks around the building to where we stand.

She's dressed in leggings and a long-sleeved, oversized sweatshirt. Her blonde hair is up in a ponytail, and she has bright green eyes.

"Rachel, this is Logan Murphy. He's Dylan's gentleman friend."

My brow quirks, and Rachel snorts a laugh. "I don't think anyone says *gentleman friend* anymore, Miss G… Just say he's her *boyfriend*."

"It's so undignified." Miss Gina frowns. "Logan isn't a boy, and he's more than her friend."

"It's nice to meet you, Logan." Rachel steps forward to shake my hand. "That was a pretty gnarly injury you got there. I was watching when it happened. We all said a prayer for you."

"Thanks." It's another prickly topic.

"He doesn't want to talk about his injury." Zane climbs down the ladder, wiping his hands with a towel.

He cuts a look at Rachel, and her eyes narrow. "I can still be empathetic."

"No one likes being pitied."

"That's not what I meant!" She crosses her arms, glaring daggers at him as he continues into the greenhouse.

Miss Gina stands beside me with her hand on my arm and a preening smile on her face.

She leans closer to me, stage-whispering, "They're always bickering like two banty chickens."

"I think you mean *bantam*," Rachel corrects her. "And I don't bicker. He's just an old grump."

Chewing my lip, I don't laugh at her statement of fact.

Zane returns, closing the greenhouse door behind him. "That should do it."

"I'll check on your flowers." Rachel flicks her ponytail at him as she passes, and I notice his eyes flicker to her ass.

He quickly returns his attention to the old lady. "We're taking off, unless you need something else?"

"I think that's enough for today." Miss Gina releases my arm. "You'll be back next week, Zane?"

"Yes, ma'am." I wait as he collects his tools.

Satisfied, the old lady enters the greenhouse, and I turn on my crutches to follow him out to the Jeep. He's not saying anything, but I figure it can't hurt to poke the bear. Or in his case the broody panther.

"That Rachel's a cute girl."

"She's a nosy pain in the ass." He drops his tools in the back of the Jeep before climbing in with a little more energy than when we got here. "We were fine until she showed up. Now it's nonstop *suggestions.*"

"She seemed sweet to me."

"Well, looks can be deceiving." He turns the key, and I've just settled in my seat when he roughly jams it into gear and takes off down the road at a rapid clip.

If I didn't know better, I'd think he didn't want to talk about it anymore, which makes me chuckle. The wind whips around our heads, and I think about the old lady and her mischievous expression as she observed them.

"Miss Gina's something. Sometimes I think she's tricking us all, and she can really see."

"She sees things." Zane doesn't take his eyes off the road. "Just not like you and me. Probably because she's blind."

I've learned my lesson about suggesting he's being woo-woo, so all I say is, "Maybe."

We arrive at the house at the same time as Dylan rides up on her bike, and seeing her in a leotard and tights with a little ballet skirt around her waist tightens my stomach.

She's been through so much, and she still keeps going. Hell, she was there when I got injured, even after all she told me, and she stayed by my side.

I think about what Miss Gina said about change and not being able to control where your life takes you—and moving on to the next great thing.

Her eyes light when she sees us, and she skips down to where I'm standing beside the Jeep. When she reaches me, I lift her off her feet in a hug, bracing myself with my crutch.

It makes her laugh, and she wraps her legs around my waist, kissing me slowly. I'm not going to lie, it makes my dick twitch.

"How was your day?" I love the sound of her voice.

"It just got a whole lot better."

She wriggles, and I lower her to her feet. I take out my other crutch, she walks with me slowly to the house.

"What did you do today?"

"We stopped by Miss Gina's so your brother could fix her greenhouse, and I met Rachel."

"Oh, I love Rachel! I want to start doing yoga with her on the weekends."

"She seems nice. Your brother does not agree."

"I have no feelings either way." Zane's tone is flat as he passes us on his way to the house.

Dylan's eyes cut up to mine, and my eyebrows rise. I'm pretty sure we're thinking the same thing. *Sparks.*

"Well, I've got to get changed and get to the restaurant." She rises on her toes to kiss me once more.

"See you there."

She squeezes her brother's arm as she passes him. Zane puts his bag behind the coat rack, but frustration twists my stomach as I watch her disappear upstairs.

"I don't like the way *certain people* talk about Dylan."

"None of us do." He glances in the direction his sister went. "Jack's wife dealt with the same thing. The only difference was, she deserved it—not that you heard it from me."

"Dylan doesn't deserve it, and she's been through enough."

"It's best to ignore it. Otherwise, it gets worse. Then it gets ugly."

"I don't know." My mind is working. "I'm not good at ignoring things."

And I'm even worse at seeing my girl treated badly. I'm making a call.

Chapter 28

Dylan

THE CHRISTMAS SHOW IS NEXT WEEK, AND WE'VE BEEN REHEARSING after school every day. Austin and Mia dance like true partners now. They predict each other's movements, and he hasn't dropped her since that time before Thanksgiving. Confidence guides them, and I'm so excited for her auditions.

Invitations are slowly filtering in, and she brings them to me every time. It's almost like it's happening to me again, which I know is silly.

The entire class stays after for rehearsals now. They're performing a modified version of "Waltz of the Flowers" from *The Nutcracker*, and Josh and Sally are doing a modified version of "Mirlitons," or "The Dance of the Flutes."

We're finishing up for the day, and Mia and Austin are moving through the combination of little jumps, arabesque, and the lift. They come down with a plié bow, and the entire class breaks into applause. Josh even lets out a sharp whistle.

I can't keep the smile off my face. As important as teaching them ballet has been to me, I've also done my best to foster a non-competitive, supportive environment—something I didn't always have in my own classes.

"Good work, everyone!" I smile, giving them the signal they can go, and they begin collecting their books and backpacks, changing their shoes.

I've got to get to the restaurant. It's Thursday, and Logan wants to learn to make this week's Dare dish with me. Craig says he's nuts, but I'm excited.

He's been spending a lot of time with Zane, and he's finally off those crutches, which had a bigger impact on his attitude than I realized. He's less angry, and he even seems eager, like he's formulating a plan.

I wish I could keep him here with me always, but I know he had things he wanted to accomplish this year. I'm glad he's gotten his second wind, even if it means once he's strong enough, he'll be headed back to the city.

My heart sinks when I think of having to watch him play another season, of us being separated, and all the longing. I don't know what I'll do if he's hurt again, but that's the life of a football WAG… something I never dreamed I'd be.

"Miss Dylan?" Mia's voice halts me as I'm headed for the door.

The worry lining her young face makes my stomach drop, and all my fears are momentarily set aside. "What's wrong?"

She nervously looks around the space as if to be sure everyone is gone. Then she steps forward, clutching my arm.

"Did you ever feel like you couldn't do it? Like it's all too much?" She releases me and paces away. "It's all happening so fast, and yeah, I'm good *here*, but I'm not New York good."

Pressing my lips together, I collect my thoughts. Her back is to me, and I see her shoulders rising and falling rapidly with her panicked breathing.

"Hey." I slowly walk across the stage to where she's standing, taking her hand in mine. "Of course, I felt that way. Everybody does, but you dance through it."

"It's more than that." Tears are in her eyes, and her face drops. "Who am I to think I can be a prima ballerina? I'm just a girl from Newhope, Alabama."

"It's true. Right now, that's all you are." Dipping my chin, I catch her eye. "Natalie Varnum was just a girl from Dothan, and now she's a lead dancer with the Houston ballet."

Mia's brow furrows, and she swallows her tears. "I'm so afraid."

Stepping closer, I pull her into a hug. "If you weren't afraid, I'd be worried you were a narcissist. Everyone is afraid. No one knows if they're good enough or what directors want, but we keep trying anyway." Releasing her, I touch her chin. "But I think you're good enough. I believe in you, and I can't wait to see how high you fly."

Her lips press into a smiley-frown, and tears spill onto her cheeks. "Thank you, Miss Dylan."

I exhale a smile, tapping my fingers against my own eyes. "I've got to get to the restaurant, but you keep that chin up."

"Parallel to the floor?"

"Always."

"I'm so proud of you. I knew you'd be the best teacher." Craig beams at me from a safe distance on the other side of the metal table in the kitchen at Cooters & Shooters. "That little Mia has no idea the torture we endured under Ms. Westwood. Was she Russian?"

"She wasn't Russian!" I lean forward with a laugh. "She was just old-school."

Logan was supposed to help me with the recipe tonight,

but at the last minute he got all mysterious, saying he had a big surprise for us. Then he took off in Zane's Jeep.

"What do you think that old bat would've said if you'd started crying and said you didn't think you were good enough?"

"Oh, man." I shake my head, picking up a spoon to scoop the middle out of an avocado. "She'd have probably said something like if I thought that, then I probably *wasn't* good enough."

"Then she'd have made you do seventeen minutes of pirouettes."

"Until someone cut those red shoes off my feet," I cry, quickly slicing a plum tomato and tossing it into the bowl.

"God, that story." Craig does a full-body shiver. "What was wrong with Hans Christian Andersen?"

"He was Danish."

"The old ways weren't the best ways." Thomas leans his head in as he passes us on the way to the stove. "You did the right thing for that little girl, and *you* were better than good enough."

"Thank you, Thomas." I call after him.

I grab the kosher salt, a lemon, a lime, a pinch of cilantro, then it's time for the star ingredient.

"Trinidad Scorpion." My eyes widen as I lift the round, red pepper.

It's about the size of a small tomato with wrinkled skin and a pointed tip.

"Where did you find that thing?" Craig lifts the bar towel over his nose and mouth.

"Crosby, Mississippi—can you believe it?" I slide on my gloves and grab a knife. "These little guys are almost as hot as the Carolina Reaper, but it's a sweet heat that builds and builds and builds…"

Allie breezes into the room, scooping up her apron. "Ooo, who's this little guy?"

She steps over and leans in to watch as I slice off a long sliver. "Trinidad Scorpion."

Her eyes widen. "What's the warning tonight?"

"This one's wild." I carefully chop the sliver into tiny pieces before transferring a teaspoon into the bowl of guacamole. "If you took a bite of this raw, you'd have like five seconds of happy thoughts before your whole mouth went numb, then you'd start sweating and hiccuping uncontrollably."

"Hiccuping!" Craig yells from where he's standing beside Thomas now. "Put that thing in the freezer before Logan gets back and eats it."

"I'm pretty sure he knows better than to eat anything in this kitchen without asking." I walk over to start another batch of the scorpion guacamole. "I think the avocado oil will make it a little less potent, but we've got to warn people just because they don't feel it right away, don't eat more too fast. Put out plenty of ice cream for them and honey. A teaspoon of honey will neutralize it."

"Gotcha." Allie nods.

"It's an inferno." Craig nods, pulling out his phone. "I've got just the song for it."

"What's this I heard about your ballet star having a meltdown after rehearsals this afternoon?" Allie leans her hip against the table, crossing her arms.

"How did you hear about that?" My eyebrow arches, and I know. "Austin?"

"He was worried about her." She shrugs. "I think he's crushing hard, but Mia is *very* focused on dance schools."

"She's a senior." I wrinkle my nose, returning to the guacamole.

"Is she okay?"

"Yeah, imposter syndrome is a bitch, but I hope I talked her off the ledge. She's so talented." I glance up at my friend. "Austin's actually pretty good himself. He's strong from his football workouts, and he's flexible. Who knew football and ballet went together so well?"

"Anybody who knew your family," Thomas calls from where he's mixing the ground beef.

"Anybody who knew our family, what?" That loud, boisterous voice makes my heart jump… seconds before I'm swept off my feet and over a broad shoulder.

"Garrett!" I squeal, holding the hot pepper by its stem and away from my face. "What are you doing here?"

Allie's eyes are wide, and she grabs a bowl, running to hold it out for me to pass her the killer fruit.

"Surprise!" Logan says with a laugh. "I managed to get this idiot to fly home for the holiday."

Garrett sits me on top of the metal table. "What else was I going to do? All my people are down here now."

"I'm so glad you're home." Joy surges in my chest, and I'm smiling so hard my cheeks ache. Just as fast, I point at him. "Don't touch anything! I'm making guacamole with Trinidad Scorpion pepper, and it won't just melt your face off—"

"Uncontrollable hiccups," Craig says as he walks past in a blond wig and Santa hat.

"Craig, my man!" Garrett grabs him around the waist, lifting him off the ground in a hug.

"Put me down, Beast!"

"Uncle Grizzlaaay!" That little voice makes him laugh, and he drops Craig before taking a knee.

Kimmie Joy runs straight to him, and he throws her into the air. "How's my little Peanut doing?"

"I'm a mouse!" she squeals, and he swings her around onto his back.

"A mouse?"

"Dylan has all the kids in *The Nutcracker*." Jack enters the room, patting his brother on the back before shaking his hand. "She convinced Mrs. Laverne to be the lady with the big skirt, and all the kindergarteners are mice."

"You put the principal in the show?" Garrett cocks a brow at me.

"She asked me to teach ballet." I shrug. "It was the least I could do!"

"It's going to be so cute!" Allie coos.

"Rehearsals have been hilarious, that's for sure," I say, "But everybody loves it when the little kids run around and shake their tails."

I carefully put the pepper in a plastic bag and label it with a *TS* before tossing it into the freezer and disposing of my gloves. Then I step to the sink and rub coconut oil all over my fingers, hands, and nails before washing them with dish soap.

"Let's get out there and do this," I call, glancing at the clock.

"Best welcome home party ever." Garrett laughs, grabbing a blond wig and Santa hat and wrapping an apron around his waist like a dress. "What's our song, Cray?"

"You'll see."

They head out, and I hang back when Logan levels his eyes on me. He only has a slight limp when he walks to where I'm standing by the table. "Good surprise?"

"Second-best Christmas present ever." I place my hands on his shoulders.

His chin lifts, and he frowns. "What's the first?"

"Having you here with me." I stretch higher to kiss his lips. "Seeing you smile like you're happy and not pissed at the world."

"I'm very happy to be here with you."

He leans down to seal his lips to mine, and I part them, curling my tongue with his. A groan is in his throat, and he pulls back. "Do we have to stay for the Dare dish?"

Craig's voice on the mic reaches us. "Dylan's got a special surprise for you all this Christmas. Get out here, Danger!"

I look over my shoulder and back at him, giving him a little smile. "Sounds like a yes."

Warmth is in his eyes as he looks down at me. "We can't keep your fans waiting. Except that little Oliver Duck kid. I think he has his eye on my girl."

"Oliver Duck." I shake my head, laughing. "That kid is something else."

Our fingers are entwined as we exit the kitchen, going into

the full dining hall that's decorated with colorful Christmas lights, balsam wreaths, and red cinnamon candles.

Everyone is dressed up in ugly Christmas sweaters, and I see Rachel sitting in a booth with Miss Gina. I wave at her, and she smiles and waves back, leaning down to whisper in Miss Gina's ear.

Zane stands at the back wall, not too far from where she sits, doing his very best to act like he doesn't notice her. He's in a navy sweater and jeans. His square jaw is set, and his arms are crossed. Still, I catch his blue eyes drifting to where they're sitting.

Kimmie is on the bar with Garrett and Craig, and the waitresses are wearing headbands with reindeer antlers and lights on them.

Allie reads off the warnings for Trinidad scorpion. "As always, water or beer will not put out the fire. We have vanilla ice cream and honey stations if you need them in the back."

The lights change to red and green, and Craig hits the button. A driving baseline starts right away, and I laugh when I recognize the intro to "Disco Inferno."

Logan has me around the waist, and we start to sway. Customers line up, doing funny disco moves as they make their way to the front to try out the fiery guacamole.

It's a hilarious, Christmas dance party, and Logan leans down to my ear. "Will you get on the bar for me?"

The hunger in his tone sends a flush of heat from stomach to my core. My nipples tighten, and I turn to face him. I'd never danced sexy, until I started dating a football star hotter than every pepper on the Scoville scale.

Rocking my hips, I shimmy, pointing to him with a naughty grin as I make my way to the bar. Everyone's dancing, and I'm about to hop up beside my big brother when the back door opens.

Two men enter the restaurant frowning, and all my sexy thoughts freeze in my chest.

Chapter 29

Logan

GARRETT HOPS OFF THE BAR WITH A HEAVY THUD. HE WHIPS OFF the wig and apron, and his voice is a low growl. "What the fuck is he doing here?"

My brow lowers and adrenaline surges through my veins when I turn to see Davis Kent standing in the back of the room with his arms crossed.

He's dressed in his usual khakis and light blue golf shirt—in the middle of December—and standing right next to him is someone I've been waiting to see again. Peter Krall.

Instinctively, my hands fist at my sides. My jaw is tight, and I step in front of Dylan as if I'll shield her from these bastards. I'm struggling with the urge to wipe the floor with their asses.

"I think we need to take these losers to the parking lot." Jack's voice surprises me, and I turn to see my former football hero with fire blazing in his eyes.

"Are we doing this?" Zane steps up beside him.

Craig is off the bar at once. "Not without me!"

I've never been in a gang, but I understand the appeal now that I have four men at my side all thinking the same thing.

"Wait!" Dylan's voice is worried. "Don't… It's Christmas."

"Too late for that, Sis." Garrett's eyes are leveled on Davis and Peter. "These assholes came here looking for trouble, and we're going to help them find it."

"Logan?" Dylan puts her hand on my arm. "You're still injured."

The worry in her voice twists my stomach, but I can't let these guys walk.

I put my hand on her cheek, slicing my thumb across her bottom lip. "Don't worry, babe. We'll just have a little meeting of the minds."

"In the parking lot?" Her brown eyes are round, and I lean down to kiss her lips briefly.

She reaches up to touch my face, and I see the leather bracelet on her wrist. *Mine* is stamped on the side, and defending her honor is the only thing on my mind.

"This won't take long." I nod to where Allie is in the middle of the girls scooping up guacamole and watching us. "Take care of your people."

She doesn't go to her friend, but I can't wait any longer.

I rejoin the guys as we walk to where Davis is glaring at us with a disgusted expression, and Krall has his eyes leveled on me with something like hatred. As if he has a right.

"Hello, Davis." Jack takes the lead. "What brings you here with this guy?"

"Hello, Jack." I'm ready to slap the smug smile off his punk-ass face. "My friend Pete here wanted to know where he might find your sister's new boyfriend. I told him I knew right where to go."

"Let's take this outside," Garrett growls, seeming to grow larger.

Davis blows air through his lips. "You think I'm stupid enough to go to the parking lot with you, Garrett?"

"No." Garrett spits out the words on a taunting laugh. "I think you're way stupider than that."

"What do you want, Peter?" I'm working hard to keep my tone level.

"We have a beef now." This guy's a defensive lineman, and he's as big as Garrett with light brown hair shaved close to his head and dark brown eyes.

"Oh, yeah?" Standing taller, I'm mad enough to whip his ass by myself. "How do you figure that?"

He leans down in my face. "You ended my career."

A meaty hand fists the front of his shirt, shoving him back. "You got what you deserved, asshole," Garrett seethes. "You tried to kill my best friend."

"Fucking bullshit. I only broke your streak, *Lightning*."

The sarcasm in his tone is like a match to the gasoline in my veins.

Jack must see I'm about to go off, and he quickly steps into the mix. "Outside. Now."

Thomas has joined the group, but Zane puts his hand on his arm. "Stay here, friend."

The older man's dark brow furrows. "You might need help."

Zane nods at the girls. "We need you to watch over Dylan and Kimmie if things go sideways. You don't need to be in this."

Thomas's lips tighten as if he'll argue, but he glances at the five of us and chuckles. "Let me know when you need the shovel."

Davis has both hands up. "I didn't agree to take it outside."

Zane's eyes flash fire, and he steps closer. "Then you shouldn't have opened your lying mouth about my sister."

He grabs Davis's shoulder, turning him and shoving him through the door. We're all out the door, our boots scuffing against the gravel parking lot.

"I've been waiting for this." Craig hustles up, getting in the rich prick's face. "I've been ready to kick your ass since you put your hands on her."

The match is struck, and my fury explodes. "What did you just say?"

"Give me a break. I grabbed her fucking arm." Davis rolls his eyes, blowing air through his lips. "She wouldn't listen, so I had to—"

My fist slams into his mouth before he even finishes speaking. He takes a staggering step back, then drops to one knee. Craig rushes forward and hits his shoulders hard with both hands, sending Davis all the way onto his back with an *Oof.*

"What?" Craig yells in his face. "I only pushed you down. Give me a break!"

Craig pulls back his foot, ready to kick him in the stomach, but I reach down and grab Davis under the arms instead. I stand him on his feet so I can punch his lights out again.

My fist is raised, but he holds up both hands, ducking and whining. "Don't hit me again!"

Blood covers his mouth and chin, and my fingers itch to pulverize this sniveling coward. Tension tweaks all my muscles, and only one thing is strong enough to hold me back—Dylan and Christmas and not spending the weekend in jail.

Instead I shake him hard, throwing him on the ground again. "Don't show your fucking face here ever, or it'll be the last time. Hear me?"

"Yes," he whines, curling into a ball.

Jack steps up beside me, and he reaches down to grab Davis by the collar, jerking him off the ground with his fist raised. "You hurt my sister, *and* you lied about her to *TMI*?"

"No, man!" Davis holds up both hands over his head, whining. "It was a misunderstanding. Just let me go home. I won't come back."

"You're fucking right you won't." He shoves him back hard onto the gravel, then he kicks him in the stomach.

Reaching out, I grab his shoulder. A small crowd is forming, phones are coming out, and I'm the only one who won't suffer for what's happening here. As head coach at the high school, Jack could lose his job.

"Go on back inside. I'll finish up here."

He's breathing hard, looking down at that fucking prick on the ground, but I manage to get him to turn. I grab Craig's arm and pull him over.

"You two go back inside. Take care of the girls."

"Take care of him." Zane nods to where Garrett and Peter are circling each other behind us with their fists raised.

"Shit like that doesn't go unanswered by me." Garrett lands a punch to the side of Peter's face, but the big guy only takes a half step back.

"Then you'd better have more than that in you." Peter swings, but I'm there to block it with my forearm.

"I've got more." Not wasting a beat, I step forward quickly, pulling with my stomach and using all my weight to drive an uppercut straight into the bottom of his jaw.

His teeth rattle and he snorts a grunt. I actually see his eyes roll before he staggers to the side. Garrett is right there with a finishing jab to the chest, and the asshole falls like a tree, a knockout punch.

We stand over him, breathing hard when red and blue lights flash through the trees. A police car is headed this way, and in an instant, the crowd starts to disperse.

Behind us, Davis has crawled to his Rover and is now dragging himself inside it.

Garrett grips my shoulder, shaking me and laughing. "What the fuck was *that*?"

I look at the Goliath on the ground. "College boxing."

"Boxing?" His voice is loud, and I can tell he's happy. "What the hell?"

"I took it as an elective. Probably the smartest thing I ever did."

"Man, that felt good. He hurt the whole team with that tackle."

"I'm sorry." I hadn't considered how we lost the game, and with me off the team, they've been struggling to replace us.

"Whatever, we're big boys." He grips my shoulder. "It's the fucking holidays. Let's get inside."

Garrett and I hustle into the restaurant where the party is still going strong. A brassy version of "Sleigh Ride" is playing, and everyone is dancing.

The place seems oblivious to what just happened in the parking lot. I don't see Craig, Jack, or Zane, but when Dylan's eyes meet mine, she heads straight to me.

"Allie took the guys to the kitchen. Oh—your hand!" She lifts my swollen hand, pulling me in that direction.

"I'm ready to dance!" Garrett is on the bar at once, dancing with the waitresses.

Kimmie jumps up and down beside him, and he lifts her onto his hip. We pass Craig on the way to the kitchen, and he's in his wig again looking for all the world like nothing just happened.

"I'll deal with the sheriff," he says as we pass, and Dylan nods.

In the kitchen, Thomas has a bowl of ice on the large silver table. Dylan leads me to it, wrapping my hand in a thin towel before dunking it in the ice bath.

"Not too swollen." Jack inspects the damage. "I doubt you have a fracture."

"I only punched the soft spots." I glance at Dylan. "You didn't tell me he hurt you."

"It was only one time." Her lips are tight as she dries my hand. "It was after we broke up, and he came here to talk…"

"The marks on your arm?" I remember her playing it off that night in the kitchen so long ago.

"You remember?" Her brow furrows, and I reach for her, pulling her to my chest.

"Don't ever hide something like that from me again." I kiss the top of her head.

"You should've seen your man here, D." Garrett blusters into the kitchen with a beer in his hand and a smile on his face. "Dropped Krall like a rock, and from half a foot below."

"Look at your hand!" She grabs Garrett's fist and puts it in the ice.

"I'll be fine." He looks up at me. "We got him, bro. He won't mess with you again."

"I hope not."

"If he does, we'll be ready for him." Garrett nods around the room at the five faces smiling back at us. "The Bradford boys."

"Does that include me?" I tease.

"Hell, yeah, it does, and we take care of our own."

Christmas is almost here, and my knee is getting stronger. My physical therapist prescribed walking, so I'm strolling along the bay in the direction of the old cinder-block radio station.

A cool breeze coats my face, but it's nothing like the winters up north. I'm far away from that level of cold these days.

The resident flock of pelicans glides silently in their *V* formation, dipping their beaks into the water, and it reminds me of being on a team.

For so long, my life has been about football. It was where I went to escape the loneliness of my home. It was where I went to find a family.

But football ends, guys retire, and I've grown older. I think about that night at Galileo's last July, when I was disillusioned with everything and so frustrated with my prospects.

Then Garrett brought me here.

Watching the games from this distance, sitting beside Dylan as she hides every time her brother gets tackled, I think about going back for a tenth season. I think about leaving Dylan behind and returning to the days of phone sex and hand signals and stolen weekends.

She's in even less of a position to move to New York, and I wouldn't ask her to do it anyway, not after seeing her with her students. Teaching brings her joy and healing. Her family and her support network are here.

What about my support network? My dad said I should go for the MVP trophy and retire. It was his goal for me. I went into this season with my sights set on proving I was more than just a cog in the wheel, a player who'd better get the fucking pigskin across the line.

Breaking records and proving I was still relevant was my goal, and even if my season was cut short, they'll be talking about what I did and sharing my highlight reels for years to come, for better or worse.

Most of it's better, but last week I stumbled across another replay of the hip-drop tackle that landed me in the hospital. Commentators debated the merits of banning Krall from the league. My injury didn't end my career, they'd argued, so was it fair to end another player's?

My jaw tensed in anger, but it got me thinking about how next season I'll start from a place of recovery. All the records I've set will be overshadowed by my comeback, and everyone will be watching to see what happens.

It's possible I'll make it back to where I was before I was injured, but it's more likely my days of being the fastest wide receiver have passed. There's no guarantee I won't be injured again, and another injury could be worse.

Walking up to the small building, I study it for a few moments. A truck is parked in the back lot, and a man is inside behind the desk.

It's easy to see the new path in front of me. It's not complicated, and I don't hesitate.

I walk straight to the door and open it.

Chapter 30

Dylan

B Y THE NIGHT OF THE CHRISTMAS SHOW, EVERYONE IN TOWN KNOWS what happened in the parking lot of the restaurant, and everyone in town seems to have taken a vow of silence.

A few videos have popped up on social media, but they're shot from behind the guys. All we can see is Logan's prize-winning uppercut and Davis crawling to his car like the shitty coward he is. He won't be back, and I'm quietly pleased by how the boys closed the book on that situation.

When I peek through the curtain at the side of the stage, I see my brothers, Allie, Rachel, and Miss Gina all sitting together in the seats I reserved for them in the middle section. Garrett had to fly back for Christmas Day games and to get ready for the playoffs.

It's time to begin, and I step away, clasping my hands together as Mrs. Laverne is wheeled out in her giant "dress" with all the little mice beneath her skirt. It's a modification of the Mother Ginger role because none of them are dancers.

The kindergarteners all run out, grab hands, and skip around in a circle while the high school principal waves and blows kisses at everyone. Then the little mice line up in front of her and drop onto all fours, stick up their booties and happily wag their tails.

Everyone laughs, and they jump up and circle again before going back under her skirt and rolling her off the stage again. I can hear their giggles and squealing from the opposite side of the stage, and the audience claps and cheers.

Up next is "The Waltz of the Flowers." My entire first-year ballet class does a beautiful, modified version of the classic waltz, and to my relief, no one falls and no costumes malfunction.

Josh and Sally go next, doing their Mirlitons dance. It's not as intricate as Mia and Austin's piece, but it's impressive enough to get a hearty applause and whistles.

My heart squeezes as the curtain sweeps closed, and Mia and Austin take their place for the final dance of the evening. She looks at me, and I nod, swallowing my nerves.

The curtain rises, and the violins begin. They move across the stage with confidence, executing every step with perfect timing. Mia is graceful and controlled, and Austin watches her, reading her movements and anticipating her steps.

"They're as good as we were." Craig's whisper in my ear makes me jump.

"I think I was holding my breath." I laugh, putting my hand on my chest. "He's nowhere near as good as you were, but he's good enough."

"At four months in?" Craig cocks his head at me. "I'd say he's very good."

We watch as they reach the final steps—the three little hops, arabesque, and the lift. They turn, and Austin lowers her for the final plié and the bow.

The auditorium bursts into cheers, with everyone rising to their feet. I jump up and down clapping.

Tears are in my eyes as I grab Craig's arm. "Tell me we got that on video!"

"Of course." He wraps an arm around me in a hug.

The dancers all return to the stage for their bows, then Mia and Austin motion for me to join them. I almost feel guilty walking out there, like I'm taking away from their spotlight.

As soon as I emerge from behind the curtain, a low voice breaks into a yell, and I duck. Covering my face with my hands, I laugh as I see Logan on his feet, clapping as hard as he can like my biggest cheerleader.

Holding up my hand, I cross my thumb and index finger, giving him our signal, and he does it right back to me.

Mia's mother is in the wings, crying and mouthing *Thank you*, and I put my arms around my young dancers as we all bow together. Mrs. Laverne pats my back, and Kimmie Joy runs to jump into my arms.

The curtains fall, and Logan was right. I took the first, trembling step. I was brave enough to face my fears, and love has healed the loss.

The Christmas tree glows with white twinkle lights, and candles are on the hearth above the fireplace. Cinnamon and pine scent the air, and I'm sitting on the floor facing Logan like we did that night on the beach so long ago.

I remember him holding my hands and saying he wanted me to be his girl. He wanted me to be on the sidelines cheering for him. It's a treasured memory I replayed in my heart so many times when we were apart.

"I was so proud of you tonight." Logan takes my hands in both of his, and I gaze deeply into his blue eyes. "Those kids were really good, and they looked like they were having fun, too."

My heart squeezes, and I reach for his cheek, leaning forward to kiss his soft lips. "Thank you. I'm not sure I'd have done it without your encouragement."

"I have two gifts for you this year."

"What?" My eyebrows shoot up. "I only got you one."

"You shouldn't have gotten me any."

"But I did." Pulling the small bag from my pocket, I take his hand. "I was walking by the bay and this girl was selling handmade leather jewelry."

He exhales a soft laugh. "Hey, I know that girl."

Taking the chunky, dark leather band from the pouch, I slide it onto the third finger of his left hand. "I got her to stamp it with a ghost pepper here." Then I turn it. "And here it says, *Mine.*"

Lifting his hand, he turns it, inspecting the ring. "I like this a lot."

He cups my face in his hands and pulls me closer for a kiss, parting my lips and sweeping his tongue inside to find mine. The touch sends heat burning to my core, and I exhale a whimper.

When he lifts his head, his eyes hold mine with so much intensity. "I was going to wait and do this second, but I can't."

My brow furrows. "Okay?"

"I love you, Dylan. I've said it before, but every time I say it, with every day that passes, it grows stronger." Lowering his hands, he shakes his head. "I didn't even think that was possible the first time I said it, but it's true. You're the best thing that's ever come into my life, and I never want to spend another day without you in it."

A knot rises into my throat. "What are you saying?"

His large hand slips into his pocket, and I can't breathe as he takes out a small, robin's-egg blue pouch with the words *Tiffany & Co.* stamped on it. My fingers tremble as I watch him pull it open and slide out a sparkling, princess-cut diamond with a brilliant pavé diamond band.

Tears are in my eyes as he lifts my finger so gently. "Will you marry me, Dylan Bradford? I talked to Jack, and he said it was a good idea. Garrett wanted to know why I waited so long. Zane said we make a good match—"

"You asked all my brothers?" I exhale a laugh.

My heart is beating so fast, I can't breathe right, and a tear falls onto my cheek.

His brow furrows. "I know they're important to you. I didn't have a chance to talk to Hendrix, but I didn't want to wait any longer."

Leaning forward, I place my hands on the sides of his neck. "You don't have to talk to anybody—my answer is yes!"

A straight white smile breaks across his gorgeous face, and that dimple I love appears. "That's my girl."

He slides the ring onto my finger, and I hold it to my chest, looking into his eyes. "I love you, Logan."

Strong arms go around my waist, and he drags me onto his lap. He kisses the side of my neck, moving his lips higher to my ear and leaving a trail of fire in their wake.

"My wife." It's a low rumble.

My eyes slide closed, and I lift my chin as I exhale a delighted sigh. "How can two words fill my entire body with so much joy?"

"It only takes one word for me."

Looking down, I hold his cheeks in my hands. "What's that?"

"Mine."

Our mouths seal together, then they open and our tongues curl. His cock hardens beneath me, and I'm ready to lose these clothes and do more than kiss. "Let's take this party to our bedroom."

"Shit, I wanted to take you right here in front of the fireplace and the Christmas tree."

Dropping my forehead to his, I close my eyes, wrinkling my nose. "Zane would kill us."

"I have one last gift to give you."

"I can't imagine anything that could top what you've already given me."

He takes out his phone, taps the screen several times, and he hands it to me. "How about this?"

Scooting back, I sit on my butt in front of him, studying the bold-type headline. *Her Feet are Bare, but Her Heart is GOLD!!!*

Frowning, I look up at him confused. "What...?"

"Read it." He nods at the device.

Scanning the story quickly, I see it's a follow-up to the original article about me by Callum Cross.

New information from model-turned-influencer Natalia van Norse sheds light on Logan Murphy's mystery lady, and she's a country girl with a Heart of Gold...

It goes on to describe how my background as a "rising star" in the ballet world was cut short by a career-ending injury. It details how I took care of my brothers after our parents died within months of each other. It even talks about my current work with the high school kids, and how I'm...

"Helping the daughter of a poor single mother achieve her dreams?" I read it out loud, lifting my eyes to Logan's. "How would Natalia know about Mia?"

His eyebrows rise, and he twists his lips with a shrug. "She's an influencer. I guess she realized she hadn't done her research before she ran her big mouth the first time."

I hiccup a breath, placing my hand over my lips. "You told her." Energy burns in my stomach, and I read the final quote. "She's the one person who understands best what he's facing. They have a lot more in common than we knew."

"That's more like it." His tone is protective and satisfied, and possibly a bit smug.

I don't even know what to say.

"You made it right." My chest surges, and when I blink, a tear hits my cheek. "No one's ever done something like this for me."

He reaches up to cup my face again, sliding the moisture off my cheek. "Well, get ready. I'm going to do more than that for you, Dylan. You'll never suffer for being mine again."

I dive forward, wrapping my arms around his neck. "I love you, Logan. You've only ever made me happy."

"That's all I want. Forever."

Cupping my cheek in his hand, he leans down to kiss me again. It's strong and possessive, and the start of something real. Then he lifts me off my feet, carrying me to the bedroom.

As we kiss and touch and slowly shed our clothes, I'm lost in the sensations of his body against mine. I'm flooded with all the memories of our first days, fearfully sharing our dreams and fears.

He kisses his way down my chest to my stomach, and as desire floods my veins, I moan and sigh and think of the first time he covered my pussy with his mouth. My entire body came alive.

"Oh, God!" I cry out as my body tightens with orgasm and my thighs start to shake.

"That's right, baby, come for me." He gently bites the side of my stomach, and I yelp. "I love this body."

He kisses his way up to my breasts, cupping them in his hands and kissing, sucking, circling my hardened nipples with his tongue. Rising all the way, he covers my mouth with his, curling his tongue with mine.

My knees rise, and we both groan with relief as he thrusts deep into my slippery core. His hips rock fast, and I'm moving with him. It's cold outside, but it's hot as Pepper X in this bed.

Orgasm surges again and again like the waves on the sea, and I cry out as he goes deeper, hitting that sweet spot in my body.

He's thrusting fast. Our bodies are slippery with sweat, and I bite his shoulder when the pleasure grows too intense. Salt is on my tongue and he groans, stiffening and shuddering as he finishes between my thighs.

His body trembles, and my legs wrap around him as he holds me firmly, filling me, making us one.

I tried to build a wall against him before I ever knew who

he was, but he broke through my guard rails. He helped me face my fears and showed me how not to be afraid. He taught me to be strong, and when I couldn't, when the hits were too much, he stood up and fought for me.

He's my dream come true, my strong defender, and the way we touch fits all the puzzle pieces into place.

Epilogue

Logan

Two months later...

NEON LIGHTS SHINE THROUGH THE THEATER IN THE MANHATTAN Center in Midtown. A crowd of celebrities has turned out for the annual league honors, and I cover Dylan's small hand with mine as we sit together in the balcony.

She's beautiful in a red strapless dress that hugs her curves and hangs in a flowing skirt to her muscular calves. I'm so glad she finally agreed to come with me, even if it was pretty last minute.

Garrett called and insisted we attend, even though I'm completely out of the running. He guaranteed me I wouldn't have to watch Ricky win the MVP trophy, and he threw in a carrot for Dylan—their brother Hendrix is also here.

Once she agreed to come, I gave in and said yes. The carrot for me was being able to stay in my apartment with all the privacy features I installed after our last encounter with the gossip sites.

Now we're in our seats watching highlight reels and listening as award after award is announced.

Lifetime achievement winners are assigned along with the Man of the Year award, whatever that means.

I slide my palm down the front of my charcoal-gray Armani suit. The ring Dylan gave me at Christmas never leaves my finger, and her sparkling engagement ring is on hers.

The second *TMI* article put an end to all the bad-mouthing and dragging her reputation. Once the list of everything she's overcome and achieved became public, followed by how faithfully she stood by me during my recovery, anyone who dares to dunk on her comes off looking like the biggest asshole in the business.

Word of how we handled Krall in the parking lot also trickled through the media. It was all speculation, of course, since nothing could be verified on tape or video.

We have never addressed the rumors, but after the guy who cut my record-setting run short with an illegal tackle was found with his clock cleaned in the parking lot of the Bradford family restaurant, they put two and two together.

"How much longer?" I shift in my seat, clapping when a friend from another team wins the Comeback Player of the Year award.

"Too long," Hendrix quips from where he sits on Dylan's other side.

His date is an actress from LA, but Dylan is so excited to see her brother. She holds his hand and leans her head on his shoulder, and it's one of the few saving graces of the night.

Hendrix is a cocky little shit, but he still has that Bradford heart—even if he tries to hide it behind a mask of celebrity. He's wearing a sharkskin suit, and he has his championship ring on his finger. I'm surprised he didn't roll up in his tricked-out Range Rover, but he used a car service like the rest of us.

Then the stage explodes with neon lights, and a new video begins. Shifting in my seat, a surge of nerves hits me when I realize they're playing my highlight reel from the past season.

"He set record after record until he was unfairly taken down at the pinnacle of his success," the narrator says, and they show that fucking replay of the hip-drop tackle.

Even though my knee is fully healed, Dylan's eyes are fixed on her hands in her lap, which tremble as she moves her diamond ring around on her finger.

Reaching over, I cover her hand with mine, and when she looks up at me, I lean over to kiss her forehead. "We made it, babe. Don't be afraid."

She nods, and I've already made my decision. I've just been waiting for the right time to tell her.

The video ends, and a comedian I like walks to the microphone to announce the offensive player of the year award.

He hesitates, then says my name, and the entire place erupts with applause and cheers. Everyone is on their feet, and Garrett stands beside me, clapping.

I look up at him with a wry smile. "You could've warned me, bro."

I grasp his elbow, and he pulls me in for a hug. "Why would I ruin the surprise?"

Turning back, I catch Dylan's hand and give her a kiss before heading down to the stage, passing players I've encountered on and off the field all wishing me well.

Ricky stops me on the floor, catching my hand in a firm shake. "I'm ready to take you on again next year!"

I nod, not stopping as I hustle up the steps on my fully healed knee to the man holding my trophy. He passes it over and congratulates me, then steps aside for me to take the mic.

It takes a bit for the applause to die down, and as it does, I try to pull together something of a speech in my mind. I start by thanking my coaches and my fellow teammates. I thank the league and the other players who've sent encouragement.

"This is a big surprise." I scratch my forehead with my thumb. "I guess I have to thank Garrett for getting my ass here or I'd have missed it."

That elicits modest laughter, and I wait.

"Finally, I'd like to thank my fiancée Dylan Bradford for standing by me through all of this, even though she insisted she only dated golfers…" More modest laughter. "I somehow managed to change her mind, and I want to thank her for her bravery and her unflinching support through the hardest times."

Clearing my throat, I look up to see she's on the big screen smiling and tapping tears out of her pretty amber eyes. Warmth surges in my chest, and I realize the time is now.

"I hadn't planned to announce this yet, but after my accomplishments this year, I've decided to make it my last. I'm retiring from the league at the end of this season." A collective gasp sweeps the crowd, but I don't stop. "I've had a great run. I've made some great friends, and now it's time to move on to my next great adventure. Thank you so much for this, and I'll see you soon."

I hold up my hand, waving at the crowd, who are on their feet again clapping. Ricky is frowning at me, but when I look out and see Dylan's smiling face, I know I've made the right decision for us.

"You said I didn't warn you. You could've warned me!" Garrett's voice is loud over the noise of the bar.

"You?" Dylan pushes his arm. "He didn't even tell me!"

"I thought you were going to win the MVP before you retired," Garrett complains.

"That actually wasn't my idea." I lean back, taking a sip of my whiskey. "I realized it was what my dad said I should do, and again, I was busting my ass hoping to hear him say he was proud of me."

"I'm sorry." Dylan's bottom lip pouts, and I lean forward to kiss her.

"It's okay, babe. I decided to stop living my life to please him when I met you."

"But are you sure you're ready to retire?" Her brow wrinkles.

"I've never been more sure of anything—except you." I pull her to me. "It's given me a whole new perspective, then Miss Gina took it a step further."

A smile curls her lips. "Then it's a good thing. Miss Gina always knows."

"She does." I nod, leaning down to kiss her and thinking about our future.

Flying back to Newhope after the ceremony, Dylan curls up beside me on the small sofa. Her head is on my shoulder, and she takes my large hand in hers, sliding the leather ring around my finger.

"I'm sorry you didn't win the MVP award." Leaning her head back, she looks up at me. "It sounds corny, but you'll always be my MVP."

Smiling, I kiss her lips slowly, tracing my tongue along hers. She tastes like wine and chocolate, and she smells like lavender and vanilla. She fits perfectly in my arms, and every part of my being is satisfied.

"It's not corny." My voice is warm. "It's what I want to be."

She blinks a few times, her soft brow furrowing. "I hope you didn't retire just for me, although I'm glad you did."

Tightening my arm around her shoulder, I hug her closer. "I did it for us. I've achieved everything I wanted. I set records that will stand for a while, and I was recognized for it." I glance at the trophy lying on the seat. "I didn't want to take the risk of another bad tackle, and I didn't want to go another season separated from you like we did last year. I chose you, but I also chose us."

By May, Dylan wraps up her first year of teaching. Mia got invitations from her top three ballet programs, including the American Ballet Theatre in New York. At her graduation, she made a special speech, where she thanked my girl for helping her get there, for being an inspiration, and for showing her what it means to be strong.

I couldn't have said it better myself.

Walking through the house before heading to the restaurant, where everyone's preparing for another wild Dare night, I take a minute to call my dad.

"This is unexpected." His low voice is surprised, and I hear his hesitation.

By contrast, I'm fully confident in what I'm about to say.

"I'd like to start by apologizing for not being ready to forgive you at the hospital last year. Thank you for being worried about me and for making the effort to extend an olive branch."

"Okay…" He takes a breath. "Apology accepted. And congratulations on winning player of the year."

"Thanks." This is feeling better already, and with a smile, I say a silent thank-you to Miss Gina for insisting it's never too late to forgive.

"I'd like to work with you, Dad—just not in the way you described. There's an old radio station here, and I just closed on the paperwork to purchase it."

"You did?" More surprise.

"It's a good station with a strong AM signal. I'd like to affiliate with your network and use it to broadcast interviews with local sports heroes and celebrities in the region. We could do some sports talk and basically see where it goes."

He doesn't answer, so I finish. "I think it's a good idea. Don't you?"

"You're certainly qualified." Hearing him say that, after how long he dismissed my degree, goes a long way to erase the bitterness in my chest.

"I'll write up my proposal and send it to you."

"I look forward to reading it."

We disconnect, and I nod. It's the first step in our next great adventure, but first, I have to get down to the restaurant and see what my girl is cooking up for her masochistic, fire-eating fans.

A cheer rises from the group the closer I get, and I hustle the rest of the way. When I open the door, I'm confused to see Craig standing in the center of the room holding the mic like he was caught mid-announcement.

His cheeks are bright pink, and an embarrassed smile is on his face. He covers his eyes with his hand, and a guy I don't recognize pulls him into a big hug before planting a big, sloppy kiss right on his mouth.

"Whoa!" I shout, laughing and clapping along with the entire room.

Allie grabs the mic from Craig's hand. "I'm not sure if tonight's recipe will top that on the Scoville scale, but we'll see!"

Dylan stands in the doorway to the kitchen with her hands on her cheeks, and she's smiling as well, her eyes misty.

I hustle over to her, pulling her close. "What the heck did I miss?"

"Closeted Clint just professed his love for Craig in front of God and everybody! Isn't it wonderful?" She throws her arms around my neck, and I lift her off her feet.

"Absolutely, and you're going to have to catch me up. Who's Closeted Clint?"

"He's going to be the florist for our wedding!" She kisses my lips. "Now help me bring out the rest of these fried habanero poppers."

Allie announces the usual warning, and as soon as she's done, the PA system starts blasting "Hot Stuff" by Donna Summer.

It's an oldie but a goodie, and as the girls dance on the bar, my beautiful fiancée kicks off her flip-flops and hops up there with them.

Her eyes are on mine as she rotates her hips, and her long hair dances in waves around her shoulders. Her red toenails taunt me, and my fingers curl when she shakes her cute little round ass in those cutoff blue jeans.

I'm the luckiest guy in the world getting to spend the rest of my life with her. She's barefoot and beautiful, a little piece of spicy-pepper heaven. She's dangerous and everything I'll ever need, and together, we're the family I've been searching for my whole life.

Thank you for reading *The Way We Touch*!
Be sure to download your Free Bonus Scene here:

Up Next is The Way We Play!

Since his career-ending injury, Zane Bradford doesn't need anyone, especially not sage-burning, yoga practicing, massage therapist Rachel Wells. Their banter, their enemies-to-lovers vibes, their spicy sports romance is going to curl your toes and warm your heart...
Available in Kindle Unlimited, paperback, and on Audio!

Learn about all of my books on TiaLouise.com/Books, including a downloadable Reading Guide.

The Way We Play
The Bradford Boys, Book 2

*He's a grumpy, retired kicker who says he only breaks things.
I'm a thirty-year-old virgin with something he can break (and I
don't mean my heart)...*

How does one get to be a thirty-year-old virgin?
In my case, start with being risk-averse and cautious, focused
on building your career, then inherit your 12-year-old, special-
needs brother. *Done!*
Zane Bradford appeared at the perfect time.
He takes my brother to equine therapy, he gives me rides to
work, and he rescues me when I collapse in the shower. (*Yes,
he saw me naked.*)
He says he only breaks things, but I only see him fixing
everything. Heck, his *job* is as a repair man.
This grumpy, angry god with lean muscles, silky dark hair,
and ice blue eyes has taken himself out of the game.
But massage therapy is *my job*, and I'm ready to play.

Hello, I'm Zane Bradford, and I break things.
Starting with my little sister's dreams, followed by my football career.
Yes, I'm grumpy and distant; I'm following the script: *No attachments; no one gets hurt.*
Rachel Wells is ruining everything.
She walks into my workplace and argues with me, talks back, defends herself.
She gives me romance books to "improve my mood," and insists on massage therapy to ease my pain.
Chronic pain isn't my problem—she is, with her bright green eyes and sassy attitude.
Then she tells me she's never been kissed. (*What's wrong with the men in Birmingham?*)
The more she tempts me, the more I feel my resolve weakening.
She wants to play, but I'm not going to break.

(THE WAY WE PLAY is a small-town, grumpy-sunshine, sports romance with close proximity, enemies-to-lovers vibes, and a virgin FMC, and an over-protective alpha hero. No cheating. No cliffhanger. No third-act breakup.)

Prologue

Zane

Twelve years ago

"THINK FAST!" THE FOOTBALL FLIES AT MY FACE, BUT I CATCH IT before it bounces off my nose.

I level my gaze on my youngest brother Hendrix, who recently turned eighteen. "Don't do that."

His blue eyes sparkle, and a grin splits his cheeks. "Or what?"

"I'd hate to have to kick your ass on Thanksgiving day right here in front of those girls."

A pair of teenage girls has stopped walking to watch us, and he gives them a wink and a wave. "Happy Thanksgiving, ladies!"

The girls laugh and wave, and I suspect they know him from school, where he's both a senior and the starting running back on the football team. To be fair, everybody knows my brothers and me in this small town, and any time we start playing, people stop to watch.

"Don't taunt the kicker, dumbass." My other younger

brother Garrett grabs him around the shoulders, attempting a headlock. "What makes you think they're looking at you? You're so ugly, the doctor slapped the wrong end."

Hendrix does a quick twist, escaping our oversized brother's grip. "Get off me, sasquatch. You're so ugly, the cat ran away."

"The cat did run away."

"That's why!"

"Lame." Garrett shakes his head as Dylan, our baby sister jumps onto his back, which is quite a feat, considering she's an entire foot shorter than he is.

"I'm on Grizz's team!" She calls out, riding piggy-back out to the waterfront park a few blocks from our house.

It's the first time we've all been together for the holiday in a few years. Our oldest brother Jack is in Texas now, making a name for himself as starting quarterback for the Mustangs. Garrett is building his reputation in Tuscaloosa, and I've been in Baltimore a year as the starting kicker.

It might also be the last time we're together for a while, since Hendrix got an offer from the University of Southern California and Dylan has auditioned for the American Ballet Company in New York. We're all just waiting for that acceptance letter in the mail.

Our parents would be proud, and thinking of them looking down on us makes me nostalgic for the days when they'd be here watching us, Mom playfully scolding and laughing.

We lost them almost four years ago, and I always feel it during the big holidays.

"Hendrix, go long!" Jack shouts.

He takes off like a gazelle, and Garrett stands beside me, watching with Dylan on his back.

"He runs the way you dance." I glance at our baby sister.

Her dark hair is in a high ponytail and her amber eyes sparkle with happiness. She's always happy when we're all together. Losing our parents hit us all hard, but I know Dylan lost the most when we buried our mom.

Dylan was her favorite, but ultimately, we all spoiled our only sister. After four failed attempts, Mom finally got her wish of having a little girl, but with Hendrix only eighteen months old, she was pretty overwhelmed.

She handed Dylan to me in the hospital, and it was all hands on deck.

I'd never seen a baby with such big, dark eyes. She was so little, and her expression was so serious. I didn't know what to do. Mom told me to read to her, and as time passed, it became our thing.

Dylan would sit on my lap and listen so intently. We started with a book about pooping, because Mom said it would help her learn to go potty, then we graduated to books about dancing mice.

When she was four, Dylan announced she was going to be a ballerina just like Angelina, and she started ballet. She was quiet like me, but she worked long and hard to make her dream a reality—just like Jack and Garrett and Hendrix.

I wasn't like them. I didn't sleep with my head on a football as my pillow. I didn't watch every single game all weekend long. I liked the game, but I liked other things, too.

Still, when Dad told me to be a kicker, I said okay. Looking back, I realize Mom probably played a hand in that directive.

Now we're all poised for success, aided in no small party by the celebrity of our football-star father. Walking out to the field now, I can still see Mom on the porch laughing and cheering us on.

She loved her sons, even if they were wild animals, and she loved her only daughter, the light of her life.

"How was that?" Hendrix passes the ball to Jack, clear on the other side of the park, and I think of all of us, he was the most obsessed, the most like our dad. "Jack and I are going to clean the field with you two."

"I'm playing, too!" Dylan skips sideways, holding Garrett's arm.

"You cover Zane, and I'll take butt-face over here." Garrett nods at our brother.

Jack catches the pass easily, and the four of us line up facing each other with Jack a few feet behind Hendrix waiting for the snap.

"You're so fat, you have your own weather system." Garrett loves to trash talk on the line.

"You're so fat…" Hendrix falters, and Garrett straightens waiting.

"What?"

"You're fat."

"Bruh, your burn-game is embarrassing. We gotta work on it before you leave for LA."

"Yeah, but my ball-game is strong. Watch me!" Hendrix makes the snap and shoots straight forward like a rocket.

Garrett's on him, and I cut to the left, getting out of the clump before turning back to where Jack is looking for who's open. Obviously, it's me. Garrett is the best lineman I know, and Dylan's a shrimp.

What I don't expect is her to be keeping pace with me, tracking my moves like a real cornerback. Jack makes the pass, and I reach out, swiping it right out of her hands.

"Dang it!" Dylan jumps up and down with the graceful style of a ballerina.

"Way to hustle." I pass the ball to Jack before patting her shoulder.

"Seven-zero!" Hendrix yells, all fired up. "Nice try, Swan Lake!"

"Don't be hasslin' my girl!" Garrett lifts Dylan off her feet in a hug. "That was a good run, Dee!"

We're back at the line, and this time Jack plays QB for Garrett and Dylan, who takes off running as fast as our younger brother. Hendrix is right on her heels, reaching easily over her head to steal the pass.

She gives him a shove, and he laughs, yelling, "Illegal contact!"

"I was the receiver!" She pushes him again, and he laughs more, running to the center of the field before Garrett stops him.

Dylan's arms are crossed, and she's pouty on her way back to the lineup.

"Don't hate the player, hate the game!" Hendrix does a shuffle step, which makes her sulk more.

"Just because you're all a foot taller than I am."

We line up again, and I'm inclined to give Dylan a break, since she's working so hard. Hendrix knows me too well, and insists I cover Garrett this time.

It's how we spend the afternoon. Until the sun slowly makes its way to the horizon, and the chill in the air grows a touch more distinct. It never gets too cold this far south.

More people have stopped to watch us, clapping and cheering as each side runs it in for the score. Everyone in this small town knew our dad, and they know we're continuing his legacy. I guess it is a little thrill to see us play, even if it's just for fun.

With one goal separating us, our youngest siblings won't stop until we have a clear winner. Garrett manages to keep Hendrix at bay long enough for Dylan to complete a pass and run it in, and she does a little pirouette in the end-zone.

"Excessive celebration—call it back!" Hendrix yells, and Dylan flips him the bird, which makes everyone laugh.

"Looks like y'all need one more player to even things out." Dylan's dance partner Craig runs onto the field.

"It's my boy, Cray!" Garrett immediately grabs him in a bear hug. "Get out here, so we can win this thing!"

I don't bother pointing out Jack. Hendrix, and I make two and a half pro players versus their one college athlete and two dancers.

"We call Jack!" Hendrix yells, and our oldest brother shakes his head, looking down.

"Pretty sure that was always the plan, Einstein." Garrett quips.

"Last play," Jack calls. "It's sudden-death overtime."

As the oldest, Jack slid easily into Dad's role. He has both the patience and the natural leader-quality that makes him a good team captain.

While I tend to be more of a loner, Jack steps up and checks on everybody, making sure we're all okay and giving us advice if we need it.

Hanging back, I watch our small clan laughing and rough-housing as they approach the line, and I think we've made it. I think we're going to be okay.

Just goes to show what I know.

We line up for the snap, and Hendrix and Dylan are practically nose to nose. "Don't go soft on me, Zane."

I shake my head at his ferocity. "It's only a game."

The snap is made, and Jack falls back, his eyes scanning Garret hulking over Hendrix and Dylan skipping around me.

Craig makes a beeline for him, and he's forced to throw it. My eyes are on the brown pigskin spiraling like a bullet straight to me. It's a perfect pass, and I seem to be wide open. Dylan's not in my sights as I reach for the ball.

It's higher than I expected, forcing me to jump. Hendrix yells, but I've got it. The only problem is I'm a kicker, not a runner, and I'm not used to calculating how fast I'm moving. I realize as I'm flying through the air, I'm going to hit the ground hard. Shit.

Clutching the ball to my chest, my muscles tense as I brace for impact. It all happens so fast, yet so slow at the same time. I feel her small body under mine. My chest seizes, and I try to twist away from her.

It's too late, and all my weight comes down hard on my little sister. Throwing out my arm, I try to fight my velocity, but at six-foot-two, I can't stop it. She screams, and I lose the ball, doing everything I can not to hurt her.

We hit and bounce, and I hear the crunch of bone. Another scream, and I know without looking I've broken something that can't be fixed.

I'm on my feet fast when we stop moving, but Dylan doesn't get up. She rolls to the side, holding her leg, her foot bent unnaturally.

Her cries echo in my ears, and it's not just the physical pain. This injury changes everything, but not only for Dylan.

It's the first in a series of breaks that will change my life.

Get *The Way We Play* today!

Also available on audio.

Acknowledgments

Kicking off this new football series (*get it?*) has been ***so much fun***, and I've had the most amazing team of family, friends, and readers helping me—***I love y'all so much!***

Huge thanks and so much love to my husband "Mr. TL" for his encouragement and feedback, and his ongoing interest in every new adventure.

I'm so excited to welcome my amazing daughter Kat to the team, who is helping me with marketing now, and returning illustrator, my incredible daughter Laura, who made all the cover and all the character art and logo for the story. I can't even begin to describe how full my heart is having you two with me!

Thanks so much to my alpha readers Jen DeJong, Renee McCleary and Leticia Teixeira for your song suggestions, laughs, and swoons! Y'all keep me going…

Huge thanks to my *incredible* betas, Maria Black, Corinne Akers, Amy Reierson, Courtney Anderson, Jennifer Christy, Heather Heaton, and Michelle Mastandrea. You ladies are my rockstars!

Thanks to Jaime Ryter for your eagle-eyed edits and to Lori Jackson and Wildheart Graphics for the killer cover designs, to my dear Wander for the *perfect* image, and the amazing Stacy Blake, who helps me make my gorgeous paperback interiors!

Thanks to my dear Starfish, to my Mermaids, and to my Veeps for keeping me sane and organized and helping me spread the word.

I can't begin to put into words how much I appreciate the love and support of all the influencers on BookTok, Instagram, Facebook, and to my author-buds! I love you all so much…

I hope you adore this new world, these quirky characters, and all the love! I'm so blessed to have you. Thank you for helping me do what I do.

Love, football, and spice,
♥ *Tia*

Books by
TIA LOUISE

ROMANCE IN KINDLE UNLIMITED

THE BRADFORD BOYS
The Way We Touch, 2024*
The Way We Play, Oct. 2024*
The Way We Score, Jan. 2025*
The Way We Run, 2025*
The Way We Win, 2025*
(*Available on Audiobook.)

THE BE STILL SERIES
A Little Taste, 2023*
A Little Twist, 2023*
A Little Luck, 2023*
A Little Naughty, 2024*
(*Available on Audiobook.)

THE HAMILTOWN HEAT SERIES
Fearless, 2022*
Filthy, 2022*
For Your Eyes Only, 2022
Forbidden, 2023*
(*Available on Audiobook.)

THE TAKING CHANCES SERIES
*This Much is True**
*Twist of Fate**
*Trouble**
(*Available on Audiobook.)

FIGHT FOR LOVE SERIES
*Wait for Me**
*Boss of Me**
*Here with Me**
*Reckless Kiss**
(*Available on Audiobook.)

BELIEVE IN LOVE SERIES
Make You Mine
*Make Me Yours**
*Stay**
(*Available on Audiobook.)

SOUTHERN HEAT SERIES
When We Touch
When We Kiss

THE ONE TO HOLD SERIES
*One to Hold (#1—Derek & Melissa)**
*One to Keep (#2—Patrick & Elaine)**
*One to Protect (#3—Derek & Melissa)**
One to Love (#4—Kenny & Slayde)
One to Leave (#5—Stuart & Mariska)
*One to Save (#6—Derek & Melissa)**
*One to Chase (#7—Marcus & Amy)**
One to Take (#8—Stuart & Mariska)
(*Available on Audiobook.)

THE DIRTY PLAYERS SERIES
*PRINCE (#1)**
*PLAYER (#2)**
DEALER (#3)
THIEF (#4)
(*Available on Audiobook.)

THE BRIGHT LIGHTS SERIES
Under the Lights (#1)
Under the Stars (#2)
Hit Girl (#3)

COLLABORATIONS
*The Last Guy**
The Right Stud
*Tangled Up**
(*Available on Audiobook.)

PARANORMAL ROMANCES
One Immortal (vampires)
One Insatiable (shifters)

GET THREE FREE STORIES!
Sign up for my New Release newsletter and never miss a sale
or new release by me!

About the Author

Tia Louise is the *USA Today* and #4 Amazon bestselling author of (*primarily*) small-town, single-parent, second-chance, and military romances set at or near the beach.

From Readers' Choice awards, to *USA Today* "Happily Ever After" nods, to winning Favorite Erotica Author and the "Lady Boner Award" (*lol!*), nothing makes her happier than communicating with fellow Mermaids (*fans*) and creating romances that are smart, sassy, and *very sexy*.

A former journalist and displaced beach bum, Louise lives in the Midwest with her trophy husband, two young-adult geniuses, and one clumsy "grand-cat."

Sign up for her newsletter and never miss a new release or sale—and get a free story collection!

Signed Copies of all books online at:
https://geni.us/SignedPBs

Connect with Tia:
TiaLouise.com
Instagram—@AuthorTLouise
TikTok—@TheTiaLouise